Bonnie

Enjoy!

8/16/08

Soft Target:
The Air

by

Joel
Narlock

ISBN 978-0-89754-226-5 // $18.95

Fiction

Cover design by BestBookCovers.com

This book is a work of fiction. Any resemblance to any person, living or dead is coincidental.
Only the Entomopter is real.

Dan River Press
PO Box 298

Thomaston, ME 04861

Acknowledgments

My heartfelt thanks . . . .

To those who defend freedom in an uncertain world;
To those who earn a living in the sky;
To those who put up with my incessant questioning.
And to my wife Terri, for your love and support.

Author's Note

Soft Target: The Air uses realism and fiction to describe aviation terror on U.S. soil.

The idea came to me when there was neither a global war nor an enemy so emboldened and publicly defined.

The story features the Entomopter, a pigeon-sized micro-air vehicle created by Robert C. Michelson, Principal Research Engineer, Emeritus of the Georgia Technology Research Institute. Professor Michelson designed the Entomopter to harmlessly explore Mars. I gave it a far more sinister purpose than collecting rock samples.

The easiest way to see an Entomopter is by entering the word at any Web search browser.

Some may think that even fictional accounts of remote-control flying devices harassing U.S. commercial aircraft may offer the wrong kinds of ideas to the wrong kinds of people. However, I believe that evildoers will continue to plot with or without the help of a novelist. Certainly, if I can discover and exploit an aviation industry weakness, so can those who mean us harm.

By beating them to the written punch so to speak, we might

deter a desperate enemy from actually employing these tactics. This was on my mind.

The Lord will bring a nation against you from far away, from the ends of the earth, like an eagle swooping down, a nation whose language you will not understand, a fierce-looking nation without respect for the old or pity for the young.

Deuteronomy 28: 49-50

Introduction

From: **ERRI DAILY INTEL REPORT-**Tue, January 8, 2002-
Vol. 8, No. 008
TODAY'S CENTRAL FOCUS:
Newspaper Asks *Was The Shoe-Bomber A Trial Run?*
[Terror Group Reference: al-Qaeda]
SAN FRANCISCO: Investigators on both sides of the Atlantic
are still gathering evidence, looking for any possible links between
would-be airline shoe-bomber Richard Reid and the al-Qaeda terrorist organization. According to a report over the weekend in the San
Francisco Chronicle, intelligence officials are seriously considering
a disturbing theory: that Reid's bombing attempt may have been a
"trial run" for future, simultaneous attacks against jetliners to be carried out by supporters of master terrorist Osama Bin Laden.

According to the report, U.S. and British intelligence officials
believe that Reid, a British national, on American Airlines Flight 63
from Paris to Miami on 22 December was a "foot soldier" sent to
check the destructive power of a shoe bomb. One senior British intelligence official said there are indications that "more than a few,
but less than a dozen" individuals may be preparing similar attacks
in the near future. Counterterrorism officials cite similarities with a
weapon developed by the infamous Ramzi Yousef, who plotted a
series of simultaneous attacks on U.S. airliners in the mid-1990s.

One unnamed, high-ranking intelligence official said: "There
is a definite pattern here with Yousef's past attacks that we would
be foolish to ignore. They have tried this before, and they are trying
it again."

A preliminary study by the Federal Bureau of Investigation
indicated that Reid's black suede high-top basketball shoes contained between 8 and 10 ounces of the explosive *triacetone triperoxide*
(TATP) — dubbed "The Mother of Satan" by Palestinian militants,
because its inherent instability makes it dangerous to both the victims and bomb maker. The TATP in Reid's shoes was said to have
been "blended" with an explosive called *pentaerythritol tetranitrate*

(PETN), which can be ignited with a normal cigarette lighter. PETN is a key ingredient of Semtex, the Czech-made military explosive used to down Pan Am Flight 103 over Lockerbie, Scotland, in 1988.

A British intelligence official explained to the Chronicle: "These bombs are sophisticated devices. They would have been difficult and dangerous to produce. Reid could not have done this himself — he would have trouble tying his own shoelaces. It seems we may have an expert bomb maker on the loose in Europe."

Investigators are also looking into the origins of the money used by Reid, who has no visible means of support, as he traveled to seven different countries in 2001. Among the cities Reid traveled to was Amsterdam. The *Binnenlandse Veiligheids Dienst* (BVD), the Dutch security service, is attempting to reconstruct Reid's movements and to establish whether an *al-Qaeda* cell there may be plotting attacks on passenger jets.

The newspaper said Reid has told FBI agents that he contacted Dutch arms dealers on the Internet and paid $1,800 for the explosives. But intelligence sources speculate that Reid obtained them from an al-Qaeda explosives expert in Amsterdam, who adapted the shoes in preparation for Reid's attempted attack. FBI and British anti-terrorist sources have concluded that the shoe-bomb plot originated with the ideas of Ramzi Yousef, an early al-Qaeda operative who suggested flying airliners into buildings. While moving around in Afghanistan, Pakistan and the Far East, Yousef reportedly trained other bin Laden terrorists in the use of explosives and told them of a plan he code-named "Project Bojinka" — "bojinka" means "explosion" in Serbo-Croat. Designed to be a terrorist "spectacular" event, Yousef planned to blow up 11 U.S. passenger jets scheduled to fly simultaneously over the Far East in January 1995 by using tiny, undetectable bombs.

Yousef is said to have produced a stable, liquid form of nitroglycerine from an array of chemicals, including sulfuric acid and *nitrobenzene*, and fashioned them into devices that were undetectable by airport security devices. He converted a Casio digital watch into a timing switch, hid the liquid nitroglycerine in a contact lens case, with cotton wool as a stabilizer, and then used two 9-volt batteries to power light-bulb filaments to spark an explosion. Yousef hid the bomb components in the heels of his shoes, knowing most airport security systems do not scan the soles of feet.

Associated Press — Thu August 10, 2006 7:53 PM ET

British: *Thwarted Plot Involved 10 Jets*

British police said Thursday they thwarted a terrorist plot, possibly just days away, to blow up U.S.-bound jetliners over the Atlantic and kill thousands. Chilling accounts leaked by investigators described a plan on the scale of Sept. 11 that would use liquid explosives concealed as everyday carry-on items and common electronic devices to bring down 10 planes in a nearly simultaneous strike.

The bombs were to be assembled on the aircraft apparently using a liquid explosive — most likely peroxide — and detonated by such devices as a disposable camera or a music player, two American law enforcement officials told The Associated Press. The officials spoke on condition of anonymity because Britain asked that no information be released.

A federal law enforcement official in Washington said that at least one martyrdom tape was found during ongoing raids across England on Thursday. Such a tape, as well as the scheme to strike a range of targets at roughly the same time, is an earmark of al-Qaida.

British authorities arrested 24 people based partly on intelligence from Pakistan, where authorities detained up to three others several days earlier. More arrests were expected, the official said. The suspects were believed to be mainly British Muslims, at least some of Pakistani ancestry.

The official said some suspects were cruising the Internet looking for flights to the United States for several different days in recent weeks. He said some had gone to Pakistan recently.

American investigators praised Britain for preventing a catastrophe. "If this plot had actually occurred, the world would have stood still," Mark Mershon, assistant director of the FBI, told the AP in New York. Terror threat levels were raised to some of their highest levels and hundreds of flights were canceled worldwide. Passengers stood in line for hours and airport trash bins bulged with everything from mouthwash and shaving cream to maple syrup and fine wine. Governors in at least three U.S. states — California, New York and Massachusetts — ordered National Guard troops to help provide security.

"We want to make sure that there are no remaining threats out there, and we also want to take steps to prevent any would-be copycats who may be inspired to similar conduct," said U.S. Homeland

Security Secretary Michael Chertoff.

Experts said the nature of the plot could herald a new age of terrorism where attackers have access to explosives that are easy to carry and conceal. Emergency security measures quickly implemented on Thursday provided a stark vision of the possible future of air travel.

Mothers tasted baby food in front of airport security guards to prove it contained no liquid explosives. Liquids and gels were banned from flights. Travelers repacked their luggage in airports, stowing all but the most necessary items in the hold.

Although plots to blow up airliners using liquid explosives are not new — such an attempt was foiled more than a decade ago — the U.S. government has been slow to upgrade its security equipment at airport checkpoints to detect explosives on passengers.

U.S. authorities did not say how long the security measures would last. "We are taking the step of preventing liquids from getting into the cabin to give us time to make adjustments," Chertoff said.

The raids in Britain on Thursday followed a month long investigation, but U.S. intelligence officials said authorities moved quickly after learning the plotters hoped to stage a practice run within two days, with the actual attack expected just days after that. The test run was designed to see whether the plotters would be able to smuggle the needed materials aboard the planes, the officials said, speaking on condition of anonymity. Security experts warned it was possible attackers could hide their bomb ingredients in containers for talcum powder or medicine bottles and then assemble the weapon once behind a locked restroom door.

U.S. counterterrorism officials said United, American, and Continental airlines bound for New York, Washington and California were targeted by the terrorists. Los Angeles Mayor Antonio Villaraigosa said the individuals plotted to detonate liquid explosive devices on as many as 10 aircraft bound for the United States.

"This nation is at war with Islamic fascists who will use any means to destroy those of us who love freedom, to hurt our nation," President Bush declared.

The plane bombings could have come just ahead of the fifth anniversary of the Sept. 11 attacks carried out by al-Qaida. The terror group's leader Osama bin Laden and his No. 2, Ayman al-Zawahri, are believed hiding along the Pakistan-Afghanistan border and have repeatedly issued tapes threatening new attacks.

"In terms of scale, it was probably designed to be ... a new Sept. 11," said Jean-Charles Brisard, a French private investigator who works with lawyers of many Sept. 11 victims. "It involved the same tools, the same transportation tools and devices."

The close call also shifted attention once more to Britain's Islamic community just over a year after the London transit attacks. Three Britons of Pakistani descent and a Jamaican convert to Islam carried out those deadly bombings with a peroxide-based explosive that trained operatives can make using ordinary ingredients such as hair bleach.

In Pakistan, an intelligence official said the arrest of an Islamic militant near that border several weeks ago played a role in "unearthing the plot." The official, who spoke on condition of anonymity, said some suspects arrested in Britain were linked to al-Qaida. However, authorities stopped short of accusing al-Qaida directly for the plot.

A senior Pakistani government official, also speaking on condition of anonymity because he was not authorized to comment on the matter, said "two or three local people" suspected in the plot were arrested a few days ago in the Pakistani cities of Lahore and Karachi.

French Interior Minister Nicholas Sarkozy said the group "appears to be of Pakistani origin," but did not give a precise source for the information. Britain's Home Office refused comment. A British police official, speaking on condition of anonymity because of the sensitivity of the investigation, said the suspects were "homegrown," though it was not immediately clear if all were British citizens. He said authorities were working with Britain's large South Asian community.

Tariq Azim Khan, the Pakistani minister of state for information, said "these people were born and brought up in the United Kingdom. Some of them may have parents who were immigrants from Pakistan."

Raids were carried out at homes in London, the nearby town of High Wycombe and in Birmingham, in central England. Searches continued throughout the day, and police cordoned off streets in several locations. Police also combed a wooded area in High Wycombe.

Hamza Ghafoor, 20, who lives across the street from one of

the homes raided in Walthamstow, northeast of London, said police circled the block in vans Wednesday and that they generally swoop into the neighborhood to question "anyone with a beard."

"Ibrahim didn't do nothing wrong," Ghafoor said, referring to a suspect. "He played football. He goes to the mosque. He's a nice guy."

The British government raised its threat assessment to its highest level — critical — which warns that a terrorist attack could be imminent. The U.S. government, following suit, raised its threat assessment to red alert, also its highest level, for commercial flights from Britain to the United States.

United States Department of Homeland Security
Transportation Security Administration (TSA)
Air Travel – Prohibited Items

If you bring a prohibited item to an airport checkpoint you may be criminally and/or civilly prosecuted or at the least asked to rid yourself of the item. A screener and/or Law Enforcement Officer will make this determination depending on what the item is and the circumstances. This is because bringing a prohibited item to a security checkpoint - even accidentally - is illegal.

Your prohibited item may be detained for use in an investigation and if necessary as evidence in your criminal and/or civil prosecution. If permitted by the screener or Law Enforcement Officer, you may be allowed to:

Place the prohibited item in checked baggage;

Withdraw with the item from the screening checkpoint at that time;

Make other arrangements for the item such as taking it to your car;

Voluntarily abandon the item.

Some items are allowed in your checked baggage, but not your carry-on.

The TSA's prohibited and permitted items list is not intended to be all-inclusive and is updated as necessary. To ensure everyone's security, the screener may determine that an item not on this list is prohibited. The list of items applies to airline flights originating within the U.S. Please check with your airline or travel agent for restrictions at destinations in other countries.

Airline travel in the United States…it has never been safer.

Chapter One

Islamic Cairo, Cairo
Wednesday, April 29th
2:00 P.M.

Ali I Naimi neatly folded his Wall Street Journal and laid it beside him on the bench seat of a booth in El Fishawy's, a 200 year-old foodless tea house famous for old world atmosphere, backgammon and apple-flavored tobacco, a smooth blend with a pot-like aroma that lured unsuspecting tourists and their wallets into Khan el-Khalili Bazaar.

Weathered black-brown with deep cut lines, Naimi's face resembled that of the late Greek shipping magnate Aristotle Onassis, but without the ghoulish expression. His salt-gray mustache was stained with nicotine and his stately white suit portrayed a compassionate grandfatherly demeanor. An odd label for someone who once hacked the limbs off of Soviet Special Forces soldiers during guerilla raids in Kabul, Afghanistan. Too old for field operations, Naimi was now head of al Qaeda's majis al shura, a consultation council that discussed and approved major operations. Osama bin Laden and Muhammad Atef both sat on this council. Even terror networks had think tanks.

Naimi spoke Arabic to his guest across the table. "Infidel bastards and their color threat levels. It is not enough to profile Middle-Eastern adults, now they harass our children for explosives hidden inside stuffed animals. The Americans remind me of children. Frightened and paranoid. They dream of lutadors. Why bother with toys that have no space for even a false bottom? Our soldiers have carried nitrocellulose through airports in Madrid, Heathrow, and even New York. Not one was discovered or detained. Yes, that spiced aftershave with the ship on the bottle. Now even bottled water is suspect." He shifted to English. "An ocean voyage will be good for you. The Abuzenima is an Egyptian vessel that sails the Saharan coastal routes. Remind me to give you the rendezvous date and coordinates. Did I mention that my brother has been captain for many years? He lives in Portugal sixteen kilometers east of Aljezur.

13

A small, peaceful farm with sweet potatoes and peanuts. You can tend his livestock. To his crew he is Captain Ramon Naimi, but you must call him Raman. Then he will know and trust you. Do you understand? Raman. Change the letter in his name from O to A. A simple but effective code we have used for years. He will have your new identity and you will become family. Yes…the fertile valleys of Aljezur are beautiful. Do you know any lutadors, professor?"

I am not a fool and your banter will not distract me, Professor Faiz Al-Aran thought. Deep in concentration, elbows propped on the table, fists clenched against protruding cheekbones, Al-Aran was preoccupied with things far more complicated than substituting vowels or translating the Portuguese word for terrorist. He felt a faint tickle on his bald scalp. He slowly raised one hand and, with lightening speed, splattered a fly.

Naimi offered a napkin. "My mantis still has patience and good reflexes. Do your students at this Georgia Technical Institute know that name?"

"No one calls me mantis but you. I still don't see the resemblance."

"I see." Naimi smiled suspiciously. "Then I receive electronic mail from some other professor named Praying Man? Perhaps there is another insect on your mind?"

"Perhaps."

Osama-tall and thin with the same wide-set, lifeless eyes, Al-Aran's triangle-shaped head looked exactly like that of a praying mantis. His pointed ears and a jaw that stretched forever thanks to a sculpted black goatee painted a Christian portrait of Satan without horns.

Al-Aran removed a small spiral notepad from his shirt pocket and drew out a series of zigzag lines. Finished, he sent the design to the next department for approval—a department run by his eyes. They dutifully darted back and forth, following invisible pathways, testing the feasibility, evaluating the tactical benefits. The final proposal flowed up to headquarters.

Rejection.

Frustrated, Al-Aran unleashed a violent but dry spit at the notepad and deliberately pushed it off the table.

Naimi shook his head at the antics and picked it up. He perused the pages, pausing at one labeled: McDonnell Douglas MD-80 Series Nose Landing Gear Design. He closed the notepad and offered it back. "Temper, my mantis. One day your mind might burst and then you will be old and feeble like me. If that happens, you must not lead soldiers."

An old and feeble lion with teeth and hunger is still dangerous, Al-Aran wanted to speak, but refrained. He tucked the notepad away and resumed his concentration, pressing his brain to the limit. At this desperate juncture, taking his own life was certainly an option, but would bring no honor. As a leader, he was neither incompetent nor sentimental, but he despised the thought of seeing his soldiers fight so valiantly only to be scooped into a single body bag and hung upon a nail like meat. Banished to a realm of black nothingness. All because they followed his plan. Who could tell when they would be summoned to fight the infidels again? Those damned white infidels.

After another minute, Al-Aran broke from his trance and looked up. All strategies had failed; he knew it was hopeless. His attack force had started with fifteen men and one woman. A lopsided ratio, but the woman was extremely powerful. Her skill level equaled that of the men combined. Unfortunately, even she was now dead. Only three had survived. Al-Aran felt a strange calm. Some inner contentment. His anger was still present, but controlled. A potent recipe for revenge. There would be another day. At peace with the decision, he reached for his teacup and used the lip to gently signal surrender.

The black king tottered over onto the chessboard.

Chapter Two

Both men were pipe smokers and followed an unwritten rule that the first to indulge must earn the right. Naimi inserted his snuggly into the corner of his mouth, the taste of the stem a precursor to a fitting reward. "Do you know why we cannot resist chess? Even in the face of certain defeat, one can still do severe and repeated damage to an enemy. That itself purports victory. I'm surprised, my mantis. Air, earth, fire, water…your plan attacks America's very foundations, yet you hesitate to show aggression in a simple board game."

A noise was building in the cafe. In English. Soft at first, it grew to a crescendo.

"Suck suck suck suck suck suck suck……"

The men turned towards a table in the center of the room filled with what appeared to be western students. A young female had boldly straddled her legs around a shisha (water pipe) and, goaded by the raucous chant, was sensuously sliding her lips back and forth over the mabsam. Once carved from the finest ivory and shared, the potential for hepatitis had turned the mouthpieces synthetic and disposable. Finished with the vulgar display, she inhaled. The syrupy tobacco smoke instantly swirled through the coiled plastic tubing and into her lungs. She choked violently. Caught in mid-swallow, one student laughed so hard that two symmetrical beer streams shot from his nostrils and doused the table's candle.

Disgusted, Al-Aran turned to Naimi. "Hesitate to show aggression? How can I even think when I must witness pigs like that? Infidels were never allowed here, now even women come and do as they please and good Arab men say nothing. I despise that culture and I will never accept it. Never."

"Times change, my mantis, even in old places," Naimi declared. "I doubt that your American colleagues would approve such ego. And speaking of ego, I commend you again; a four-pronged attack on America's homeland is truly brilliant. But to entrust the success of one element to this…mechanical insect?"

Al-Aran produced his pipe and tapped the bowl vigorously against his palm. His eyes burned angrily at the students. "My colleagues favor technology over ideals. Liquefied nitrocellulose is

16

still common lacquer. Clear and highly explosive, yes, but thanks to those London amateurs and their peroxide toys all U.S. airports are on high alert and scanning system deployments are being accelerated. The Rapiscan Secure 1000 will detect liquid density differential even when mixed with a companion. The x-ray beam can penetrate one tenth of an inch below skin to locate the outline of polymers, plastic, ceramic, glass, vials, and even wooden objects. All in eight seconds."

"But you are not worried," Naimi observed.

"Our insect can carry many things. Liquid, powder, even a military-grade compound with a metal flake accelerator."

"It is not our insect until we acquire it," Naimi reminded. "I thought you had abandoned C-4 and Semtex explosives because of chemical signatures?"

"We did abandon them," Al-Aran reassured.

"Then what will you use? Acetone?"

"Refined potassium. It has ten times the power and the spent residue is virtually untraceable. Deciding how to transport and camouflage it is a non-issue. The way to defeat x-ray scanners that screen passengers and carry-on luggage is to bypass them entirely. I defy airports and their incompetent security. Soon I will never set foot in one again. Let them search forever and direct resources to an aircraft's interior. I will concentrate on the exterior. Remember, it is not my plan that is brilliant, but the tool with which to accomplish it. If God allowed our soldiers to pass chemicals through an airport, he will also bless my plans."

Naimi removed his pipe and nodded. "God is surely with us. Your people...are they safe?" He meant operatives.

"My students have always traveled freely. The Mexican routes are foolproof. Almost too easy."

"I agree, Faiz, it is too easy. I have been told that we can enter the United States from the south with little or no resistance."

"From the south or north," Al-Aran corrected. "The Minnesota route is still our most productive."

"Minnesota...a northern state," Naimi affirmed. "What is the name of that border crossing station again?"

"Fort Francis on the Canadian side, International Falls on the U.S.," Al-Aran answered. "Unfortunately, they are scanning vehicles. Thirty miles to the west in a place called Baudett, there is no such scrutiny. Ten soldiers a week cross Rainy Lake in recreational fishing boats to Highway 11 on the U.S. shoreline. Drivers coordinate pick-ups and then travel to Minneapolis without the slightest concern. The American Department of Homeland Security demonstrates the height of ignorance from its senior management to the lowest levels. Thanks to the strength of the federal unions, unqualified workers occupy key positions and are rarely fired for even the gravest incompetence. I know a middle-aged African-American woman in Atlanta who worked for our campus cleaning service. She vacuumed my floors. Then the TSA was formed. Now she is a supervisor in charge of baggage and x-ray security at Hartsfield-Jackson Airport. These are not professionals, Ali; these are novices. Hired to meet race or gender quotas. America's entire border is a tattered wineskin and their ports are like gaping holes. Think of it. A country's security entrusted to novices. The chaos in the INS is also beyond reason. They have long abandoned plans to develop a tracking database of foreign nationals. My students returning from their beach vacations are rarely screened thoroughly. Even the Congress continues to resist the issue for fear it will harm immigrant labor. And now Cale Warren and his amnesty plan. God has given us a window of opportunity."

"The American president is not stupid," Naimi countered. "He has called for their National Guard and would not propose something as foolish as amnesty without recourse. Perhaps it is an elaborate trap?"

Al-Aran scoffed. "Ten thousand miles of trap? I could personally drive a herd of camels from Mexico into Arizona and the immigration patrols would tip their hats and point us to water."

"CNN reported on this Arizona," Naimi recalled. "The U.S. government will increase its aerial surveillance. Do you know on what? An endangered sheep."

"Praise God for environmental priorities." Al-Aran frowned at Naimi. "Why are you laughing?"

"I am sorry, Faiz, but that is a sight I would pay to see. My mantis high off the ground on a camel clutching the cantle horns. A quiet voice singing in the moonlight."

"There is already a voice, but it is neither mine nor the Bedouin. And it certainly is not quiet. Day after day the Irish sing for more border security."

"The Irish?"

"American news correspondents." Al-Aran blew smoke at his

18

match flame. "One is named Sean Hannity. The other is the bastard who exposed Sami. His name is O'Reilly. Both spew poison and both have a tremendous following." He referred to Bill O'Reilly of the Fox News Channel and his probing interview of a University of South Florida professor that resulted in the man's dismissal and federal indictment for alleged fund raising for the Palestinian Islamic Jihad. He was subsequently acquitted.

"One day they may lose their voices," Naimi warned.

"All in God's time. Now there are other challenges."

Chapter Three

"Who will fly this insect?" Naimi asked pointedly.

"Leonardo Damiano Sinani."

"An Italian?"

"He has many identities. His father is Egyptian."

"Where is he now?"

"He also has many addresses," Al-Aran answered. "A college campus."

"Studying like so many others," Naimi presumed. "Miami?"

Al-Aran shook his head. "I advised him to leave Florida and its bulletins. "He attends Marquette University in Milwaukee. A city north of Chicago."

"We have many soldiers in middle-America. Unfortunately for your earth operation, this mad cow business has already increased livestock security."

"It was unfortunate, but expected. There is still opportunity. The FBI insists that the potential for bringing such a plan to fruition is low."

Naimi nodded thoughtfully. He recalled seeing a similar news report related to U.S. water supplies. "And how does Mr. Sinani manage so many addresses and identities?"

"He is young, but disciplined. Unknown with an average face. He understands western nuances and blends well. He has a taste for their vile music and games of chance. A typical American youth. His light skin will not draw attention."

"And your funds?"

Al-Aran smiled slyly. "You forget that I am a tenured professor who travels. I have more than I can spend. We have a safe arrangement."

Naimi finally lit the tobacco in his pipe bowl and drew several deep puffs. The tight brown ball flamed orange. "When a young lion matures he becomes restless. When a mane appears he is driven from the pride and not given the opportunity to make a mistake. Discipline is a fine quality, but is this man committed to our success?"

Al-Aran took another sip of tea and folded his arms defensively. The skin below his left eye twitched. It always did that whenever someone questioned his judgment. "A difficult term."

"Commitment or discipline?"

"Sinani is an American citizen with valid identification. He carries legitimate Canadian, French, and Italian passports. His electronics ability is without question. He is also a chemical genius."

"An ugly skill," Naimi observed. "But one that all of our soldiers must learn and exploit. It is critical for success."

"Success also depends on compensation and some measure of maturity. He will not make an ass of himself like that idiot, Jdey."

Al-Aran referred to Abderrouf Jdey, a Tunisian who left a public suicide message on videotape recently recovered by the FBI in Afghanistan. In it, he demonstrated a maniacal machine gun dance that ended with a promise to die fighting non-Muslim infidels. His color photograph was now posted across America in a terror alert.

"Jdey single-handedly fashioned and delivered the materials used in the London subway distractions. He is now established in New York City," Naimi added. "A brilliant bomb maker and a true man of God. He can design anything. His exuberance may prove useful. Does Sinani share such commitment?"

"To his very soul."

"And this insect...he knows it?"

"We have all studied the design."

"Studied but never operated," Naimi clarified.

"I have operated the device," Al-Aran boasted. "When the project team was formed. It is like a toy."

Naimi frowned at that. "Disbursing a liquid or powdered chemical over water or a cattle pasture, yes. A remote-control toy traveling in a straight line can be managed by anyone. But Sinani's operation...we are not speaking of a straight line. Are you confident?"

"Yes," Al-Aran insisted. "Sinani is aware of the unit's specifications and capabilities. It is very easy to maneuver. It will fit."

"Show me."

Mildly annoyed, Al-Aran opened his travel bag for his laptop computer. Raising the cover slightly, he placed his hand between the screen and the keyboard and made a circular motion. "When a plane's flaps are extended there is adequate dead space."

Naimi's eyes narrowed. "We have known each other too long. Your confidence has weakened. Why?"

Al-Aran's jaw muscles flexed as he raised the screen complete-ly. He pressed the laptop's power button and inserted a wireless broadband access card. The operating system came to life. "There is space underneath a wing to hide and even detonate an explosive, but I cannot guarantee the results. Even a large hole might not be enough to destabilize an aircraft. The bond of airfoil and fuselage is simply too strong."

"Is that all?" Naimi brushed the admission aside.

Al-Aran rubbed his eyes with his palms. "The timing for a pi-lot to lower flaps on a departure runway is also unpredictable. There is no set schedule to complete preflight checklists. Manipulating the insect with such a constraint is too dangerous. I'm sorry, Ali. It was a foolish idea."

"Neither you nor I are perfect, my mantis. We all make mis-takes from time to time. What sets God's people apart is our ability to adapt. The ability to recover and survive under adversity. God gave you a mind that easily understands the world's technology. I have no such skill. If you have discovered a weakness with aircraft landing gear then I will support it. I am confident in whatever you decide. This insect has legs that can cling tightly, no? Can you not leverage that?"

"God has already allowed me to consider it, Ali. I will not fail."

Chapter Four

"You seem to have everything in hand," Naimi concluded. "But what of this award contest in Rome? If the insect wins then the entire world will notice."

"Notice what? A flying assassin that destroys America's economy or an insect that carries rocks on Mars?"

"Your colleague, the inventor...what is the name of his hotel?"

Al-Aran fished a business card from his pocket and scribbled something on the back.

Not wanting to bother with his glasses, Naimi tilted the card toward the wall sconce. "Atlante Star, suite four hundred."

"It is near the Vatican."

Naimi tucked the card away. "The targets...how many have you chosen?"

Al-Aran carefully glanced around the café and then lowered his voice. "Fire, water, earth, air. Fifteen American forests will burn; nine filtration reservoirs will be poisoned; twenty-seven livestock feedlots will be infected; four passenger aircraft will fall from——"

Conversation abruptly stopped as a waiter approached with a refill of mint tea. Al-Aran accepted. Naimi waved him off.

"The targets are spread throughout America. Each was selected to allow for the widest impact. Access has already been established. With respect to the airport cities, there was good proximity. I simply await confirmation. Do you wish to know the names of the other leaders and specific details of their plan—?"

"Which operation will bring immediate fear?"

Al-Aran paused for a moment and then he answered. "The air."

"Show me these cities."

Al-Aran set the laptop aside and reached for four chess pieces. He placed one on the right-hand side of the board, two in the center, and one on the left-hand side.

Naimi recognized the configuration as the outline of the U.S. mainland. He touched one chess piece—a rook—with his pipe stem. A thin but prophetic smoke swirl drifted upward from the rook's crest. "Los Angeles International?"

23

"There was bad proximity," Al-Aran replied. "San Diego."

Naimi nodded approval. He motioned to the remaining pieces. "New York, Chicago and this?"

"Milwaukee's Mitchell International," Al-Aran explained. "A major airport near water. It will begin there. The proximity was excellent."

"What do you request of the council?" Naimi asked.

"Permission. I wish to undertake all operations simultaneously."

Naimi reached for his newspaper and unfolded it with a sharp snap. "Four operations with fifty-five targets is a bold undertaking. When do you expect to receive this airport...confirmation?"

"In a few moments I will speak with all four leaders over the Internet. I will tell them which operations have been approved; they will confirm the target locations and commencement dates."

"Target locations, dates, electronic mail messages...our best plans displayed for everyone to see? You are aware that President Warren and his NSA monitor Internet traffic with impunity?"

"I am," Al-Aran said smugly. "And I am also aware that he is under severe criticism for doing so. Judges have ruled against him. One report suggests the outrage is so great that there will be official censure and perhaps even impeachment."

Naimi wanted to laugh. "Take caution in your political conclusions, my mantis. Especially with the propaganda that flows from the American news media. I doubt if they have studied the U.S. Attorney General's brief in defense of the matter. Mr. Warren will clearly demonstrate on appeal that he has the power and authority to continue his so-called protective surveillance."

Al-Aran shrugged. "CIA or NSA wiretaps will make no difference. They will never discover us. The most secure communication in the world is that which appears in plain sight. A conversation on a public website works well as long as one thinks and types like an infidel."

Naimi turned back to the newspaper and quoted the headlines. "U.S. aviation still vulnerable; Delta and Northwest Airlines eliminate pension plans; high threat level costs U.S. taxpayers $1 billion per day."

"Mere pennies," Al-Aran observed.

There was a moment of extended silence as if everyone in the café had knowledge of the conversation and waited for the pronouncement.

"You may attack America's airlines," Naimi calmly ordered. "The earth, fire, and water operations must wait."

"God is great," Al-Aran whispered fervently.

Naimi lowered the newspaper slightly. "God is great. But the destruction of four commercial aircraft will require four insects."

"Five. One will be tested."

"I wager two or three will achieve our goal," Naimi observed. He tucked the newspaper neatly under his arm and rose from the table. "Guard yourself and this insect technology, my mantis. May God bless young Sinani and your new life in Portugal."

"And you, Ali," Al-Aran said, stuffing the chess pieces into a cloth pouch and pulling the drawstring taught. He looped the string over a nail on the wall and gave his attack force a farewell pat. He smiled at the irony. An ancient Persian board game foretelling the demise of the American economy. Two or three insects might do. But the mantis was prepared either way.

Al-Aran's finger deftly rolled over the laptop's touch pad. He browsed through several Internet websites and stopped at Virtual-VacationWorld.com/travel/forum. He glanced at his watch and waited another minute.

Praying Man has logged in.

Praying Man: Does anyone have any vacation ideas or suggestions that are athletic, healthy, and fun? I'm open to some female companionship with the right person. I prefer something in the U.S., but I'm flexible.

Campfire Girl: How about hiking or camping in a national forest?

Praying Man: Sorry, Campfire Girl. I'm not interested. Some other time.

Jessica21: What's your idea of fun???

WetnWild: Do you like the water?

Praying Man: Sorry, WetnWild. I'm not interested. Some other time.

Earthy Lady: Want to rodeo with a real cowgirl?

Tuna Reefer: Hey, WetnWild…I dig all kinds of water sports.

Praying Man: Sorry, Earthy Lady. I'm not interested. Some other time.

Air Babe: How about something high and exciting like parasailing or skydiving?

Praying Man: I suspect that the rush of the air can be quite exhilarating, but I'd prefer something safer.

Air Babe: What about a luxury cruise?

^Satan^ has logged in.

^Satan^: Hell-o-Hell-o-Hell-o-Hell-o-Hell-o-Hell-o-Hell

Praying Man: A cruise sounds interesting. Tell me more.

Air Babe: The Cunard Line sails the best ships in the world. My aunt booked a trip on the Queen Elizabeth II. Twenty-one days in the Atlantic for $87,000. She lives in Milwaukee, but flew from Chicago and boarded in New York City. She said it was the trip of a lifetime. Great food, regal atmosphere, very elegant. Everything was planned perfectly. She had considered a Pacific cruise from San Diego, but confirmed the QE2 itinerary instead.

Praying Man: Sounds like a winner. Didn't Cunard build that new ship, the Queen Mary II?

^Satan^: SlutSlutSlutSlutSlutSlutSlutSlutSlutSlutSlutSlut

Air Babe: Yes, the QM2 is the QE2's replacement sister.

Monicalewd: Hey, Praying Man…if you're not a priest then I'd make a great travel companion. I love ocean romances and know how to please someone who's financially secure!

^Satan^: virusvirusvirusvirusvirusvirusvirusvirusvirusvirus

Praying Man: I'll have to do some coordinating. You wouldn't happen to know the QM2's next sailing date or when you have to confirm?

Travelking: I get huge discounts on travel, especially cruises. Let me show you how to save big bucks. E-mail me at travelking. com**^Satan^:** travelSCAMtravelSCUMtravelSCAMtravel

Air Babe: I think that you have to confirm by May 18th, but I'm not a travel agent. You should browse Cunard's website or call them directly.

Praying Man: May 18th. Thanks, I'll check it out. A cruise may be just what I need. You've been a big help.

Travelking: I think Satan jerk should find a kiddie chat room where he obviously belongs. Stupid little kid.

^Satan^: kidDIEkidDIEkidDIEkidDIEkidDIEkidDIE

Chapter Five

General Mitchell International Airport
Thursday, April 30th
4:30 A.M.

Milwaukee's airport was quiet. A handful of business travelers, a few young people. A custodian and his cart. Shop lights flickered on. The terminal smelled of fresh bakery and coffee mingled with an occasional wisp of gasoline-like fuel that had sneaked through the jetways. The security lines were empty.

Sitting at a Starbucks kiosk, local Fox News investigator Neela Griffin booted her laptop and opened a Microsoft Word folder named Carly Simon. She scrolled through a list of text files and double-clicked on You're So Vain.doc. She stared blankly at the 1973 hit song lyrics and sipped extra strong Americana. The caffeine buzz rolled through her body like a warm electric shock. Her senses steadily improved and she spotted her cameraman, Terry Lee at the cash register rolling his T-shirt sleeve over his bicep and exposing a new Celtic sunburst to a young female server.

Lee's official union title was 'remote broadcast specialist'. Twenty-eight years old with rugged dark features, his unshaven beard and unkempt hair somehow rang GQ. He had natural on-air confidence and occasionally expressed interest in the opposite side of the lens. Sadly, the average news viewer would never get past the body ink.

Lee set his breakfast on Griffin's table and flopped dejectedly into a chair. "This is going to be a great day; I just got trashed."

"Good morning to you, too," Griffin said, checking her cell phone messages. "You are looking pretty scary."

"I wasn't rude or anything. All I did was ask where she hangs out and then she says have a nice day." Lee held a bottle of apple juice up to the light and shook it vigorously. "I hate getting up so flippin' early. My head hurts, my arm is sore and everything just feels out of sync."

"Any more complaints?" Griffin asked. "For your information, Have a Nice Day is a dance club on Old World Third Street next to the Bradley Center. It's rated as Milwaukee's best."

Lee stared at his co-worker. "At least she liked my tattoo."

"I'm surprised you had any bare skin left. How many is that now?"

"Women or tattoos?" Lee smirked, chewing open a packet of Philadelphia creamed cheese. "Five. Maybe I'll do my name next just for you. A letter on each knuckle like my cousin."

"The Motley-Crue-Pamela-Anderson cousin? You're such a B-esser."

"I swear Tommy Lee is my cousin," he defended. "I talked to him just last week. He's coming here next month for some radio gig and we're going to hang together. I'll introduce you." He peered at Griffin's laptop screen. "Tell me, what's the difference between B-ess and ob-sess?"

"I am not obsessed," she shot back.

"Yeah, right. I listen to a lot of music, but that old tune is all you ever think about."

"I'm simply trying to unravel a mystery about the ident..."

"You told me a hundred times," Lee interrupted. "Too bad there is no mystery. Everybody knows Carly Simon wrote that song about the lead singer from the Rolling Stones, Mick Jagger."

"Wrong."

"Then it's that Playboy Magazine guy."

"Nope."

"The actor she used to date?"

"It's not Hugh Hefner or Warren Beatty." Griffin's face had a Cheshire grin.

Lee sat forward. "You know something."

"Possibly."

"And you're going to stop playing games and tell me, right?"

"Maybe," she teased.

"Gimme a break. That's like the number one media secret in the world. What makes you so sure?"

"Because I've spent the last year of my life on the Internet researching archives from 1972. That's the key. Newspapers, political issues, media stories. I had to experience the same events, influences and lifestyles that Carly would have encountered when she wrote it. I had to get into her mindset."

"C'mon, one hint," Lee begged. "I promise I won't——"

"I found eleven pointers."

"What's a pointer?"

"A confidence indicator. When I dissected the song line by

line I found eleven new facts that all pointed to one prominent individual. It was incredible. He's such a perfect fit I'm surprised no one has ever suspected him before. I'm about ready to go public."

"Public as in a news story?"

"Uh-huh. I've got an outline for the whole segment. I've just got to convince Gillespie to let me produce it my way. If it's done right it'll mean national exposure."

"Please?"

Griffin scrolled through the text and then turned the computer screen toward Lee.

You're So Vain and I'm So Smart
Alternate Title: Searching for Mr. Vain
By: Neela Griffin

Pointer #1 — Son of a Gun

The song's whispering introduction mimics Joey, one of Mr. Vain's closest gang members and opening act. Joey had this trademark phrase sewn onto his bathrobe.

Lee nodded thoughtfully, trying to hide the confusion on his face. He smiled politely and spun the laptop around. "Look, I know you're really into this and it's probably none of my business, but there's more to life than Internet hobbies. I'm serious about my cousin. He's a cool dude and definitely not a cop. You should start seeing people."

Griffin stared into her coffee. The comment hurt. Her brief, abusive marriage was over. Her life and spirit were finally healing and she was gaining both physical and emotional strength. At thirty-five years old she was forced back to college. Independence University. The classes were hard and bitter and she wondered if she could ever trust another man again. She closed the laptop and slid it into her briefcase. "I don't need matchmaking, especially with some burned-out rock star. And the fact that my ex is a police officer has nothing to do with anything. Dennis was a bad person and I'm glad it's over. Let's drop it."

"No problem; I said my piece," Lee said rather dismissively. He gulped the last of his juice and let out a muffled belch. "Okay, so why are we at the airport at such an ungodly hour?"

"We're meeting a man named Brad. He sent me an e-mail

about a hole."

"A hole? What kind of hole?"

"Airline security," she answered. "Ticketing and passenger boarding."

"Which airline?"

"He didn't say."

"What's he look like?"

"I don't know that either. He said he'd be wearing a Green Bay Packer jacket, but not green and gold."

Lee frowned suspiciously. "Do you trust him?"

"How should I know? We've never met."

"Neela, you're freaking me out. The guy could be a nutcase. They call in crank news tips like this all the time."

"Possible, but his story could be big. It might have a terrorism angle."

"Oh, great." Lee threw up his arms. "Just like the time you called the FBI about the suspicious white van parked in front of the courthouse downtown. It turned out to be a window washing service and we almost got fired."

"Someday I'll break a major news story, mister and you'll be begging to film it."

"Nutcase," Lee mumbled through a mouthful of bagel. "Just trying to get on TV."

Griffin had her own reputation at Milwaukee's local Fox affiliate. Supporters labeled her investigative style as aggressive and bold while jealous detractors called it lucky ignorance. She was currently assigned to the station's Crime Stoppers Tipline, a position that afforded maximum face time in a major news market, but one that also saw her career path running parallel to the anchor desk instead of intersecting with it.

She lifted a cheese-filled croissant with both hands. The huge bite left a sticky white mustache. Pausing in mid-chew, she spotted a lone customer browsing in the gift store next to the entrance to Terminal D. Average build, balding, mid-forty-ish, his black leather jacket bore a tone-on-tone Packer chest emblem. He pretended to read a magazine, but Griffin could feel him peering. She was used to stares. Stunningly attractive, her body was thin and muscular. Her long, jet-black hair and white complexion were often referred to as black-Irish. But attractive had a downside. A consultant's report showed that male television viewers lost a full seven seconds of comprehension of opening news content evaluating appearances of female commentators.

"That's him," she said to Lee. "Get your camera and make sure those security guards are in the background."

"Umm, those are Federal TSA screeners," Lee clarified. "The airport's okay with this, right?"

"Trust me. But we need to move fast."

Lee gave a skeptical look as he fished a thin aluminum tripod from his equipment bag. "Some anonymous guy sends an e-mail and you grant him a taped interview. You have no idea who he is and the topic is airline security. And you want this to run on Wednesday's 9:00 segment."

"You should have been a producer."

"So what's the title? Brad loses his ticket?"

She hesitated. "Not exactly. There's a gun involved."

"What?"

"A hidden gun."

"Jesus, Neela, you can't even joke about that around here. I need to know where this is headed right now or I'm gone and so is my camera."

Griffin rose from the table and waved. The man promptly set the magazine down and walked over. She extended her hand. "Bradley Marshall? Thanks for coming. We're setting up now."

Marshall casually surveyed the area and noticed several TSA personnel beginning to take an interest. "Do you have to use my real name?"

"This lighting sucks," Lee sung from behind the viewfinder. "Try moving left."

Griffin placed her hands on Marshall's shoulders and gently nudged him sideways. She noted that Marshall's voice had a slight lisp, but his tone was deep and would carry well. She clipped a tiny microphone to his collar. "Your name is key to the story and by the way, that's my friend, Terry Lee. He's actually a very talented professional when he keeps his mouth shut and acts like one." She flashed a brief smile. "He's going to film everything you say so please talk freely. We'll edit the rough spots. Viewers will concentrate more on the subject than your name. Just relax and start at the beginning."

"Do I tell the truth?"

"Yes, of course. You tell the truth." She nodded to Lee.

The camera turned on.

31

Marshall cleared his throat and took a deep breath. "A week ago Monday, that would have been April 20th, I walked up to the Midwest Airlines ticket counter in Ft. Lauderdale International Airport and told the agent that I was flying to Milwaukee. I also mentioned that I had a firearm."

Chapter Six

"You attempted to take a firearm on a passenger aircraft," Griffin clarified. "What kind of firearm and for what reason?"

"Uh-huh, well, no, not exactly on the plane. I mean, not on me personally. A Beretta 92FS. Nine millimeter with a fifteen-round clip. I collect pistols and I like to shoot. It's perfectly legal to fly with a handgun as along as you declare it and carry it in a locked, hardened case inside your checked luggage. It's really no big deal." Marshall unzipped his jacket. His hand was trembling. "I'm a little nervous doing this right in front of Midwest's terminal. Why'd we have to meet here anyway?"

"It adds drama," she replied. "Please, go on."

"Well, the ticket agent inspected the Beretta and then gave me a form that said I could carry it on the plane." Marshall produced a 5 x 7-inch pink slip from his pocket. The camera zoomed in.

NOTICE TO ARMED INDIVIDUALS

PLEASE READ THE FOLLOWING PROCEDURES: THEY OUTLINE WHAT IS EXPECTED OF YOU WHILE IN BOARDING AREAS AND IN-FLIGHT.

If your weapon is concealed, you must keep it concealed at all times.

The Captain and Flight Attendants and other armed passengers will be informed that you are armed.

Our Flight Attendants and Pilots have been instructed how to handle passenger disturbances without assistance from other passengers and do not expect your help. Discharge of a firearm aboard an aircraft could cause a situation far more dangerous than the original disturbance...and this includes hijacking. If the pilot were accidentally disabled, the flight could end in disaster. Also, behind the walls, under the floor, and above the ceiling there are many fuel lines, control cables, electrical wires and hydraulic systems all essential to safe flight and all subject to damage or destruction by a stray bullet or ricochet.

As a person having a weapon accessible to you in flight, you

33

will not be served alcoholic beverages.

If you are accompanying a prisoner, the following procedures apply in addition to items 1 thru 4 above:

Prisoners who are considered a "maximum risk" must be accompanied by at least two armed law enforcement escorts and no other passenger may be under the control of those two escorts. No more than one passenger classified as a maximum risk will be carried on the airplane.

You must be equipped with adequate restraining devices. Midwest Airlines will not accept prisoners in leg irons.

You will be pre-boarded and you will be assigned a seat in the rearmost available row of seats in the cabin. You must sit between the passenger and the aisle.

You must accompany the prisoner to the lavatory as necessary.

At your destination you must remain seated until all other passengers have left the aircraft.

If you are connecting to another flight, you must identify yourself to the connecting flight's gate prior to boarding.

You and your prisoner will not be served alcoholic beverages.

Interline Carriers must complete their own form.

BY YOUR SIGNATURE BELOW AND BY PRESENTING PROPER DOCUMENTS, YOU ARE IDENTIFYING YOURSELF TO MIDWEST AIRLINES AS BEING AUTHORIZED TO CARRY WEAPONS; THAT YOU ARE ON OFFICIAL BUSINESS FOR THE AGENCY NAMED ABOVE; THAT SUCH WEAPONS MUST BE ACCESSIBLE TO YOU DURING FLIGHT AND THEREFORE EXEMPT FROM 14 CODE OF FEDERAL REGULATIONS 108.11.

"Why would Midwest Airlines give that form to you?" Griffin asked.

"I have no idea."

"You signed it?"

"Yes, but I didn't read it thoroughly and that was my mistake," Marshall admitted. "It's a five-part form with extremely small print. I thought it was just a formality."

"What were you supposed to do with the form?"

"She told me to give it to the agent at the boarding gate."

"Are you a police officer?"

"No, ma'am. I'm an accountant."

"Are you absolutely certain that you didn't hint at or otherwise imply that you were somehow involved in law enforcement?"

"Positive. I never said anything to that ticket agent but my name. I figure she got confused and thought I was one. You know, a Federal Air Marshal."

"What happened next?"

"I carried my suitcase to the checked baggage station. The security people x-rayed it and sent it off to the aircraft. Then I walked to the terminal."

"So, at this point you have no weapon, correct?"

"That's correct; it's in my suitcase. I have no weapon."

"Okay, continue."

"When I arrived at the boarding gate I handed the form to the agent as instructed. He looked at it briefly and then simply waved me through. No one asked me for any ID; no one verified my name against any master list; and no one requested any official letter or document stating exactly who I was and why I was carrying a firearm—nothing. I just took my seat. For the next fifteen minutes I watched the crew discussing the form at the front of the plane and when they started looking my way I knew that I was in trouble. I figured that some passenger list or cross-check log had raised a flag and they were simply stalling until airport security arrived. All I could think of was a news headline. Milwaukee CPA arrested for impersonating an officer. Then a flight attendant walked over and handed me this pink copy. It was signed by the Captain. She told me to have a nice flight."

"Okay, I'm trying to see an advantage here," Griffin announced. "Let's play this out to a worst-case scenario. You're in the air on a commercial aircraft and you're a terrorist. And the crew on that aircraft believes that you're carrying a concealed loaded firearm. You're not really, but they think you are. You could probably create panic, especially if you jump out of your seat and started waving a toy handgun, but it's only a bluff. Ultimately, to cause real harm to the passengers, crew, or the aircraft itself, you'd need a real weapon, right?"

"Or have access to one."

Griffin paused briefly. "I'm not following."

"All armed passengers who fly, including legitimate Law En-

35

forcement Officers and Federal Air Marshals are quietly introduced to each other before takeoff so they can study each other's appearance and learn where they're seated. That way if something happens in-flight, like an attempted hijacking, they'd presumably know where help is. It's a professional courtesy thing."

"How do you know that?" Griffin wondered.

"Look, I don't work for any airline, but one of my clients is a pilot and he showed me the regulations. I also know a couple of flight attendants."

"Okay, so there is a Federal Air Marshal on board. You continue your charade and the two of you are introduced to each oth— ohmygod," Griffin's voice trailed off. "You'd know who's carrying a real firearm and where they're sitting."

"Bingo," Marshall confirmed. "There's your terrorist advantage. Get yourself a pack of forms—-forms that no one verifies— and keep boarding commercial aircraft. Sooner or later you'll be introduced to someone who has a weapon. Someone you and your accomplices can overpower in the air. I'm not an engineer, but shooting inside a pressurized cabin at say, 37,000 feet probably isn't good. Take it one step farther. If no one is introduced to you, you can safely assume there's no Air Marshal on board. Welcome back to terror in the sky. And that's not all. My friend said that flights at Reagan National in Washington, DC always carry two Marshals and that they always mouth who they are to the flight attendants in plain view of other passengers and that they always sit in first class. And this business about introducing armed passengers to one another pre-flight? It's true; you can look it up for yourself. It just proves that paper rules won't stop anyone intent on breaking those rules for evil. And the first step needed to gain access to a loaded firearm on an aircraft is acquire, steal, or reproduce a harmless form—a form that no one is validating at all. I really think that it's a security hole." Marshall unfolded another piece of paper and handed it to Griffin. "You're the reporter and I don't mean to tell you your job, but I wrote something that I thought we could use to lead off the story."

She tucked it into her pocket. "Have you contacted anyone at Midwest about this?"

"Sure. I e-mailed their Consumer Affairs group and told them there was a firearm security failure in their boarding process. Seven days later a woman called back and accused me of being the problem. She said that the ticket agent who gave me that form was a contracted Delta employee—she used the term 'newbie'—and that it was a simple training mistake. She said the situation would never have turned dangerous unless I was dangerous. I also e-mailed the facts to Florida Congressman James Micha, Chairman of the U.S. Subcommittee on Aviation Safety. He never responded at all. That really pissed, er..upset me. I figured someone in the media should know. That's why I contacted you."

Griffin faced the camera. "For those of us who fly, especially in today's aviation environment, a very scary situation. Stay tuned for an exclusive follow-up with officials from Midwest Airlines and the Department of Homeland Security. Reporting for Crime Stoppers Tipline at Mitchell International Airport, this is Neela Griffin, Fox News."

The camera stopped.

She unclipped Marshall's microphone. "This is great material. Thanks for coming forward. It needs to be told. I'm leaving for Europe tonight on special assignment and I'd appreciate it if you wouldn't talk to the other news stations, okay? I think we can do at least two more segments after we confirm a few facts."

"Yeah, no problem. I'm happy this'll finally get out." Marshall shook Griffin's hand and headed down the airport corridor for the parking structure.

Griffin walked over to Lee. Her face carried an obvious smirk. "You were saying something about a nutcase?"

"So Miss Paris Hilton is tooling off to Europe without her favorite cameraman and no one tells me anything."

"I wanted to yesterday, but I forgot," Griffin apologized as she unfolded Marshall's note. "Gillespie assigned it to me personally. I'll be back on Sun—"

They Think I'm Armed

Dear Mr. Bin Laden,

Nice try, but it's my distinct pleasure to inform you that your little form loophole—or should I say rat hole—has been discovered. Homeland Security is filling it with concrete as we speak. Too bad you're not in it. Chalk up another one for the good guys.

Chapter Seven

Rome, Italy
Saturday, May 2nd
7:00 P.M.

Michael Robertson stood up from the commode in the men's restroom of the Palazzo Taverna and braced himself inside the stall until everything stopped spinning. He listened quietly, almost able to hear the remnant echoes of the violent 'hoo-wah…hoo-wah' that only moments before had burst from his lungs and bounced off the red-black marble walls. It was both humorous and frightening that a forty-year-old male human being could make such outrageous noises. Thankfully he was alone.

Noting the pungent smell on his breath and hands, he twisted the door latch and gingerly made his way to the sinks. His face was still warm and his heartbeat elevated, but his swallowing reflex had slowed indicating that for the moment what little was left in his stomach had opted to stay. He swished a mouthful of water from cheek to cheek and spit. He envisioned the lead story in the Atlanta Constitution: Finalist Vomits at Pirelli International Technology Awards Ceremony. *Damn!—didn't that happen to someone else?* He wondered. Yes. President George Bush, Sr. at a state reception. All over the Japanese prime minister. Wonderful.

The scarlet towel draped over his shoulders protecting his suit made him look like an escapee from some princely barbershop. He patted his face with more water and examined the outline of his month-old beard. It had filled in nicely. His wife was right; he did look more European. Every little bit helped.

Michael folded the towel and then his hands. He wasn't an overly religious man, but occasionally chatted with the Almighty whenever he needed a break. This was such a time. "Dear God… please make the food disappear, and please…don't let me get sick in front of three hundred people and world media. If I do, then let it be on the Germans. Amen."

He didn't even consider asking about winning; that would be pushing.

Michael returned to the dining room and his seat at the head table. The ever-attentive waitstaff had collected the dishes and whisked them away.

One prayer answered.

The food had been sickeningly rich, drenched in a buttery sauce and fried. Even the appetizer—bread piled with tomatoes and thin-sliced meat—dripped with olive oil. He should have known from the stench that something was wrong. Ham was not supposed to be translucent blue. It had obviously outlived an expiration date. How could they call it a delicacy?...no—how could they even serve it? No one else complained which meant it was either a conspiracy against Americans or the Italians had simply developed a tolerance for rotten pig strips cooked by nothing hotter than the mountain sun. Then the main course. Oily breaded sea-something with an odor so strong it reminded him of catfish stink bait. After just two bites whatever it was sent his already roiling stomach over the edge.

Linda Robertson bent sideways for her purse and caught a whiff of her husband. "Oh my god, did you throw up?"

"Of course not," he squeaked in a voice an octave higher than normal. "Why would you think that?"

"Your knees are dusty and I do have a nose. Michael, look at me. You did, didn't you? Are you drunk?"

He thought for a moment. He had sampled three different wines. "The fish. I think the fish had a funny aftertaste."

She checked the time. "We still have a few minutes. Do you want to lie down? There's a lounge upstairs."

His only response was a belch of sour air.

Linda noticed the master of ceremonies, Carlo Burno making his way down the lengthy table greeting each of the ten finalists and their spouses. She tore open a roll of antacids and then motioned to the back of the room. "Michael Charles Robertson. See that saxophone player? If you make a scene at this table I'm going back to the hotel with him. Chew."

Carlo placed his hands on Michael's shoulders. "You barely ate anything. Perhaps we should have prepared something a little more American? I hear Georgians are partial to fried chicken." The remark drew a table chuckle.

Michael stopped munching the chalk-like tablets and exhaled a long breath. "My stomach's upset. I need a minute to close my eyes."

"It's the competition," Linda added. "This is all he's thought about for months. He's a little queasy; he'll be fine."

Carlo smiled sympathetically. "Parasites. Sometimes they hide in the suction cups. It's rare, but it happens. Let me know if there's anything I can do. I'm reminding all the finalists about the press conference. The winner will have a few minutes to address the media. With so many reporters here we might as well take advantage of the publicity. Good luck."

Suction cups? Michael felt his stomach undulate. His mouth filled with saliva. *Focus. It'll help the fight. Concentrate on the audience...no—read something.* He snatched the ceremony's program booklet. Candidate biographies. The inflow of information successfully routed his brain waves away from stomachs and food. *Yes, much better.* He'd never seen his name in gold leaf before. *Jesus, had it been that long since college?* He flipped to the back page and an English version of the menu. His eyes widened as he read the entrée preparation instructions:

...remove eyes, outside skin and intestines...cut off head and tentacles...combine ingredients into cavity and sew closed...

"I'm sorry I missed such a delicious meal. Calamari imbottiti is an Italian tradition," a wheezing voice announced in a thick German accent. "Good to see you again, Michael. Thank you anyway for at least saving my place. I'm so pumped I really don't feel like eating. The world's most prestigious technical competition can ruin an appetite, even in Rome."

"Hello, Gerhard," Michael managed to respond. He set the program booklet aside and closed his eyes again. "I thought Germans were always so prompt?"

"Ya, well, you know how it goes. I was trimming my acceptance speech. It's much too long."

Michael ignored the boast. "Gerhard Bender, my wife, Linda."

"Ahhh, the sexy kindergarten teacher." His eyes boldly followed the slit in her black dress up her exposed thigh. He sat down, breaking wind in the process. He nonchalantly waved his cigar behind him before setting it in an ashtray. "Somehow I thought you'd be younger. I represent Innovation Technologies."

Linda uncrossed her legs and pulled the fabric taught. "I represent Decatur High School," she clarified with a nasty look. They shook hands.

He pulled her face closer. "Forgive me, but I'm so pumped. I insist on a dance after the minor formality of winning." He glanced over her shoulder. "Your husband won't mind, will you Michael? Michael—wake up. Are we boring the king of the flying bugs? Are you and your British friends at Cambridge still staying up nights peering into a microscope and counting the wing beats of the hawk moth? Or are you now collaborating with those zookeepers at MIT who train rodents to search for earthquake victims? What was that project name again…ratbot? You know, working with animals is not that difficult. Neither is flight. Birds have been doing it for years. Flap a wing and into the air you go. Speaking of that, it's a real shame you came all this way just to go back with nothing but air. You can always say you gave it a good American try."

Chapter Eight

Linda held her breath, trying to avoid Gerhard's methane that had unfortunately drifted into her space. She had an uncontrollable urge to simply slap the man, but feared his fleshy jowls might burst. She glanced at a knife on the table. *If you ever fart near me again, I will stab you.* She peeled his clammy fingers off her hand. "And what exactly is your winning entry?"

"Networld. A completely paperless society. Free Internet hardware and software for everyone. We've tested a Berlin market for over a year. All media that comes into the home will do so electronically via high-speed access. Magazines, newspapers, business and legal documents, advertising, every piece of mail—all digitized. You decide what you want to print. It will transform the world. We even sent a team to interview your American postal service. Unfortunately, when they understood Networld's ramifications, things got a little hostile. Innovation always has a winner and loser. And trust me, they would be big losers. The projected cost savings gained by eliminating all the human mail carriers was huge. We haven't yet extrapolated the benefits to the global environment by saving all those trees. A little more practical than a flying bug, isn't that right, Michael? I'm so pumped." He splashed wine into a glass. "To Networld and the end of all paper."

Michael whispered to his wife. "If he wins, do me a favor and pour that into his crotch."

"I'd never find it," she whispered back.

The room lighting dimmed.

The musicians providing the background music noticed the cue and began casing their instruments.

Michael cautiously felt his stomach. So far so good. He'd never won anything in his life except a disappointing white ribbon in a fourth grade spelling contest. He glanced outside to an open veranda overlooking a terraced fountain. It was a bit ironic. The Italians definitely loved flowers.

Perennial. p-e-r-e-n-i-a-l.

I'm sorry son, but we needed two Ns.

Linda squeezed her husband's hand. "How much is 250,000 euros in U.S. doll—?"

"Shhh," he interrupted. "That's bad luck."

Conversation in the room quieted. Overhead spotlights beamed onto a podium in the center of an elevated stage.

"Ladies and gentlemen...." a voice boomed in English through the speaker system. The room went silent...."Pirelli Managing Director of Research and Development, Carlo Burno."

Applause.

Carlo strode to the podium and gently adjusted the microphone. "For over a thousand years, Roman conquerors returning from the wars enjoyed the honor of a triumph, a tumultuous parade." He turned to the head table. "On behalf of Pirelli International, I welcome you, the modern-day conquerors who have left your own wars to be with us this evening. One of you will indeed enjoy triumph. Not by means of a victory over a traditional enemy, but rather a victory over technology. You are here not by chance but by skill, dedication, and most importantly, design. We at Pirelli believe that design excellence must be recognized and rewarded on a world scale. As you know, the Pirelli Award favors a diverse scientific culture and is a further testament to research and development especially when humanity benefits from new ideas and technologies. Our international jury has evaluated over one thousand entries and culled them down to you, a select group of conquerors. I should also mention, while it's not a guarantee, all six previous winners went on to a certain Scandinavian capital to solidify their achievement in science. But such triumph tends to arrive suddenly with much fanfare and leave just as unexpectedly. Cherish this moment. The conqueror always rode in the lead chariot, prisoners marching before him with spoils from the captured territories. A slave stood behind the conqueror holding a golden crown and whispering in his ear a warning, that all glory is fleeting."

Three giant overhead screens lowered, framing the room.

Carlo turned to a group of nine men seated at a table off-stage to his left. "Has the jury made a selection?"

"We have," Ilya Frigogine, jury coordinator and former Nobel Laureate for Chemistry responded. He approached the stage and transferred an envelope.

Carlo calmly sipped water from a stemmed goblet before breaking the seal. He took another agonizingly long ten seconds to examine the contents and then placed the envelope onto the podium. He smiled at the head table. "Ladies and gentlemen, as part of a manned mission to Mars..." Michael buried his face in his hands "...planned by a United States NASA endeavor in the years 2013 through 2017, I present to you a device. A truly wonderful and revolutionary device that can operate beyond the boundaries of atmosphere. One with the ability to both fly and crawl. It is my privilege to announce that this year's winner of the Pirelli Award for best new technology in any school, college, university or research center worldwide is...Entomopter created by Professor Michael Robertson and his team from the Georgia Technology Research Institute, USA."

The room erupted. Guests rose to their feet. Media cameras whirred as the overhead screens showed animation of two tiny butterfly-like mechanical creatures fluttering above a terrain rover that was rolling across the Martian landscape. Each creature alternatively set down on a platform on top of the rover and picked up a slender tube before flying off.

Still seated, his skin prickling with excitement, Michael opened his eyes. He never felt Linda shaking his arm and shoulder, almost violently.

Reporters rushed to the front of the stage.

Temporarily blinded by spotlights now trained on him, Michael pushed out his chair. The walk to the podium felt dream-like. Unbelievably, he had completely forgotten about his stomach. Adrenaline was a great antacid.

Carlo presented a mahogany plaque fitted with a large gold medallion. After an admiring glance, Michael set it aside and waved to the crowd appreciatively.

The overhead screens now showed a field-level view from inside Georgia Tech's football stadium. A pony-tailed man stood on the midfield grass extending one arm. The Entomopter appeared and gently set down like some trained mechanical parrot. Knees bent, the man heaved the device skyward like a falconer. The camera followed the Entomopter as it sailed through the air toward the end zone and passed between the goalposts. It circled back and deftly perched sideways on one of the uprights.

The applause grew to a crescendo.

Michael considered raising his arms referee-like, but controlled the tacky impulse. Instead, he reached into his suit and slid out his glasses and a 3 x 5 note card. "Wow, what a thrill." The audience sat. "Thank you, Carlo. I want to express my appreciation to the members of the jury, the Pirelli family, our Italian hosts, distinguished colleagues, my wife, Linda and especially the other finalists and their respective teams who also put forth tremendous effort and resources. Yes, even to my competitive German friends."

Arms folded, Gerhard offered a stern but conciliatory nod.

Michael cleared his throat and motioned to the overhead screens. "Instead of a football theme, we considered flying the Entomopter into a soccer goal. Unfortunately, insects don't take too kindly to nets." The audience chuckled. "We scientists tend to lean toward the introverted side of the gregarious scale. People say that I fit somewhere between boring and bullheaded because I make unilateral and often wrong decisions. I respectfully disagree. For example, the last decision I made on behalf of the Entomopter team was to either allow or not allow my research assistants to travel to Italy and attend tonight's ceremony. I simply determined that most young single men would prefer to hang out in a campus laboratory rather than cavort through wine-filled Italian taverns with beautiful women and the most gracious people in Europe. I freely admit that I may have been wrong." The remark drew a generous laugh. "It is fitting that our technology is recognized in Europe. Its very name ento-insect, mopter-split-wing originated here. I accept this award on behalf of Georgia Tech, and my research team, brilliant, dedicated workers every one. Before we get into questions, and in keeping with the tradition of this award, I would like to once again reaffirm my personal and professional commitment to use the Entomopter to benefit humanity. I pray that its ultimate owner, I certainly hope it's NASA, will honor that same commitment. Thank you, again. I'm very grateful."

Chapter Nine

The audience stood and offered another long ovation.

This time Michael did raise his arms and for a moment looked like the Pontiff concluding mass. "Yes, sir."

"Darren Beel, Reuters. I don't think many of us have ever seen this ento insecto mopter before. Would you mind giving us a brief rundown on its specifications, capabilities, and significance to a space project?"

"Certainly. As Mr. Burno alluded to in his remarks, it's all about a planet's atmosphere, or lack thereof. The Martian airspace at ground level is like Earth's at 100,000 feet. Unstable and extremely difficult to fly through, linearly speaking. We've all seen the limitations of ground rovers. Truly, the most efficient way to explore Mars is from the air. Unfortunately, a conventional fixed-winged aircraft would have to fly 250 mph just to stay airborne. That makes landing, collecting samples, and mapping virtually impossible. On the other hand, the Entomopter can achieve radically high lift by flapping mechanical wings, just like that of an insect. Being a multi-mode vehicle with retractable legs, it can fly slowly over rough terrain, literally cling to whatever it lands on, collect or deposit samples, recharge, communicate and even download data before returning to its original launch point. As far as physical design, think in terms of a dragonfly with a front and rear set of wings. A dragonfly the size of a pigeon. When insect or Entomopter wings flap through air, the low-pressure vortex created above the wingtips gives tremendous lift. For those of you struggling with the scientific name, dragonfly is really more appropriate. We use D-Fly for short." He shielded his eyes from the lights. "Yes, on the left."

"Thank you. Judy Chin, Hong Kong Commercial Daily. Can D-Fly walk and is it for sale?"

"Yes, it can actually crawl forward and backward, but its specialty besides flight is its ability to clamp pincer-like legs together and hold itself in position. The simulation video you just saw showed the Entomopter attaching itself to the Mars rover's roll bars and hanging on for the ride. Two sets of legs can literally pick up objects in a certain weight class. The capability is especially useful for grasping, transporting, and releasing. A tool or rock sample, for instance." He looked at his notes. "I'm sorry, what was your other question?"

"Can I buy one?"

His smile slowly vanished when he realized the reporter was serious. "Sure. Assuming we get to that point. The retail price will probably start around $2,500. I suppose NASA's not the only one with interest, but there are patent and ownership considerations and frankly, we haven't worked all those out. I'd have to get back to you with a better answer. Yes, ma'am."

"Debra Vaser, CNN. Two questions: How is the D-Fly machine powered? And how much has NASA, I assume it's NASA, appropriated for program funding, and what effect, if any, did recent budget cutbacks have on your project?"

He paused briefly to write down keywords. He noted the woman had actually asked three questions. He couldn't remember if the budget number was proprietary. "First of all, it's not really a machine in the sense that it has no stored or combustive power source. Without getting too technical, we developed a liquid propellant that flows to a muscle-chemical reciprocator, or MCR. That's Entomopter's real claim to fame. The MCR consists of two parallel shafts that, when forced by propellant and catalyst gases, push pistons in opposite directions and move both the leg and wing sets. Suffice it to say that it's not powered by a traditional engine or motor, but rather a chemical reaction. A reaction that not only allows the wings to flap, but also creates enough electrical energy to power a few small sensors. A camera for instance. With respect to the reaction, we combine polynitrogen, common RP-1 which is a hydrocarbon similar to kerosene, and a catalyst. I'm sorry I can't be more specific about the composition; we do need to keep some trade secrets. I'm certainly not a spokesperson for NASA or the military, but I think it's simply coincidence that the Institute for Advanced Concepts and the Pentagon have both invested heavily in their own robotics programs. You really should ask them."

"Sir, for the record, it says in this program that your full name is Michael Charles Robertson," a British correspondent spoke up. "Would that be accurate?"

This drew a suspicious frown. "Umm, yes. But I think they've turned some of my work history around."

"Professor Robertson, seeing that your NASA is a taxpayer-funded body and under severe criticism for arrogant safety failures,

I wonder if you can be more specific about similar venues and projects...and was it also a coincidence, sir that this MCR apparatus carries your initials?"

Michael blushed slightly, caught with his ego exposed. He knew when he coined the muscle technology that he might pay a price. He spotted the reporter's ID. Damned BBC. "Caltech's Micro-bat team built the first battery-powered flapping wing micro-aerial vehicle small enough to fit in the palm of your hand. Then there's Berkeley's MFI, micro-mechanical flying insect. A ten-millimeter device capable of autonomous flight just like true flies. For years the Massachusetts Institute of Technology tried to combine the flight mechanics of insects with neurobiology, structural engineering, and aerodynamics. It's an unbelievably difficult challenge. Even the most brilliant scientists are learning that it's one thing to build an airplane, and quite another to build a bird. Unfortunately, there had been a general loss of enthusiasm for space ventures after the shuttle incident. I'm confident that NASA can rekindle public confidence. President Warren certainly supports an aggressive Mars project. The initials were pure coincidence."

"But if NASA can't or won't accept your invention, wouldn't that suggest that the Ento...D-Fly might be available for other applications including military?"

"I really don't know," Michael dodged. "We built D-Fly exclusively and in good faith for planetary exploration. The beneficiaries are NASA and Georgia Tech's bank account, in that order. At this time I'm not aware of any plans for either private or military usage other than minor reconnaissance. Our first priority is strictly planetary. Yes, ma'am, in the front row."

"Neela Griffin, Fox Cable. Is the D-Fly project classified, and if not, would we be able to see an up-close demonstration?"

"Good questions; thanks for asking. Let me make this very clear, again. D-Fly is absolutely not classified. In fact, you've already seen the preferred test site. Our stadium has lots of camera angles. D-Fly's components are modular and almost toy-like in design...very easy to control and very sturdy. They have to be with all the Martian rock structures. Even if the wings bump into something during flight, they'll simply snap off and are easily replaced. The most aggressive pilots are under age twelve. My two sons learned to hop it back and forth across those goal posts in no time. I guess it's all that video game experience. They loved it. If any of your organizations want a crack at the controls, I'd be more than happy to make the arrangements."

"What's the operational range?"

"Approximately one mile. We're working to extend that."

"Could the Entomopter be used as a weapon of mass destruction?" Griffin blurted.

A hush spread through the room. Even the waiters who were quietly collecting the tableware paused.

Michael peered over his glasses at the TV station letters on the woman's ID. "I'm sorry…did you say you were with Fox?"

"Yes, their local affiliate in Milwaukee, Wisconsin."

"You're quite a ways from home."

"I'm on a working vacation." She maintained a straight face.

The audience chuckled nervously.

Michael smiled briefly. "The Entomopter was developed to serve as a Mars surveyor and collector. I don't think it would do very well in a military venue."

"You didn't answer my question," she pressed. "I asked you if a terrorist could possibly use your invention as a weapon of—"

"The answer to that is a categorical no," he shot back. "We're not, I'm not interested in destroying humanity, I'm interesting in improving it."

The audience applauded.

Carlo gently interjected himself between Michael and the podium. "Thank you, ladies and gentlemen, but we're running a little behind. This concludes our official program. Please join us out on the terrace for an evening of romance with the Riccardo Perrici Ensemble. You'll also find a delicious selection of wines and desserts. They tell me tonight's specialty is Zuppa Inglese, Italian Tipsy Cake. We hope it lives up to its name. Buon appetito."

Chapter Ten

Washington, DC
NTSB Office of Aviation Safety
Monday, May 4th
7:30 A.M.

National Transportation Safety Board investigative specialist Tom Ross squinted at his reflection in a metal letter opener. The
rounded blade distorted his hair even more. He licked his palm and
tried to smooth down an unruly lump. He angled the makeshift mirror and examined the side of his face. *Relax. It's just a band-aid, not
the end of the world. People wear Band-Aids all the time, even at work.
Pimples, cysts, sores. Shaving. If anyone asks, I cut myself shaving.* He
ran the backside of his hand over a night's worth of whisker stubble.
He always was a horrible liar. Tall with sandy-blonde hair and a fair
complexion, his face blushed every time. The women in the department teased him unmercifully. They said he looked like a vulnerable
Harrison Ford. Thankfully, his boyish good looks and honest reputation would give credence to any facial excuse he used.

Satisfied with the band-aid's adhesion, he reached in a drawer
for a small plastic baggie. He emptied the contents onto the desktop
and herded his breakfast into a neat pile. Pumpkin seeds. The white
coating fed his salt addiction and, in some quirky way, methodically
eating the seeds one by one lowered his stress level. That's how he
rationalized it. The medical truth of the matter disagreed. Sodium
simply raised his blood pressure. He didn't want to think about
that.

He reached for a thick bound set of papers in his in-basket
that was stamped: Courtesy Copy. He shook his head at the eleventh
revision of the latest Department of Homeland Security organization chart. Thank God the NTSB wasn't part of it. There weren't
many advantages of working exclusively for and under the scrutiny
of the United States Congress, but this was definitely one. On paper
the new DHS resembled an electrical wiring schematic for a 1960s
refrigerator. There were black boxes and lines everywhere. Dotted
lines. He found the section he was looking for and ran a finger down
the reporting hierarchy. The poor souls in the FAA were told that the

transition into a new structure would be seamless and that the final result would produce a smooth running anti-bureaucracy. That was a pipe dream. Government was government. Too many chiefs, too many super-chiefs, and too many dotted lines.

After several confusing minutes of paging back and forth and interfiling addendums, he finally pinpointed key TSA counterparts. He wondered how many would be physically transferred and on which effective date. Relocation was always hell, especially on families.

Family.

Like a powerful magnet, the word pulled him away from the office to a quiet neighborhood in Arlington, VA, a house, and a relationship he'd hoped would lead to that. He owned the duplex outright and leased the upper flat to Marcia Davies and her two daughters. He'd been intimate with Marcia for about two years—a joint inner hallway conveniently morphed the separate living quarters into communal space—but the spark had grown dimmer the more her true character unfolded. Their relationship had regressed into that of roommates of different nationalities occupying the same land but with internal borders. They tolerated each other's presence for the children's sake and together churned out a gross domestic product of arguments. The quota was reached nearly every day. Ross had reduced himself to logging Marcia's accusations in hopes of countering them with some form of evidence. At the NTSB, he lived and breathed evidence.

> never home
> not interested in commitment
> no help with chores
> no help with Rachel and Kristin
> loves job more than her
> pumpkin seeds in the wash
> not interested in making love

That was pure bullshit, and she knew it, Ross cursed to himself. She was the one who always brought up wanting another child, yet she was the one with the migraines. Pregnant? God help humanity. Marcia and her ex-husband had already produced and raised the incarnate spawn of Medusa without the head snakes. At 13 and 14, her daughters were unbelievably spoiled brats—-no, they were worse. Disrespectful little bitches. A harsh sentiment, but appropriate. Fights with their mother and especially each other had become cat-violent and routinely involved four-letter words. Once he'd gotten into a confrontation with the younger Rachel and had no choice but to pin her to the floor—a position that stopped the flailing youth in her tracks, but raised cries of abuse. The incident taught him a bitter lesson about the thickness of blood.

Damn terrorists. Ross crumpled the paper. It all started with 9/11. They destroyed 3,000 physical bodies that September morning along with untold thousands of lives of survivors, but it went even farther. No one cared about the untold fractures to families and loved ones on the investigative periphery. There was still a ton of backlogged work.

Dysfunctional family.

He touched the band-aid again. The inch-long fingernail scratch still stung smartly. It would heal in a day or two. The wounds to his relationship might never.

Ross was part of NTSB's Go Team, an elite group of investigators on-call for immediate deployment whenever there was a major transportation accident. As a member, he was expected to have his personal affairs under control so as to arrive at a designated departure airport within two hours of notification. Two hours. That meant stashing extra clothes in his DC office, ensuring that his cell phone and pager were fully charged and activated 24/7, and understanding that nothing but death should keep him from meeting the deadline. No personal commitment was unbreakable. Disciplinary measures were routinely threatened and meted out. There were times during the 9/11 investigations when he literally survived on four hours of sleep. He had managed one precious day off to attend a parent-teacher conference when Flight 587 crashed in Rockaway-Queens, New York.

Marcia just didn't understand.

NTSB staff specialist Ron Hollings poked his head inside the office and immediately noticed his boss's disheveled appearance. The term bedhead came to mind. "Morning. You won't believe it, but guess where we found the file on that 747 that crashed near Madrid in 1976? The one with the wing failure."

"The men's room storage closet," Ross replied off-handedly, his tongue locked in fierce struggle with a stubborn shell fragment.

"How'd you know?"

"It used to be a pre-archive holding room, but no one followed up. Boxes just started accumulating." Ross's own stack was nearing the ceiling.

Hollings glanced at the pumpkin seeds. A solid mood indicator. True to their gender—no matter what the daytime soap writers scripted—most men weren't comfortable talking about personal relationships. They needed a shove. "Things warming up any on the home front?"

"About as warm as Antarctica," Ross said matter-of-factly, showing the battle scar on his cheek. "She started in again this morning, so I just left. I never even shaved or showered. You won't believe what happened yesterday."

Chapter Eleven

Hollings quietly found a chair.

Ross rose from his desk and gazed blankly out of the window. "Dammit, I just don't have the strength anymore. I live in a crazy house and can't handle the violence. Marcia's always been high-strung because of her job. Public accounting firms just beat the hell out of people. It all started when Arthur Anderson collapsed after that Enron thing. She hired on with Ernst and Young, but entry-level tax consulting is brutal. She drags home every night physically and mentally exhausted. Her kids are experts at pushing the guilt buttons. She won't discipline them for anything and when I try all hell breaks loose. She keeps everything inside and then unloads on me in some berserk rage. The littlest thing sets her off. She told me the other night that she works hard and therefore has every right to act that way."

"Menopause," Hollings concluded. "Either that or she needs professional help."

Ross loosened his necktie and sighed. "You tell me. Yesterday I invited the three of them downstairs for dinner. Roast turkey, stuffing, mashed potatoes, homemade bread, and cranberries. The whole house smelled like Thanksgiving in spring. I even made a pumpkin pie. Right after we say grace, Marcia starts in about me not taking our aroma therapy classes seriously and, get this, that she knows about my secret conspiracy to make her submissive."

Hollings' entire face squinted. "Conspiracy?"

"Secret conspiracy."

"You're joking."

"I am not joking," Ross said sternly. "Wait, it gets worse. When Marcia and I first started talking marriage, I told her that I didn't feel comfortable sleeping together with her daughters upstairs. If they were at their father's house, fine. I know it's old fashioned, but that's my rule. Anyway, she makes a nasty comment about me needing Viagra and then brings up this thing with the telephone directory and the fact that my name is listed first because I intentionally switched the..."

"Hold it, you lost me," Hollings interrupted. "The what?"

"Our names. You know, the Arlington White Pages. When

it looked like we might make a go of it, she told me to take out a joint phone listing just like we were married. So I did. Ross, Tom and Marcia. I never even thought twice about it. She said her name should have been listed first because M comes before T and that I switched it on purpose to make her look submissive. She said she wasn't going to eat a single bite until I called Verizon about printing a correction sticker for all their phone books. On a Sunday afternoon!"

Hollings shook his head repeatedly. "Tom, that's not normal behavior. I don't know what to say."

"I don't either," Ross spoke dejectedly into the windowpane. "She just sat at the table glaring at me like my mother. I was dumbfounded. Then like an idiot I tried to lighten things up by saying that the aroma class didn't work because I had Beagle poop on my shoes. It was definitely the wrong time for humor. Out of nowhere, she picked up her plate and flung everything on it clear across the kitchen. Lueeze was laying in her bed and a wad of mashed potatoes landed right on her head. Scared her half to death. She started pawing it off, but then scrambled for her life when Marcia came flailing with a dishtowel. The girls were in tears at the table watching their hysterical mother chase my dog through the living room, who by the way was peeing on the run and tracking gravy all over the carpeting. How's that for a pleasant family meal? Part of me wants to give up; another won't let me. It might be time to get out."

Hollings bit the insides of his cheeks. "Of the relationship or the house?"

"Both." Ross spit a seed hull into the wastebasket and flipped through his calendar. "To hell with this place, too. I need to think. Tell Jennifer I'm taking the rest of the...damn! Is today the fourth?"

"Uh-huh," Hollings nodded.

"I can't win," Ross said softly.

"Nope."

"Another terror presentation?"

"Yup, ten minutes," Hollings noted. "I saved us front row seats."

Ross opened his office door and peered down the hallway. Employees were already making their way to the conference center. "I can't win." He reached for his suit coat and a notepad. "Damned security consultants. I've heard enough of them to last the rest of my career. What's the scare topic this time? Anthrax-laced toilet paper?"

"I'm not sure, but Barrens arranged it personally. I don't think it's a consultant. Some hotshot from Homeland Security. He's definitely got Bridge's ear. Barrens wants the whole department there. Another of his mandatory edicts."

Ross stared at the calendar for a few moments and then defiantly reached for his briefcase. "What could be important enough to bring the Secretary of Homeland Security to this place on a Monday morning? A silver-tongued hotshot? To me that means one of two things: the guy's either bucking for some TV job, or he's running for office. Screw it. I'm leaving anyway."

"Tom, that's not a good idea. This is a departmental meeting. It's mandator—"

"Damn that word," Ross cursed, slamming his briefcase to the floor. "My life is mandatory. This job has sucked every living drop of energy out of me and now it wants my soul. Well guess what? I'm not giving it."

Hollings let his boss vent. He knew it would pass. Ross rarely showed this kind of emotion especially after being named NTSB's backup IIC (investigator-in-charge). His workload had doubled with the responsibility. It was both sad and somehow reassuringly human that, when faced with mounting personal and professional pressures, even the best had breaking points.

Ross sat down and shook his head. "I'm sorry, Ron. I'm not sure I can handle another motivational speaker telling us how far to bend over during a Washington nuclear attack. I've heard it all before. I'm just sick of it."

"Hey, I understand," Hollings assured. "If it'll make you feel any better, this guy's spiel is supposed to be pretty good. A buddy of mine over at Justice heard it and said it shook him up—bad. Nancy Petri's been attending the presentations and publicly challenging some of the content. We might see some fireworks."

Ross rolled his eyes and glanced at the time. "Petri's a political hack and the only thing hotshots know how to do is breed fear. You mark my words. I will get my life in order."

Chapter Twelve

The NTSB conference center was a theater-like room with two aisles wide enough to accommodate even the largest of public press venues. Every seat was filled.

"Good morning," Roger Barrens, Chief of Major Investigations Division announced. "I'm very pleased that the Secretary of Homeland Security, Samuel Bridge was able to join us this morning." The room gave out strong applause. Bridge remained seated and acknowledged the audience with a wave. Barrens produced a fact sheet and continued. "The speaker you're about to hear is Jack Riley, Assistant Deputy Director of Homeland Security Intelligence. Mr. Riley hails from Georgia where he graduated from Emory University with a master's degree in mathematics. He served in the United States Air Force achieving the rank of captain. In Desert Storm, he was in charge of the placement, encryption, and synchronization of all satellite-to-ground voice communication links. He carries a third-degree black belt in Tae Kwon Do and also has, dare I say, the unique honor of reporting directly to Secretary Bridge and is therefore allowed to bypass all those evil Under Secretaries." This drew a collective chuckle. Barrens' brother headed the Directorate of Border and Transportation Security. "As I understand it, Mr. Riley's topic today is something called the Komodo Twins. I haven't seen the presentation myself, but I do know it's being packaged as a video feed to all federal, state, and local law enforcement agencies in the nation. President Warren has also seen it, and that about sums up the gravity. Secretary Bridge has expressed very strong support for the theory based on its, and I quote, 'on-target significance'. With that, let's begin. Mr. Riley?"

The spitting image of a youthful Sidney Portier seated next to the Secretary sprang from his chair and approached the podium. He appeared physically fit with a strong jaw line, symmetrical facial features, and an unusually grim visage. He clipped a wireless microphone set to his belt and necktie, but apparently forgot to turn it on. He placed his hands behind his back and walked regally down the center aisle. His dark blue suit gave off a subtle metallic flash.

"Thank you, Roger. Good morning. My Christian name is Prince. Prince Jackson Riley. I want you to know that I'm neither

Irish nor next in line for the British or any other throne. My mother named me Prince because she thought I looked like African royalty when I entered this world. My friends still call me that. You may call me Jack. I'm the Department of Homeland Security's lead terror investigator for any and all major threats; specific or potential. Bombings, cluster cell identification, motorized incidents, WMD, you name it. But don't let the impressive title fool you. My staff and I work in the trenches hand in hand with every federal enforcement agency. It's all about teamwork. For some strange reason, my boss doesn't believe in letting people take time off. He keeps sending me out on assignments anytime and anyplace." Riley turned to the front of the room. "How long has it been since I've had a vacation Mr. Secretary? Three years or four?"

"Write your senator," Bridge responded to a throng of laughter.

It was four years. A day here or there was fine. Bridge once told his department heads that they could take extended vacation when the nation's terror alert level dropped down to guarded.

Riley shook his head and turned back to the audience. "I guess you could say that I'm terror's point man. Perhaps we'll meet somewhere sometime in some official capacity, but I hope not. Terror is never a pleasant thing." He pointed to the large U.S. flag standing in the corner. "Take a good look at the symbol of American freedom, people. It's the last time you'll ever think that."

A cell phone's annoying musical scale interrupted the mood.

Riley took note of the location and casually strolled toward the owner. "My presentation today has just five slides. Five."

He clicked an overhead projector and the first appeared:

You can't defend against the unthinkable
without thinking about it in the first place.

"And now, the unthinkable." Riley clicked the next slide.

The audience chuckled at two adult Komodo dragon lizards, mouths agape, spaghetti-like streams of saliva dangling disgustedly. The subtitle said: 'al Qaeda.'

"By a show of hands, how many in this room think the next nine-one-one-level terrorist attack on American soil or against American assets will involve one of these?"

Riley clicked the third slide.

CRUISE SHIP
SHOPPING MALL
NUCLEAR FACILITY
GOVERNMENT EMBASSY
NATIONAL MONUMENT
BRIDGE/TUNNEL
SUBWAY/RAILROAD
SKYSCRAPER
NATIONAL SPORTING EVENT
MILITARY FACILITY
LEVEE SYSTEM
WATER/FOOD SUPPLY

Every hand raised but one. It was the woman with the cell phone.

She finished her conversation and quietly tucked it into her purse.

Riley's eyes took a snapshot of her appearance. African American, thirty-ish, medium build, short hair, attractive Halle Berry-ish face. He read her nametag ID. "Patricia Creed-Riley, TSA Aviation Operations. I'm glad to see that we have a mix of agencies with us this morning. No relation but we used to work for the same C-O-O. Nice to meet you."

"Nice to meet you. I prefer Tricia."

"Okay, Tricia Creed. You didn't raise your hand. Don't you like my targets?"

"I'm really sorry," she whispered. "I wasn't listening."

"And why weren't you listening?" Riley raised his voice.

"I had an important call," she responded evenly.

"Not a problem, Tricia. I'm addicted to cellular phones myself. Mine even vibrates and then displays text messages so I can receive information without disrupting anyone else. The next nine-eleven?"

Creed folded her arms and studied the slide. "I think you might have missed one."

Riley nodded thoughtfully to the audience. "She says I missed one. Okay, I suppose that's possible. Brief us."

"Excuse me?"

"Enlighten us, Tricia. Share your insights. I'm sure we could all benefit."

Creed straightened in her seat. "Well, I'm a damned good transportation investigator, but not exactly familiar with terror tactics. What about an attack on the general population by chemical or biological weapons spread over large urban territor—?"

"We get the message," Riley interrupted rudely. "Not a bad idea. One more question, Tricia, before we move on. I wonder if you wouldn't give us your definition of freedom."

"Huh?"

"Freedom. I want you to define it."

"Um, the constitution. Speech, liberty, the pursuit of happiness. Our freedom is guaranteed by rights in the U.S. constitution, specifically the first ten ammend—"

"No!" Riley's voice boomed into the now activated microphone. The volume was so loud that several people jumped in their seats. The audience gave out a collective murmur. "Words on a piece of paper do not constitute freedom. Ms. Creed, you are a highly-trained professional in the field of American law enforcement, yet thirty seconds ago you admitted to God and country that you're not, what was the word you used?...familiar with terror tactics. You carry a weapon. I suspect that if push came to shove, you'd use it on me if you had to. Please know that I would use mine on you. You're wearing a skirt and are therefore presumed to be female and thus physically weaker than most male counterparts in every other enforcement and security agency. Do you know the primary combat function of women serving in the Israeli Defense Force? Border police. You other females in this audience...raise your hands if that bothers you or you think that's unfair."

Most complied including several males.

Riley scanned the responses. "Golly, folks, I'm real sorry. Did I just ruffle those feathers in another paper document called Title VII, Discrimination in the Workplace? Perhaps a politically correct apology is in order; or another set of quota regulations for women and minorities; or even a lawsuit? Well, tough. In al Qaeda's world, paper documents, rules and regulations, and political correctness are totally meaningless. More importantly, they will kill you. Freedom is won and maintained through physical force or lost for the lack of it. A society clinging to a list of paper rights can't provide it. Neither can this country. Take another look at those targets, America. Raise your security threat levels to fire engine red. Activate and deploy your military and civilian soldiers, guards, officers, and agents on every street corner in every city. Confiscate the lethal nail clippers, hatpins and aftershave bottles, and then yank the shoes off every passenger in every airport. Spend your physical and monetary resources guarding, preventing, disrupting, and generally wasting time, effort, and my tax dollars defending against something that may certainly materialize, but never produce much more than a few box cutters and a few mangled bodies. Americans don't have one damned clue about protecting freedom."

Chapter Thirteen

Riley made his way to the front of the room. He definitely had everyone's attention.

"What I'm about to show you is a fuse. A fuse that will light the mother of all terrorist actions. By numbers alone, more than twenty-five times deadlier than 9/11. You can count on it. If I had the mind-set, I'd sure as hell give it a whirl. It is not about the destruction of any of the so-called traditional target potentials on this screen. Why? Because they're too well-guarded. And it won't happen via another airborne assault on New York skyscrapers, presidential residences, or five-sided military buildings. Those were appetizers. Damned lucky wake-up appetizers. You will not see some wild-eyed foreign radical running through downtown Manhattan waving a dirty bomb. No one will poison the water supply or inject himself with typhoid or bubonic plague and start greeting shoppers at Wal-Mart. Nobody's going to swallow plastic explosives and blow up in the front row at the Academy Awards. And no one's going to start picking off shoppers in the Mall of America on a Saturday afternoon. No, my friends...the next major attack will be the shortest in duration, unimaginably brutal, highly coordinated, and involve the smallest military invasion force in history—one hundred and forty soldiers to be exact—who in just thirty minutes will attempt to destroy the freedom of the United States of America. And they will succeed. Why? Because we're vulnerable as hell. And more importantly, our constitution guarantees it."

Riley clicked the fourth slide. Twenty-five names appeared. He let the audience digest the information.

KOMODO ONE

Disney's Animal Kingdom – Lake Buena Vista, FL
Six Flags – St. Louis, MO
Paramount's Kings Island – Cincinnati, OH
Universal Studios – Orlando, FL
Seaworld – San Antonio, TX
Disney's MGM Studios – Lake Buena Vista, FL
Busch Gardens – Williamsburg, VA
Six Flags – Gurnee, IL

Epcot – Lake Buena Vista, FL
Six Flags – Austell, GA
Rye Playland – Rye, NY
Disneyland – Anaheim, CA
Six Flags – Arlington, TX
Magic Kingdom – Lake Buena Vista, CA
Universal Studios – Hollywood, CA
Seaworld – Orlando, FL
Six Flags – Valencia, CA
Coney Island – Brooklyn, NY
Paramount's Great America – Santa Clara, CA
Six Flags – Darien Lake, NY
Six Flags – Aurora, OH
Knott's Berry Farm – Buena Park, CA
Worlds of Fun – Kansas City, MO
Cedar Point – Sandusky, OH
Seaworld – San Diego, CA

"Theme parks. You know these places. You've packed up your families and traveled there. Perhaps you've even seen some identified as potential terror targets. But you've never seen the tactics. On the perfect date, let's call it K-Day, one hundred guests will enter these twenty-five theme parks across the U.S. Did you catch that? Not terrorists, not soldiers, not enemy combatants…guests. One-zero-zero. Four in each park. And trust me…none will comply if asked to hand over the weaponry strapped under their clothing. One MP-5 machine gun, two Glock automatic handguns, and 1,000 rounds of 10mm ammunition in fast-load clips. For those of you who at this very moment are so anal as to want to calculate the weight of 1,000 such rounds, I'll save you the trouble. Less than thirty-five pounds. Easily concealed and carried inside normal attire. The guests will assume offensive paired positioning throughout the event. Follow? Two pairs of shooters in each park. One protects the other. At a precisely coordinated P.M. hour, they will engage in open and random firing, and continue until all ammunition is gone. Ever hear the expression shooting fish in a barrel? These fish will include women and children. Young and old. At the end of Komodo One, seventy thousand Americans will lie dead or wounded."

Riley clicked the fifth slide.

63

KOMODO TWO
Wrigley Field – Chicago, IL
Fenway Park – Boston, MA
Yankee Stadium – New York, NY
Oriole Park – Baltimore, MD
Coors Field – Denver, CO
Jacob's Field – Cleveland, OH
Turner Field – Atlanta, GA
Dodger's Stadium – Los Angeles, CA
Safeco Stadium – Seattle, WA
The Baseball Park in Arlington – Arlington, TX

"Precisely coordinated with the date and clock timing of K-One, forty fans will enter these ten baseball stadiums. Four-zero, same weaponry. Sound familiar? They will pack identical armaments and take seats near home and visitor dugouts. Within seconds of the theme park attacks, they'll enter the field of play, calmly open fire at bench and active players, and then continue targeting the general stadium population until their ammunition is spent. At the end of K-Two, you can add another ten thousand to the casualty list..." Riley paused for effect. "...and twenty major league baseball teams will cease to exist."

The audience sat stunned.

Riley clicked the projector off. "The shooters will drop their gear and melt into the chaos, and believe me, there'll be chaos. Authorities will never be certain of their exact number. Within the hour, al Qaeda will release videotape to major news outlets throughout the world declaring jihad against all infidels inside the United States. K-Day. It will be quite historic for at that precise moment, we'll all need to sign up for Yiddish class. America will have become Israel. Military curfews, roadblocks, checkpoints, religious persecution. Anyone with dark hair and a suntan will feel racial mistrust and bigotry so severe it'll make slavery in the old south seem like, Disneyland. In the aftermath, Americans will start making life-altering decisions to avoid major cities in a panicked attempt to live and raise their families in terror-free environments spelled r-u-r-a-l. People will establish virtual safety zones and any excursions beyond those zones or into crowds will carry overwhelming tension and suspicion. Fear will bear on every decision to either congregate in large numbers or travel, and millions will simply stop. In the next segment, we're going to examine why K-Day will happen, why we won't or can't stop it, and why the incredible violence and subsequent threat of open warfare in our beloved country are only a means to an end. Remember, I said Komodo is only the fuse. I have not yet explained what it leads to. But first I suggest we all take a break. Based on the facial expressions, it looks like some of you could use it. Fifteen minutes. Oh, and Ms. Creed? So much for freedom."

Chapter Fourteen

Rome, Italy
Atlante Star Hotel

Linda Robertson sat on the edge of the Jacuzzi and stared dreamlike out of the fourth floor window at the surreal sight of St. Peter's Basilica in the distance. The setting sunrays had formed a golden halo around the dome just like so many artists portrayed in the radiant face of Christ. Chainsaw-like buzzing interrupted her mood. Annoyed at first, she had actually gotten used to the popular motor scooters racing through the downtown area. She turned off the water spigot and helped her husband remove his underwear. She smiled. After all these years, she still liked to look at his butt.

Michael gingerly stepped into the 100-degree water. His whole body ached with flu-like symptoms and every inch of his skin carried thorny pain that emanated from his intestines. He eased himself down. The warmth provided soothing relief evidenced by a long moan.

Linda laid a cool washcloth across his forehead. "Know what I think I'll do?"

"Find a new husband," he said jokingly. "One who doesn't ruin a wonderful vacation in the world's most romantic city. We should cancel the dinner reservations. I'm really sorry; I feel terrible."

"You shouldn't worry. People get sick. There's always room service." She dried her hands and placed the towel within his reach. "I saw an interesting jewelry shop next door. Do you need anything else?"

"Thanks, I'm fine." He drew her hand to his mouth and kissed it. "I'll just sit here and sulk. Be careful."

She dimmed the room lights and left.

Michael let his body submerge until his mustache met the water. His finger touched a button. Soft jets rolled up and down his back like an undulating snake.

There was a knock at the door.

Michael raised himself slightly and glanced at the nightstand next to the bed. *Damn—she forgot her key.* He bunched a towel around his privates and carefully stepped across the marble floor for the door. He never considered the security peephole.

"Professor Robertson?"

Startled at the male figure and voice, he slipped backwards as the towel fell to the floor. He quickly retrieved it. "How can I help you?"

Ali Naimi removed his brimmed hat. "My name is Ibrahim Al-Assaf. I apologize for the intrusion, but I was unable to attend your ceremony last evening. We have a mutual friend...a Professor Al-Aran. I believe he is a colleague of yours? He mentioned that you were staying here. May I come in?"

"Um, sure." Michael instinctively turned to verify that his wife was presentable. Confused at remembering she wasn't there, he opened the door and stepped aside.

Naimi hesitated. "I've come at a bad time. Would tomorrow be...?"

"No, it's fine. Please, sit down." He noticed the man's deep complexion and well-spoken manner. He set the room key on the bar and motioned to a chair by the window. "Excuse me, for just a minute."

Naimi carefully sidestepped two suitcases. One was packed with children's T-shirts.

Michael emerged from the bathroom somewhat drier and wearing a white terrycloth robe. He tossed a towel on the floor and foot-swiped the water. "Can I get you something?" Naimi declined. Michael opened the refrigerator and wrestled with the cap on a bottle of mineral water. "Faiz and I have shared office space at Georgia Tech for three years. Seems like they're always remodeling. Sometimes we even cover each other's lectures. How do you know him?"

"I work for the Minister of Petroleum and Mineral Resources for the Kingdom of Saudi Arabia," Naimi explained. "If I could speak freely, there is a certain, business proposition."

Michael frowned deeply. "What sort of proposition?"

"Well, you may know that our Kingdom produces one quarter of the world's oil with new resources being discovered faster than current reserves can be used. Our newest field at Shaybah is already the fourth largest. We are also very proud of the fact that at one dollar per barrel, our production costs are three times less than the

67

world average. Dr. Al-Aran is currently working at Shaybah on an Arab-Exxon development venture. He is in charge of laying out new airport runways. I'm afraid the desert is quite inhospitable."

"Faiz has a PhD in operations research from George Washington University. He's an expert in that area. What's it got to do with me?"

"We wish to evaluate a new form of surveillance at our production sites including security cameras that are reliable, highly mobile, and easy to operate. These insects of yours...when Faiz described the project, it piqued our curiosity."

"You want to use Entomopters for security?"

"Evaluate," Naimi quickly corrected. "On a platform—literally. We need something that has the ability to position itself atop strategically placed platforms and observe production operations. Can your insects do this?"

"Platforms? What kind of platforms?"

"Observation stands attached to existing equipment and framing. Derrick steel, for example. Both flat and round. We wish to evaluate the possibility of deploying a series of moveable sentries that can quickly reach certain high-risk areas and monitor our assets. Not only in Shaybah, but potentially all our fields. But this must be done very quietly and without drawing attention."

"I'm confused," Michael said suspiciously. "What's wrong with traditional options like good old security guards?"

"Intolerable." Naimi's hand gave off a dismissive wave. "A series of fixed surveillance cameras is both limited and vulnerable and, I'm afraid a human military presence is something we cannot afford." He meant trust.

Misinterpreting the comment as a monetary issue, Michael's frown grew even deeper. The Saudi's weren't exactly known for frugality. "What about unmanned aircraft or helicopters?"

Naimi maintained his courteous demeanor. "Professor Robertson...you don't understand. The Royal Family is committed to solving this rather delicate problem of wide area security in the quietest way possible. We cannot abide armed patrols or military aircraft littering the skies above the Kingdom. It's an extremely sensitive situation, particularly with the current value of petroleum. You must know that the Saudi government, under the leadership of the Custodian of the Two Holy Mosques, his Royal Highness King Abdullah must manage the region with the utmost reverence. It is related to appearance, but frankly, there is another reason. One that is somewhat unpleasant."

Chapter Fifteen

"You may think it unusual for Arabs to be overly concerned with terror, but certain individuals have made repeated threats regarding Saudi oil. The largest prize in the world for the west to capture and terrorists to destroy. Threats that we must take seriously. Faiz has explained that your Entomopters have some dexterity and also a small profile?"

Michael sipped his water thoughtfully. Now he understood. The terrorist bombings in Spain, London, and most recently, Saudi refineries. Bin Laden's network. The Royal Family was running scared. "Very limited dexterity. But we're already negotiating with NASA. I wouldn't be able to look at any other offers until our position with the space program is finalized."

"Completely understandable," Naimi acknowledged. "But certainly you would be agreeable to a trial evaluation for a brief period, say, thirty days? Something that would allow us to see these Entomopters in action."

"I'm not sure that's possible," Michael countered. "I'd have to talk to my university. They would have to approve something like that."

"I mean no disrespect, Professor, but there is a sense of urgency in this matter. And with you on vacation and unavailable for conference, well, Dr. Al-Aran has already conversed with the appropriate trustees. They were most enthusiastic in expressing preliminary support for such a trial. Arrangements have already been made on your campus in Atlanta for us to acquire the necessary system components. If we like the Ento—"

"Excuse me?" Michael interrupted. "What did you say?"

"We've arranged for a point of transfer."

"No, before that. You said something about trustees. What trustees?"

Naimi gently stroked his mustache. "I recall the name Garton. Yes, that's it. Dr. Al-Aran has had direct conversation with a Winford Garton. He was most enthusiastic about the prospects."

He would be, Michael thought. Garton was Vice Chair of Georgia Tech Research Corporation, a non-profit entity that secured and managed research funds. He was also a primary sponsor of the

Entomopter. He'd sell freshmen on the black market if it meant a grant commitment. "Okay, let's back up. You apparently don't need my permission so why are you even here? It's obvious that this is a done deal."

Naimi folded his hands, prayer-like. "Michael, we need your expertise, or that of your program staff, particularly with technical nuances and hands-on training. We prefer to borrow several Entomopters for a very brief time period, evaluate them on site at the Shaybah location, and make a final decision. We certainly wish to keep you in the loop so to speak, at least in the short term. Of course there will be compensation made to your campus research facility. An initial deposit of fifty percent. If we like the system, we will make a second payment that will constitute a full purchase. You obviously will retain patent rights and may serve as a general advisor during the trial. The Kingdom is very flexible in these matters. If we decide the Entomopters are not feasible for our oil fields, then we shall return them immediately and you may keep the deposit. In any event, your university gains adequate compensation."

"How adequate?"

"Ten million dollars, U.S. Five million has already been issued and is in Dr. Al-Aran's possession."

Michael lifted the water bottle to his lips, but didn't drink. His mind was trying to comprehend what he just heard. The sudden air gasp brought on a coughing jag. "You're willing to pay five million dollars to perch a flying camera on an oil rig? Are you crazy?"

Naimi bunched the sheer window fabric aside and gazed outside. "Again, you must forgive what I say. I am an honorable man and do not wish to appear condescending. Saudis are taught at a very young age never to boast of wealth. At current trends, our Kingdom's net export oil revenue for the current production year is projected at 250 billion dollars. Net revenue, professor. That is far more than even your Wal-Mart will earn on 320 billion dollars in gross sales. I can assure you of two things: the monetary aspects of this arrangement can be compared to a purchase of…" He glanced at the suitcase…"a child's souvenir. It is indeed trivial; and, I am indeed not crazy."

"I'm sorry, I didn't mean it that way," Michael apologized. Ten million dollars still wasn't trivial. "You mentioned a transfer point?"

"Dr. Al-Aran has attended several OPEC conferences in the

U.S. Members of the Royal Family feel comfortable with him, but more importantly, they trust his judgment. As an Arab, he understands the...eccentricities of our business culture, not to mention the language. We wish to have him take the lead in this matter. He has informed us that he is knowledgeable enough with the Entomopter's design to transition and even operate the system. Do you share that assessment?"

I'll be damned, Michael swore to himself. His colleague was literally stealing his project. "I do not," he said flatly. "The good Dr. Al-Aran might be well advised to consult with me before making any more commitments. I need to speak with him before this goes any further."

"Of course." Naimi casually peeked at his watch. "That reminds me...how many Entomopters are currently in existence?"

Michael's head was spinning. "Huh? I'm sorry. Um, twelve. Twelve are assembled and ready to fly. We can make more on site right from our own lab. All the parts are modular. How many units do you figure you'd need?"

Naimi pursed his lips thoughtfully and then shrugged. "If I recall correctly, Dr. Al-Aran has stated that five Entomopters should give us more than enough insight to make a decision. We've worked closely in the past. He understands the Kingdom's rather straightforward methodologies." Naimi rose from his chair. "Five units. May I presume that we have your tentative support?"

Michael nodded reluctantly. "An offsite transfer might require some special licensing, but overall, I don't think there'll be any opposition, especially if it's a temporary thing. I suppose my team could help make it a smooth transition."

"It has been a sincere pleasure, Mr. Robertson." Naimi offered his hand. "Enjoy Rome. I wish you safe flight Thursday and congratulations again on the technical award."

Michael closed the hotel room door and untied his bathrobe. He sank back into the Jacuzzi and let his head submerge completely before turning on the jets. He felt like he could throw up, but he was too furious. *That sonofabitch Faiz. What the hell was going on? Tromping off to some oil field in the desert with a bunch of Entomopters? My Entomopters.* He wanted to pick up the phone and stop the whole ridiculous idea. The patent issues had never been resolved and if push came to shove, he really didn't know his position on ownership. *Was it his invention or Georgia Tech's?* They hired him to head a research team and develop something that could fly on Mars. *Been there, done that. Jesus, am I expendable now? Funny how word of the Entomopter had spread so quickly, but after all, the Pirelli Award was an international event. Relax,* he told himself. This was probably the first of many weird offers. And this Al-Assaf character and his Saudi money...*talk about weird. It really wasn't a proposition at all,* Michael recounted. Propositions meant you had a choice. The Saudis were known for dangling huge sums of cash in front of academia, especially when they wanted something. Knowing an insider certainly helped. No wonder Faiz had shown increased interest in the project's timeline. Rome or not, now Michael was even more anxious to get home. He spit a stream of water across the Jacuzzi fountain-like. He wondered how Al-Assaf knew his flight left on Thursday.

Chapter Sixteen

NTSB Conference Center

Jack Riley waited politely as a few stragglers hurried to their seats. There wasn't much talking; there never was. He walked to the center of the room and brought up slide number two. "Okay, why is K-Day so powerful and so perfect? Two reasons. The first is obvious and once cost a U.S. president a general election. Anyone? George Bush, Sr? Clinton victory? One of the best ways to significantly wound the United States of America is to wound the economy. So, let's talk about airlines. Since 9/11, this fiercely competitive industry has lost a combined ninety billion dollars. Two weeks after the attacks, carriers needed fifteen billion in government loans just to keep operating. A sagging global economy, terrorism, and wars in Afghanistan and Iraq didn't help. A weak recession suddenly became severe. Economic losses extended to vacation, travel, food, hotel, and motor transport industries. Entire lengths of resort beaches were virtually empty. Key West for example lost eighteen percent of its small businesses. All across America, cruise lines, rental car companies, restaurants, hotels, local retailers dependent on tourist dollars are finally starting to recover. Last time I checked, airline layoffs had reached 200,000 positions including technical, management, and skilled and semi-skilled workers. With respect to America's resolve and the U.S. military's Middle East campaigns, no terrorist organization will ever be dumb enough to face-off with us again. That includes borders and all of the traditional targets I've shown you. Terror will turn both high-tech and guerilla lethal. One more thing: In my humble opinion, I believe our intelligence agencies are being fed information for no other reason than to burden our security forces and keep true motives hidden. Thanks to the Spanish rail and London subway incidents, just one piece of disinformation can shut down entire transportation systems. One anonymous phone call threatening a chemical or explosive attack in New York's tunnel or subway system will alert 25,000 defenders and cost 24 million dollars. Think about it. One incredible call. And that's just one alert in one city. How long can any budget hold out under that kind of pressure? Is it any wonder why our federal deficit is the highest ever? Questions?"

"With all due respect, Mr. Riley, I think you, your presentation, and all it represents are preposterous," Illinois Congresswoman Petri spoke up. One of the three political appointees, she headed the NTSB's Office of Public Relations. "The Shapiro Report on Terrorism showed that cities can survive even the largest calamities. You do remember that after 9/11 our financial markets opened and operated without a single major problem. The American people have an uncanny ability to rebound. And you're obviously misinformed about theme parks. Just last week my family and I attended the pre-season opening of Great America in Gurnee, Illinois. They unveiled state-of-the-art metal detection equipment and every one of us had to walk through. In addition, they hand-searched backpacks, purses, and even baby strollers. As far as your baseball scenario, I highly doubt that such a thing could ever transpire. Think about what that would mean to the country's psyche. I'm actually feeling sick to my stomach just hearing such nonsense."

"Preposterous isn't the right word, ma'am," Riley countered. "Try devastating. The truth is we don't like to hear reality. Americans tend to live in a figurative world where everything, and I mean everything is taken for granted with respect to open freedoms. The ramifications of target vulnerabilities are just starting to emerge, and they are crushing. 9/11 cost New York City eighty-three billion dollars and sixty thousand jobs. We estimate that the sporting event we used to call America's pastime would be completely shut down for at least two seasons. The initial forecast of economic losses to cities with host stadiums is in the hundreds of billions. Six small market teams would never recover. They'd simply be lost to history. But it's more than that. The psychological impacts would last years. And of course, we haven't discussed the date. That, my friends is utterly unthinkable. The explosion at the end of the fuse. K-Day is a fixed secular holiday; a national celebration; and a time when citizens go about their daily lives having fun and enjoying traditional summer activities. Want to permanently imprint a terror tattoo right on America's forehead? Destroy the sanctity of its birthday. That's right. The Fourth of July would signal the beginning of the end of our precious open society. The major cities within the U.S. would become military guard posts. With respect to theme parks...every single one schedules an evening fireworks celebration. The crowds will be enormous, loud, unconcerned, and anticipating noise. If you think 9/11 damaged the airlines, Komodo One alone will sound that industry's death knell especially on routes to those locations. And to prove that, let's talk for a moment about travel. Last year, U.S. theme park attendance rose 6% to 324 million visitors, a number that's expected to increase steadily through 2010. Can anyone here spell target rich environments? Of those visitors, only one percent will be American minorities. Baseball game attendance is even worse. Why? Because they can't afford it. The way admission prices are rising just to walk through the gates, I can't afford it. You may not like to hear this but that place in Florida with Mickey and the seven little guys? It might as well be called White Disney World. African and Latino-American minorities just don't go there. So who does besides the Europeans and Japanese? Caucasian suburbanites. Families with medium to upper incomes. Disposable incomes. Parents who panic if their kids take ten unsupervised steps away from the back door on their own property. After K-Day, an entire generation of prime spenders will never take their precious offspring to a theme park again no matter how safe the physical conditions are portrayed. The mere potential that something so horrific and violent could happen again will be enough to dissuade the travel. Think about it. How many families move to Colorado just so their kids can enroll at Columbine? They won't go, period. But don't miss the point, people. This isn't a forever thing. Time will heal the effects of even mass carnage, but by then the damage will have been done in beautiful and complete fashion. How long can any business survive after losing an entire generation of customers? The U.S. economy will flirt with the country's second depression primarily because people will be in an extended state of shock-fear. And for those of you who need financial gravitas, we hired the Brookings Institute to construct a model of the economic impacts. As to the Congresswoman's statements on the strength and resiliency of our markets, all I can say is ignorance is bliss. I won't bore you with details, but after the events of K-Day, the Dow Jones Industrial Average starts snowballing downhill for twenty-six consecutive months before leveling off at...you ready for this?...fourteen hundred. If you think that your 401(k)s have bottomed out at fifty percent of their previous values, then try swallowing account balances at zero to three percent. We call it the Komodo Effect. A relatively small but dangerous reptile waits in ambush for prey many times its size. With a single bite, infection starts almost immediately and is always fatal."

75

Petri rose from her seat. "I resent being called ignorant and I certainly don't have to sit here any longer and listen to unsubstantiated speculative propaganda about lizards. This administration is fear-mongering. If you'll excuse me?" Flanked by two aides, she stormed out of the center.

Riley gave his boss a surreptitious glance and pressed a button on the remote. The overhead screen retracted into the ceiling.

"Based on that pleasant little episode, I've decided to end the presentation here. But I'll leave you with one final albeit sickening thought: al Qaeda's official declaration of jihad will be announced before the attacks take place. Therefore, according to our illustrious Supreme Court, any combatant captured will technically be eligible for Geneva Convention prisoner protection. Don't be surprised when some of our own citizens actually try and enforce those rights." Riley glanced at his watch. "No part of this presentation is confidential. In fact, Komodo needs to be shown and publicized to as many people as possible. But as you just observed, that's a tall order, especially when entrenched bureaucrats have their heads stuck up their...in the sand. They don't want to know. Why? Because they don't believe in taking preemptive measures to stop potential threats. They claim it tramples on the constitution. Many don't have the funds to do anything about it anyway, even from a planning perspective. Secretary Bridge and the president have already listened to my preposterous rambling—twice. It's one of their top priorities. Needless to say, they're already receiving plenty of heat from people who share the Congresswoman's opinion that yours truly is crazy and such events could never happen. Meanwhile, protective resources continue to flow toward those big name targets. I'm sure you've all heard rumors of Iranian and Hezbollah sleeper cell activations. Just the other day five thousand law enforcement officers in San Francisco went on alert after someone saw a suspicious rubber boat puttering around the Golden Gate Bridge. The so-called prisoner abuse scandal at Abu Ghraib has actually produced an increase in sympathy levels for those who want to kill us. Some enemy combatants held in Guantanamo Bay, Cuba have already been awarded civil liberty status. Let me remind you...walking a terrorist prisoner on a dog leash is not an atrocity. Torturing a U.S. soldier and then mutilating his body is. Anyway...I'll be at the Martin Luther King Federal Building in Atlanta on May 11th and the Peck Building in Cincinnati on May 18th. If you have contacts in the FBI offices there,

I'd appreciate it if you'd give them some feedback. My video should be finished by then. We're distributing it for free. Before you leave I have one more comment about accessing so-called protected locations that deploy state-of-the-art metal detection equipment. Great America at Gurnee, Illinois has an employee entrance staffed by a seventy-year-old security guard named Fritz. Have a safe day."

Chapter Seventeen

Milwaukee, WI

Leonardo Sinani drove his black 2000 Toyota Camry into the parking lot of a tavern off Layton Avenue. He lowered the window and peered at the address. A stiff spring wind managed to water his eyes, but couldn't budge his curly black hair. A tear ran down his cheek. A rarity—he rarely cried for anyone or anything—he wiped it away. He despised cold weather. He wasn't born in it and vowed never to get used to it. Satisfied that the building's painted block letters matched those in a newspaper clipping, he shut off the engine and unzipped a pocket inside his jacket. He drew out a small red book and rubbed his thumbs lovingly across the gold leaf lettering. He pulled on the end of a thin cloth ribbon and the Holy Qur'an split open. Transfixed, he read from the text aloud. His voice was filled with passion as if he were re-dedicating himself to some lover or deep cause. In essence, he was.

Surah 9. Repentance, Dispensation

1. A declaration of immunity from Allah and His Messenger, to those of the Pagans with whom ye have contracted mutual alliances:

2. Go ye, then, backwards and forwards, as ye will, throughout the land, but know ye that ye cannot frustrate Allah by your falsehood but that Allah will cover with shame those who reject Him.

3. And an announcement from Allah and His Messenger, to the people assembled on the day of the Great Pilgrimage, that Allah and His Messenger dissolve treaty obligations with the Pagans. If then, ye repent, it were best for you; but if ye turn away, know ye that ye cannot frustrate Allah. And proclaim a grievous penalty to those who reject Faith.

4. But the treaties are not dissolved with those Pagans with whom ye have entered into alliance and who have not subsequently failed you in aught, nor aided any one against you. So fulfill your engagements with them to the end of their term: for Allah loveth the righteous.

5. Then fight and slay the Pagans wherever ye find them, and seize them, beleaguer them, and lie in wait for them in every stratagem of war; but if they repent, and establish regular prayers and practice regular charity, then open the way for them: for Allah is Oft-forgiving,

Most Merciful.

He kissed the book and tucked it away. He dialed a number on his cell phone. After four rings, an answering machine picked up. The voice was female and seductive.

You've reached Nick's Velvet Touch Escort and Massage. We're located on Pacific Drive across from San Diego International Airport. Our hours are noon to three A.M. Tell us what you need and remember, we've got that special touch just for you......beeeep.

Sinani looked at his watch. "This is Dean Sogi and I'm calling about the apartment. I just wanted to make sure that everything's all set. I'm in Milw, er..Minneapolis right now doing some last-minute packing. I hope you got my deposit. It'd be nice if I could move in a day or two early to clean. If it's all right with you I'll even pay for paint. I'll try later and thanks——"

"Hola. Um, hello." A soft-spoken Spanish voice answered.

"Hello, who is this?" Sinani asked.

"Marissa. It's six o'clock in the morning, senor. Everyone is still sleeping. Can you call back?"

"You're not sleeping," Sinani said playfully.

She yawned. "I know. My kids woke me up. They're hungry."

He frowned into the phone. "Is this The Velvet Touch?"

"Si, I mean, yes. I work here, but I also live here, temporarily. I don't exactly have my own place."

"I see," Sinani mused. "I need to leave a message for Nicholas Karkula. I sent him a deposit check for an apartment I rented. Do you know if he received it?"

"Nick is the owner. I think he did, but I'm not sure. You'll like the place; it's right above us. The last tenants didn't take care of it so Nick had to throw them out. He gets really mad when people drink and make noise. He has a bad temper."

"Thank you, Marissa. That's good to know."

"Don't mention it. I hope it works out for you. Maybe I'll see you when you get to San Diego. You sound like a nice guy. We don't get too many of those around here. Bye bye."

"I am a nice guy and I really like kids," Sinani replied, awkwardly attempting to prolong the conversation.

He cleared his phone and dialed a second number.

A receptionist answered. "Good morning. O'Hare Aerospace

Center. Cohen Leasing and Management. May I help you?"

"Dennis Cray, please," Sinani replied. The transfer rang once.

"This is Dennis."

"This is John Ghoacci. I wanted to follow up on my contract?"

"Yes, John, we've been waiting to hear from you. I've got your application file right here. PC Doctors, fourth floor, office forty-two west. The occupancy lease is signed and approved for six-months commencing May 1st. We have your deposit. Will you need any administrative support or housekeeping?"

"Not right away," Sinani lied. "But I'd like the option."

"No problem; we have daily rates. You can sign up anytime. When will you be arriving?"

"I haven't made all the arrangements, but I'll probably move some things in this week."

"That'll work," Cray assured. "Always a pleasure to have a new tenant. You'll love the location. You have a wonderful view of the airport and western sunsets. We use keyless entry and this month's lobby access number is triple five. Your office door code is one-one-nine. Will there be anything else?"

"Nope, I think I'm all set."

"I'm glad we could do business, John. Have a good one."

"Thanks. You, too." Sinani clicked off and dialed a third number.

The woman's voice that answered was grandmother sweet, but her speech was slurred. "Kenny? Kenneth Wory by the saints where are you, lad and how is your poor mother? I've been a worried soul."

"There's good news, Mrs. Timmons." Sinani announced. "They think the pneumonia's under control. She's home now and resting. I'm going to stay here a few more days."

"Take your time, lad. New York won't run away. My brother Bernard has been keeping me company. All the way from Ireland to finally visit that Statue of Liberty. He's the only ting I've got in the world now. I sure hoped the two of you might meet."

"I'll try Mrs. Timmons. See you in a day or so. Bye-bye."

Chapter Eighteen

Sinani stepped into the parking lot and pressed his key chain. The Camry responded with a high-low tweet. He gave a wary glance to two warring bookends—a full-sized M-60 tank and Apache attack helicopter—that flanked each side of the building.

American Legion Post 154
MEMBERS ONLY

He stared suspiciously at a vintage pineapple hand grenade cemented to the door's metal frame. He complied with the instruction and pulled the pin. Across the street to the south, Mitchell International Airport was layered in light fog. A Midwest Airlines jet sped down a runway and lifted into the air. Recent business reports had touted the company's much-improved financial condition. A leaner more productive workforce; 34% profit increases; competitor Northwest Airlines had exited several lucrative passenger routes. The future looked bright.

A return buzzer sounded and the door latch popped open.

Sinani stepped inside. "Helloooo, Marianne?"

"She's not here and we don't open 'til ten," a raspy male voice sang out from the end of a long oval-shaped bar.

"Are you the owner?" Sinani inquired.

"Every legion member is an owner here, son. Who wants to know?"

"Michael Waleu. I spoke with someone last night about renting an apartment. I think it might have been your wife?"

"Not unless that fancy phone on your belt has a number for Heaven. My wife's been dead for four years."

"Oh, I'm sorry. I didn't mean—"

"Sorry for what? Everybody dies sometime. Marianne's one of our bartenders. Tightest little cheeks on Layton Avenue. The vets fill this bar every day just to get a peek if you know what I mean. I'm Chief Jerry. Jerry Watts." He reached across the bar. "Everybody calls me Chief. Sit down. Be with you in a minute."

Sinani straddled a stool and examined the bar top, a solid

wood surface that held a collage of foreign coins and heroism medals embedded in a thick layer of decoupage varnish. He surveyed the room décor. Every square foot was covered with some sort of military memorabilia in a nostalgic tribute to war. Camouflage netting, photographs, flags, rifles, hand-held weaponry, and even a shoulder-fired missile launcher suspended from the ceiling. Next to the cash register, an empty 155mm artillery shell served as a tip jar.

"I've never owned a cell phone in my life," Watts said proudly, tucking his black POW-MIA t-shirt into Marine utility fatigues that hugged his 60-year-old trim waistline. "One of these days I'll have to bite the bullet. My grandkids call me all the time. Do you mind?"

Sinani reluctantly unclipped the phone from its holder.

Watts examined the features menu. "Sony-Ericsson. Is this a good one?"

Sinani wrinkled his nose and shrugged. "On a scale of one to ten it's probably a three. Pretty basic. Full Bluetooth. MP3 audio library, MPEG video, infrared port, GSM/GPRS Internet access with real-time sports scores. It even has a 3.2 megapixel digital camera complete with xenon flash and video stabilizer. It can take four pictures before you even press a key."

"You're shittin' me?"

"Most phones have that capability. To be honest, I'm not sure how everything works. I've never taken the time to figure it out."

"Yeah, that's the problem." Watts returned the phone. "There's so much crap stuffed into those things that nobody can."

"Is it still available?" Sinani asked, somewhat irritated by the man's slow pace.

Watts carefully added three scoops of horseradish to a large plastic container filled with red liquid. He tightened the cover and shook it vigorously. "The apartment? I've been trying to rent that sucker all year. Today is your lucky day. I'll throw in the utilities and give you half the garage if you take it. Bloody Mary?"

"Thank you, but no," Sinani said, referring to the mixture.

"What's the matter? Afraid of a little vodka?"

"No, I'd rather just fill out an application."

"Jesus, a college kid who doesn't drink?"

"I drink," Sinani defended. "I prefer Grey Goose."

"Only the good stuff, huh?" Watts poured himself a glass and topped it off with a heavy sprinkle of caraway salt. He stabbed his fingers into a jar trying to corral the last few green olives. "You are a student?"

"Is it that obvious?"

"Ten-four." Watts sifted through a manila folder next to the cash register. "You want a sandwich or something? You probably haven't eaten in a week. I bet you don't go more than one-fifty. I was a Milwaukee cop and a small town police chief for twenty-eight years. I always had pretty good instincts."

Your instincts have faded like your dyed hair, old man. Sinani thought, fishing a pen from his jacket. His hand brushed against a Glock 25 .380 handgun fitted with a smooth extended silencer.

A thin smile came to Watts's face as Sinani filled in the occupation line. He noticed a gold chain around the youth's neck and his excessive use of cologne. "Forget the references. I can tell just by looking at you that you're a good kid. Not like some with all those damn piercings. Why do you want to live out here? You work at the airport or something?"

"No particular reason," Sinani answered, twirling his pinky ring. "I need a quiet place for the summer semester. Preferably off campus. Far away from the frat houses."

Watts scanned the application and smiled fondly remembering his old patrol routes. Milwaukee's 3rd district jail cells were often crammed with students sleeping it off until morning. "No offense, kid but you don't look old enough for Marquette grad school. Don't tell me, I bet you're a dental student."

Sinani smiled and shook his head.

"Law?"

"Information technology."

"Thank Christ." Watts made the sign of the cross. "There's enough stinking ambulance chasers in the world."

"I guess you could say that I'm a bona-fide computer geek," Sinani admitted. "Especially with hardware. Someday I'll have my own business. A PC doctor who makes affordable house calls." He walked to the array of musical equipment on a stage at the end of the bar. A neon beer sign illuminated the tobacco sunburst color of an electric guitar propped in its stand. "May I?"

"Knock yourself out," Watts replied. "If you want sound, the power switch is on the wall behind the drums."

Chapter Nineteen

Sinani lifted the instrument and gently eased the strap over his shoulder. Mesmerized, he wrapped his hand around the thin neck and strummed a fingernail across the strings. "Gibson ES335. Semi-hollow with a single cut. It's beautiful. Who plays it?"

"Neil Bauer. He's a buddy of mine from 'Nam."

"This should be cased."

"Neil was a little preoccupied with the ladies last night," Watts said. "He had other things on his mind."

Sinani set the guitar in its stand and returned to his seat. "That's worth five thousand dollars. It's a replica of Jerry Garcia's Wolf."

"He a friend of yours?" Watts asked innocently.

Sinani gave an incredulous look. "You've never heard of Jerry Garcia and the Grateful Dead?"

"Not really, but we need somebody to play Saturday night for the women's auxiliary. Can you get me their number?"

"I'll see what I can do," Sinani said, chuckling.

"Guitars I understand. Computers? Who needs 'em," Watts growled. "I've got two pieces of junk in the back room that aren't even worth fixing. Then there's my grandkids. That's all they do is play video games. Click click click all day long on that whatchama-callit gizmo they hold in their hands. One's a teenager who just spent four bills for some Z-box or Y-box that lets you play sniper with kids all over the world."

"X-box."

"Yeah, that's it. Four hundred bucks just to stare into a TV screen? I couldn't stand it. When I was a kid I had to be outside playing something. Stickball, army, kick-the-can…anything but sitting on your ass. We'd leave the house in the morning and be gone all day. Nobody could even find us until we came home for supper. Cell phones were something from outer space. Hell, you probably never even heard of kick-the-can." Watts stirred his drink and licked the thin straw clean. "What nationality is Waleu?"

"French Canadian."

"You look Italian," Watts observed.

"My mother is from Italy. I was born in Rome. My parents live in Minneapolis. My father travels a lot. I think he's in Bangkok right now. International hotel management. We've lived all over the world."

"Bangkok as in Thailand?"

"Uh-huh. I speak four languages. Je prendrais volontiers du café." (I could do with some coffee.)

"Pretty impressive, kid," Watts sighed. "I was a supply sergeant in the Marines for four years and the only language I learned overseas was, 'GI, GI, sipp sipp pokemo'. Know what that means?"

Sinani shifted uneasily. "I think I can figure it out."

"Yeah, good times in 'Nam," Watts reminisced. "One day in Da Nang, a big-ass aircraft carrier pulled in with supplies for the Air Force. Well, suffice it to say that four pallets of beer and six thousand steaks got redirected. My Marines ate like kings that night. Even our captain knew. We had so much meat left over that we had to bury it. Damned Air Force prima donnas can suck my shorts. Were you in the service?"

"I'm afraid not," Sinani replied.

"No big deal. Let's see your horn."

"Excuse me?"

"C'mon, even half Italians have lucky horns." Watts pulled out his neck chain and displayed the traditional bent charm.

Sinani slid a chain from under his shirt that held a small cross. "First communion."

"Ten-four for the Catholic Wops, kid. I'm half Italian and half Polish, so that makes us paisan. We'll get along just fine." He took a huge sip from his glass. "Anyone ever tell you you look like that shortstop for the New York Yankees. What's his name…Darrin or Daryl something?"

"Jeter. Derek Jeter." Sinani fanned the edge of a deck of cards resting on a wooden board on the bar. "I hear that a lot."

"You play cribbage?" Watts asked.

"Nah…I prefer the money games. Blackjack or Texas Hold 'Em."

"A real gambler, huh? Okay, cut ya' for a thousand," Watts joked and pinched off half the deck. He displayed the ten of clubs.

Sinani lifted the king of spades.

Watts cursed. "Good looking and lucky. Jesus Christ, the horny old gals who come in here are gonna love you. Follow me; I'll show you the place." He stuffed the rental application into his back pocket.

The two men walked through the bar into a hallway past the restrooms and up a narrow set of eighteen stairs. The bottom three creaked.

Watts opened the apartment door and sniffed. Thankfully there was no odor of stale beer. "There are two entrances; this and one in the kitchen off the porch that leads out back. Doesn't bother me which one you use. It's not much for a mother-in-law flat, but at least it's clean. This room doubles as a bedroom. Four hundred a month including utilities and appliances. But I'll be honest, with all the planes flying over it's not the quietest place for studying. Not to mention us old fart veterans. We usually have a helluva crowd on the weekends, especially when there's live music. Sometimes Elvis shows up."

Watts knelt on a foldout day bed and stretched for a cord hanging in a large picture window. The roller shade snapped up allowing the bright southern sun to fill the room. "One nice thing is the view, if you're into flying, that is. That runway is only a stone's throw away. Jets line up for takeoff just beyond that fence. There's a radio in the kitchen. If you tune to 85.5 FM you can hear pilot chatter. There's even a public observation lot up the road."

Sinani peered at the scenery briefly and then turned away, seemingly more interested in the cleanliness of the bathroom shower stall.

"It's yours if you want it, but I'll need a deposit today," Watts pressed. "I'll even give you a break on meals. We cook some damn good chow for a bar. Tomorrow night's dollar tacos. We'll put some meat on those bones."

"I love Mexican," Sinani admitted. "But I have a crazy schedule. Driving back and forth to Minnesota spending time with my girlfriend. You know how that is."

"Hey, it's none of my business," Watts assured. "You come and go as you please. Nobody keeps tabs around here except at the bar. Case closed. What do you think?"

Sinani walked into the kitchenette and observed a chained door that led onto a small porch. A rusted barbecue grill hid the fact that half the railing was missing. He opened the refrigerator and turned the cooling dial to high. The compressor kicked in with a mild hum. "I'll give you seven hundred, cash. Three for the current month's rent and four for the security deposit. I just need a receipt."

"Sold." Watts pumped Sinani's hand. He consummated the

deal with a long cigarette drag. His face swelled up like a red beet. "You'll be here in time for my {choke} birthday party on the seventeenth. I've got my {choke} rent book {choke} downstairs. Don't go anywhere. I'll get the keys. "

Sinani waited for the distinctive three creaks before returning to the front window. He produced a small pair of binoculars. Mitchell International Airport averaged 230 daily commercial flights. Runway 19-R(ight) was 9,690 feet long and 200 feet wide with no end identifier lights. He judged the departure point at 390 yards. Considerably farther than a stone's throw, but that didn't matter. The morning traffic on Layton Avenue was mild. It would even be less traveled at night. All in all this American Legion Post seemed like a relatively quiet location. The proximity was excellent.

He tucked the binoculars away and knelt on the floor.

Surah 84. The Sundering, Splitting Open

19. Ye shall surely travel from stage to stage.

20. What then is the matter with them that they believe not?

21. And when the Qur'an is read to them, they fall not prostrate,

22. But on the contrary, the Unbelievers reject it.

23. But Allah has full knowledge of what they secrete in their breasts.

24. So announce to them a Penalty Grievous.

25. Except to those who believe and work righteous deeds: For them is a Reward that will never fail.

Chapter Twenty

Atlanta, GA
Tuesday, May 5th
9:15 P.M.

Kevin Jones set his guitar—a Taylor acoustic six-string—firmly against a table in the Georgia Institute of Technology Space Science and Technology Laboratory and reached for a pair of binoculars. He rolled his fingers over the focus dial until the west campus dormitories came into view. The warm evening air flowing through the lab's open casement window smelled delicious thanks to a Pizza Hut delivery carrier scurrying across campus like a pollinating bee—a sure sign that exams had started. Grade-nervous and summer-restless students coped the only way they knew how. Party.

Jones lowered the binoculars and turned his signature fluorescent pink baseball cap around on his head. "Hey, Zee, Pavlov was right."

Roman (Zee) Zibinski stopped trimming the rough fiberglass edge of a newly molded Entomopter wing and paused thoughtfully. He'd heard the name before in some distant lecture hall and associated it with canines, but it along with a gazillion other facts lay in his brain like dormant soldiers until summoned for duty. He visualized Cesar Millan, the Dog Whisperer. "Who?"

"Pavlov, the father of stimulus-response. You know…ring a bell, a dog salivates. See a pizza delivery car, a research assistant salivates. Pavlov was right; I'm starving."

"You're always starving. We've had pizza three nights in a row. I'll pass."

"You can't pass. You're too weak. Besides, you're living proof of Pavlov's most famous theory, INR."

Zee frowned at his friend. "So now you minored in music and psychology?"

"Your shirts," Jones announced. "Every single day of your college life. Long-sleeved striped shirts. You're a living tribute to Pavlov. INR, involuntary nerd response."

"You should talk. A longhaired hippie who wears pink caps and worships Simon and Garfunkel. Talk about a nerd."

"What can I say? They're my heroes. And I'm a diverse guy who plays diverse music."

"Give me a break," Zee scoffed. "First of all, nobody under forty even knows who Simon and Garfunkel are, I mean, seriously, they're like, ancient. Granted, Paul Simon was pretty hip in his younger days when he hosted Saturday Night Live in a turkey suit, but that was a hundred years ago. Secondly, both of them are rich white boys. Third, folk music is heading the same direction as polka music. Garfunkel just keeps getting busted for pot. So much for musical diversity."

"That's where you're wrong, nerdboy," Jones argued. "You obviously don't know squat about my man. Paul Simon was the first musician to recognize and embrace true African music, even if it took a little media criticism to get moving."

"Criticism?"

"Uh-huh. He did a concert once in the summer of 1983 for forty thousand people and some music critic actually counted the number of minorities. Three. Pauly knew that he needed something innovative so he bought a ticket to South Africa. The rest is musical history."

"Ancient history," Zee corrected.

"You just don't get it. People still dig Simon and Garfunkel songs. Especially chicks. Young, old, and in-between. And when they're gone, it'll be up to me to keep the legacy alive. Listen to the only folk guitar player in the country who figured out the exact picking progressions to Scarborough Fair."

"Huh?"

"Scarborough Fair, dummy. It's a canticle with a secondary melody and lyrics sung over the first."

"Sure, anything you say."

"Not only are you a nerd, but you're totally devoid of culture. Haven't you ever watched The Graduate? You know, Dustin Hoffman and that Mrs. Robinson babe?"

"I've seen the film," Zee quipped. "I'm a college student remember?"

"Then listen and marvel."

Jones lifted the guitar to his lap and carefully placed his fingers at points on the third and fourth frets. He plucked a series of notes with his right hand fingers while smoothly sliding his left hand up and down the neck. The result was a perfect rendition of the song's unforgettable melody. After four measures, he set the instrument down.

"That's it?" Zee asked incredulously.

"Cool, huh?" Jones beamed. "Someday I'm going to get up the nerve to play in public. A new renaissance in sidewalk folk music. They'll call me Pavlov with a guitar. Guaranteed to make women salivate."

Zee stretched a rubber band and snapped it across the room. Amazingly, it landed on the back of Jones's shoulder-length mane. "You are truly disturbed. Instead of listening to *The Sounds of Silence* every day you might want try the sounds of scissors and get a haircut. Seriously, what are you going to do?"

"Ponytail."

"Not that, I mean your future," Zee clarified. "You can't hang around a research campus strumming guitars forever. The Entomopter project is finished. There's nothing more for anyone to do except negotiate with NASA and neither you nor I have any say in that."

Jones slowly picked each note of a D chord and heard a slight off-key wave. He gently twisted the tuning knob of the stubborn B string and set the guitar in its case. "I guess I'll just have to move to a place where I can work on my tan and sing for the women. You know, somewhere warm and sunny like that city with the Padres and Chargers."

Zee set the wing down and propped his glasses onto his head. "No way. You got the fellowship? In San Diego?"

Jones smiled. "Three years."

"You ass, why didn't you tell me? Dude, congratulations. That's awesome. Which one?"

"Space and Naval Warfare Systems," Jones replied. "I don't know, I felt kind of guilty. I was hoping there were two openings."

"Nah...don't worry about me," Zee said, the disappointment obvious on his face. "What project?"

"Several, actually. Three-dimensional fighter simulation, transonic airfoil design, and 15cm MAV (micro-air vehicle)."

"That is so cool. I'm really happy for you," Zee pumped Jones's hand. "You'll be working with DARPA/CBS (Defense Advanced Research Project Agency/Controlled Biological Systems). That's Danny Liepmann's team. He just finished his Bootpie analysis. It's a great breakthrough."

Piezoelectricity was the ability of certain mineral crystals to change shape and produce voltage when under pressure. The word stemmed from the Greek *piezein,* which meant to squeeze or press. Bootpie was a U.S. military subproject of Energy Harvesting that powered battlefield equipment by piezoelectric generators in soldiers' footwear.

Chapter Twenty-one

A soft glow of intermittent red and blue light rolled through the lab.

Jones lifted the binoculars. "Zee, check this out. I think our friendly campus police busted another Spam party. Half of the freshman body just bolted across Northside Drive for the undergrad living center...wait—oh man, not again. That dumb little shit."

"Your brother, Tyler?"

"My stupid brother, Tyler."

Zee peered through the window and shook his head disgustedly. "Spam in the park. Sexually Prolific Academic Males. Now that brings back memories. Bad memories."

"The meat or the parties?" Jones wondered.

"Both. Remember them? One huge bash where freshman pay ten bucks for a plastic cup and the right to drink, pee and puke. Talk about patterned response. I used to hate standing in beer lines. Are you sure it's your brother? This'll be his second time."

"Third...and don't knock Spam. When I was a kid my mom used to grind it up with cheese and onions and then broil it on buns." Jones propped his elbows on the window sill. "Yup, it's him. Damn, he's standing next to a Chevy Tahoe. That means Burby, the toughest cop on campus. If he gets busted again he'll get kicked out. Stupid freshman. He's really starting to annoy me. It's like he just doesn't care. My parents will definitely freak. Why is it always up to me?"

"It's totally not," Zee protested. "Just because you're his brother doesn't mean you're his...brother. I say let him fall."

Jones lowered the binoculars and rubbed his eyes. "That made a lot of sense. I can't just let him fall. But I swear this is the last time. Then he's on his own. Pick a color."

Zee froze suspiciously. "Kevin Jones, don't you dare."

"A diverse color."

"No, I won't."

"Zee, relax. Just pick one."

"Kevin, no. You might not think so, but we've earned a certain level of prestige on this research team. Not to mention working our butts off. We can't afford to blow it. We could get in mega trouble especially with your fellowship and this Pinella Technology Award. Please, don't."

"Don't what? Shut up and pick a simple color," Jones growled. "And it's the Pirelli Award. Pinella's a baseball coach."

Zee exhaled a deep breath. "Black."

"You chose wisely, my son."

"Dammit," Zee cursed to himself. "I hate it when I do that."

Jones walked to a large metal cabinet and turned a combination dial. He slid a plastic case from a shelf and brought it to the table. Inside, six Entomopter frames rested between twenty-four sets of colored wings. Blue, yellow, red, and black. He lifted a set and turn-clipped four together, twisting each pair into locking slots on the rear and front sections of the Entomopter's thorax. Next, he inserted four metal but pliable legs coated with rubberized silicone into the frame's underside. Each leg tip had a textured pad that, when pressed towards its counterpart, locked into position to grip and hold. The assembly took less than a minute.

Zee opened the lab's refrigerator and removed a foam carton. "Award-winning but incredibly stupid researchers busted for incredibly stupid prank," he mumbled. "I can't believe we're doing this. One or two?"

"Dos," Jones answered in Spanish and propped one Entomopter upright on the table. The unit looked like some evil queen hornet. He plucked a thin plastic cartridge from the case and held it up to the ceiling. Next, he inserted a plastic syringe into a container of bright orange liquid labeled polynitrogen propellant and drew back the plunger. "I figure the distance is a quarter-mile one way. How much juice?"

"Just fill it and don't worry," Zee said. "Fifteen minutes will be plenty of time."

Jones injected the liquid and snapped the cartridge cover tight. He turned the Entomopter upside-down and removed a thin plastic shield from the tip of a camera lens. "Be a good roommate and get the window, lights, and door."

"Anything else, your highness?"

"Yeah, toss me your phone."

Jones gently clamped each pair of legs around the raw cargo and turned the Entomopter upright. Finished, he pressed the fuel cartridge into position. The Entomopter's wings twitched twice, then instantly blurred.

Zee slid his cell phone across the table. He opened a laptop and connected several sets of cables. "Hold on. I need you to focus."

Jones reached for a crescent moon-shaped plastic control box with two thin stems, one for lift and the other for motion. He pushed one stem and the Entomopter eased forward off the table and slowly floated out of the window. When he rolled the stem tip between his fingers the insect obediently turned and pointed its camera lens into the lab.

Zee's screen came up showing his fuzzy image sitting at the laptop. He adjusted the picture quality and then raised one thumb.

Four blocks away, campus security officer Nathan Burby shifted his 280 lb. weight on the curb and clicked a pen. "Name?"

"Jones. Tyler Jones."

"Let's see your Buzzcard, son."

Tyler slid his campus ID from his wallet.

Burby eyed the youth's facial features. Satisfied, he handed it back. "Okay, one more time…you don't know any of the students who ran and you were simply looking for a friend. And that beer can you were carrying was on the grass empty. You recycle them for the money."

"That's right, sir. That's exactly right," Tyler confirmed with a straight face. His cell phone chirped. Burby nodded. Tyler turned away and brought the phone to his ear. "Hello?"

"You dumb little shit. You can't keep screwing up like this. I'm serious. They'll kick you out. And if that happens, guess who mom'll blame? Not to mention your student loan."

"Kevin?" Tyler whispered. "Can you hear me? Where are you? How do you know where I am?"

"Unfortunately, it's my job. I'm probably a fool, but help is on the way. I hope you like breakfast. This is the last time. Do you understand?"

"Thanks, big brother. I love breakfast." He flipped the phone shut, fighting the urge to look skyward.

Burby tucked his notebook away and reached for his handcuffs. "I'm sorry, son but I've got no choice. You're under arrest for possession of alcohol and underage drinking. I need you to put your hands on the truck and spread your legs."

"Sir, please, you've got it all wrong. See them?" Tyler pointed to a group of students sitting in lawn chairs in front of Maulding Residence Hall. "They've been getting high and rowdy out here all night. I'm not a squealer or anything, but there's been talk around campus about some kind of police ambush."

Burby craned his neck at the youths, unimpressed. "C'mon, I said spread your ..."

thump-splat......thump-splat

The first egg hit the Tahoe's windshield. Symmetrical streams of yolky matter spread out across the hood. The second egg landed two feet away from the officer splattering his pants and shoes.

"What the hell—?" Burby turned angrily.

Tyler ducked theatrically and covered his head with his arms. "See? I told you. They're crazy drunk. Those came right over the trees."

Burby crouched behind his vehicle and touched the squawker button on his shoulder. "Dispatch, this is four-one. I just got egged at Northside and Tech Parkway. Send some support, quick." He motioned to Tyler. "Alright, son, you get a pass tonight. Thanks for the tip on those little sons-a-bitches. Now I'm pissed. Take off."

Tyler sprinted toward campus.

Chapter Twenty-two

"Mission accomplished, sir," Jones shouted across the lab. "Damn, I oughta be in the military. Precision guidance system pilot extraordinaire."

"That was pretty cool," Zee admitted. "Are we about finished with the teenage adrenaline rushes? If Robertson ever knew about this he'd kick our butts from here to Italy."

"Relax. He's eating his own pizza with the Pope," Jones smiled. "For at least three more days. Besides, I know for a fact that the D-Fly's going to win first prize so it's time to celebrate. Toss me a brew. I'll bring the B-1 bomber home."

"Winning would be awesome, but I'll believe it when I see it." Zee opened the refrigerator and dug out two cans of Budweiser. "Weird. I wonder what he'd say about NASA's prized flying insect dropping eggs on cops?"

"Correction. It's still our flying insect until someone officially buys it. NASA hasn't committed to anything."

Jones guided the Entomopter back through the lab window and brought it to rest in his left hand. He carefully pulled the fuel cartridge and watched the wingbeats peter out. He briefly examined the frame before removing the legs. He popped open his beer and took a long drink. "Okay, back to the important stuff. How about cheese, sausage, and mush...?"

There was a loud knocking on the lab door.

Zee capped his beer with his hand and bolted for the refrigerator.

Jones set his in a cabinet and quickly disconnected the laptop cables. He managed to close the Entomopter case an instant before the metallic door latch clicked open.

"Who is in here?" The voice was male and stern. He wasn't from maintenance. "Mr. Jones? Mr. Zibinski? Why is this door locked?"

"Dr. Al-Aran, sir...um, we were just finishing," Jones squeaked, standing guiltily at attention. "It's been a long day. How are you? No particular reason, sir. We just feel better about privacy with the project and all."

Al-Aran gave the room a general glance. Satisfied there were no naked women, he tucked his security access card away. "I saw the lights and thought you'd be interested to know that the Entomopter was named top Pirelli prize winner. Professor Robertson sent a departmental e-mail. Your research budget just got a quarter of a million dollars richer. Are you sure you're all right?"

"Yes, sir, we're fine." Zee confirmed.

The refrigerator door slowly swung open and banged into the countertop.

Al-Aran removed the open beer can and set it on the table. He scooped his pipe through a tobacco pouch. "I suppose we might overlook any punishment for the sake of celebration. I'll enjoy a smoke and we'll talk about the Entomopter. Any problem with that?"

"No, sir," Jones said, relieved.

Al-Aran sucked several deep puffs. He dropped the match into Zee's beer. It sizzled briefly. "Gentlemen, you should be proud. You've come a long way with your little flying gold mine. Did Professor Robertson ever mention that I helped design the wings for the first prototype? We cut them from Atlanta's world-famous aluminum cans and called it the *Coke Roach* until their lawyers objected."

"They're on the wall in Robert, Professor Robertson's office," Zee noted. "But we're way beyond that now. Everything's synthetic. Here, let me show you." He opened the case and removed one unit.

Al-Aran set his pipe on the table. "I forgot how light...like a toy. I remember it being heavier. But that was some time ago. Can it still carry its own weight?"

"More than double," Jones answered.

Al-Aran motioned for the laptop. "Walk me through startup."

Zee pulled up a chair and patiently explained the Entomopter's boot program.

Jones inserted the wings and re-snapped the fuel and catalyst cartridges in place. Five seconds later, the wings blurred.

Al-Aran picked up the control box and applied slight pressure to one toggle stem. The D-Fly rose from the table and fluttered in mid-air. It looked like some giant insect from a science fiction film. He gave the other stem a gentle push and the Entomopter began a slow circular flight. "Fascinating. It's hard to believe something can fly this easily. It almost moves by itself." He lowered the unit.

"Refresh my memory. You must have a laptop if you want video, correct?"

"Right," Jones answered. "With high-end graphics."

"When will the wings cease?"

"When it runs out of fuel or loses a cartridge. The one on the right is the catalyst. Each set lasts approximately fifteen minutes. Don't worry about touching the wings when they're moving because they'll just snap off."

Al-Aran made a mental note. "One more question... who is most qualified to provide technical answers regarding flight performance?"

"Robertson." Both assistants answered in unison.

"But I know just as much as he does," Jones spoke up. "Why do you ask?"

"I need you to gather five Entomopter frames and all related components. We're lending the system for a while."

"Huh?" Jones asked incredulously. "To who?"

Al-Aran relit his pipe and shook his head. "Six years of higher education should have taught you something about prepositional objects. To whom, Mr. Jones. A Saudi evaluation team is considering purchasing the entire system for asset security."

"Are you serious?"

"Arabs are always serious about security, particularly when it involves oil."

"Don't we need some kind of permission?" Zee questioned

"You're absolutely right. I almost forgot." Al-Aran reached in his pocket and unfolded a piece of paper.

The first thing Zee noticed was that the check was drawn on the Bank of Riyadh. His mouth hung open at the dollar amount.

"Five million dollars buys a lot of permission," Al-Aran said smugly. "And this is only the down payment. If our Entomopters perform well, there'll be another just like it. I know it's late, but I need everything packaged and in my office before you leave. Do me another favor and print out a detailed set of operating instructions. Something that's complete and easy to follow."

"Sure, but what about Professor Robertson? He won't be back until Friday. Shouldn't we at least let him know? Who's going to explain the system?"

Al-Aran folded the check and tucked it into his pocket. "I am."

Chapter Twenty-three

East Elmhurst, NY
Thursday, May 7th
1:15 P.M.

Sinani sat with his feet propped on the kitchen table in his frame two-story rented flat. He finished his second Big Mac sandwich and made a point to recover the last French fries from the bottom of the bag. He lifted his shirt. His stomach was expanding nicely. He scanned a flyer that some local protesters had handed out at the restaurant's drive-thru exit. He was mildly concerned by the black and white photo on the flyer featuring a row of homes that supposedly received the brunt of LaGuardia Airport's noise pollution. His flat was centered in the photo along with his Toyota that was parked on the street. Thankfully, no other meaningful identification was apparent. He crumpled the flyer into a tight ball and buried it deep in the trashcan. There was work to do.

He retrieved the last two plastic gallons of bleach from six cardboard cases in the bedroom and set them on the kitchen table. He filled a measuring cup with salt substitute (potassium chloride) granules until the needle on a small vegetable scale read sixty-three grams. He poured one bottle of bleach and the granules into a large metal pot on the gas stove and turned the burner to medium-high. The liquid reached a slow boil in six minutes. He dipped a battery charge suction tube into the mixture and watched the plastic balls float upward to the full-charge calibration line. He turned off the heat and set the pot in the refrigerator next to two others. Each was labeled with masking tape to indicate where it stood in rotation en route to a final cooling temperature of thirty-three degrees. A heavy crust of crystals had formed around the rim of a pot at the front of the production line. Sinani gently scraped the excess into a cup gun mesh funnel from a local paint store and tapped the filtered material into a drinking glass. It was already half full. He carefully measured out fifty-six grams of crystals and added it to a container of one hundred milliliters of distilled water. This was also boiled and cooled into a secondary (fractionalized) crystallization process. After another round of gentle scraping, this time with a plastic tool to

99

avoid sparks, a white powdery substance finally appeared—potassium chlorate. He placed the powder into a flat pan and heated it to drive out any moisture. Next to that pan, he heated an even ratio of Vaseline and wax melted with a small amount of white camping kerosene. He poured that mixture over ninety parts of the potassium powder and allowed the kerosene to evaporate. He kneaded the now gooey gray-brown matter together and pressed the finished product into a rectangular plastic tray separated into six-ounce cubes. Finally, he poured a layer of melted wax over the tray until each space was waterproof. He updated a label on the container indicating the name and the birth date of the charge. A charge with the explosive power of one stick of dynamite and a room temperature decomposition lifespan of four days.

Sinani booted his laptop and connected to the Internet. He clicked on 'Favorites' and then scrolled through www.madscientist. com.

KILLING MADE EASY
PREPARATION OF POTASSIUM CYANIDE (KCN)

Heat ammonium formate crystals by flame in an environment containing as little oxygen gas as possible. The ammonium formate decomposes into formamide ($HCONH2$) and further into hydrogen cyanide. Condense the gas given off in a rubber, plastic, or glass tube that has one end immersed in a beaker containing a solution of potassium hydroxide (KOH). Position the tube so that any liquid in it will run off into the beaker of potassium hydroxide. The hydrogen cyanide will quickly react with the potassium hydroxide to form approximately 65.1 grams of potassium cyanide crystals. Hold your breath and dilute 900 to 1000 mg in any drinkable liquid. Victims will fall into coma almost immediately. Timeframes depend on stomach contents, but death generally occurs in less than two minutes. KCN is virtually untraceable and its symptoms mimic myocardial infarction (heart failure). Antidotes, even if administered immediately after ingestion, often cause severe and irreparable brain dam...

The kitchen door handle began to turn followed by a squeaking of metal hinges.

Sinani reached for his Glock pistol and flattened himself against the refrigerator.

The door continued to open stopped only by the latch chain.

"Kenny, are you in there, lad? I fixed the light in this hallway so you can see again. I don't know why those damn bulbs burn out so fast."

Sinani quietly crept into the bathroom and closed the door. "Yes, Mrs. Timmons, I'm in the shower. Thank you for doing that. I always forget."

Timmons pressed her face into the door crack. "When did you get in, lad, and what's that smell?"

"This morning," Sinani spoke over running water. "Probably bleach. I was cleaning."

"Now don't you fuss. You come right down when you're finished and meet me brother before he leaves. We're conversing in the living room. You'd better hurry because the taxi man is on his way. My word, did ya' hear that, Kenny? Two glasses of wine is all it takes to work up me brogue again."

"I'll be down in a few minutes, Mrs. Timmons," Sinani answered. "Should I bring anything?"

"Just that coin trick you promised from that mall in Minneapolis. And even though I'm your landlord, there's no need to be so formal. You might refer to me as Mary."

Sinani waited for the lower porch door to slam shut. This was a problem. A petite Irish-Catholic with a constant smile and hosiery balled at her ankles, Timmons was in her late seventies. The recent loss of her husband forced her to manage the two-family dwelling alone. Her alcohol consumption had increased with the responsibility. She needed the courage. Thrilled with the extra rental income, but obviously ignorant about New York tenant law, barring an emergency, it was illegal to enter a residence without cause or advance notice. Sinani couldn't tolerate such uninvited intrusions, especially if he wasn't there. He was becoming the son she never had.

Downstairs, Timmons flopped into the living room sofa and filled a wine glass from a carafe on the coffee table. She raised a toast to her brother sitting in a chair across the room. "Bernie, I really like that skinny kid. If I were thirty years the younger I'd go for him meself. He's only been here a month, but I can tell he's a good one. And quite a worker, too. What other young man would clean that whole apartment so you could lick the floor and not taste a bit of dust? Wouldn't let me pay for a ting. I never in me life saw so much bleach. He must have carried a hundred gallons. What in the world was he tinking? But then the place was filthy. The Olsons who lived up there before were as near to pigs as pigs could be. Their mongrel dog used the dining room for his own private yard. Did his jobs right on the carpet until there was a ring around the whole table. Left his filth for God and the world to see. Can you fathom a stench like that? How on earth could people with working nostrils tolerate such a...?"

"Mrs. Timmons?" Sinani's voice spoke through the screen door.

"Come right in, Kenny. I've been swearing up a storm about the previous tenants when I should be tanking the Savior for who I have now." She tried to rise, but couldn't. "Master Kenneth Wory, this is me brother, Bernard Sloan."

Chapter Twenty-four

Countryside Irish, Bernard was a hairless clone of his sister, complete with rosy cheeks and perpetual smile. He stood and extended his hand. "It's afinepleasuretomeet'yaMr.Wory.Mesister's toldmequiteabitaboutyouandyoursickmotherandIsurelyhopethat she'smakinggoodprogressbacktotheworldofthehealthy."

There was a moment of awkward silence as Sinani struggled to comprehend the fast forward monotone. He noted the strength in the little man's grip. It was icy from caressing a huge beer glass. "I've never been to Ireland, but I hear it's beautiful."

"Oh,it'sfarmorethanthat.Somanytinkthepopulacelivesinthebi ggertownsbutthere'sawawhole'nutherworldoutthereamongstthegr eens."

"What part of Ireland?"

"GreencastleCountyDownisrightalongthecoastoftheIrishSea aboutanhour'sdrivetothesouthofBelfast.Wecanseetheferrysmaking theirwayuptoUlster.Beenalobstermanallmelifebutthat'sonlyforsixor sevenmonthsoftheyearsothenItryangetagoodpricefortheshellfish."

Sinani nodded as if he fully understood the coordinates. For a moment he thought the language was some form of old Gaelic. He managed to hear the words lobster and fish in the diatribe and correctly concluded the man had something to do with the sea.

"Greencastle is a medieval fortress that sits on the hill behind our old homestead," Timmons clarified. "Would you believe that Bernard and I used to play up there when we were just six years old? The Normans built it all from stone in the thirteenth century. We could see all the way down to the cellar through the holes in the floors. We'd jump across without any fear at all. Bernard would hide and then scare me half to death with his screams. Pigs stayed in that place and they'd chase after us. What I wouldn't give to hear them snort again. But that was ages ago."

"It sounds very nice," Sinani said, glancing at his watch.

"Kenny's a bartender, Bernard. I'm sure the two of you would've hit it off," Timmons continued. "And he's a trickster, too. But only at night. In the daytime he attends the university."

Bernard nodded curtly at that and gave his glass a congratulatory tip. "That'salwaysafineplacetostartoutnowaslongasyouknow whatyou'rewantingtostudy."

"Yes, I study quite a bit," Sinani affirmed.

"It's gadgets, Bernard," Timmons said. "He tinkers with everything. And that reminds me, Kenny. Why in the world would you have so many of those cellular telephones lined up on your sink? Plugged into the wall like kittens drinking their mother's milk. The other day I tink there were five. God rest his soul, me husband Dermott hated those things. He said they were the toys of the Devil himself."

Sinani smiled broadly. "I, um…gifts. I bought them as gift phones for my family. They were on sale."

Timmons accepted the flimsy excuse. "You're sure a thoughtful son, Kenneth. Will you join me for dinner tomorrow? I bought a beef roast fat enough for the whole neighborhood."

"I'm really sorry, but I can't. My mother's been asking for me again. I have to leave in the morning. I should be back in about a week."

"Well, that's a shame, but family comes before all else in this world. God speed to you when you travel then. And speaking of travel, did you happen to find a spare set of Scotch and Soda in the stores?"

Sinani winced at the ceiling. "Damn, I completely forgot. I promise on my soul that I'll get it for you."

Timmons frowned at a curse spoken for such a trivial thing. "Did you bring yours then? I know you never go anywhere without it."

Sinani reached in his pocket and pulled out a plastic case the size of a cigarette pack. Scotch and Soda was a vintage coin trick that made a quarter disappear from a person's closed hand. In reality, it elegantly slipped inside two hollowed-out halves of an American half-dollar.

A loud rumble shook the room. The wine carafe rattle-walked toward the edge of the table. Timmons steadied it. "Oh, that damned LaGuardia," she cursed. "It's near to the end of the world when those jets leave. As sure as Jesus rode a donkey, one day they'll take my hearing and I'll sue that airport for its millions. Then and only then will I go back to Ireland. And this old neighborhood will be the sadder for it. The colored are taking over anyway. I should've given this place up after poor Dermott passed."

A vehicle horn beeped twice.

Sinani completed the magic trick with his usual dramatic flair and tucked the plastic case away. In a respectful gesture, he lifted Bernard's suitcase and walked to the door.

Bernard hugged his sister in a long embrace, pressing moisture from his eyes with a handkerchief. "IguessI'mjustnotusedtothat odorcomin'fromupstairs."

"Now don't you try and blame Kenny's bleach for that you old crier." Timmons smiled through her tears. "Even though there's enough to scrub the whole neighborhood. I'll miss you, too."

Sinani set the suitcase down and eased the Glock from his waistband. This could not pass. One bullet per head. They'd fall together onto the sofa in some final act of macabre incest. There was a fruit cellar in the basement and a heavy roll of plastic that could easily mask body decomposition for perhaps ten days.

"Somebody call a cab?" A voice shouted through the door.

Sinani stuffed the pistol away and puffed out his shirt. He walked Bernard to the curb.

"You call me when you get home or I'll worry through the night," Timmons shouted from the porch stoop above the roar of another aircraft.

Bernard shook Sinani's hand and then blew his sister a kiss.

The taxi sped off.

Sinani walked upstairs to his apartment and tied the curtains back in the dining room exposing an unobstructed view of LaGuardia's Runway 4/22. He estimated the departure point distance at 410 yards.

He opened his beloved *Qur'an*.

Surah 48. Victory, Conquest

1. Verily we have granted thee a manifest victory.

2. That Allah may forgive thee thy faults of the past and those to follow; fulfill His favor to thee; and guide thee on the straight way.

3. And that Allah may help thee with powerful help.

4. It is He who sent down tranquility into the hearts of the believers, that they may add faith to their faith; for to Allah belong the forces of the heavens and the earth; and Allah is full of knowledge and wisdom.

5. That He may admit the men and women who believe, to gardens beneath which rivers flow, to dwell therein for aye, and remove their ills from them; and that is, in the sight of Allah, the highest achievement for man.

6. And that He may punish the hypocrites, men and women, and the polytheists men and women, who imagine an evil opinion of Allah. On them is a round of evil: the wrath of Allah is on them. He has cursed them and got hell ready for them, and evil is it for a destination.

7. For to Allah belong the forces of the heavens and the earth; and Allah is exalted in power, full of wisdom.

8. We have truly sent thee as a witness, as a bringer of glad tidings, and as a warner.

9. In order that ye may believe in Allah and His Messenger, that ye may assist and honor Him, and celebrate His praise morning and evening.

10. Verily those who plight their fealty to thee do no less than plight their fealty to Allah. The hand of Allah is over their hands: then any one who violates his oath, does so to the harm of his own soul, and any one who fulfils what he has covenanted with Allah, Allah will soon grant him a great Reward.

Chapter Twenty-five

Decatur, GA
Friday, May 8th
5:03 A.M.

Linda Robertson opened her eyes, alerted by footsteps in the hallway outside the bedroom. The clock on the dressing table suggested pre-dawn, but the room was nearly black thanks to the room-darkening window blinds. There had been a recent string of morning break-ins in this normally quiet suburb ten minutes northeast of Atlanta. Her mind raced to remember if she'd activated the alarm system. She slithered her hand under the covers and tapped her husband. Michael didn't respond. She pinched his thigh hard and received a mild snort for the effort.

The noise in the hallway stopped.

She turned her head and whispered. "Someone's in the house."

Michael sat up and when he did, he felt instantly nauseous. His eye sockets throbbed trying to focus across the room. Incredibly, the curved French door handle began to turn. He watched helplessly as the crack grew wider. He squinted through the dim light at something easing itself inside.

The unmistakable outline of a handgun.

Michael felt like he was living an out-of-body experience. He could see and comprehend what was happening, but couldn't activate a single muscle. He knew he had to react. "That's far enough, buddy," he blurted. "If you come in this room, I'm going to tie you to a tree and squirt you with the garden hose."

Ignoring the silly warning, the assassin calmly entered the room and took aim.

Realizing there was no escape, Michael did the only thing he could to save his life.

He whipped the covers over himself leaving his wife exposed.

Linda screamed, taking hits to her face and chest. She fled into the bathroom and slammed the door.

Unmerciful, the assassin turned to the lump under the covers.

"Alright, that's enough!" Michael coughed, his forehead dripping wet. "Hand it over, please."

Daniel, their six-year old son relinquished the squirt gun and proceeded to turn the bed into a circus trampoline. "How come you didn't wake me when you got home?" he pouted.

"You were sound asleep," Linda answered, tackling her son to the mattress. She caressed him tightly. "Mmmm, I missed you. Where's your brother?"

"Playing Spiderman on his computer. Did you bring me anything?"

"Did you behave?"

"Mom." He protested the obligatory parental question and proceeded to bounce higher. "We always do. You can even ask Aunt Tina. Did she go home? She taught me a new song on the piano about a lady with a man's name. It's called 'Go Tell Aunt Rudy' and it's about a goose that gets dead. Then we played a game called Molopoly and I had all the cool hotels and I was a racecar and Teddy was a dog and Aunt Tina was a dumb iron. She said that's the one you always pick. I won because I bang-rupted everybody. What happened with D-Fly? Did dad win? What's a morgadidge? We saw a cool black snake outside. Did you get me a video game?"

"Yes, your father won, but he doesn't feel well." She slowed the boy's trampoline routine and gently turned him around toward the door. "A mortgage is a piece of paper that says you own something and have to pay for it. Aunt Tina left last night. Time to shower up, please. School today."

Grumbling, the water assassin shuffled off.

Michael noted the squirt gun's water level before shamming it into his pajamas.

Linda ran a brush through her hair. "Are you going to campus?"

"I have to," he said, fighting a giant yawn and twisting his neck from side-to-side. There's a surprise party. I'm not supposed to know."

"You don't sound very enthusiastic."

"It's the flu."

"Do you want me to call the doctor? I'm sure he could give you something."

"Nah, I've just got a funny feeling. It's probably nothing."

"About what? Your stomach?"

"NASA, what else? Or to be more specific, NASA's budget. Everything in that agency is about money. If they can't make a commitment, the Entomopter Project is stuck and that means so am I."

"Professor, stop worrying," she ordered. "I'm sure it'll work out. And if it doesn't, then you'll just have to find someone else who's interested."

"Sure. There's all kinds of companies planning trips to Mars. Maybe I could write to Steven Spielberg."

"What about that oil field security thing with the Saudis?"

He frowned. "The flying cameras? I'll find out more about it today, but I guess it's moving forward. I heard that my good friend Faiz is arranging an on-site trial for some delegation. I'm not giving it much credence. The Entomopter wasn't designed for security. I didn't want to burst any bubbles, but I've got a feeling they'll take a close look at the mechanics and pack the system right back up. It's not that sophisticated."

She noticed anger in Michael's voice. "You're mad at him aren't you?"

"Why should I be mad? I like being kept in the dark about my own project."

"So in other words you like being in control."

He smiled at his wife's perceptiveness. "I don't like being irrelevant."

She kissed her finger and touched it to his chin. "Stop fretting and stop selling yourself short. You just earned a huge award. Something you can be proud of for the rest of your life. No one can ever take that away. The Entomopter's a great invention. Whatever happens, I love you."

"Me, too." He hugged her and then motioned to the unmade bed. "Wanna fool around?"

She felt something rigid press against her. "I thought you were sick, professor?"

"Dad, could you come here?"

He sighed and gently kissed the top of his wife's head.

She closed her eyes and took a deep breath. "We'll make up for it."

Michael strode to the door. "Hey, teach, thanks for the pep talk. Don't know what I'd do without you. Sit down and close your eyes. I've got a present."

Yes! That black onyx necklace slide from the hotel gift shop in Rome. She smiled warmly and complied.

Four streams of water arced through the air.

Michael barely managed to close the bedroom door before the retaliation pillow slammed into it.

He placed his hand over his stomach and gingerly walked upstairs. He peeked into a bedroom. "Hey, bud. What's up?"

"Hey, dad," ten-year-old Teddy acknowledged, his eyes fixed on the computer screen. "Josh lent us Spiderman. Check it out."

The boy's thumbs and fingers expertly pressed buttons on the controller. In synchronized rhythm, the screen character sprang sideways from one building to the next, simultaneously shooting streams of webbing at an array of menacing attackers dressed in black camouflage and brandishing automatic weapons.

Michael simply shook his head at all the hand-eye coordination. "That's pretty good, mister. How about your reading?"

"Spiderman can stick to things just like D-fly," Teddy remarked. His fingers made a final series of clicks on the controller. The video character leaped across the screen to a flagpole protruding from the side of a building and then raised both arms in victory. A musical tone filled the speakers and a voice offered congratulations at defeating level three of ten. "Do you think I could fly it again sometime?"

"When school's over and if you improve your reading grade." The sound of running water flowed through the wall. "Okay, Spiderman, hop downstairs and say hello to your mother and then hop in the shower with your brother. Deal?"

"Deal." Teddy high-fived his father's hand and hurried out of the room.

Michael picked up the controller and examined the buttons. He pressed one. The video game came to life from the beginning of level one. The attackers appeared and immediately walked toward Spiderman, weapons blazing. He randomly pressed buttons in a frantic attempt to bring the motionless hero to life. Nothing worked. Streams of bullets easily found their mark. The game ended abruptly with a digital voice announcement. "Sorry, Spiderman. You lose."

Chapter Twenty-six

Kenosha, WI
Sunday, May 10th
10:45 A.M.

Faiz Al-Aran pulled his rented Buick Regal sedan off the exit ramp and turned into the parking lot of the Brat 'n Beer Truck Stop at the intersection of I-94 and State Highway 50. He shut off the engine and arched his body in a deep stretch. So deep that his hands reached the two suitcases resting on the back seat.

A man approached the vehicle and tapped the passenger's window.

Al-Aran unscrewed the cap on a thermos before touching the door lock button.

Sinani slid inside.

There were customers milling outside the restaurant, so the men refrained from traditional greeting kisses. Sinani extended his hand instead. "God is great, Faiz. I am happy to see you. Follow this road behind the restaurant and turn left on—"

"Patience, young lutador," Al-Aran said through another yawn. "We will sit a moment and talk in English."

Sinani folded his hands on his lap.

Al-Aran downed the last of his drink. "This coffee is as cold as the northern climate. Are you finding what you need on the Internet?"

"The information is endless," Sinani observed warily. "If you are asking how long it will take to become proficient at flying the insect, the answer is not long at all. There are Web games that require the same skills. Is there a problem?"

"Not at all. The last billing statement I received showed over thirty hours of access. Soon all of my students will have online capability." He handed Sinani a thick roll of bills. "Your face is changing, my lutador. You are gaining weight."

"God has given me nearly fifteen pounds," Sinani said, tucking the cash into his jacket pocket and exposing his *Qur'an.* "Why do you choose to drive? And what is this lutador?"

"May I?" Al-Aran extended his hand. Sinani passed him the

111

book. Al-Aran perused the worn pages. "A meaningless Portuguese word. Flying means airport x-ray machines and surveillance cameras. Baggage opened and inspected on a security conveyor is photographed. No one must see our toys. And no one must see this." He kissed the *Qur'an* and buried it in the glove compartment. "The tactics have changed. Have you set the Milwaukee timetable?"

"I have chosen Midwest Airlines. A morning flight. Changed how?"

"Suffice it to say that you will not have to negotiate close-quarter maneuvering near the flaps." Al-Aran started the ignition and turned on the heater. "You will fly the insect to the front of the aircraft and attach it to the strut of the nose landing gear. It will be swallowed inside like poison."

"You mean the main landing gear?"

Al-Aran saw the confusion on Sinani's face. "The nose," he calmly repeated.

"But there is no fuel in the nose." Sinani knew that the original plan attacked the center tank. "What damage can be done in that area? If we simply destroy the front wheels, an aircraft can still land safely."

"There are many vulnerabilities inside a gear bay, specifically cables and hydraulics. Newer aircraft with fly-by-wire systems transmit commands from the cockpit via electric wires to actuators on the control surfaces themselves. Trust Allah, my lutador; it is in his hands," Al-Aran reassured. "I assume you have a device assembled and fused?"

Sinani reached inside his jacket, but quickly withdrew it as another vehicle pulled alongside. The State Patrol deputy gave the two men an unconcerned glance and walked toward the restaurant. Sinani waited until he was inside. "The insect's legs…if the harness should somehow fail, I need to know the precise grip strength. The potassium charge cannot tolerate friction or pressure above fifty-one pounds per square inch. And I must know the maximum radio communication distance."

Al-Aran mused softly to himself. He scribbled something on a piece of paper and handed it to Sinani. "This man is Kevin Jones. An original project team member. When you contact him, speak directly on my behalf. Make up whatever you like. You have music in common. Have you arranged a test?"

"There is a small rock quarry ten minutes from here. A farmer owns the property and will not go there. If we park on the access road, no one else can enter."

"We will not park anywhere. You will test the insect alone. The risk is great whenever two or more of God's people appear together. I will eat a meal and be on my way. Atlanta is a long ride."

"As you say, professor. What else must I know?"

"Everything you need is in those cases. Laptop, control box, and five Entomopters. There are two types of cartridges. Fuel and catalyst. You must choose a mid-sized aircraft with engines attached to the fuselage, not the wings. If God gives us a victory, then you may use your discretion on the next."

Sinani nodded at the instructions. He examined the note. "There are two names."

"Jdey is a soldier of God. I have already contacted him. He knows nothing about this operation except that he is to serve you. Use him at any time and in any manner you choose. He is loyal and completely fearless. We will not meet in person again. I have already made my travel arrangements. My itinerary fits perfectly into our schedule. Learn and remember the tactics, my lutador."

"How will we communicate?" Sinani produced a pen and small notebook.

"After today we will speak only English in public chat rooms on the Internet. My userID will be derived from the calendar and will change daily. If it is Sunday, May the tenth, then my ID will be SMT followed by the numbers 0510 representing the numeric date and month. If it were Monday, May the eleventh, my ID would be MME0511, and so forth. Your userID will be derived from a global website and will also change daily. We will use two communication windows; one at 17:00 and the other at 23:00 Greenwich Mean Time. Ten minutes before each window you must access CNN.com. Make sure that your timing is precise. There you will see a list of major news headlines. You will take the first two letters of the first word in the first three headlines as your ID. I will wait in the chat room only ten minutes for you to appear. If other members are present, they will never suspect or care about our conversation. Do you understand?"

"Yes, but what chat room?"

"That also will be derived and will change depending on the date. If it is the tenth of the month, then you will enter the words 'Internet Dating Service' into CNN's search browser and then scroll to the tenth website displayed. That site will serve as our meeting room. No law enforcement agency on earth could discover our movements."

"May God smile upon us on May 18th." Sinani squeezed Al-Aran's hand and then tucked his notebook away.

Al-Aran exited the vehicle first and scanned the headlines in a row of newspaper boxes at the restaurant's entrance.

Sinani opened the glove compartment and retrieved his *Qur'an*. He waited a few minutes before transferring the suitcases to his Camry.

Chapter Twenty-seven

Sinani drove west on Highway 50 to County Highway J, and then turned south on Quarry Road for another mile. The site was nothing more than an abandoned dump surrounded by gravel mounds and littered with shredded tires and rusted appliances. Broken glass was everywhere. He parked in the middle of the access road and dialed his cell phone. After six rings, someone picked up.

"Hello?"

"Kevin? Kevin Jones?"

"Speaking."

"My name is Omar Yassin," Sinani said in an exaggerated Middle-Eastern accent. I'm calling from Al Hufuf, Saudi Arabia. Can you hear me okay?"

Jones was in his new San Diego apartment sitting on a stool in a spare room that he'd converted into a makeshift recording studio. He reached over a microphone and paused the tape on an audio mixer. "Yeah, I can hear you fine."

"Excellent," Sinani replied. "Dr. Faiz Al-Aran gave me your name as a knowledgeable contact for the Entomopter. I apologize for the interruption, but I have a few technical questions."

"Not a problem; it's cool. I was just jamm, er..playing a little music. No big deal." He slid off his guitar strap and shifted the phone. "How can I help?"

"Well, at this time we have three issues. I determined that you might save us time and effort if you've already encountered them. The first is environment. Can you give me any insight regarding the machine's tolerance with airborne particles or debris? Secondly, with respect to the appenditures...do you recall the precise amount of grip pressure exerted when the legs are closed? We certainly could calculate it ourselves, but I thought you might save us the trouble."

"Sand is no problem at all. We logged sixteen hours in a wind tunnel at category three hurricane strength and added silica to the airflow. It rolled over the wings just fine. As far as the leg grip strength, I can't recall the exact pressure, but it was at least forty-two or forty-three pounds per square inch. The compression springs are completely removable and should maintain tension coil for eight months."

"That's exactly what I needed to hear," Sinani confirmed.

"What's the third issue?"

"Oh, yes...maximum distance to receive radio signals from the controller?"

"That's easy. You'll see severe degradation at one mile."

"Perfect," Sinani said almost gleefully. "I'm jealous."

"Excuse me?"

"Dr. Al-Aran told me that you have exceptional musical ability. I, too have a talented voice. Unfortunately, when I sing the Fennec foxes start to howl in the desert. I often wonder what it would be like to be an American rock and roll star who can play, how does one say it...a mean lick? Sometime you must give me a lesson."

"Anytime, Omar. I'm not a star yet, but if you're ever in southern California, then look me up. I just got out here. Rockin' in the desert with Fennec foxes sounds pretty cool to me. You take care, okay?"

"Thank you, Mr. Jones. Nice talking to you."

Sinani clicked off. He exited the Camry and carried the suitcases fifty yards. As he approached the quarry, he noticed a sour stink in the air emanating from surrounding cabbage farms. He retrieved an old kitchen table and propped it up parallel to the prairie-like field to the south. He scanned the far perimeter with binoculars and gradually let his vision focus on an abandoned tractor sitting in the tall grass three hundred yards away.

He opened a suitcase and removed one Entomopter thorax from its foam cradle. It was the first time he'd ever touched the device. He noted the unevenness in the seam glue. Obviously handmade. The unit also was lighter than he expected. He inserted a front and rear set of wings into the body slots and then flattened a single piece of paper onto the table with numbered instructions. He opened the laptop and inserted the control program diskette. The screen showed a positive frequency acquisition to a wire-thin two-inch receiver antenna on the Entomopter's tail. He connected two sets of plug-in cables from the controller to the laptop and when he pushed the toggle stem forward the Entomopter's wing angle changed. The unit was receiving properly. He read the next instruction and chuckled to himself at the terminology. *Verify tension on surface locomotors.* He pinched the legs together and then pulled them apart. Satisfied, he unfolded a brown paper bag from his jacket and spilled out the contents. He briefly examined the Radio Shack receipt and cursed at the $4.98 price of the 555 timers—six times the cost in hardware stores. Next, he reached for his personal laptop and slid out the battery pack. Inside and to the left of that compartment was a small hollow space framed by two memory chips. He tilted the laptop sideways until four fully assembled switches dropped out. He examined each switch to verify the soldering. He opened his wallet and unfolded a hand drawn schematic, written in pencil and labeled: *computer memory board layout.* Of all the times he'd passed through airports, security screeners had often removed the battery, but never bothered to question the excess chips.

The 555 timer was simple yet elegant with one backup relay to guard against premature ignition. When fully assembled, the device consisted of ten button-cell watch batteries taped and wired in parallel, two switches, one capacitor, one resistor, the timer, relay, and a three-inch long socket board. A pocketed nylon harness held the potassium charge. The contraption resembled a pony express mail delivery system complete with four small saddlebags draped over a giant dragonfly instead of a horse.

Where is the fuel? He wondered. After a few moments, he spotted a separate compartment inside one suitcase and pulled the Velcro flap. He plucked two cartridges and laid them on the table. Next, he gently lifted one potassium cube from a static-free container in his jacket. He tore off a strip of clear duct tape and wrapped one fuse packet to the cube leaving two exposed strands of wire dangling from the tiny circuit board. He repeatedly pressed a small black button on the timer delay until the digital readout said 00:06:00. He carefully inserted the two wires into the clay-like potassium and packed the entry holes tight. He reached for the fuel and catalyst cartridges and snapped both into place in the Entomopter's thorax. The wings immediately responded by flapping at a parallel angle. He pushed the toggle stem on the controller and the angle changed again producing slight forward lift. Careful to avoid the beating wings, he pressed the timer button one last time. The digital readout started a descending countdown in one-second intervals.

Like a skilled pilot, he manipulated the controller and watched from the laptop screen as the insect lifted into the air and floated effortlessly across the quarry. Spotting a pile of rusted cans, he deftly lowered the Entomopter to the ground and then picked one up. He couldn't help think that, contrary to practicing on so many Internet video games, operating the physical device itself was difficult. The unit responded poorly and he was thankful that he didn't have to negotiate it into dead space underneath an aircraft's wing while the flaps were extended. That scheme would have certainly failed. This was indeed a rudimentary invention, but one that would serve his purpose. God would see to it.

He flew the Entomopter back to the table and gently allowed the thorax to hover at head level. He touched a single button on the controller. The Entomopter's legs released and the can dropped to the ground.

Sinani looked at his watch. There were two minutes of flight time left. He directed the Entomopter south over a barbed wire fence and into the grassy field. It took a full minute to reach the tractor. Preferring to watch the event through binoculars rather than the laptop's screen, he gently eased the Entomopter forward until the legs were positioned around the tractor's steering wheel shaft. He touched the controller again and the legs clamped together. The circumference of the shaft was thinner than that of an average landing gear strut, but for this test the placement motion would be the same. The insect predictably rotated sideways and slid down the shaft and into the tractor's dashboard. Three wings snapped out of their socket joints and flailed through the air. The harness with the potassium cube held firmly.

Sinani lowered the binoculars long enough to get a fix on his watch. He refocused on the tractor and counted the last few seconds out loud. "Three...two...one..."

A split second later there was a powerful but muffled explosion. The force of the impact sent pieces of the tractor's gear shifter and steering wheel high into the air. He smiled to himself as the fourth Entomopter wing gently fluttered back to earth.

Chapter Twenty-eight

Milwaukee, WI
Monday, May 11th
8:10 A.M.

Fox Television general manager, Bud Gillespie removed his glasses and sat at his desk grimfaced. His station had again retained sole possession of last place in southeast Wisconsin's viewer ratings. It was now four periods in a row.

Neela Griffin poked her head through the doorway. "You wanted to see me?"

He pointed to a chair. He folded his arms and stared at her. It was the same stare a father would give to his teenage honor roll daughter after retrieving her from police custody and a shoplifting arrest. "You had quite a trip to Italy, young lady."

"I can explain."

"Explain what? The meaning of the word ethical?" He rose and sat on the edge of his desk. "Ms. Griffin, I'm going to be frank. I like you. We all like you. Your tenacity and reporting skills have stayed above average even with all your personal problems. I for one had serious doubts as to whether you could maintain your professionalism through a public divorce and spousal battery. But you did, and I'll tell you here and now that I was wrong. Additionally, your on-camera demeanor in this market still portrays trust. That's something very important to me, your co-workers and this station." His wording was a veiled compliment to her physical appearance, but he had to be careful. He'd recently reassigned another female reporter from the anchor desk and she immediately filed suit. Management claimed it was performance related, but everyone knew it was due to excessive weight gain. "However, your Ohio State journalism degree doesn't give you the right to tromp through Europe posing as a foreign affairs correspondent for a major news network. We sent you to Rome to investigate a theft ring involving Harley-Davidson motorcycle parts. How on earth did you end up at some scientific award ceremony asking questions about weapons of mass destruction? Correct me if I'm wrong, but you did introduce yourself as someone from Fox Cable? When exactly did you make that career move?"

"I thought that there might have been a big story——"

Gillespie pounded his knuckles into the desktop. "Dammit, we're all looking for a big story, but you're not paid to freelance. Now I have to write three apologies; one to this Georgia Tech professor; one to the Pirelli Consortium; and one to our owners, who by the way will be even more upset when they see our ratings. Neela, I'm not a reporter any longer and I hate typing."

"It won't happen again," she apologized. "I promise."

Gillespie returned to his chair and reached for a pen. "Whatever happened to the entertainment piece you were developing to identify the mystery person in that Carly Simon song? What was it again? Something about he's so vain or being vain?"

"You're So Vain."

"Yes, now there's something newsworthy."

"I'm still working on it," she sighed. "And with all due respect, that's not exactly the kind of story that'll benefit society. I have a new lead that exposes a security hole at a major airline. A passenger can gain access to a firearm on board a commercial aircraft just by having the right form. A form that no one is cross checking or verify——"

"Gillespie threw his hands in the air. "See? That's exactly what I mean. You need to tone down the drama and keep a lower profile. So far none of our competitors have picked up on your little stunt. I hope for your sake it stays that way. We'll have to wait and see. I'll give you one more chance. I know we talked about a change, but I've decided to keep you on the Tipline and out of trouble. No more special assignments and no more travel. I want you working local and nothing more. I think it'll give you some time to learn a thing or two about patience."

Georgia Tech

"Quiet. Here he comes," Sharon Tillman announced, dimming the overhead lights.

On cue as if by some distorted magic, the scotch tape on one corner of the 'Congratulations Professor Robertson' banner that was strung across the research lab's ceiling let loose.

Zee quickly climbed onto a stepladder and awkwardly straddled a metal file cabinet.

"Zee, get over here," Jones whispered loudly. "Nothing's happening."

"I can't. This won't stick. Try track fifteen."

Michael opened the door and flicked the light switches.

"Welcome home-a from Rome-a!" A chorus of mock Italian voices shouted. Simultaneously, a melody began playing from speakers on a portable CD player. It was the theme from The Godfather.

The roomful of university staff and coworkers reverently bowed their heads.

Michael put his hand on his chest. "In deference to the late Marlon Brando, I made them a mopter they couldn't refuse."

Laughter turned into cheering.

Zee hopped off the counter.

The banner drifted to the floor, entangling the head and shoulders of Dr. Winford Garton II. He freed himself and waited patiently for the congratulatory crowd to dissipate. He approached Michael with an extended hand. "Well done, professor. I suppose you'll want a bigger office?"

"Thank you, sir. I may take you up on that." He removed his jacket. "You wouldn't believe all the media. I've never dealt with that many news stations before. There had to be at least a dozen. I agreed to demonstrate the Entomopter system at an Orlando Symposium at the end of the month. I hope that was all right?"

"Certainly, but not before we lock down the second half of this Saudi thing. I'm sure you know that we've finalized a deal with Mr. Al-Assaf. Dr. Al-Aran has made all the arrangements. My God, man…all we have to do is let them fiddle with your bugs for a few weeks and it will be a windfall for the university. I repeat, I want you to make sure Faiz has everything he needs to satisfy their requests. Five million dollars is a helluva payoff, son. All those hours of dedication. A tangible and fitting reward. You should be proud."

They're not bugs, Michael wanted to scream. "I'm happy for the university, sir. It's a nice round figure. I hope you understand that we're still in a developmental stage. I'm not an expert on desert oil fields, but I do know that they're huge. The Entomopter can't possibly cover such distances with its current radio signal strength. I just don't want to raise false expectations. The device might not be suitable for a security plat…"

"Nonsense," Garton interrupted, unconcerned with technical limitations. "Not another word. Faiz can work through that. He has everything well in hand."

"I'm sure he does," Michael said through clenched teeth. He scanned the room. "By the way…where is Faiz?"

"I hear you're not feeling well," Garton dodged. "Why don't you take a few days off? You've certainly earned it."

"Thanks. I am feeling a little better, but I just might—"

"I'd love to chat, but I have another commitment," Garton extended his hand. "We mustn't forget NASA. That project has my favorite kind of potential: fat and federal."

"Very true, sir," Michael agreed. "Mars could be at least a five to six year run with enough guaranteed income for second and third generational upgrades."

"You're certainly on a roll," Garton beamed and glanced at his watch. "You just brought five and a quarter million dollars into our coffers not to mention keeping Tech's good name in the spotlight. I know it and so does the Board. That brings solid credibility. If this Saudi venture pans out, I'll personally see that the new research center bears your name."

"I appreciate that, sir."

"You've earned it, son. Look me up next week; I'd like to take you to lunch. That is if you can stand lowly American food again. I hear the Italians really know cuisine. Keep me posted and I'll do the same."

Robertson Research Center. Michael envisioned the exterior lettering. When his digestive system got back to normal, he would eat a cheeseburger for lunch. A large American cheeseburger with fries.

Chapter Twenty-nine

After the obligatory mingling, Michael corralled his research team into his office and slammed the door. "Looks like you two have been busy."

"I knew you'd be upset," Jones said apologetically. "We wanted to call you, but Dr. Al-Aran said he'd take care of everything. He kind of just took control. What were we supposed to do?"

"Whoa...why would I be upset?" Michael said sarcastically. "Someone literally overtakes the project without my knowledge or permission? But, wait...maybe I'm overreacting. After all, I only invented the thing."

Jones turned to Zee. "Didn't Al-Aran say he'd keep everyone in the loop, especially about the hotel demonstration?"

Michael raised one eyebrow. "What hotel demonstration?"

"The Swissotel," Zee peeped.

"The what?"

"In Buckhead. One of the Saudi representatives leased a meeting room for some sort of demonstration. Meal service, private waiters. I think his name was Ibrahim something. He and Dr. Al-Aran were even considering making a videotape."

"Faiz is flying my Entomopter in a hotel?" Michael checked his watch. "When does it start?"

Jones shifted. "Um, Dr. Al-Aran figured he could handle everything himself."

"When does it start?" Michael seethed.

"I'm not sure," Zee stammered. "Wait, I think they changed the schedule."

Michael's face welled red. He dialed the phone. "Buckhead, Georgia...the Swissotel, please."

Sharon Tillman cracked the office door. "Excuse me, Professor Robertson, there's a Mr. O'Neill from NASA on line two. He says it's urgent."

Michael slammed the phone onto its cradle. "Sharon, find Professor Al-Aran for me right now. I don't care where he is or what he's doing. Find him."

"I'm sorry professor, but Dr. Al-Aran is on a cruise for the next three weeks."

Michael sat stunned. "This can't be happening."

"Do you want to speak to Mr. O'Neill or should I take a message?"

"Huh? No, put him through." Michael touched the speakerphone. "Stuart?"

"Michael, there's no easy way to say this, so I'll get right to the point. We're trying like hell to make our numbers work, but the whole shuttle program is under severe scrutiny. Everyone is running for cover. The Mars mission is still alive, but with certain reductions. I'm afraid you've been impacted. We're releasing the official announcement shortly. I wanted you to know before Garton. I'm sorry."

Jones and Zee tiptoed outside.

Michael's face turned ashen. He sat motionless staring across the room at the set of red and silver Coca-Cola can wings pinned inside a glass display case on the wall. "Impacted how?"

"The Entomopter Project has been canceled. Funds have already been reallocated. You need to put all your schedules and any other work in progress on hold indefinitely."

"What about future planning? Couldn't we at least continue to test the—"

"Don't you understand what I'm telling you? It's over. There is no mission to Mars for the Entomopter. We estimate that it will take four years just to restore some kind of confidence in the base program. Congress has concluded that the entire shuttle fleet needs regeneration. Orbiters, support equipment, and people. In addition, we've just made the decision to go back to the moon with a permanent base station. Substantial resources are being diverted to that. I wanted to tell you in person."

"The moon? That's the dumbest idea I've heard this year. What the hell for? We've already been to the damn moon."

"I'm sorry."

Michael leaned into the speaker. "You're sorry? Tell that to the students on my research team who turned down other highly-sought after appointments and worked their asses off to meet your timeframes. Tell that to benefactors who donated the lab funding just to satisfy your needs. Tell that to the Pirelli foundation who just became the world's biggest fool for giving a golden plaque to something that's already been canceled. Exactly where would you like me to stick that?"...dial tone.... "Hello? Stuart?"

Washington, DC
Outback Steakhouse Restaurant
Friday, May 15th
6:30 P.M.

tap..tap..tap...tap..tap..tap

Tom Ross handed four menus to the waitress. "And we'll have two orders of coconut shrimp. Thanks." He leaned sideways and pecked Marcia's cheek.

Marcia's younger daughter Rachel nudged her sister Kristin and gave a disgusted look. "That is like so gross, especially in public."

"Speaking of public, another year of high school is winding down," Ross observed. "Would either of you girls be interested in NTSB summer work?"

"Ohmygod, it's Robbie Billings and Aaron Hill." Kristin ignored the employment offer and slunk low in the booth. She frantically dug through her purse. "I am so busted. I knew I should have fixed my hair. They're like the hottest seniors in the whole school. I can't believe I'm sitting here with my parents."

"Would it help if we put bags over our heads?" Ross asked. "Good grief, we're not that horrible are we? You shouldn't worry so much about what other people think. True friends should accept you for who you are. Just be yourself."

Rachel rolled her eyes. Obviously bored, she shifted the fork to her other hand and continued tapping her water glass.

"Rachel, would you please stop that?" Ross asked politely.

"Yeah, a big plastic garbage bag," she said matter-of-factly.

Ross folded his hands prayer-like. "Okay, let's all relax and play something. Tell us the best thing that happened to each of you in school today. Kristin?"

"Well, I had my solo in band which was like pretty awesome and then I found out that Justin might be getting a car and if he does then I won't have to like ride that lame bus next semester."

tap..tap..tap...tap..tap..tap

Ross nudged Marcia suspiciously. "Oh, and why didn't we know about that?"

tap..tap..tap...tap..tap..tap

"Rachel, please. Tom asked you to stop."

125

"I'm just being myself. Besides, my real dad says I don't have to do what Tom says." She made a sneering face. "This game is stupid and I don't feel like—"

"Alright, listen," Ross raised his voice. "Your mother just got here and she's had a very long day. So let's try and make this a special dinner for her, okay? Rachel, it's your turn. Tell us what happened in school."

"I got up; I went to class; and then I came home. School sucks."

tap..tap..tap…tap..tap..tap

Ross took a deep breath. "Please stop."

"So what if I don't? Are you going to like make me be a dorky government worker and wear a dorky band-aid on my face like you or send me to bed without supp…?"

He snatched the fork from her hand and knocked over the condiment rack in the process. She instinctively flinched backwards. Conversation in the booth across the aisle stopped. "Watch your mouth little girl." Ross lowered his voice. "Now tell us about your damn day."

Rachel straightened and placed both hands flat on the table. "Okay, in first hour biology we got to like touch a real human skeleton. Guess how many bones there were?"

Ross set the fork down.

She snatched it back.

tap..tap..tap..tap..tap..tap..tap..tap..tap..tap..tap..tap

Ross shimmied out of the booth. He found the waitress and gently put his arm around her shoulders. "We're having a little problem tonight. I want you to cancel the medium rare sirloin, please. One of my daughters just lost her appetite. She won't be getting it back, understand?"

He returned to the booth. It was empty.

126

Chapter Thirty

Marcia was standing alone in the aisle, car keys in hand. "Rachel is upset, so we're leaving. Maybe if you showed a little more understanding you two could get along. Sometimes I think you forget that she's just a child. We'll be at home."

The waitress appeared with two plates of shrimp. "Did everyone lose their appetite?"

"Bring me some Dewars scotch, please. On the rocks." Ross sat down. He opened a Ziploc bag and spread out a pile of seeds.

"Little family dispute, eh?" A man's voice spoke through the wood slats in the next booth. "I couldn't help listening."

Ross was about to politely tell the eavesdropper to mind his own business, but recognized the voice. "This is really embarrassing. I'm sorry you had to hear that."

Jack Riley boldly sat down and extended his hand. "You should have been raised in my family. My father would've slapped the hair off my head if I spoke to him that way."

"I'm Tom Ross. I was at your presentation on the fourth. I really enjoyed it."

"Most people do." Riley opened his cell phone. "I thought I recognized you. NTSB, right? I hope you don't mind. I like to have a broad range of contacts."

They exchanged phone and pager numbers.

"Congresswoman Petri was wrong," Ross stated.

"She's always been a pain so I'm used to it. I try to ignore politics. It gives me a headache."

Ross noticed Riley eyeing the appetizers. "Help yourself. Nobody else gives a damn about eating."

"Thanks." He scooped a shrimp through plum sauce. "What are those? Pistachios?"

"Pumpkin seeds." Ross flicked one across the table. "I started when I was a kid. I guess I got hooked."

Riley frowned warily at the morsel and then touched it to his tongue. He made a painful face and placed it on a napkin. "That's quite a spunky girl. Looks like you've got your hands full. If it's any consolation, you were right in sticking to your guns. There has to be consequences for bad behavior. Kids have to learn." Ross shook his head. "I don't get it. Both of them are honor roll students and musically talented, but have absolutely no discipline. You should see when they go at each other. The younger one throws some of the worst tantrums I've ever seen. Unfortunately, her mother's a big part of the problem."

"I take it you're not their biological father?"

"It's complicated," Ross admitted. The waitress brought a fresh cocktail. He took a hefty swallow. "So, you were in the Air Force, huh? Did you fly in the Gulf War?"

"Nah, I'm not a pilot. I was in charge of technical teams that trekked out into the desert and set up satellite receivers. Most were trained at Langley, AFB. We made sure everybody could synch up with whiz-vee."

Ross paused thoughtfully. "I've heard of that. It's a military radio communication system."

"Wideband Secure Voice is the ultimate avionics radio communication system. ARC-164 is a UHF frequency hopper that's totally uncrackable. Every aircraft we fly has it. It's the same system the president uses."

"Hmph. Sounds impressive."

"Impressive and top-secret. After the war, several units mysteriously appeared inside some Saudi F-15s, accidentally installed by some of our own incompetent contactors. I raised hell up and down the chain of command and probably ruffled the wrong feathers. I never was very tactful with bureaucracy. After that, I figured my chances at reaching major were nil, so I got out."

"And now you've got your own bureaucracy at Homeland Security."

"Not exactly," Riley chuckled. "One secretary and one office assistant."

"You're joking."

"Apparently you weren't listening very well during my presentation. I evaluate threats and point the appropriate federal enforcement agencies in the right direction. I'm the guy who makes sure that everyone and everything gets plugged in. Other than traveling my butt off day and night, it's a great job. I get to work alone and still carry a pretty big stick."

"Besides attacking theme parks, what else do you think al Qaeda might do? Be honest."

"You don't want to know," Riley warned. "Trust me."

"I do," Ross said adamantly. "Tell me the truth."

"With all due respect to Jack Nicholson, you can't handle the truth."

"Try me."

Riley shrugged. "They'll make a statement. A very poignant statement."

"Like what?"

"Well, Mr. NTSB, put it this way…here's what I'd do." He finished munching his third shrimp and washed it down with water. "I'd order my U.S. sleeper cells to pick random but prominent Americans and shadow them. Members of Congress for instance. Day in and day out. I'd memorize their routines and schedules; learn their neighborhoods, homes, and patterns. Then on a given date at a given hour, I'd execute their family members in a horribly brutal way. I'd send videotapes everywhere."

Ross was visibly taken aback. "That's really sick. I'm sorry I asked."

"Hey, get a grip," Riley raised his voice. "And get ready because that's exactly how al Qaeda operates. Their next statement will be so public and so shocking that it will be incomprehensible to every civilized human being. All in hopes that Americans will simply cave to fear like our European friends. And the sad part is, those same cowards—including some in this country—will say they told us so. It's unbelievable that so many people have no idea who we're dealing with. The terrorists we're fighting are cold-blooded animals, period. Animals that prey on the weak and innocent. Life to them means nothing. They thrive on making their enemies as angry as possible solely for a reaction. They'd like nothing more than to whip us into a state of murderous revenge. It's all about keeping the cycle of fear and violence alive."

"Do you think something like Komodo could really happen?"

"Do you know any radical Islamic fundamentalists?" Riley volleyed back.

Ross broke into a chuckle. "Nope, can't say that I do."

"How about enemy combatants?"

"I know who they are. Soldiers who fight against us, right?"

"Captured soldiers," Riley clarified. "The worst are interned at Guantanamo Bay, Cuba. Well, one in particular arrived in November 2001. We think he specifically targeted and killed CIA operative Johnny Spann in the prisoner uprising in Mazar-e-Sharif, Afghanistan. To this day he's never spoken a single word to anyone. He sits in his cage down there and does three things: eat, sleep, and chant. Day after day, every waking minute of every hour. Know what he chants? Verses from the Qur'an. He starts at the beginning and reads every word in every Surah, er..chapter and then starts over. The guy's like a broken record. Or worse yet, a machine. An evil machine. We think he lives in a state of permanent psychosis. A real Hannibal Lector. The guards can't take their eyes off of him for a second because he'll do anything to kill an American. Anything. We don't know much about him except that he attended one of those Wahabi indoctrination schools funded mostly by Saudi money. The kind where kids sit cross-legged all day long rocking and reciting over and over until their minds are so fixated that they literally become religious robots. And you can bet they're not memorizing anything about love thy neighbor. Wahabi Islamic ideology teaches two fundamental principles: Israel has no right to exist; and America has no moral right to rule and is therefore the central enemy of Islam. Fortunately for us, these robots aren't that smart. I mean, they don't have the ability to strategically plan attacks. They're more suited to brute force."

"You mean homicide bombings?"

"Especially homicide bombings. Granted, they're still completely brainwashed, but I'd rather deal with them than some of the other fighters we've been hearing about."

"Other fighters?"

"Uh-huh. We've gotten credible information from some Gitmo prisoners that members of Al-Adl Wal Ihsane (Justice and Charity), Morocco's biggest Islamic movement have formed a splinter faction of Western-savvy assassins called the Salafi, a.k.a. super-terrorists. Most have Syrian roots. With respect to ruthlessness, these guys make Hezbollah seem like nuns in a convent and they do have the ability to plan. They're extremely intelligent and skilled, mainly because of the education that the west has conveniently provided. We think they're the ones who've been probing our planes. We call them carpenters."

Chapter Thirty-one

"Carpenters?"

"As in ants," Riley explained. "There are designated soldiers within an ant colony that literally go out and probe territories for new nest sites. They report back to the colony and the queen before making a decision to attack. It's the same with the Salafi. They evaluate, test, and learn all they can about the mechanics, operation, and layout of potential targets. They're the ones who provided the intelligence to those kids involved in the commercial aircraft attacks in London. The ten planes that were targeted for mid-air destruction. I can't tell you any more than that, but trust me; they're here and they're real. They legally board planes and soak up information. Information that they plan to use against us in some form of terror. And we can't do a damn thing to stop it. Neither can the airlines. No excessive questioning or racial profiling allowed. In fact, if they try, the FAA doles out hefty fines. The London carry-on bombers were either Salafi terrorists or trained by them."

"Fines?" Ross mumbled around an ice cube. "What idiot made that rule?"

"The Secretary of Transportation. No airline can question or detain more than one person of Middle-Eastern descent at a time."

"So, you're telling me that these Salafi can plot God-knows-what evil plan and we can't do anything about it?"

"Yup. Not a thing. And the sad part is we know for certain that they're scoping U.S. aircraft just trying to figure out a way to sneak combustible liquids on board, assemble an explosive device, and detonate it in-flight. The components by themselves are harmless and generally undetectable while passing through screening systems. Israel would lock these bastards up in a heartbeat and we can't even slap their wrists for fear of violating their human rights. Isn't the U.S. Constitution great?"

"I'll be so glad when we win this damn war," Ross sighed.

Riley frowned deeply and shook his head. "Win-the-war-on-terror. The five dumbest words in the world. Why? Because it's impossible. It can't be done. Now don't get me wrong, I'm one hell of a patriot, but that's the biggest line of political B-S ever. There is no such thing, yet everyone from the president on down speaks it. We're not ever going to win the war on terror. That's like saying we need to win the war on crime or drugs or sickness. It'll take every ounce of our collective will and energy just to survive and control it. The war on terror is really an endless battle of attrition on a world stage fought against an endless army of pop-up killers. Killers who hate us and want us dead, period. And that hate just keeps rolling and gaining strength every day. No prisoners, no bargaining, and no peace. Dead."

"That's what I don't get," Ross admitted. "Where does it all come from?"

"The hate? Good question. Sometimes even I get confused. But beyond all the socio-political and territorial issues, Americans do stupid things."

Ross bristled at the Michael Moore-ish comment. "What do you mean?"

"Easy, Sparky. I'll rephrase it. Some Americans do stupid things. Specifically, the guards at Guantanamo by way of some rather unique interrogation methods."

"Torture?"

"Physical torture is illegal and after that Iraqi prisoner abuse scandal, there are too many human rights groups watching."

"What then?"

Riley smiled seductively. "You'd be surprised how effective a CD can be. A little ghetto rap music turned on at prayer time works better that a beating. Especially the real raunchy stuff like Ludacris or Eminem. It literally drives the detainees nuts. Some have negotiated information for silence. Get it? Even the U.S. military plays its little games. But then last October, on the first day of Ramadan to be precise, a twenty-year-old American soldier single-handedly took the war on terror to another level by committing a real atrocity down there. One that had reverberations throughout the entire Muslim world."

Ross leaned closer. "Are you telling me that the stories about flushing religious literature down toilets were actually true? But, I thought that Newsweek...I thought they retracted..."

"The flushing stories were false," Riley said matter-of-factly.

"Then what was it? A music atrocity?"

Riley shook his head. "Hardly. This kid was drunk on duty and thought he'd be funny by dropping his pants right in front of an entire open cellblock. Word got out through the visitor channels like a bolt of energized lightening and the ramifications were unbelievably disastrous. It was an atrocity of the worst kind. Trust me. That lone stupid act did more to enflame Osama bin Laden's terror base than one thousand Abu Ghraibs. It's something you'll never hear in the media."

Ross gave a doubting look. "So one dumb guard pulls down his pants and moons prisoners. What's the big deal?"

Riley stared at Ross for a full five seconds. "The big deal is... he squatted over a copy of the Qur'an. You can figure out what he did next."

Ross closed his eyes and lifted his head to the restaurant's ceiling. "You've got to be kidding?"

"So...what were you saying about wining the war on terror?"

"I'm so glad we had this little chat. I feel like I could throw up. Either that or move to some remote island in the middle of..." He lifted his glass at the waitress, but suddenly clutched his side. He let out an audible groan.

"Are you alright?"

Ross sat motionless. "Oh, man...I hate that. Every once in a while I get a sharp pain. Always in the same spot. It comes and goes. I'm fine. Where were we? Oh, yeah, a remote island. You mentioned the Florida Keys the other day in your presentation. What's down there?"

"Not a helluva lot except ocean breezes and palm trees. And my retirement job. I'll tell you about it sometime."

"No terrorists, huh?"

Riley chuckled and shook his head. "Like I said before, a Salafi soldier would blow up a kindergarten class and think nothing of it. But even that kind of damage, for lack of a better term, is manageable. Sure, people usually die violently, but so does the terrorist. What we're hearing about the super-terrorist is that he'll orchestrate the destruction of an entire city, and then quietly and carefully move on to the next. That's the guy I fear. One time in Norfolk I escorted four Saudi nationals to dinner. Radio technicians. They get in my car and I politely ask them to fasten their seatbelts. They refused. They said if Allah wills that they die in an accident, so be it. And speaking of that mentality, I majored in math, so let's do some.

Chapter Thirty-two

No one knows how many Muslims live in the U.S., but estimates range from one to seven million. Take the low end. Say ninety-nine percent are peaceful, law-abiding citizens just like you and me. If just one half of that other one percent support radical fundamentalism, then that's five thousand people who are here and ready to die for their beliefs. Five thousand potential pop-up killers as opposed to nineteen who were responsible for 9/11. Twenty if you count that sonofabitch Moussaui. Go ahead and call me a racist because I don't give a shit. And you'd be wrong anyway. Racism doesn't have a damn thing to do with it. It's radical religious fanaticism. Remember the Danish newspaper that printed those caricatures of Mohammed? People were killed over cartoons. In America, so-called artists can paint and display a portrait of Jesus covered with feces and all you get is a threat to withhold tax dollars from some publicly-funded institution. Instead of the Da Vinci Code, just imagine an American filmmaker creating the Mohammed Code. I guarantee that within twenty-four hours the entire production cast would be assassinated and Hollywood would become a suicide war zone. Religious fanaticism. You can't reason with it, you can't change it, and you certainly can't kill it. All you can do is keep fighting on and on and on. So, in answer to your question about Komodo...yes, it can and it will happen. And believe me, we're talking all out war. You and I go about our daily lives. Rise, shower, work, relax. Eat salad, sip wine, and go to bed. Routines, routines, routines. A little passion when we have time. Not romantic passion, but things you absolutely-love-to-do passion. Golf, travel, shop, hunt, collect things, read, whatever. Contrast that to Mr. Super-terrorist's passion——to destroy the enemies of Islam, period. In case you're wondering, that means you and me. He has complete and utter faith in his god, Allah and all he stands for. No timeframe, no diversions, and no pause in the action to pack up the family and head to Disney World. And all this talk about Islam being the religion of peace? It may be for most, but not for Mr. Super-terrorist. Therein lies the problem. Do you know where he is right now? In America learning two things about his enemy: how to exploit cultural and emotional weakness, and how to become an expert at modern technology. Komodo exposes the former."

"This whole world seems so scary. How do you deal with it?"

Riley gave an incredulous look. "How do you deal with being first on the scene of an airline crash involving hundreds of people? I can't imagine it, but then we both continue to fly, right? You and I have the ability to turn it on and off. Problem is, I don't believe most people can. Americans are simply too damned nice. We hold feelings high on a pedestal as if they really matter to a terrorist. Wanna know something? They don't. That idiot, er..Congressional rep Petri is a perfect example. Don't get me wrong. Liberal thinking may have its place, but not in a war on terror. They just don't want to accept the fact that the world has dangerous people. The far-left really scares me because most of them are in denial about the menace and will never consider preemptive military action. We need to remember history. Kinder and gentler just ain't gonna cut it in our future. The bottom line is this: if we don't or can't bring war to the terrorists, they'll bring it here."

"So, what else do you do when you're not chasing the Salami, er..Salafi?" Ross said, feeling the alcohol.

Riley smiled to himself and methodically licked his fingers. "I already told you. The Keys. I have a small place on the water right smack in the middle near Marathon."

"Aren't you afraid of hurricanes?"

"Hey, we're not talking about a New Orleans soup bowl. If a category five storm hits the Florida Keys head on, then all that's left is sand. Did you get that? The sand is still there. You rebuild. It's the chance you take to occasionally visit paradise and drive a 32-foot Boston Whaler 305 Conquest with twin 225 hp Mercury OptiMax outboards. My one and only toy. Whenever I get the chance I head south and chase a Jewfish...oops, sorry, I'm not supposed to call it that...grouper. I've been after him for three years now and one day I'm going to catch his miserable ass."

"A grouper is a fish that sort of looks like a bass, right?"

"Uh-huh. But Osama is much more than a fish."

"Osama? That's cute."

"Cute, but appropriate. I named that ugly bastard myself," Riley said proudly. "Osama bin Grouper. The baddest of the bad. He's got a bad ugly head with bad ugly lips lined with bad ugly hooks. My hooks. I figure he goes at least one hundred pounds."

"One hundred pounds?" Ross asked skeptically.

"Groupers can get huge. Some reach eight, even nine hundred pounds. The largest was twelve feet long and weighed fifteen hundred. There's an unofficial report that it ate a diver. Well, every time I hook Osama he burns me. He hangs out in a series of underwater caves in a deep channel off Duck Key. Problem is, he never stays in one spot. He keeps moving around just like the real Osama. I've made it my life's ambition to catch that fat sonofabitch and when I do, I'm going to pack him on ice and introduce him to a new dark cave right in my backyard. It's called a Weber grill."

Ross chuckled at that. "So what do you call your boat? Osama-Killer?"

"Not a bad choice, but I named it after the island. Just-Duck-Key. Get it?"

"And where's home up here?"

"My wife, Charlene and I own a place thirty miles west near Dulles. It's got room for horses."

"You own horses, too?"

"Not me, pal. That's her little hobby. She has five of her own and boards two more right now. Horses don't like me and the feeling is mutual. They can sense uneasiness in certain people and I guess I'm one."

"Big money in horses?"

"Don't go there," Riley said, pinching the bridge of his nose. "I keep telling my wife if you want to make a million dollars on horses, then start with two million."

"Family?" Ross asked.

"Just one very smart daughter in first year law. She wants to specialize in corporate real estate. You?"

"I live in Arlington downstairs from...um...well, you already met them."

The conversation abruptly stopped. Riley figured it was time to leave and glanced at his watch. "I know you NTSB folks can't spend a nickel on meals, so why don't you let me pay for this?"

"No way. I appreciated the company. Even though you did give me indigestion."

Riley slid out of the booth and peeled off a few dollars. "My boss may not let me take extended vacations, but he sure as hell doesn't skimp on much else, especially when terror's involved. Don't tell anybody, but I can use his plane whenever I want. Someday you and I might have to conduct some official business in southern Florida. It's a G-1159 and fast as hell. Seats eleven. If I were Joe Shmoe, a round trip would cost twenty-three grand."

Ross recalled a recent media report about Homeland Security lavishly overspending on employees at a local DC hotel. He wanted to mention that the NTSB also leased a private aircraft whenever rapid transport was required, but he let it go. A modest Learjet 25, it seated half as many and cost 1/3 less to operate. He extended his hand. "Maybe I'll see you again sometime."

"If there's ever an aviation incident on your watch you can count on it," Riley promised. "Fair warning. I can be a real pain in the ass."

"I'll try and remember that."

Riley nodded curtly. "Do me a favor and ease up on the booze and the salty white seeds. You should check out diverticulitis on WebMD, too. You got an umbrella?"

"Why? Is it raining?"

"Not yet." Riley picked up a fork and tapped Ross's glass. "But there's one helluva storm brewing at your house tonight. Peace."

Chapter Thirty-three

Milwaukee, WI
Saturday, May 16th
8:45 P.M.

Fox cameraman Terry Lee used his legs to steer the company mini-van as he scrolled through a list of artists on his new I-pod.

Neela Griffin gripped the armrest in the passenger's seat as the vehicle turned sharply from Lisbon Avenue onto West Lloyd Street. The tires gave off a slight squeal; she gave off a nasty glance. She was listening to her station's Tipline, alternately erasing the usual number of crank voicemail messages, and jotting down those that were potentially newsworthy. The last message played out.

....Saturday, May 16th...2:15 P.M... "Hello, my name is Dave from Mequon. I just wanted you to know that there's a Pakistani guy who lives in a twenty thousand square foot house on Pioneer Road. He lets his teen-age son run around the property with an AK-47 assault rifle. They spent $285,000 on landscaping last year and the kid blew every one of the sap-lings in half. I've seen him shoot from the road. I heard that they've even got grenade launchers. You should check it out. If there's any kind of ter-rorist reward money I'd sure be interest..."

She deleted the message and tucked the phone in her purse.

Lee peered through the van's windshield trying to match a backdrop they had used on a previous filming. He gently eased the vehicle up and over a street curb and onto a bike path that ran through Washington Park. He turned off the ignition and opened the side door for his camera. "So, what happened with Gillespie and that Midwest Airlines firearm security thing?"

Griffin ignored the question and continued perusing pages of a television script entitled, 'When Cops Deal' that was scheduled to lead off tomorrow's evening news.

"Okay, I guess that's a sore subject. I'm sorry I brought it up. Let's see, what else can we talk about? Wanna see my new tattoo? It's a picture of you." Griffin's mouth curved slightly. Lee lifted his camera and focused the spotlight. "Ladies and gentlemen, introducing Fox's newest anchor. The beautiful, the awesome, the intelligent, the Pulitzer prize-winning and definitely available and longing for a decent caring partner, Neela Griffin."

She shook her head at the theatrics and clicked her microphone. "This is central city Milwaukee on a Saturday night. Your city. A city where people like Rick—not his real name—work by day and return to at night. A time when darkness is a friend that hides both movement and identity. Rick is a college graduate and corporate manager. He has a stable, high-paying job, a loving wife, and three young daughters. He lives thirty miles from here in an upscale suburb, yet someone and something urges him back to the city. That someone is a drug dealer who goes by the name of T-Man; the something is percodan, a prescription pain pill so addictive it draws users like Rick back to Milwaukee's inner city again and again no matter what the cost. By his own admission, when Rick has the urge to use, nothing matters. Money, family, fear of arrest, nothing. He's even taken his youngest daughter along for a ride into some of the highest crime areas in the city. Why? Because he has to. The segment you're about to see captures one such meeting between dealer and user. You'll witness the counting and distribution of cash and pills in the front seat of Rick's SUV. Even more startling, you'll also see District Three Milwaukee Police Squad zero-one-nine approach Rick's vehicle from the rear and appear to make an arrest. The problem is, there is no arrest. Incredibly, both Rick and T-Man are allowed to simply walk away. Watch now from our hidden camera."

"Got it." Lee stopped filming. He left the spotlight on. "Heads up."

She caught the water bottle in mid-air and took a long sip. "Okay, we insert the buy segment, Rick's interview and then reaction from Alderman McGhee. I don't think we'll have time for the Internal Affairs piece, so we'll shift that to the follow-up. Okay, I'm ready."

The camera turned on.

"Milwaukee is not unique, and neither is Rick. There are thousands just like him in cities all across America. In our next segment we'll find out what happened to two hundred pills and sixteen hundred dollars. Stay tuned for reaction from Chief of Police Louis Williams and Third District Captain Robert Oliva. Reporting for Crime Stoppers Tipline from Washington Park in Milwaukee's central city, I'm Neela Griffin, Fox News."

139

Chapter Thirty-four

Monday, May 18th
1:00 A.M.

The air inside the American Legion Post was heavy with smoke and '50s music. Guests were determined to party all night. A private club by membership, the Post was therefore exempt from normal closing time that was strictly enforced on other bars.

Elvis-like, Chief Watts donned a fur-lined white cape and had a large gold medallion strapped around his waist. His white sequined suit contrasted well with his slick hair that formed a widow-peak V on his forehead. A neck chain sported a fluffy Hound Dog, a song he personally sang to break the Karaoke ice. After that, a steady line of customers eagerly demonstrated their vocal talents. Strategically positioned television monitors flashed song lyrics throughout the bar.

Finished with his third helping of spicy chicken wings, Watts refilled his glass with a hefty slosh of Korbel brandy and headed for the stage. When he whistled into the microphone, a piercing back feed echoed through the speakers.

The crowd quieted.

"Excuse me. The King has entered the building and this is him speaking. I want to thank everyone who came here tonight to help celebrate my birthday and I want you all to know that this kick-ass party is just getting started. Why? Because it's after midnight and I'm on vacation." The crowd roared. Watts raised his glass appreciatively before guzzling the contents. "I love all you assholes and if you don't have a good time, then you can suck my Marine shorts." He spied Sinani sneaking up the back stairs. "Hey, Stan. Bring Mikey up here."

Two huge sets of arms carried Sinani through a path in the crowd and plopped him onto the stage.

"Attention everyone," Watts announced. "I'd like to introduce you to my Cench Franadian brother from the north, Mikey Waleu. He finally got smart and moved to the best damn country in the world where he plays major league baseball for the best damn team in the history of the world. Case closed. Ladies, get ready to throw your underwear up here because this little shitter uses a fake name.

Wanna know who he really is?"

Sinani's eyes widened and he tried to make his entire body small hoping that Watts would simply release him and move onto another subject.

"I'm proud to present the sexiest shortstop in baseball, the New York Yankees, Darrin, er.. Derek Jeter."

The crowd let out a raucous cheer.

Watts pressed his lips into Sinani's cheek. "I love ya, Mikey. C'mon, this is for you." He touched a button on the Karaoke console.

"Take me out to the ball game,
Take me out with the crowd..."

Sinani squinted at the monitor lyrics, and was quickly two measures behind. No one cared. By the middle refrains the audience had forgotten about him completely.

Watts dragged him off stage toward the bar and ordered another round of shots. He hugged Sinani sideways. "You're a good shit, Mikey. Let's have another cocktail and play some poker. We've already got six. Are you in?"

"No way; I can't," he protested. "I think I'm about finished."

Watts frowned deeply at someone actually refusing to travel into the euphoric land of party world. "C'mon, it's early. You need some tequila. Or better yet, why don't you run upstairs and bring down some of your fancy vodka."

"I need my bed," Sinani yawned. "Yup, need to go upstairs right now. Goodnight, Chief. Happy birthday."

"G'night, Mr. Jeter with the little Peter," Watts said, raising his glass. "Sleep tight you little Yankee shitstop."

Sinani waved a weak acknowledgement and pretended to stagger upstairs.

Inside his apartment, he locked the door and tuned the kitchen radio to the pilot chatter on 85.5 FM. He opened the refrigerator and slid out a plastic tray. His watch said straight up 2:00 A.M. Good timing, he thought. The potassium chlorate cubes needed three hours to reach room temperature. Closing the door, he paused and gave a wary glance to a Ziploc bag isolated on a lower shelf, imprisoning a tiny eyedropper bottle filled with potassium cyanide.

Mitchell International Airport
Monday, May 18th
5:20 A.M.

It was ten minutes before general boarding.

Midwest Airlines Captain Joseph Falk felt like a delivery boy as he hurried down the passenger ramp clutching a bag of donuts and a six-pack of large coffee cups. The early flight crews flipped coins to eat. This was his third loss in a row. The Starbucks ladies always added dark chocolate to Falk's coffee and marked the cup with a distinctive red 'F'. He told them that drinking it while flying was better than joining the mile-high club because it lasted so much longer.

He distributed breakfast to the crew of Flight 309 and took his seat in the cockpit. Even with 11,000 hours, he was still considered a junior captain based on seniority and spent most of his time on standby waiting for work. The boredom had gotten so bad that he found himself pestering the dispatch center to see if any pilot had called in sick. Falk had flown since he was sixteen and had earned his commercial certification piloting trans-Atlantic cargo to Africa. Once over the coast of Namibia, he drifted over a plateau so close to a herd of zebra that he could count stripes. It was the only time he'd fallen asleep flying an aircraft.

Boeing's MD-80 twinjet actually referred to a series of models (MD-81/82/83/88) certified by the FAA in 1980. An upgraded DC-9, the MD-80 was best known for its quiet fuel efficiency that produced some of the lowest operating costs in the aviation industry. The Pratt and Whitney JT8D-217 engines were fuselage-mounted.

The morning flight to Boston was routine. Still, Falk preferred westbound routes—Denver in particular due to its pilot-friendly layout. No matter where a plane set down, it could reach a terminal without having to cross another inbound runway. Eastbound flights usually meant Boston's Logan or New York's dreaded LaGuardia with its complex routing points, congested skies, and temperamental controllers. Mitchell International was just the opposite. The FAA used it to break in rookies. That meant by-the-book procedures and maddening distance spacing between approaches, sometimes up to three minutes. It was common knowledge among commercial pilots that on a clear day, one could see training wheels at the base

143

of Mitchell's tower.

First officer Tim Haas had never flown with Falk before and was anxious to make a good impression. He reached for a clipboard that held one of three pre-flight checklists. He craned his neck briefly and noticed that the lead flight attendant had closed the cockpit door, a signal that the cabin was secure. He turned to Falk. "So you're the one."

"The one what?" Falk asked suspiciously.

"The guardian. The keeper of the box. Will, Penny, Dr. Smith, the robot. Warning, warning. Gosh, when I was a kid I loved that old TV show, especially that nerdy robot. Do you mind if I hold it?"

"Sorry. You can look, but not touch." Falk held up his authentic Lost in Space lunchbox. It had become the Ark of the Covenant among flight crews.

Haas peered at the character imprints and monotoned one of the robot's most famous lines. "I-am-your-loyal-and-faithful-servant."

Falk set the lunchbox down. "Okay, loyal and faithful servant, let's get back to work. Where are we?"

"Before-start checklist. Hydraulic pumps on, fuel on."

"What's the volume?"

"Twelve thousand pounds. Navigation lights and rotating beacon are on. The maintenance log is on the aircraft." Haas scanned a dispatch release. "We are in fact flying to Logan. Oxygen system is set and checked. Pressure is set for elevation. FMC (flight management computer) is set and checked. Parking brake and pressure, checked. Rudder and trim set to take-off settings. Seat belt sign is on. We're all filled up and the doors are closed. Before-start checklist is complete, Captain."

Falk spoke into his microphone. "Ground crew, how about a push?"

"Ready for push, sir," a tug operator's voice responded from outside on the tarmac. "Release your brakes."

"Mid-Ex 309 at gate D-30 requesting clearance for pushback."

"Mid-Ex 309 you are cleared for pushback at D-30," a ground controller's voice answered. "Advise ready for taxi."

Chapter Thirty-five

Haas initiated the engine start-up sequence.

The tug pushed the aircraft back from the gate.

Sinani followed it through binoculars. The distant engine whine was masked by voices in the American Legion's parking lot below his apartment. The poker game had finally ended.

Watts escorted the players to their vehicles and turned back for the building. He spotted Sinani's silhouette in the window. "I see you up there ya' little shit. What are you looking at those jets for?"

"I can't sleep," Sinani answered quietly. "Is everyone gone?"

"Yup. Along with my money. The only thing they left was a mess."

"Do you feel like a nightcap?" Sinani offered. "I could give you a hand?"

"Hell yes I'd like a nightcap. Get your ass down here and bring that Vodka."

"Okay, Chief. I'll be right there."

Sinani withdrew from the window and flew into his kitchenette. He filled two plastic cups with Grey Goose. Next, he pulled on a pair of nitrile gloves. He opened the refrigerator and carefully removed the cyanide. He held a deep breath and delicately squeezed a full eyedropper into one cup. He swirled the mixture gently and then exhaled down the stairs.

The two Midwest pilots completed the before-taxi checklist.

"Mid-Ex 309 requesting clearance for taxi," Falk stated.

"Mid-Ex 309 you are cleared for taxi on Bravo-Gulf-Echo. Proceed to runway one-nine right and hold for departure."

5:47 A.M.

Sinani returned to his apartment empty-handed and lifted a suitcase onto his daybed. He removed the yellow Entomopter frame and two sets of legs. He reached for one timer assembly and tightly wrapped four windings of duct tape around the insect's thorax. A

145

second layer of tape held the pouched circuit harness and four po-tassium cubes. He pressed the sets of exposed wires into the cubes and then wound more tape across the entire assembly. It held to-gether firmly. He twisted the wings into their sockets and removed a tiny cap from the front of the camera lens. He positioned the con-troller and laptop next to one another until the screen came into fo-cus. Next, he set the digital timer at 00:06:00. Finally, he snapped the fuel and catalyst packets into position and clutched the control box firmly. He reached for one of his cell phones and dialed a number. He spoke a brief sentence and then clicked off.

The Entomopter fluttered across Layton Avenue onto airport property and continued south across the public observation lot and over a steel fence monitored by two security cameras. Both were angled down at the gate crossing.

Flight 309 was stopped at the end of the taxiway.

The Entomopter approached the aircraft from the rear. Sinani knew that the MD-80's nose landing gear folded forward so he had to maneuver the insect the length of the fuselage to get in position. This was accomplished with relative ease.

6:00 A.M.

Captain Falk spoke into his mouthpiece. "Mid-Ex 309 in de-parture position at runway one-nine-right. I still need a minute to finish my numbers. Is it alright if we wait?"

"Roger, Mid-Ex 309. Hold for departure in six-zero."

Falk turned on the cabin speakers. "Flight attendants prepare for departure."

Sinani pressed a button on the control box and the Entomop-ter's legs clamped securely around the outer housing of the jet's front gear strut assembly one foot above the wheels. The device resembled some mechanical parasite clinging to its unknowing host.

Falk tucked his clipboard away. "Mid-Ex 309 ready for depar-ture."

"Mid-Ex 309 you are cleared for take-off on runway one-nine-right. Proceed to five thousand and heading zero-nine-zero. Winds are south-southeast at three knots. A few rain clouds moving in, but you'll be well ahead. Have a safe trip. G'day."

The jet quickly reached 165 knots and lifted smoothly into the air at an angle of 20 degrees nose-up. The climb rate was 3,500 feet

146

per minute.

The landing gear folded neatly inside.

One minute and thirty seconds into the ascent, the aircraft slowly turned east.

The digital timer on the Entomopter harness reached 00:00:00.

Chapter Thirty-six

15.5 volts sparked into the potassium chlorate and the subsequent explosion released four powerful blast waves in four directions thanks to the square shapes of the cubes and the fact that they were draped evenly over the sides of the landing gear strut. One horizontal wave shredded the plane's nitrogen-filled tires, but deflected sideways sparing the weather radar dish in the nose. The second horizontal wave dispersed aft through the steel braces on the strut and produced a mild shudder under the main cabin. The more violent upward blast tore through the first of two floorboards beneath the cockpit and carried enough force and material to sever two 3/16 inch braided steel cables that ran the length of the plane. The downward blast blew out the relatively thin bay doors sending shards of aluminum spiraling into the external airflow. They were instantly sucked up and over the left wing and into the engine. This foreign object ingestion had happened before on MD-80s when condensation ice had formed on the wings over the center fuel tank. Internal warming blankets had solved that problem.

The shrapnel ripped through the engine's brittle titanium fan blades creating a second tighter vortex of jagged missiles shearing through the compressor, burner cans, and finally the fuel injectors.

The entire aircraft shuddered.

"What the hell was that?" Falk asked Haas.

"There's a problem. Do you have the airplane?"

"Goddammit, I don't know."

"Captain, we need air fast," Haas pleaded. "We're rolling."

"What's the status of EN1 and 2?"

"EGT (exhaust gas temperature) is good on two. Number one is rising. It's working too hard."

Falk steadied himself. He instinctively knew that he'd lost an engine. It was the second time in his career. The first had happened on Denver approach and although unnerving, was manageable. His mind flashed back to training: The MD-80 flies well with one engine, even on takeoff. But you must compensate, quickly. Stay calm. Lower the nose to maintain airspeed, and apply opposite rudder to maintain wings level.

Falk tightened his grip on the control column and pushed the rudder pedal.

Nothing. No cable tension whatsoever. His foot went clear to the floor.

He saw the alarms as recovery logic raced through his brain. Think. Where was the rudder? Gone. How? From what? Wind shear? Had it been hit? By what? His heart sank. He tried to compose himself a second time, but the wave of internal panic was too great. He immediately thought to use the ailerons to bring the wings back, but remembered that that was a classic rookie reaction. Any deflection past five degrees would extend the jet's spoilers and severely increase drag, a devastating condition on takeoff with an engine failure. He frantically searched for a way out. There was none. He needed the rudder, a rudder that wasn't there.

The aircraft rolled through 120 degrees in some surreal aerobatic maneuver gone wrong. The physics produced a 2-G pull toward the ground, one from the weight of the aircraft, and one from the reverse curve (pull) of the now upside down wings. Approaching 200 knots, it quickly passed Lake Michigan's shoreline and careened toward the water like some giant twirling lawn dart.

Liquid hurtled through the cockpit and drenched Falk's head and face. Some entered his mouth. Hot and sweet, it was the opposite of that which was fast approaching in the windshield. Helpless, he closed his eyes and spoke the last word of his life. "Starbucks."

The jet's low velocity and angled descent prevented it from exploding into the usual millions of pieces typical of a perpendicular crash. The tail's vertical stabilizer skimmed the water first, and then the left-side horizontal. The drag of a twenty-foot wide sea anchor forced the tail cone's roof to split open in a gaping crack. The plane briefly skipped back into the air high enough to make one quarter turn. The right wing sliced the water and the enormous stress broke it away. Weakened by the underside blast, the nose section bent backwards like play dough. Moving in what had appeared to be slow motion, the aircraft now flailed wildly like some out of control floor exercise competitor, one arm extended, off balance and spinning on a great tumbling mat, somehow attempting to regain control via a clumsy maneuver, trying to make the best out of an awkward position. Completely out of its element, the jet did an awesome half cartwheel and came to rest standing on its tail rocket-like as though preparing for liftoff. With both ends of the fuselage open, all buoyancy was lost. The craft started to sink. Still at full power, engine number two blew valiantly; sucking and churning like some giant blender. Fully submerged, it choked out on massive amounts of water. The last sound waves sped back to the shoreline in a deafening roar and were gone.

Finished, the hapless aircraft-gymnast stopped, exhausted and embarrassed at the end of a botched routine, awash in deductions, broken and unable to keep even one wing in the air before tearfully spotting the coach on the sidelines and then slinking into the water tail first. Seagulls perched along a concrete breakwater chattered in conference at the altogether poor performance. The judges were not impressed.

Waukesha, WI
6:32 A.M.

Neela Griffin was asleep sitting up in her bed, a pen in one hand, and the other cradling a cordless mouse. Papers were strewn everywhere. Each time her hand moved, the laptop's screen saver retreated into its secret hideaway and a Microsoft Word document appeared.

You're So Vain and I'm So Smart
Alternate Title: Searching for Mr. Vain
By: Neela Griffin

Son of a gun
The song's whispering introduction mimics comedian Joey Bishop, Mr. Vain's close friend, fellow gang member and opening act. Joey had this trademark phrase sewn on his bathrobe.

Mr. Vain's name has an 'e' in it
And also an 'a' and 'r'. Carly Simon's only public hints. She revealed Mr. Vain's full identity to one person, NBC executive Dick Ebersol who paid $50,000 at a charity function in August 2003. He signed a confidentiality agreement never to tell.

Your hat strategically dipped below one eye
That classic look. Mr. Vain and his short-brimmed fedoras were inseparable. They went together like love and marriage. Or

150

perhaps a horse and carriage.

Your scarf it was apricot

So was Mr. Vain's world-class Lamborghini Muira. His favorite color was orange and he had an excellent eye for arancio tones in his collection of French impressionist paintings.

You had one eye in the mirror as you watched yourself gavotte

Gavotte—a lively French dance. Mr. Vain started his career as a 15 year-old singer-dancer. He learned to 'swing' with the best.

And all the girls dreamed that they'd be your partner

Perhaps Mr. Vain's most (in)famous attribute. Crooning to throngs of adoring teenagers.

You had me several years ago when I was still quite naïve

Carly's collective lament for all those immature, adolescent, and inexperienced virgins that Mr. Vain had 'under his skin'. He once ate breakfast off a hooker's chest.

You said that we made such a pretty pair and that you would never leave

Carly was both jilted and betrayed by Mr. Vain's shocking political exodus from left-wing liberal Democrat to staunch Republican.

Well, I hear you went up to Saratoga and your horse naturally won

Mr. Vain was appointed director of the Berkshire Downs Racetrack in Massachusetts and regularly performed at Saratoga. Comfortable in casinos, he was also spotted in Las Vegas a few million times.

You flew your Learjet up to Nova Scotia to see the total eclipse of the sun

It was actually over Nova Scotia—twice. He named his jet after his daughter Christina and it was really a Grumman Gulfstream equipped with a bed and bar. In the summer of 1972, Mr. Vain left America in a political huff and flew roundtrip across the North Atlantic for England. The flight path followed the precise track of the famous July 10th solar eclipse.

You're with some underworld spy or the wife of a close friend

The FBI literally developed thousands of pages of testimony on, from, or about Mr. Vain. He chummed with mob figures Lucky Luciano, Sam Giancana and Carlo Gambino. He even shared women with his personal friend, President John F. Kennedy.

Mr. Vain is.....

Griffin's phone rang on her dresser and she leaned out of bed as far as she could before slowly sliding onto the floor. Early morning calls were always ominous and usually involved family.

"Neela, it's Marty. A commercial passenger jet just crashed on takeoff at Mitchell International. It's hitting the news wires now."

"Oh, no," she said, putting her hand to her mouth. "Bad?"

"We're not sure. We're hearing either Northwest or Midwest. Gillespie just called and said he wants you there a-sap. They're shutting down the airport and...hang on, someone's on the other line."

She hurriedly typed one more entry.

Francis Albert Sinatra

She closed the file and laptop and then flew into the bathroom.

"Neela, that was Terry. He said it's Midwest and it went into the lake right over Grant Park. He's on his way with the news van and said you should take Lake Shore Boulevard to 5th Avenue and then to Marshall. He'll meet you at the South Milwaukee Yacht Club. It's across from the water filtration plant. Don't forget your cell phone. He'll call you."

"Thanks," she sighed, but didn't mean it. Thanks for what? Turning the rest of her day into one filled with horrific sorrow? She'd covered one plane crash before, but it was a small single engine type. A pilot took his neighbor's kids up for ride in his Cessna. At three thousand feet the propeller shaft literally disintegrated sending the blade twirling through the air toward the ground. Oil completely covered the windshield. Luckily, he had enough skill to safely glide into a hayfield, but that wasn't where his good fortune came from. It was the fact that the whole propeller had spun off. If only a portion had broken away, steering would have become aerodynamically impossible.

Griffin clicked the TV remote. There was breaking news of a Metra train derailment in Chicago.

Chapter Thirty-seven

Arlington, VA

"Give it back, you little bitch," Kristin demanded and pressed her sister's head deeper into the bathroom sink. "You're making me late."

Rachel clutched the hairspray bottle tighter against her chest. "Get off me you fat slut."

"Bitch."

"Slut."

With each volley, the tones grew more intense. The two teenagers were locked in struggle until Kristin decided to lift the faucet handle.

The cold water didn't really cause Rachel any pain, but the shock was enough to ignite a burst of energy coupled with a catlike scream. She twisted sideways with a handful of Kristin's hair.

Tears streamed down both girls' cheeks, but neither was willing to let go.

Marcia slammed her hairbrush onto her dressing table and stormed into the hall.

Downstairs, Ross stepped out of the shower. He could hear the fight through the ceiling. Like clockwork, cursing had greeted another day. He dried himself and turned on the TV. The screen was filled with emergency personnel in Chicago. He managed to catch the end of the scrolling text that said something about a five-car two-engine commuter train on fire and 125 injured. What a way to start Monday rush hour, he thought. Thankfully no one was killed. The instant the word jurisdiction entered his mind, he heard the telephone.

"Tommmm," Marcia screeched from the top of the stairs.

He sat on the edge of the bed and picked up the cordless.

"Mr. Ross, there's been an incident," a female voice from the NTSB Communications Center said. "The Go Team is being alerted. The Learjet is standing by at Dulles. I'll need your ETA."

"Yes, ma'am. I just caught the news broadcast." He thought he heard the woman say something about the Midwest and wondered why he was even being notified. Assuming there was no tampering with the rails themselves, the first point of concentration for a train accident should be on area crossing switches and Chicago satellite photos. "Ma'am, they're confirming no fatalities, so I'd like you locate a Mr. Gerry Cooper and log him in on this one. He's with the Bureau of Rail and Tracked Vehicles."

The operator paused. "Sir?"

"The derailment. Tell Gerry to call me first."

"Mr. Ross, we have a downed commercial aircraft. Midwest Airlines in Milwaukee, Wisconsin. My procedure is to notify you, sir. I'm afraid I can't deviate from that."

Ross scrambled for the remote and clicked through the channels. Nothing. "I'll be at Dulles in forty-five."

"Very good, sir. I've got you down."

He scooped a handful of pumpkin seeds from a bowl on his dresser. His cell phone chirped. The ID said: 'Unknown Caller'. He placed it to his ear. There was a muffled hum in the background.

"Are you chewing on those damned salted nuts again?"

"Huh? Who is this?"

"Jack Riley."

Ross paused. "Oh, geez. Sorry about that. What's up?"

"You tell me. I assume you know that a plane has crashed."

"That appears to be a true statement. I've just been advised."

"Good, now advise me. I need answers."

Ross braced the phone against his cheek and hurriedly pulled on his socks. "What are the questions?"

"I need to brief Secretary Bridge on the hour. That's ten minutes from now. Sorry, but that's a homeland security rule whenever there's an incident like this. He'll want to know three things: how it happened; number of casualties; accident versus intentional action, and if so, any threats received prior."

"Jack, that's impossible. There's no way to tell anything at this point in—"

"Mr. NTSB, I'm telling you that I need answers and I need them now. If you don't know, just say so. As a precautionary measure, the FBI is already setting up H-Q at a hotel on the northwest corner of Mitchell International. I just left Cincinnati. I'll be in Milwaukee in...fifteen minutes. My job is to relay information from their case agent and the NTSB investigator-in-charge. That means you. Three answers, please."

"I don't know; I don't know; I don't know."

155

There was brief silence. "When will you?"

Ross glanced at the time. "My team should be en route in one hour. I'll call you when we arrive. What hotel?"

"We're on approach into Mitchell and I'm losing you. It's the Marriott."

"Marriott," Ross repeated. "Got it. I'll see you there."

The engine noise crackled out. The connection went dead.

Ross pulled a shirt over his head. Jesus, Riley. You are a pain in the ass.

"See who at the Marriott?" Marcia's voice startled him. She was standing in the doorway in her bra and slip. Her arms were folded defensively.

"There's been an airline crash in Milwaukee. I'm sorry. I have to—"

"That's just great. I'm supposed to meet with two audit clients today and I thought you were taking off early. Now I have to deal with my period and Kristin's dentist appointment while you go off on another one of your junkets. Fine, go. I'm sick of you and this whole goddamn life. Don't bother coming back."

156

Chapter Thirty-eight

South Milwaukee, WI

The weather was unseasonably cool with intermittent sun trying to punch through heavy but fast moving clouds. A light rain began dusting Griffin's windshield. She made better time than she figured and noted that the other news stations and even the local authorities had the crash site wrong. They were too far south, almost to Racine.

Terry Lee had somehow managed to sneak the Fox News van into the Yacht Club's private parking lot. When Griffin's Volkswagen Beetle pulled up, he kicked his leg in front of the remote sensor and the electric cyclone gate drew open. She pulled straight ahead into a handicapped space next to the restaurant.

"There's a roadway that juts out into the lake about a quarter mile off shore," Lee shouted. "I can't believe the luck. Nobody's here and the view from this harbor is totally open."

Griffin counted the concrete blocks on the building. Eighteen. She spied a rickety wooden stepladder and propped it onto a nearby picnic table. From the top step, she could just reach the lip edge of the flat roof.

Lee stared at her incredulously. "You're not going to do what I think you're going to do?"

"I need three things," she shouted down to him. "Park the van on the other side of this building so it's out of sight; make sure we can handle a live feed; and then get up here with that camera. This is going to be great."

Lee completed the tasks and joined his partner.

The rooftop view was panoramic.

Griffin stood mesmerized by the horrific scene of burning debris clearly visible on the water. It looked like some flaming asteroid had exploded. Her hunch proved true in that there was no easy way for land rescue teams to access the shoreline except through the Yacht Club parking lot. They'd have to come right past a Fox News camera. Advancing sirens confirmed that fact as the first official emergency vehicles appeared on Marshall Avenue. Authorities immediately established a perimeter and began diverting non-essential people and traffic. Shielding her eyes from the reflective glare of the now cloud-free sun, she saw that there was no sign of an aircraft, at least in one piece.

"Twenty seconds," a producer's voice spoke from her earpiece.

Lee raised the camera to his shoulders.

She adjusted her microphone. After coordinating the break-in sequence, the station informed her that the feed was being picked up nationally. She straightened the fabric and logo on her company windbreaker and gave her hair a few fluffs. She was facing west; Lake Michigan was in the background.

"Less than an hour ago, a commercial passenger flight..." She paused and touched her earpiece... "We're confirming that it was Midwest Airlines...crashed shortly after takeoff from Mitchell International Airport. What you're seeing behind me is exclusive live video of the crash site and a debris field that appears to stretch from west to east. We are just now receiving preliminary information that there may have been over one hundred passengers and crew on board. We don't have any confirmation on that yet."

The network news anchor, Miles Hall interrupted. "I want to repeat for viewers just tuning in that Mitchell International is just south of Milwaukee, Wisconsin and we're speaking with Neela Griffin from our local Fox affiliate. Neela, has anyone given you any indication of the possible cause for the crash?"

"No, Miles. It's way too early. I don't see any federal officials who generally take charge of situations like this. Local emergency crews are just starting to enter the area."

Griffin noticed two men climbing onto the rooftop. Both wore dark blue windbreakers with yellow block lettering. She instinctively clicked off the microphone.

The first FBI agent rudely swept a finger across his throat. "Ma'am, you've got exactly one minute to pack up your equipment and get off this building. That goes for Kid Rock over there, too. Tell him to sign off and leave now."

She walked briskly over to Lee. "Do what they say and please don't give them any hassle. Get the van out of here——fast. See if you can set up across the street on that hill to my right. The first house on the point. The one with the flagpole. Be sure to ask permission. I'm going to nose around here for a while and see if I can get some statements. I'll meet you as soon as I can."

She'd had federal confrontations before and was smart enough to know that their jurisdictional muscle flexing was serious. Some agents even confiscated equipment and vehicles without warning or legal cause. The action wouldn't stand up in court, but it rarely went that far. The station always recovered its property, but only after bureaucratic delays that killed any chance of news exclusives.

A convoy of police-escorted vehicles appeared. The entire scene was quickly becoming federalized which meant media personnel would receive only limited information via scheduled news conferences.

Griffin's brief moment in the national spotlight had ended. She stepped back into the camera and turned on her microphone. "Miles, we've lost our video and it looks like we're being asked to move to a safer location. I don't know how much longer we'll be able to broadcast. We'll try to check in later. Reporting live from the Midwest Airlines crash site on the shore of Lake Michigan, this is Neela Griffin, Fox News."

Griffin talked with the agents until she saw the news van drive away. Finished, she straddled the edge of the roof and then lowered both feet onto the stepladder. Starting down, the ladder suddenly twisted sending her flailing sideways off the picnic table toward the pavement. Her tailbone absorbed the brunt of the impact, but the back of her head bounced off the concrete with a hard thump.

Filing through the parking lot, the first of four Chevy Suburbans lurched to a stop.

A man flew out of the passenger door. "Jesus, lady. Are you all right?" Tom Ross bent on one knee. He noticed a small circle of blood oozing from her hair. He flashed his ID and motioned to an FBI agent. "Where's medical?"

"Straight ahead and left to the shoreline about a quarter-mile farther, sir. They're setting up now."

"Do me a favor and call this in, okay?"

"But she's a reporter."

"What difference does that make?" Ross snapped angrily. "She's injured for Christ's sake."

Ross gently parted Griffin's hair and pressed a handkerchief onto her scalp. He placed his hand in front of her face. "How many fingers?"

She stared at him incredulously and then softly touched his

cheek. Tears formed in her eyes.

Ross assumed she was simply too dazed to understand. "It's alright, ma'am. Try and keep pressure on that, okay? We'll get you some help."

She noticed Ross's ID and tried to sit up. "N...TSB? Would you mind if I..."

"You need to lie back and lift your knees."

"...asked you some quest...?" Feeling lightheaded, she took his advice. After a few moments, blood and oxygen returned. "I really would appreciate an interview. It's the least you can do after trying to run me over."

"Excuse me, ma'am, nobody ran you over. You fell off the side of a building. It was an accident."

"You asked how many fingers," she said, her voice trailing off.

Ross noticed photographers gathering outside the fence and waved to his entourage. The vehicles moved on. He slid his arms under Griffin's body and headed for his Suburban. "Ma'am, it's a good chance that we've got well over a hundred fatalities to deal with out here. You're not making much sense right now and I'm afraid I don't have time to try and figure it out." Her hair pressed under his chin. It was mink-soft. "I'll give you an interview for five minutes after you get treatment and after our initial press conference."

Ron Hollings opened the Suburban's middle door and helped lift her inside.

She stretched out on the seat and rested her head on a blanket. She examined the handkerchief. The bleeding had stopped.

Hollings started the engine. "We don't have a first-aid kit. How is she?"

"It's a nasty gash, but I think she'll live." Ross closed the door. The suburban rolled forward to a gated checkpoint. Ross held his ID to the windshield and a sheriff's deputy waved them through. Ross gently wiggled Griffin's leg. "Hey, no sleeping with a head injury."

She sat up. "Can I have ten? Five minutes isn't long enough."

Ross chuckled at the woman's determination. "What's your name?"

She spotted a house in the distance. The news van was parked next to a large flagpole. Someone was standing with a camera on his

160

shoulder. "Terry."

"Terry what?"

She gave a confused look. "Terry Lee. I told him to find a place to…he's my camera—"

"Ron, meet Terry Lee. She's a reporter. You promise to keep your eyes open and I'll give you ten minutes. Try the Marriott Hotel on Howell Avenue. It'll probably be around eleven o'clock. That's the best I can do."

"A.M. or P.M.?"

"Fifteen hours from now. There'll be one helluva crowd."

Griffin tried to calculate but couldn't. Her head was throbbing.

The Suburban pulled up to the medical station—a series of tents sealed off from the weather by heavy canvas—where two emergency paramedics were waiting.

Ross helped her onto a waiting gurney. "Okay, Terry Lee. They'll take care of you from here. You'll be fine."

She motioned for him to come closer. "My name is Neela Griffin. Thank you. I'm sorry if I caused a problem. I didn't mean any harm." She put her arm around his neck and squeezed tightly for a long five seconds.

Ross didn't know why he closed his eyes, but when he did, his stomach flipped. It felt like he was on the downward slope of a thrill ride. The gurney rolled away.

"Are you going to stand there all day or would you like to get in here and close that door?" Hollings wondered.

Ross took a deep breath and gave his head a rapid shake before climbing back into the Suburban.

Hollings frowned at his boss suspiciously. "Are you alright?"

"She hugged me," he said blankly. "Do you know how long it's been since someone hugged me? And something else…she smelled great. Like vanilla and cinnamon. Man, I can't breathe."

"What the hell is the matter with you?" Hollings asked incredulously. "For God's sake, Tom, I know you have problems at home, but you just met that woman."

Neela. Ross smiled at the name. The thought quickly vanished when he saw the chaos out on Lake Michigan. Something in the water caught his eye. Rectangular-shaped objects bobbing up and down on the waves. He reached for a pair of binoculars.

Luggage.

Chapter Thirty-nine

Marriott Hotel Press Briefing
Tuesday, May 19th
1:35 A.M.

The NTSB and the FBI had leased adjoining room blocks. The hotel's largest meeting center was converted into a press site complete with a roped-off section separating media personnel from federal investigative and local law enforcement authorities. The NTSB followed the AIM—-Aviation Investigation Manual—-a thick bible-like document with procedural rules on how to conduct, handle, and manage a major air accident. The rules specified everything from the bureaucratically ridiculous (how to prevent other agencies from drinking NTSB's coffee) to the serious (how to recover underwater wreckage). It even addressed how to designate restricted hotel entrances and exits so officials could come and go without having to pass through a phalanx of reporters or cameras.

"Good morning. I apologize for the delays. Thank you for your patience and understanding on this very trying day. My name is Tom Ross of the National Transportation Safety Board. In the matter of Midwest Airlines Flight 309, I'll share a brief status on what we know at this point." He unfolded several sheets of paper. "Let me say first how profoundly saddened we are at the tragic loss of life. In deference to the families, I will not be providing any names of passengers or crew as there are representatives here from the airlines who have begun and will continue to address that aspect of today's events." He adjusted the microphone. "Yesterday morning at approximately 6:00 A.M., Midwest Airlines Flight 309 departed Milwaukee's Mitchell International Airport en route to Logan International Airport in Boston, Massachusetts. There were 147 passengers and five crewmembers on board. Approximately one minute into the aircraft's ascent to five thousand feet, the plane experienced a severe loss of both altitude and control, followed by rapid descent into Lake Michigan inside an area grid approximately three miles offshore. The main fuselage is submerged in fifty-eight feet of water. This continues to be classified as a search and rescue operation. We have seven teams totaling thirty-five rotational divers in the water and those operations will continue. I am able to make the following statement…at this time we cannot confirm any survivors. That may change. There still may be air pockets inside the wreckage. We are working with officials from Midwest to obtain a verified passenger list. As for possible causes of the crash, we have none. As you know with any water operation, recovery is made even more difficult by depth and temperature. I do regret to remind everyone that fifty-five degree water does not favor survivability beyond several hours. I can confirm that we have located the general position of both the CVR, cockpit voice recorder and FDR, flight data recorder, but they are under heavy debris. We are planning regular press updates here every eight hours…"

"Was this an act of terrorism?" A voice shouted from the audience.

Ross immediately turned and stepped aside.

Walter Ford, Assistant Director of the Milwaukee FBI office moved to the microphone. "We plan on addressing those issues separately from the crash investigation. Members of the Department of Homeland Security Rapid Response Team are on site to help ascertain all the facts. At this time we have no evidence that would bring us to any conclusions. We are still investigating. But as of now, I repeat that there is no indication whatsoever that terror is involved. We are in the beginning stages of the investigation and right now our priorities are with the families."

Ross returned to the microphone. "We're planning to hold a follow up Q&A session at 9:00 A.M. at this location. Our administrative liaison, Ed Roesler will have a media transcript available then. This concludes NTSB's remarks. I'm going to turn things over to Mr. Chuck Hill, vice-president of Midwest Airlines Customer Relations for a statement. Thank you."

Ross managed to casually sneak around the crowd unmolested and make his way to the back of the room. He opened a folding chair. "How are you?"

"Fine. It took ten stitches." Griffin looked away, embarrassed by the white pad stuck on her head.

"It's nice to see you again. I guess I was a little short today and I feel as though I should apologize."

"You're forgiven, but I have a confession, too."

"Confession?" Ross gave a puzzled look and moved closer.

163

"For what?"

"When I was laying there on the pavement, you put your hand in front of my face and asked how many fingers there were, remember?"

"Yes."

"And I didn't respond."

"It's understandable. You probably felt a little dizz—"

"There were three."

"That's right. So what's this all about?"

She lowered her eyes. "When I was ten years old, I fell off a porch stoop and hit my head hard on a concrete step. My father lifted me in his arms and took me to the hospital. On the way he kept asking me that very same question. I stayed there overnight and he went to work. He was a firefighter for the city of Cleveland. What you did brought back a really strong memory of him and I guess I got a little choked up. Thank you."

"That's a nice story," Ross smiled warmly. "So finish it. Were you okay?"

"Oh, sure, I was fine. It was a routine—" Her smile suddenly broke down and her eyes welled with moisture. "I'm sorry, I usually don't get emotional like this. It was just a bad time."

"Neela, what is it?"

"Actually it was the worst night of my life." She reached for a tissue. "My father tried to rescue a young boy in a burning apartment building when the roof collapsed. They were both killed."

Ross placed his arms gently around her body.

She laid her head on his shoulder and noticed several family members in the hotel lobby sobbing uncontrollably. "I hate covering these things."

"Me, too," he whispered, not wanting to let go. She was naturally attractive, but it wasn't that single quality that drew him in. It was her sense of caring. This was a woman who felt for others. It was something that he had always admired. He held her tighter.

She responded with an appreciative sigh. "They gave me pain pills, but I'm supposed to eat first. Are you hungry?"

"I am but I don't have a clue about the area. If you have any suggestions, I'll follow you. I've got half an hour so it's got to be simple and quick. I could use something hot. Anything but fast food. Can you drive?"

"Uh-huh, my car's out front. I know just the place."

Two miles south of the hotel and open 24/7, George Webb's was a traditional stool and counter restaurant and a Milwaukee landmark. It specialized in homemade soups and signature wall décor—two identical clocks synchronized down to the sweep of the second hand.

Ross visited the restroom before joining Griffin in a booth.

They ordered.

Griffin's eyelids were drooping slightly and she gave out a long yawn. "You know what's really frustrating as a reporter? You sit around for hours before anybody gives out any information. Everything's so secretive. Then the network people arrive and immediately get preferential access. I heard someone already asking family members how they felt. That really bugs me."

"That is bad," Ross agreed. "I'm not proud of this, but one time I got in a fight at a press conference. Some arrogant reporter from the Associate Press was badgering a woman who'd lost her son. The guy was actually demanding that she answer his questions. I grabbed the collar on his fur coat and yanked him outside. It was ugly. I was a lot younger then and guess I took things a little too personal."

"Fur coat?"

"Yeah. Full-length rabbit or something. It really set me off."

The waitress arrived with two steaming bowls of chili.

Ross reached into his jacket and tore open a plastic bag. He sprinkled the contents over the beans and ground beef.

Griffin wrinkled her nose. "Never saw anyone do that before. But I did hear that pumpkin seeds are a great source of protein."

Ross wasn't certain if she was being sincere or simply patronizing him and his quirky habit. He offered to share and she politely declined. "So, how do you like working for Fox?"

"It's okay, I guess."

"Just okay?"

"I'm sort of on probation. They think I'm a problem child."

"I find that hard to believe," Ross chuckled. "How'd you manage that reputation?"

"I dunno," she shrugged. "I try and make an impact, but then I also try and do what's right. Sometimes the whole local news business drives me crazy with all the corny coverage. Every time I suggest something they tell me that it's either too politically sensitive or doesn't fit the image. I hate fluff. I can't seem to find a happy

165

medium."

"How long have you worked there?"

"Funny you should ask. Tomorrow's my six-year anniversary and the official end of my three-year contract. I'm not looking forward to renegotiating. What about you? I suppose you were right in the middle of nine-eleven...shoot, I completely forgot. Excuse me." She flipped her phone open and touched a number.

"Newsroom," a youthful voice answered.

"Robby, this is Neela. Did Nancy add extra time to my Wednesday slot?"

"Hmmm, I didn't see her today. I don't think so, but let me check." He reached for his mouse and scrolled through a program listing. "Nope, sorry."

"But, I told her we needed...." Griffin stopped venting in mid-sentence. Robby was a third-shift editorial assistant who had no authority to make changes anyway. "Thanks. Talk to you later."

"Hey, Neela? Nice job on the exclusive today."

Griffin thanked him again and closed her phone.

A white-haired elderly man standing at the cash register couldn't stop his hand from shaking and dropped several coins. Griffin scurried after them. On her knees, she stretched under the cigarette machine to retrieve the last quarter. She returned the coins and straightened one of the man's suspenders. He smiled warmly.

Ross mused to himself. He contrasted the scene with Marcia angrily cursing at a disabled man with a walker who couldn't get out of her way fast enough in a grocery aisle. Neela Griffin. He didn't know a damn thing about her except that he felt at ease with her. She had genuineness. She was different. But why? It was crazy. He'd known her a combined two hours. Both Marcia and Neela were interesting, intelligent, and attractive women. Why the difference? Okay, one had a caring heart, the other didn't. Ross chuckled to himself. It couldn't be that simple.

Griffin returned to the booth. "What are you smiling at?"

"That was a very nice thing to do."

"He reminded me of my grandfather. I've always carried a soft spot for the elderly. I really feel that we owe them. They helped build what we have today. Sometimes I think that we treat them like a forgotten class of citizens. Between you and me, when's the last time you saw them in a protest march?"

Ross was staring at her face again.

She waved her hand. "Hellooo, anybody listening?"

"Huh? Oh, I'm really sorry," Ross apologized. "It's been a long day. Um, the elderly. I guess I never thought about that before, but I tend to agree."

"Are you really tired or am I boring you?" She wondered.

Ross straightened in his seat at that. "You, my friendly reporter, are definitely not boring. I'm just, I was, I'm a little nervous."

"I make you nervous?"

Ross smiled coyly and reached for his water.

"What is it?"

He felt his pulse quicken. Three voices were screaming. One logical, one daring, and one cautious. *Go on, say it. Tell her how you feel. Tell her you like being with her. No. She'll think you're weird. Weird or desperate. You just met. Wait for a better time. Yeah, that's it. No, you don't have any time. Just say it.* "I just wanted to tell you that I..." His pager started to vibrate. He glanced at the number and switched it off.

Griffin noticed the wall clocks and reached for the bill. She laid cash on the table and zipped her purse. "I'm really tired, too. This is compliments of Fox, agreed?"

"Are you married?" Ross blurted.

"Nope. Not any more," Griffin replied matter-of-factly.

"But you were?"

She pondered that for a moment. "Sort of."

"What does that mean?"

"Who's interviewing whom? What about you?"

"No comment. Your ten minutes have expired."

"No way, mister," she said playfully. "You don't get off that easily."

"So, I guess that means we have to continue another time. Please?"

She smiled broadly at the date-like suggestion. "I might like that."

"Not that I'm rushing things, but I might, too," Ross admitted. "How about tomorrow? We could celebrate your special day."

"I can't. I'm just swamped."

"Yeah, good grief, what am I thinking?" Ross downplayed the rejection. "I'll be lucky to see anyone for the foreseeable future. Could I, would you mind if I got your number?"

She produced a business card. She knew he meant home

phone number and saw his disappointment. She patted his hand. "No sense rushing things."

Outside in the parking lot, Ross watched her speed away. He turned for his vehicle and noticed the south wind carried the unmistakable scent of jet fuel.

Griffin accelerated her Volkswagen west onto I-894, a bypass freeway that broke off from I-94 and skirted downtown Milwaukee. At 3:00 A.M. all lanes were deserted and she could have used either route to get home. After two miles, the only other vehicle she saw was a lone county sheriff's cruiser tucked underneath a bridge. The deputy was pointing a radar gun. She checked her speed and then lowered the windows. Awake for twenty-one hours, she needed fresh air. She opened her cell phone and dialed the station's tipline. She hadn't checked it all day. There was one message.

Monday, May 18th...5:59 A.M. The caller's voice was distinctly Middle-Eastern.

Behold, America, the Flight 309. God has sent against it a devastating wind.

Chapter Forty

Griffin slammed her foot on the brakes. The Volkswagen skidded sideways for fifty feet and stopped in the expressway's center lane facing oncoming traffic. She floored the accelerator and sped toward an exit she'd passed a few moments earlier.

The cruiser's lights flashed on immediately.

She cut across a patch of median grass for an off ramp and headed east on Layton Avenue. She rolled through two red lights.

A Milwaukee Police squad car joined the pursuit and quickly closed to within a few feet of her bumper.

The Volkswagen turned into the Marriott's parking lot and came to a screeching stop at the main entrance.

Griffin flew through the lobby toward a man in a suit talking on a cell phone next to the restricted room blocks. He had a badge ID clipped to his belt.

"Please, help me. I'm with Fox News."

The first uniformed officer literally swept her into the air and pinned her against the elevator doors. A second officer snapped on handcuffs.

Media personnel in the lobby clicked cameras at the commotion and watched with mild amusement as this obviously intoxicated female with a bandage on her head was escorted outside. It was probably some domestic dispute.

Griffin yelled over her shoulder. "I need Tom Ross."

"Hold it," Jack Riley ordered from across the lobby, abruptly ending his phone call. "Bring her back here."

The officers complied.

"What did you say?"

"Please, do you know Tom Ross? It's an emergency."

"About what?" Riley asked suspiciously.

"Material evidence related to that plane crash. I'll only speak to him."

Riley conferred with the officers.

The handcuffs came off.

He escorted her down the first floor corridor and through a set of closed doors. The sign on the wall said: FBI Command Center.

"What the hell is she doing here?" Walter Ford barked from

across a huge table.

"She says she's a reporter," Riley answered.

"That's not what I asked."

"What time did that plane take off?" Griffin blurted.

"Get her out," Ford ordered angrily. "This isn't a press conference."

"The exact time."

Surprised by the woman's boldness, Riley held up his finger at Ford. "Yes, ma'am. Anything you say. The wheels left the ground at exactly six-oh-one. Now, what else would you like to know?"

Ross entered the room. Griffin embraced him tightly.

"Tom, what is going on?" Riley asked. "Do you know this woman?"

"Neela, what are you doing?" Ross whispered. "If this is about a story for your station, you can't..."

She placed a finger to her lips and leaned across the table for the speakerphone. She dialed the tipline number and turned up the volume.

The message played out.

Maintaining his demeanor, Riley put his arm on Ford's shoulder and walked him to the far end of the room. He bent next to his ear. "Walter, I don't want to tell you your job, but you need to contact Fox's communications carrier right away. I've got a hunch. Once that's started, I'll give you a few minutes to inform your chain of command before I call the Secretary. This is going to boil over very quickly. We need to stay calm and do the right things."

"What about her?" Ford peered at Griffin.

"She doesn't leave this room for the foreseeable future, agreed?"

Ford nodded once and promptly lifted a room phone.

Riley approached Griffin. "Ma'am, do you know which telephone carrier operates Fox's tipline?"

"Sprint, er..wait. We just switched. I think it's AT&T now."

After several conversations and a flurry of orders, Ford returned to his seat and positioned a telephone in the center of the table. He dialed the residence number for Charles Harrington, the man in charge of the Major Terror Division of Homeland Security and responsible for all domestic incidents deemed either specific or credible. He was the first link in the chain of command under Secretary Bridge, and also one of three division chiefs who advised the

Secretary on raising the nation's threat level.

After a private conversation, Ford placed Harrington on the speakerphone. "Chuck, we're all here. The reporter's name is Neela Griffin. She's with the local Fox affiliate."

"Good morning, ma'am," Harrington's voice said. "This is an official investigation under the authority of the Department of Homeland Security. I need to inform you that you are not here as a suspect, but as a holder of potential significant evidentiary material related to a terror threat against the United States of America. You will not need an attorney present during this discussion because, again, you are not a suspect. However, we do need to ask you some questions. You may, at our discretion, be detained in order to provide us with that information so determined by Homeland Security. If you do not voluntarily cooperate, you will be held under abeyance detention in accordance with the authority granted to the DHS under the Patriot Act of 2001, as amended. We may or may not record this conversation. Do you understand?"

Griffin turned to Ross. He squeezed her arm and nodded reassuringly.

"I understand."

"Ma'am, you claim to have a voice communication message about an airline incident currently under investigation. Is that correct?"

"Yes."

"Why would anyone call you?"

"They didn't. My news station operates a Crime Tipline that anyone may call to leave messages. It's available 24/7."

"We're confirming the call timing," Riley added.

"Who else can listen to these messages?" Harrington asked Griffin.

"Our voice and data support people have program access, but usually it's just me. I'm the only one with a password."

"Very well," Harrington said calmly. "Walter, contact Mitchell's departure control. I want two independent statements on the exact time that aircraft left the ground."

"We already have that," Riley spoke up.

"Re-verify it," Harrington shot back. "And let's get a trace started. We can make short work of this right now."

"Sir, that's in progress, too," Riley gently informed him. "Call time and termination number. We should be hearing something shortly."

"We need to play your message for Mr. Harrington," Ford said to Griffin.

She dialed the number. It played out on a second speakerphone.

"Has anyone else heard this?" Harrington's voice asked.

"Just this room," Ford answered.

Griffin quietly rose from her seat and headed for the door.

An agent casually blocked her path.

"I need to check my bandage and I'd like to make a phone call," Griffin said to Riley. "Is that alright?"

"I'm afraid it's not, ma'am," he said without looking up. "Please sit down. We need to sort some things out."

"You can't keep this quiet. That message belongs to a private business. A news business. That's why we exist. My God, a terrorist blew up that plane. People have a right to know that the whole airline industry could very well be under attack. I need to call my station. This is the biggest news story we've ever had. The biggest anyone's had. I don't understand."

"Ma'am, calm down. Let's try and confirm the facts. We don't need to start shouting anything about airline attacks, and we certainly don't want to take away anyone's rights."

"May I at least use the bathroom?"

"I'm sorry. Of course. We'll find someone to escort you." Riley nodded at a female agent and then leaned over the table for Griffin's phone—an indication that he was serious. She didn't protest.

Another agent entered the room and handed Ford two pieces of paper. He briefly scanned the information. "The official departure was logged at 6:01. Cingular Wireless received it and pinpointed the originating cell tower antenna at 830 West Layton Avenue. That's right up the street from the airport. The sonofabitch was in the area when he left that message."

"How'd you know it was a cell phone, Jack?" Harrington's voice asked. "After the Pakistanis tracked Khalid Sheik Mohammed to his safe house in Karachi, I thought they stopped using them."

"My hunch paid off," Riley responded. "Terrorists aren't dumb. You hit them over the head enough times and they learn. Believe me, they all know about cell phone tracing via SIM (subscriber identity module) cards and won't fall into that trap again. They never stopped using cell phones at all; they've simply switched to

172

disposables."

"Disposables?"

"Throw-aways. Prepaid and bought right off the shelf just about anywhere. No ID required. They'll use a phone once and then toss it. Impossible to track or trace. We can still fix a general radius from where a call originates, but only within a mile or so of the actual cellular tower. We'll have to follow up with ground investigations."

Riley rose from the table and motioned to Ross. The two men walked into the adjoining suite. Riley closed the door. "Alright, who the hell is this reporter and what is she to you?"

"This is nuts, Jack," Ross said defensively.

"You're damn right it's nuts. How well do you know her?"

"I swear I just met her today."

"Do you know that she's a constitutional time bomb? I'm talking unprecedented."

"What do you mean?" Ross asked.

"I mean she's a material witness with the ability to panic the country."

"Panic the country?"

"You heard me. All she needs to do is pick up the phone and boom...this story becomes world headlines. And I'm not sure we can legally stop it."

"You think she'd do that?"

"In a heartbeat. Some members of our beloved free press don't give a damn about keeping information secret even if it aids our enemies. I don't care if we have to take that bandage off her head and wrap it around her mouth. I will not allow her to do that. Not this time."

"I disagree," Ross said firmly. "She's not that way. I'll talk to her."

Riley scoffed out loud. "Man, are you a dreamer. You just admitted that don't even know her. Trust me. She's using you just to get a story. She wants one thing...breaking news."

Ross paused to clear his head. "So what are you going to do?"

"We," Riley corrected and glanced at his watch. "I need to get back to Washington. I've got a fair idea of where Secretary Bridge will want this to go."

"A big white house on Pennsylvania Avenue?"

"A big white house." Riley motioned to a table in the corner of the room. "Have a seat, Mr. NTSB. As far as our little constitutional problem goes, there might be an alternative, but I'll need your help if you're up for a special assignment. It's an extraordinary proposition, but these are extraordinary circumstances. I think it'll buy us some time."

Chapter Forty-one

McLean, VA
4:25 A.M.

Samuel Bridge was a fifty-five year-old veteran of war, politics, and for a brief period, acting. A three-term Wisconsin governor, Bridge was a tall, square-shouldered man with a linebacker's physique. He had a cross face like that of a freight train's engine which left his younger staff in a constant state of timidity, and his older staff in a constant state of laughter at the younger staff.

Retired from politics, Bridge had been living in western Wisconsin on the bluffs overlooking the Mississippi River when he got the call from the president proposing the DHS cabinet nomination. He accepted under condition that the administration let him secure the northern U.S. border. As governor, he had championed the issue for years, but other than modest increases in state funding, little was ever done. In his final term, reports had surfaced about comments he allegedly made about becoming more of a friend to Wisconsin's Chippewa Tribe on the state's largest reservation at Lac du Flambeau. Something about sitting down with them 'Indian-style', a gambling compact in one hand and a whiskey bottle in the other. He vehemently denied the allegations, but chose not to seek re-election.

An avid Harley-Davidson fan, Bridge was in his driveway preparing for a week-long fundraising ride in support of the Gulf Coast reconstruction.

"Sir, it's Jack Riley," an aide announced and handed Bridge a phone. "He's airborne en route to Reagan National. He says it's urgent."

Seated in full leather garb on his touring FLHR Road King, Bridge pulled off one glove and unsnapped his helmet. He bristled at the thought of a small jet being allowed into DC's airspace, but then remembered that he was the one who approved the exception.

"Mr. Secretary, it appears that we have a specific and credible terror threat," Riley's voice announced. "We just confirmed it."

"Confirmed how?" Bridge asked sternly.

"Someone advised the news media of the crash before it happened. We're thinking that there might have been an explosive on board," he theorized correctly. "There's evidence of warning and premeditation. It appears to be a deliberate action."

Bridge immediately suspected in-flight explosion tactics similar to those planned by twenty-one London terrorists. Then he considered something even more sinister: Flight 587 that crashed in Queens, NY. The investigation results suggested that the cause was due to a combination of pilot error and vortex wind from another jet, but he wasn't convinced. "Advised the media? My God. On board how and where?"

"We're not certain, sir. Luggage, in-flight assembly, suicide. It's too early to tell."

"Jack, we can't move on guesses," he warned. "If you're telling me we've got another potential shoebomber then I'm going to personally find Darryl Nadler and cut his balls off." Nadler was the TSA's Director of Aviation Operations and in charge of security screening procedures at all U.S. airports. "What's your ETA?"

"Half an hour."

"Step on it," Bridge ordered. "I'm sending a car."

"Yes, sir." Riley clicked off. Step on what? The G-1159's speed was already pushing 480 mph.

Bridge handed the phone to an aide. "Get me Bard." He swung his leg over the Harley and walked it back to the garage, slamming his helmet onto the seat.

The aide returned the phone. "Sir, Chief of Staff Bard."

Bridge removed his other glove. "Andy, I've just been informed that the Milwaukee incident was premeditated. I'll need to speak to the president. I'm alerting H-SOC (Homeland Security Operations Center)."

Bridge briefly revealed the details of what he knew.

Marriott Hotel

Ross approached a female FBI agent seated outside a room at the end of the hotel corridor. "How is she?"

"She stopped throwing things, but I don't think she's very happy," the agent answered. "We disconnected the phone."

Ross gently tapped on the door before entering.

Griffin was sitting in a chair with her knees propped up to her chin. She was wrapped in a blanket and staring at the floor.

"Are you alright?" Ross put his hand on her shoulder.

She shrugged it away. "Do I look alright?"

"You look tired. Do you want to go to bed?"

Griffin turned her head and eyed Ross suspiciously. "Thanks, but no thanks."

"You know that's not what I mean."

"Just how many rooms do you people have in this place? The whole floor? What's next? Strip search?"

"Neela, what would you say if I asked you to become part of this investigation? An actual insider working hand-in-hand with the FBI and me? You get exclusive rights to the story and can report on anything you witness as long as it doesn't compromise the crash investigation or national security. Other than some minor screening before it's released to the public, you'll have complete freedom."

Griffin raised one eyebrow. "Why would you, why would that Ford guy even consider allowing a news reporter to…what if I say no?"

Ross sat on the bed and folded his hands between his legs. "Neela, this is serious. You need to know that the FBI is looking at this from different perspectives. I want to be sure that you don't get into…"

She flung the blanket and backed away. "Into what? What exactly are you trying to say? What perspectives?"

"The Patriot Act. Specifically, sections 212 and 213. They deal with electronic and voicemail communications. You need to know that Fox's Crime Tipline has already been seized and is being monitored. No one has access. You can't reveal anything to anyone, not even to your station. If you do, you could be detained indefinitely as a material witness. I don't want anything like that to happen."

She tried to process what she just heard. "Are you telling me that I'm some kind of hotel detainee?"

"No, you're not any kind of detainee. But I did tell Jack, er..Mr. Riley that I would talk to you and that you'd listen. Hell, I must be crazy for even saying this. I don't know anything about you, Neela, other than I like you and I hoped that you and I might get to know each other socially. I think this whole thing is unfortunate. I just don't want you to get in trouble."

She wanted to believe him, but suddenly sensed a warning flag. Her own defense mechanism. A crossroad decision point to either trust someone and pursue a potential relationship or end it. There was nothing else she could do but agree. "What do you want?"

"Your cooperation." Ross's cheeks blushed.

She stared at him perceptively and then reached into her purse for her calendar. "You're not a very good liar, Tom Ross. But that's a plus with me. You want my silence and you probably want me to stay where you can keep an eye on me."

"Just until we can get ahead of this thing. You need to act as if nothing unusual has happened. File your crash story normally and inform your station's management that you've asked for and received permission to become part of our team. An embedded reporter. Just like those who travel with the military during combat."

She took all this in. "For how long?"

"I don't know. It could be a couple of days or a couple of weeks, maybe longer. It's too early to tell."

"So in other words, I keep quiet and you give me exclusives," she summarized. "I'm not a prisoner, I mean, you don't expect me to stay locked up anywhere, right?"

"You are not a prisoner. Neither the FBI nor Homeland Security could enforce that. They want assurance that your reports won't compromise the investigation. In return, you'll get information that no other news reporter will. Riley and I have agreed to merge investigations. If he can swing it, I'll be reporting directly to him. You'll be traveling and working with us hand-in-hand. We'll arrange a private room where you can assemble your stories. Consider it a special assignment. You'll attend all of our strategy meetings and have access to frontline discoveries. You'll be informed before any other media source. Riley needs your silence about that tipline message and he'll feel more comfortable if you stay close. So would I."

"Riley," she snarled. "I don't trust him."

"Jack's an intense guy. He's doing what he thinks is best for the country."

"You're willing and able to do all this for me?"

"It won't be easy. I'm talking hotel rooms, long hours, and probably spur of the moment travel. We have to exercise some editorial prerogative over what you release, but you have my word that it will be fair and won't involve censorship. Besides, NTSB's investigative process has a life of its own. It'll move forward with or without me. I can clear just about anything. That's not the problem."

"Then what is?" She asked.

"Someone out there found a way to bring down a commercial aircraft. If they did it once, they could damn-well do it again."

Chapter Forty-two

The White House Oval Office

A former senator and ex-Vietnam POW, President Cale Warren was best described as a tempered moderate. His tendency to lose that temper was an admitted personal flaw, but one that had seemingly faded with age. Friends believed that he simply learned to muffle his anger with little internal harm. To a certain extent it was true. At sixty-eight years-old he still had a full head of hair, even if it was snow white.

Chief of Staff Andrew Bard had served Warren for five years as an underling and political advisor. An unremarkable yet loyal aide, Bard spent a minimum of twelve hours each day keeping the president up-to-date on current events, and ensuring that his schedule carried a balance of recreational activities. Right now that meant preparing for the upcoming presidential election just eighteen months away.

"Andrew, this isn't Hollywood," the president said, setting his coffee cup in its saucer. "Does Samuel know the impact of that?"

"I would certainly hope so," Bard replied. "Especially if he's talking about moving to T-LOS (Threat Level One – Severe). There may be evidence that the explosion was premeditated."

"Excuse me for a minute," the president said, feeling bladder pressure. His mind was racing with strategies, but he didn't show it. There was also rage. A level he'd not felt in years. Controlled, but powerful. Next came a flurry of distasteful decisions he knew might be required. Distasteful because they would involve the entire country and impact the lives of millions of Americans. This went light years beyond simply raising a threat level. He drew a breath and closed the door. Then he opened it again. "I want to hear it myself. Irrefutable, clear, and correct facts. We cannot bring the air transportation of this country to its knees without cause."

Secretary Bridge and Jack Riley entered the room and exchanged greetings. Bard informed them that the president was engaged.

"What does that mean?" Riley whispered to Bridge.

"It means he's in the head," Bridge whispered back.

179

It was Riley's first appearance in the famous room. He was, like all other virgin visitors, immediately mesmerized. A week earlier, Riley and his wife had met with an interior designer to discuss swags and fabric-covered cornices for their living and dining rooms. The designer recommended straight-boarded window treatments that, while offering simple elegance still carried a hefty price tag. Riley stared in awe at the huge signature cornice on the windows behind the president's desk. It was curved to match the building contour.

The president entered the room and eyed Riley suspiciously. It took a few moments to make the connection. "Your theme park scenario was interesting, son," he said, putting his hand on Riley's shoulder. "What was that name again? Ah, yes, Komodo. But I'm afraid you give terrorists too much strategic credit. One would hope that we'd have enough intelligence foresight to identify a group of over one hundred individuals intent on shooting up baseball stadiums. Before long, every public venue will have solid security measures in place, especially sporting events. Don't you agree?"

"I hope you're right, sir," Riley softened his answer. He wanted to say that there was no way in hell private business or professional or collegiate sports organizations could afford such measures and even if they could, they wouldn't work. Riley decided it wasn't the right time or place to spar with the leader of the free world. The man would have enough on his plate after this briefing.

The men took seats on a set of parallel sofas. The president preferred a stiff wingback chair. His facial expression revealed nothing. "Alright, Samuel, we move to threat level one and clear the skies. For how long?"

Bridge looked to Bard for support. None was forthcoming. "One week."

The president nodded thoughtfully, weaving a subtle trap. Not to purposely entwine his Secretary of Homeland Security, but to simply arrive at a good and right decision. Warren was a man who liked to do that. Not given to snap judgments, he was known for baiting his senior advisors pretending to favor one position and then turning 180 degrees for another. He referred to the process as reaching factual equilibrium. "Does that include domestic and international flights?"

"Yes," Bridge responded at once. "Passenger and cargo."

The president turned to Bard. "Andrew?"

"Mr. President, if we do that, then the terrorists win. We should consider the subway bombings in Spain and London. Over two hundred people were killed and fifteen hundred injured. They didn't shut down their entire transportation systems."

"The Spanish authorities didn't have a recorded message announcing the threat either," Bridge shot back, but quickly corrected himself. "The voice evidence they found was after the fact and nothing more than mindless chanting."

"True, but I still think a shutdown is too drastic a decision," Bard argued. "You say someone gave two minutes of warning? For all we know this could be anything from a hoax to misinterpreting a wristwatch. What if it were simply some nut claiming responsibility after the fact? This administration would look like the biggest fool of the twenty-first century. I can't agree."

The president turned to Riley. "Options?"

"I see three, Mr. President. There's no evidence to support it, but unfortunately we must assume that an explosive was involved, perhaps smuggled on board. If we do nothing but step up pre-flight security and it happens again, the lives of those passengers are on our hands. Our first option is to search all commercial aircraft. A nearly impossible task because we have no idea what we're looking for. It could be a ready-made device or the result of post-flight assembly. Option two is we continue to fly, but under threat level one. That automatically sets restrictive airport security measures in motion. We could augment that by hand searching every passenger, every piece of checked baggage, and stopping all carry-ons. Unfortunately, that places a tremendous burden on TSA resources, not to mention the airlines."

"Andrew, make a note," the president ordered. "Get Norman and Elizabeth in here." Norman Minka was the Secretary of Transportation; Elizabeth Slavin was the current FAA Administrator. The vice-president was leading critical nuclear negotiations in North Korea. "Where's my Attorney General?"

"Sir, Mr. Broderick is still recovering from his surgery. National Security Advisor Wright is in Tel Aviv. She'll cancel if you need her. I can't support a shutdown, Mr. President," Bard reiterated. "We need confirmation."

"Like what, for Christ's sake?" Bridge asked angrily. "Another crash? Perhaps in Lake Superior? If we don't act, then we are potentially exposing the citizens of this country to murder. And I for one am not a murderer."

Bard stood. "Just who are you calling a murderer?"

"Gentlemen, please," the president calmly interrupted and turned back to Riley. "Your third option?"

Riley cleared his throat. "Shut everything down. At least until we find an answer. A similar order was issued nationwide for the first time in history after the Pentagon was hit on nine-eleven. No aircraft was allowed to move anywhere in the country. The FAA term for the event is called full groundstop and it means just that. Everything heads for the ground and stops. The FAA and TSA would have more insight into the logistics, but generally speaking, some 5,300 mainland airports under their jurisdiction literally freeze. All personnel are then dedicated to bringing airborne flights down to the nearest available runway. On September 11th, that meant 4,600 planes."

"My God, Mr. President, we have to think about the impact to the nation," Bard warned. "It would be another ground-zero."

Bridge frowned at Bard's choice of words. "What the hell are you talking about?"

"The economy of the United States of America," Bard said. "Every sector you can think of is touched by the airlines. Tourism, inventory and equipment, general boxed and flat mail, food supplies. The list is endless. The losses would start with coastal fishermen who'd have to eat their daily catches or serve up a free smorgasbord. It simply snowballs inland from there. The carriers won't last one week without income. They'll all be bankrupt." He removed his glasses. "Good grief, sir, both Delta and Northwest are desperately trying to make comebacks. United is selling its planes for cash. U.S. Air is filing for a second time. I don't need to remind anyone that this is an election time frame and the labor market is one we cannot afford to weaken. We've built a fragile credibility with the unions on job creations. The Gulf Coast is rebounding. A shutdown of the airlines would be absolutely devastating to the economy. When the Russians lost two planes under similar circumstances they didn't do it because they couldn't afford it. Neither can we."

"We are not Russia, Mr. President," Bridge argued. "And we cannot take the chance that another aircraft with crew and passengers might be at risk. Jack is absolutely right. If we do nothing and it happens again, the retribution from the American people would be unimaginable. It would be criminal. I cannot stress more firmly that we must shut the system down."

"What have we put in place up to now?" the president asked Bridge.

"We haven't made any formal announcement, but we've unofficially moved to threat level orange because it's easier to keep all enforcement agencies on board. This means substantially longer passenger lines and we are already planning to advise the flying public to arrive at departure airports three hours in advance. The airlines are prepared for this kind of slowdown. We still don't have everyone up and running with the right chemical isolation or x-ray equipment."

The president looked at his watch. "Andrew, I suppose we should move next door." He referred to the Cabinet Room. "I want everyone on the same page. We'll reconvene in one hour. I'll make a decision then."

Chapter Forty-three

Des Plaines, IL
5:45 A.M.

Dawn. Clear skies, calm winds. It was a perfect day to fly.

Sinani pulled into the O'Hare Aerospace Center's north parking lot off the intersection of Lawrence and Scott Street and made
his way into the second of three office buildings located on the
airport's eastern perimeter. He paused to view the directory board
in the lobby that showed a variety of tenants including a fledgling
security company and ironically, O'Hare's Flight Standards District
Office. The three buildings and a row of hotels were the only structures with unobstructed runway views. The airport's north, south,
and western perimeters were protected by mounded embankments,
heavy foliage, and regularly patrolled fence lines.

He rode an empty elevator to the fourth floor. The doors
opened to a dark reception area. He walked toward the west windows past a row of offices until he spotted one with the magnetic
sign that said: PC Doctors, LLC. He pressed three numbers on the
keypad and the door popped open. Average in size, the office was
fitted with basic furniture and modest décor. There was a welcome
card on the desk along with a gift certificate for dinner at the Rose-
mont Embassy Suites Hotel a few miles north. He walked to the windows and raised the mini-blinds. Across Scott Street and beyond the
first airport fence line stood a Federal Express distribution building
and concrete parking structure. To the north, ten planes waited for
departure on Runway 27-L.

Sinani opened the window and lifted his binoculars. The distance reading said 677 yards. Traffic was moving steadily and he
judged the departures at eight-minute intervals with each plane
timed to the inbound approaches on Runway 9-R. He scanned the
airport perimeter. Between the fence and runway, a group of starlings methodically moved back and forth on the grass searching for
breakfast. Considering that O'Hare was the second busiest passenger
airport in the U.S. behind Atlanta's Hartsfield-Jackson, everything
seemed to be running smoothly. He panned the binoculars north
where Scott Street dead-ended into secured airport property. An un-

184

marked dark gray sedan with an antenna on its trunk sat idling. A single occupant was reading a newspaper.

Sinani booted his laptop and propped an Entomopter on the window ledge. He rubbed a soft cloth over a smudge on the lens. He snapped the fuel cartridges into place—enough for eleven minutes of flight—and maneuvered the unit through the window and into the air. Gaining confidence, he played with the toggle stems on the control box and the Entomopter responded with near bird-like flight. He felt a strange euphoria in the manipulation. It was a hawk-like feeling knowing that he possessed both superior ability and raw power. A predator with ultimate control. Something else pleased him. It was the ability to kill without having to sense or witness the results. The prey was nothing more than a target to be eliminated. A culture target. This was not real killing, because it was not observable. It was simply meting out a godlike judgment on those who deserved it. It was all too easy. A culture of lambs or rabbits resting in some open meadow. Wandering about their daily lives with no reason to fear that which stalked them. A few would be taken, but no matter. There were many others. The predator would rest and then the pursuit would begin again.

The Entomopter continued forward onto O'Hare's property sneaking along the side of the runway. A Continental jet roared past. A United flight was next in line, the first of that airline's 590 daily departures. The Entomopter crossed the last section of grass and interrupted the starlings. They scattered into the air. Sinani smiled at his color selection. Red. He imagined the worst: a passenger gazes out of a window and the notices the device; is savvy enough to recognize the object as a terror threat to the aircraft as opposed to the blurred image of an early-morning cardinal; and raises enough concern to halt the flight. Highly unlikely, if not impossible.

Sinani reached for a cell phone.

The White House

Riley was sitting alone in the corner of the Cabinet Room next to a marble bust of George Washington. It seemed like the only place in the West Wing that offered some semblance of calm. He figured that the wait would be brief. He stared at the room's famous mahogany table, a gift from President Nixon. Each Cabinet member had an

185

assigned seat according to the date the department was established. Members also had the option to keep their chair after leaving office as a memento of government service. The president's was in the center.

Riley's cell phone chirped. The caller's identification said: FBI Comm Center.

"Sir, my name is Communication Specialist Marten. Mr. Harrington told me to contact you first if anything came across that Milwaukee tipline. Well, something just did. It lasted approximately seven seconds. It appears to be the same voiceprint. Male, Middle-Eastern accent, same cryptic reference to devastating wind. The flight number he mentioned was 241. We got strong signals on both the call origination and termination points. One thing's for sure; it's not near Mitchell International. We're tracing the locations now. It should take just take a few minutes."

Jesus, Harrington, alert your own people. What the hell am I supposed to do? Riley wondered. "Give me the origination address...quickly." He dropped to his knees and searched through his briefcase for a logbook. You're not going to give us a few minutes are you, you terrorist sonofabitch.

Marten's eyes followed a rolling display that showed a digital map of cellular traffic routes and locations. The call itself was 'dragnetted' by a Trysis Station Message Detail Reporter that pinged the incoming signal from Fox's equipment location in Brown Deer, WI through a series of cell towers that stretched south, well beyond the city of Milwaukee. A digital picture of the completed transmission path appeared on a monitor. Marten read the data aloud. "It's definitely somewhere in the Midwest region. The owner is Nextel. FCC structure registration number 1207758, file number is A0121446. The FAA study is 99-AGL-4202-OE, issue date 10-25-1999 constructed 04-07-2000. Structure type is BANT (building with antenna). Lat-long is 41-59-58.6 north—"

"Forget all that," Riley said impatiently. "We need an address."

"It's coming up right...now. Got it. 6600 Mannheim Road."

"Mannheim? Where's Mannheim? We need a city."

"Des Plaines," Marten replied. "It's in Illinois. Looks like a suburb of Chicago. Right on the edge of—"

"Shit!" Riley cut him off and frantically dialed an FAA hotline number.

"O'Hare Tower, Supervisor Harold Baines speaking."

"This is a Homeland Security emergency. I need you to find and stop flight 241, now. I don't know the carrier, so stop them all. Whatever you do, don't let it take off. I don't care if they're in the middle of the runway. You need to get everyone off that plane. Do you understand?"

"Sir, I need your name and authentication," Baines said sternly, waving his arm in the air. The assistant tower chief saw the movement and came running.

"My name is Jack Riley. The auth code is Alpha Tango Charlie 21215."

Baines reached for a marker and wrote HALT next to the flight number.

The assistant chief ran his finger down a numeric listing. Next, he found the local controller assigned to the departure. He scanned a display screen.

Baines relayed the information to Riley. "We found one. An Airbus A319. We can't stop it. It's already in the air."

"Dammit, then hail them for an emergency crash landing. Are they over water?" Riley figured if the terror method was the same, perhaps advanced warning might somehow soften the impact. It wouldn't.

Baines raised binoculars. "I've got him. He's westbound four miles out coming up on Itasca. Wait, oh no. Oh my God what's happening? Something's wrong. There's smoke. He's rolling. Oh my God they're going down."

"Baines!"

"Hold everybody. All ramps and runways," Baines screamed through the tower. He let the phone drop to the floor and then lifted another. It was the off-field fire hotline.

Chapter Forty-four

Decatur, GA

Danny Robertson shuffled into the kitchen, stood on a chair, and poured Honey Nut Cheerios into two bowls. He pointed the remote at the TV scrolling for cartoons and then he abruptly hurried to his parent's bedroom. He knocked on the door and waited patiently until someone gave permission. That was a rule. "Dad, there's another fire somewhere in a place called Illy-nose. There's a pond and the birds are scared. Cars and trucks are stopped all over the road."

"Uh-huh, that's nice," Michael groaned into his pillow.

"Don't say that." Linda poked her husband's ribs. "Come in, honey. Fires are never nice. Is your brother up?"

Danny bounded to the bed and curled up next to his mother. "I don't ever want to fly on an airplane."

The White House Cabinet Room

A throng of bodies burst through the doors.

Bridge bent next to Riley. "The circuit breakers have kicked in in New York."

Riley had a confused look and then instinctively assumed the city was somehow blacked out and under attack. "From where? The air?"

"Wall Street," Bridge replied, sitting down at the conference table. "The stock market just shut down."

The president entered the room last and took his seat. The vice-president's chair was empty, as were four others. For a moment, Riley thought he might be asked to join the single most powerful group of government officials in the nation, sans the Secretaries of Defense and State. Riley noticed FAA Administrator Elizabeth Slavin sitting well behind her boss, Secretary of Transportation Norman Minka, and figured no such invitation was forthcoming.

Secretary Bridge began. "Mr. President, I'm sorry to report that we have confirmed the loss of a second commercial aircraft.

United flight 241 has gone down in a forest preserve called Songbird Slough in the town of Itasca, Illinois approximately four miles west of O'Hare International. It missed the intersection of I-290 and I-355 by half a mile. Both freeways were filled with commuters. There were one hundred and eight people on board. The circumstances appear similar to that of Milwaukee."

The president sat quietly with his hands folded. He was trying to muster the strength to speak the inevitable. A decision that was arguably equal in gravity to approving a major military strike. A domestic order affecting the entire nation immediately and with unforeseen economic consequences. It was a decision unlike any other.

"Sir, it's got to be done," Bridge gently prodded, careful in his tone so as not to appear to be ordering the president, although that's exactly what he was doing.

"Tell me again…are there no alternatives?"

Slavin quietly handed Bridge a folder entitled: National Security Plan for Air Traffic Shutdown. It had been prepared for this precise situation. Bridge never opened it. "Mr. President, with all due respect, two planes and a total of 260 people have been lost. We are, for all intents and purposes, under siege. Both flights appear to have been deliberately targeted and the actions were announced beforehand. We were powerless to stop them. However insidious, someone, somehow has devised a way to plant explosive devices on our commercial aircraft and presumably detonate them at a time of their choosing. It is fantastic. And if such devices have somehow managed to elude our detection capabilities, for all we know there could be tens or even hundreds poised for similar detonation. It is my duty to admit the possibility that the recent London aircraft bombing attempts and even TWA Flight 800 may have shared circumstances. That flight could very well have been the first test. What we may have is a method or device so revolutionary that none of our systems can pick it up. Someone may have actually perfected the tactic. We just don't know."

"Dammit, we have to know," the president cursed. "It's got to be attached to a passenger somehow or they're building it in-flight. That's all there is to it. What if we simply disallowed all carry-on luggage or hand searched each and every pers—?"

"Mr. President," Bridge interrupted. "You once told me that I could speak my mind with you as long as it was respectful and from my heart. I hold you to your word. You're micro-managing. There are no alternatives. Shut it down."

The president bristled at the public rebuke, but he knew that Bridge was right. His party had held the White House for almost three years. His global progress fighting the war on terror was good; his domestic agenda was on the rise, but still precarious. The cyclical economy had shed all signs of recession and was poised for long-term growth. The decision he had to make was akin to disciplining a naughty child that held a dangerous weapon. Spare the rod, spoil the child. That was all well and good. This child had the ability to vote.

"How long was air traffic stopped after the attacks on September—?"

"Three days," Slavin spoke up.

The president digested that. "Three days and the economy went into recession for two years. What is your recommendation on timeframe?"

"Until further notice," Bridge answered.

"Andrew, have Mr. Dorn join us," the president requested. He turned to his Secretary of Transportation. "What we can expect and when? I want to know the immediate ramifications for our citizens."

A short, Native American with no formal education, Norman Minka's tribal mediation skills helped avoid a nationwide Teamster's strike last year. His face carried a permanent grimace forged by the fierce winds on Alaska's Chamkatka Peninsula. When he spoke, passion often gave way to grammar. He and the president regularly hunted together and he had already alerted the network of bush pilots in his home state. A shutdown would strand their customers on remote fly-ins.

Minka opened an inch-thick folder. "Well, at ground level, major cities will face massive gridlock. Rental car stations, subways, bus lines, rails, even taxis will become lifelines. We must deal with the ten largest first: New York, LA, Atlanta, Chicago, Philadelphia, Boston, Dallas/Fort Worth, Miami, Washington and Baltimore. If we have an extended no-fly zone, people need to get back to their homes. Flights already in the air will obviously be allowed to land; some will be near enough to destinations, but many won't. So, we're back to severe inconvenience."

"International flights en route over the Pacific and Atlantic

190

will be turned back unless they've passed midpoints and are low on fuel," Slavin added.

Minka continued. "That covers the first few hours. After one day, business sectors must brace for the worst. Cargo and intermediary suppliers who don't or can't keep inventory and depend on timely imports will be hurt. We must notify the trucking industry of increased volume. I have preliminary figures on the economic impact."

"Thank you, Norman. Not now."

Jeffrey Dorn, the White House press secretary entered the room.

"I'll speak to nation," the president announced and glanced at his watch. "Five minutes." He took a deep breath and turned to Bridge. "Is this country prepared to handle a severe terror threat?"

"It is," Bridge confirmed. "Down to the local levels. They know something's coming, but not the specifics."

The president faced Bridge and pointed to Riley. "I want him in charge."

Riley stood with his hand on his chest. "Sir, I don't work for Justice. This is the FBI's jur—"

"I'm not going to get into that," the president said firmly. I don't care about jurisdiction. I've already spoken with Attorney General Broderick. He understands my reasoning and has pledged his full support. You're it, son."

"He accepts, Mr. President," Bridge spoke up. "Would you inform Director Mueller?"

The president nodded and then gave Riley a direct look. "For God's sake find out how they're doing it." He turned to Slavin. "Shut it down. Everything."

All eyes in the room watched as Slavin calmly walked to a phone and dialed the number for FAA headquarters and command center in Herndon, VA. A team of senior air traffic managers was already alerted and on standby. From there, emergency advisories would be issued to all regional centers who in turn would relay the order to local hubs. In less than two minutes, all airport towers, traffic control centers, and all federal transportation facilities would receive the message. All airborne flights were to find the nearest emergency landing field large enough to accommodate the weight of their aircraft and land immediately. Once on the ground, passengers and flight crews were to exit as directed by controllers. No one would be allowed to leave. Medical air transport exceptions would have to show life-threatening urgency and be cleared by the FAA's National Operations Manager. A separate call went out to all airfreight carriers.

White House Press Room

Secretary Bridge strode onto the stage followed by key cabinet members. At that instant, all networks interrupted their breaking news coverage.

President Warren appeared and the room fell instantly silent. He approached the podium, pausing to inhale a deep breath. "As you know, there has been a second airline tragedy in Itasca, Illinois. At this time we are unable to confirm whether it or the Milwaukee incident were caused by mechanical failure, operator or other human error, or via acts of domestic terrorism. In order to take every possible protective measure to safeguard the citizens of the United States, and until we can ascertain cause, I have ordered that the nation's overall terror threat level be raised to severe. That was initiated just moments ago."

The room erupted in camera clicks and shouts.

"Please, I'm sorry, but I'm not going to answer any questions. Mr. Dorn will hold a follow-up session within the hour." The room quieted. The president paused again. "Coincident with that order and effective immediately, all domestic and international aircraft inside or approaching the borders of the United States will be grounded indefinitely. This includes all private, commercial, and government aircraft. It does not include the military."

Chapter Forty-five

U.S. No-Fly Zone Day 2
Wednesday, May 20th

The New York Stock Exchange had suspended all trading until some semblance of calm could be restored. Unfortunately, no one on its Board of Directors knew what that meant. They were simply trying to stop the largest volume stock loss in U.S. history, surpassing the previous record set in October 1987 when one trillion dollars evaporated into thin air. Even the sophisticated computer programs put in place to buffer such tsunami-like selling were overwhelmed. The Securities and Exchange Commission had instituted a series of trading curbs a.k.a. circuit breakers that would halt trading following one-day declines in the Dow Jones Industrial Average. A Level 1 Halt represented a market decline of 10%; Level 2, 20%, etc. Before the president's announcement, the skittish Dow had fallen 114 basis points. Thirty minutes after the announcement, the average had already reached Level 3. Worse, none of the usual liquidity rescuers were forthcoming. They were still trying to digest 30-day market bottom forecasts flirting with a 50% freefall and a Dow average in the 4,000 to 4,500 range—a loss equaling three trillion dollars. Precious metal current and future orders skyrocketed.

Milwaukee Marriott
7:00 A.M.

Jack Riley didn't follow the financial chaos. He was too busy trying to manage his own. He knew the sword of Damocles was hanging over Homeland Security's head...no, that was a dodge. It was his head. With his appointment, he had little trouble convincing the NTSB and the FBI hierarchy to maintain a central investigation point in Milwaukee. That way they could all track this mysterious bomber-terrorist on the first of two trails. Per the president's directive, Riley was to reinforce the fact, in no uncertain terms that he was in charge. Not the FBI, not FEMA, not state or local authorities, and

193

certainly not the NTSB. It came down to him, period. Riley believed that a good leader should use methodical means and feather ruffling, especially with investigative legwork. Criminal science models and theory were fine, but nothing could beat the kind of information a tough, smart cop could squeeze from witnesses or suspects.

The government had commandeered nearly the entire hotel and Riley had one suite transformed into his personal workspace. With respect to looks and functionality, he didn't give a damn about decor with one exception: He ordered that a 20"x 24" framed photograph be brought in from his Washington office. Captured off Duck Key, it was an odd picture of the ocean's glass-like surface at slack tide. He was about to snap the sunset when something made a noise on the side of the boat. A tail-flapping, taunting noise. When he peered below the surface, he saw his grouper looking up at him in some sort of direct challenge. The photo showed a clear outline of the size and ugliness of the monster—complete with its gaping hook filled mouth. Each time Riley looked at his nemesis on the wall, it renewed his determination for an ultimate fish fry.

"Mr. Riley, sir, Secretary Bridge is on line three," an agent announced through the open doorway.

Riley picked up the handset.

"Jack, I just want to recommit my support. If you need anything from any department or agency within the U.S. government, then you've got it. If anyone says the word no, then I want a phone call, understood?"

"Sir, I'm not convinced that I'm the right person for this. I don't think that the president realizes what's involved. I'm not exactly comfortable telling seasoned federal agents how and when to do their jobs. The FBI is funny that way."

"Since when is Jack Riley uncomfortable with anything?" Bridge brushed the comment aside. "Director Mueller was kind enough to suggest a good right-hand man to keep the investigation on track."

"The investigation or me?"

"Whatever the reasoning, he's supposed to be one of the Bureau's best, not to mention you could use a good sounding board. He's from their Investigative Training Unit at Quantico. But more importantly, he knows agency politics. His name is David Cheng."

"We've already connected," Riley said. "He's agreed to head up the ground investigation in Milwaukee."

194

"You'll do fine, Jack. Use your instincts."

"I still don't understand why the president wants Homeland Security in charge of such a high-profile investigation. I can name at least a dozen senior FBI people who could handle it. I'm missing something."

"Precisely because you are Homeland Security," Bridge answered. "This is the first time any president will show how effective his administration can be in combating terror on America's soil. He has the utmost faith in you because of your outstanding qualifications. He's told me more than once that he likes you and——"

"Mr. Secretary, I don't buy that," Riley interrupted the patronizing. "Tell me the truth."

There was silence. "It's a prelude."

"A prelude to what?"

"Consolidation."

Riley shifted the phone. "I'm not following."

"Jack, what lesson did we learn from Hurricane Katrina?"

"Not to build cities below sea level," he answered flatly.

"I mean with the federal government's structure and ability to function in a national crisis? We exposed the worst of ourselves down there and I want to see if you agree."

"If you're talking about selective response and rescue based on race then I don't agree."

"For God's sake, Jack, no sane person believes that. It's bureaucracy. We showed the world how miserable we are at coordinating and communicating through our own internal agencies. As a direct result of that exposed failure, the president developed a plan that will shake the federal government to its foundations. It'll involve the largest single reorganization in U.S. history. Agencies that have existed for over a hundred years will be eliminated and their functions will be merged together. It'll make the breakup of AT&T seem like rearranging your living room."

"The what?"

"Never mind; you're too young to remember." Bridge referred to a 1982 government antitrust case that split up the world's largest telecommunications monopoly. "The code name for the new singularity is DNS, Department of National Security. Anyone in the federal government who carries a weapon, investigates a crime, or defends our nation against an enemy or threat will be impacted. And by the way, threats include man-made or natural disasters like hurricanes.

195

During Katrina, Homeland Security looked like a bumbling idiot. The media filmed human horrors that we never knew existed. My God, while people were literally dying in the streets we were holding diversity sensitivity meetings with fire and rescue personnel. We don't want anyone put through that kind of embarrassment again. Your appointment on this case is simply a prelude. The president wants to use the outcome of your actions, the successful outcome of your actions to serve as a showcase, if you will. A showcase on how multiple agencies can and should work together permanently, not just during a crisis. In other words, it's a working model that paves the way for inter-agency cooperation."

"You mean kills it," Riley corrected.

"That's a true statement, Jack. There won't be inter-agencies. They'll all be the same organization."

Chapter Forty-six

Riley shook his head. Senior government managers were always trying to reorganize something. The Department of National Security. He tried to envision what that meant. All federal law enforcement personnel working in one seamless entity? It made too much sense. It also placed an even greater burden on him and his investigation. He didn't like being a public Guinea pig. He knew what was coming next. He even mouthed the words.

"Do you have any leads?" Bridge asked. "Anything at all?"

"No, sir. The FBI, er..my teams are still forming up here."

"What about resources? Do you need any more bod—?"

"Thank you, but we have enough people. I'm about to have a kickoff session. We'll be covering every possible avenue."

"Do you need anything? Anything at all?"

Riley paused. "There are two staffing issues."

"Shoot."

"I've asked someone from the NTSB to become a permanent part of my lead team. I wanted you to know up front in case it causes any problems over there."

"It won't," Bridge assured. He didn't know Tom Ross, but it didn't matter. "Consider it done. What else?"

Riley took a deep breath. "I need to bring someone from the media inside." He held the phone away from his ear.

There was extended silence. "For what reason?"

Riley explained.

"Good thinking, Jack," Bridge agreed. "Is that all?"

He pressed his luck. "Would you mind saying a few introductory words to my team? It might help reinforce the fact that we're in charge of this thing and not the FBI."

"You can handle it. I like your idea of splitting things by airport, but I still want all reporting to come through you."

"Thank you, sir. I'll keep you informed. There is one more thing...I'm curious...the president's singularity plan. What happens to the military?"

"Simple. The first and foremost question that will determine if you belong in DNS is...do you carry a weapon? Obviously, the answer is yes. All four branches of the military will integrate. Common commanders, common bases, perhaps even common uniforms. Everything is on the table."

"Jesus, that's unbelievable."

"I'll bring you up to speed on some other facets, but we need to get through this first. Good luck, Jack."

"I'll do my best."

"That's my boy." Bridge clicked off. He was under as much pressure, if not more.

Riley set the phone in its cradle. The Department of National Security. The president has gone crazy, he thought. Crazy like a fox. The idea would end criticism that the National Intelligence Director was simply another bureaucratic figurehead with no headcount and thus no real power. If everyone were in the same organization, he'd have the power.

For a moment, Riley actually felt equal measures of calm and confidence. Then something slapped the back of his head. It was a wake-up slap given by someone who wanted his full attention. His father, Robert (Robie) Jackson Riley had passed away five years ago. A high school business education teacher and wrestling coach, Robert had left an indelible mark. A stern disciplinarian, the rap to his son's head wasn't meant to hurt; it was meant to remind. Don't let anyone ever call you boy.

Riley walked into an adjoining room where a mix of Homeland Security and FBI team agents was seated. On one wall, a simulcast teleconference system linked the room with an FBI lead site at the O'Hare Hilton next to the main terminals.

Riley spoke into the camera. "Good morning. I don't need to remind everyone that the president and America are depending on us to make a rapid impact in finding the perpetrator or perpetrators who committed these vicious acts. To say that we are in the spotlight is an understatement. I will reiterate what Secretary Bridge told me a few moments ago. If you or any of your associates encounter resistance from either private or government jurisdictions, then I want to know. And I mean that. You can contact me anytime of the day or night with something of interest, relevance, or roadblocks to these investigations. With respect to chain of command, my personal likes and dislikes, and my leadership style...I like to see things for myself and I will take a hands-on approach. That simply means I'll be on-site whenever I can. I dislike paperwork, I expect teamwork, and

Special Agent Cheng will cover for me when I'm unavailable. Treat him as you would me. One more thing before we get started regarding my position here. The president appointed me and I realize that may rub some of you the wrong way. I have one thing to say about that. This is an inter-agency mission, so get over it. It's not about you or me or careers; it's about freedom. Whoever committed these crimes will be found and brought to justice. I will work my butt off for this country and I expect you to do the same. That said, let me share our strategy."

Tom Ross entered the room and sat down.

Riley whispered a few words before continuing. "I want each team leader to read and become fully aware of the tactics used in the London Aviation Cell operation. It includes 21 background dossiers and the types of accelerants they had planned to use to destroy 10 aircraft. London's Anti-Terror Branch calls it a summary, but it's still four hundred pages. Pay special attention to sections ten and eleven, In-Flight Pre-Detonation Placements, and Explosive Containers. The summary is a separate and accessible module that has been added to your Virtual Case File Network. And speaking of virtual, we're going to establish coverage zones for the Mitchell International and O'Hare Airports respectively, and then assign teams. The first zone is the inside perimeter. Both Midwest and United's CEOs have personally assured me of total cooperation from their employees. Let's start with Mitchell's team structures. Checked baggage. I want a face matched to every piece. Who's reviewing security station video?"

"I am," FBI agent Derrick Gale spoke up from across the room. "We already have Mitchell's tapes. O'Hare says they'll have everything to me this afternoon."

"Who's handling carry-ons?"

"Will Clark."

"Perimeter security?"

"Nelson Bennett."

"Customer service personnel?"

"That'd be Agent Cortez. His teams are covering rampers, agents, baggage tugs, wing walkers, fuelers, and caterers. If he needs help, my people can assist."

"Good." Riley nodded and returned to his list. "Anyone else?"

"Mechanics."

Riley thumbed through a Midwest contact list. "David Bitter, VP of Maintenance and Engineering in charge of hangar operations. Has anyone contacted him?"

"Patricia Creed-Riley. She's a TSA investigator and seems sharp enough. She's started interviewing employees and has already had problems."

"What problems?" Riley demanded.

"Some of the mechanics have a real attitude about talking to the government. They've got an inherent fear of having their tickets, er..licenses pulled. They're afraid of being thrown in airport jail. It's some kind of union thing."

"You tell Ms. Creed to keep pushing. I want hard interviews with every one of the people who touched that aircraft pre-flight. If anyone acts suspiciously, mentions constitutional rights, or balks at the questioning, I want to know. Anything else?"

"Sir, with respect to reporting hierarchy, what exactly is the FBI's role here? I'd rather not have any conflicting orders from our side of the chain."

Riley's first instinct was to slam his hand on the table, but he caught himself. "There won't be any conflicts. I know this is new and you may have to shift your thinking. This is first and foremost a national security investigation which means DHS is in charge. The FBI is taking the lead at O'Hare and their progress will flow through me. That goes for the NTSB, too. The gentleman sitting next to me is Tom Ross. We worked out an arrangement so that his findings at each of the crash sites will also flow through this team. No overlap, no confrontations and no media leaks. Everything comes through me. Let's move to the outside perimeter. Mr. Cheng?"

A lean Chinese-American with a marathon runner's physique strolled to a white dry-erase board. He inserted a marker into an electronic sleeve and drew out a rectangular sketch. The image was visible on a receiving board at the O'Hare site. "Mitchell International Airport covers seven square miles. There are 274 private businesses operating on the perimeter. The investigative boundaries will start at the airport property and stretch outward one mile in all directions. Our objective is to literally flood the area with bodies and interviews. We have confirmed that our perpetrator was in fact in the area when he made that the cell phone call. My people will visit every building, restaurant, gas station, office, and residence within one mile of the 800 block of West Layton Avenue. If our caller was sitting in a car on a side street along an airport boundary, then some-one saw him. As of today we have thirty-three federal agents as-signed to the street. Milwaukee's Mayor Barrett has offered as many local detectives as we need to supplement the ground coverage." Cheng sat down.

Riley nodded. "I want the local and national media to see us tripping over each other. We need to scare up some information. Okay, Mitchell International personnel are dismissed. Let's move on to O'Hare."

Chapter Forty-seven

Wisconsin Dells, WI
9:20 A.M.

"Place your bets for bingojack," the blackjack dealer announced, washing a single deck of cards in a figure eight across the table's maroon felt.

Playing alone, Sinani methodically stacked his chips into neat piles of starting funds versus winnings, a total that was approaching $15,000. He frowned at the dealer. "Excuse me?"

"Way back," the dealer said, smiling. "At least twenty years. That was when Ho Chunk Casino first opened. Hard to believe there was nothing here but a pole barn. Bingojack was the only game we offered. The dealers were tribal volunteers who didn't know squat about gaming. They miscounted so many hands it's a wonder the place stayed in business."

"I've never heard of bingojack," Sinani admitted, riffling his chips.

"Blackjack. Only all of the tens and face cards were white with a pink ball in the center representing the number ten. That way nobody could say it was blackjack, a game prohibited by Wisconsin state law. Every time a player got dealt twenty-one, someone shouted bingojack." The dealer waved his arm through the air. "The rest is Indian history."

"I'm surprised this place is so crowded with the flight ban and all," Sinani observed.

"There could be a nuclear war outside and people would still come here and gamble." The dealer raised one eyebrow. "Are you one of those poker pros here for the Hold 'Em tournament?"

"No way," Sinani replied. "I'm definitely not a professional."

"Your chip stack could have fooled me." The dealer finished his shuffle. "Las Vegas is probably dying, but nobody flies to the Dells; they all drive. Hell, this area is one of the most beautiful and scenic locations for midwestern tourists to pack up their rug rats and spend a summer vacation. Where else can you find majestic views of the Wisconsin River and giant roller coasters within five square miles? The water parks here rank among the best in the country, especially the indoor ones. This casino and hotel rivals any medium-sized operation anywhere. Granted, it's not the Bellagio, but give it time. If the Indians can force Donald Trump's casinos into bankruptcy, then they must be doing something right. Their U.S. gaming revenues exceed that of Las Vegas and Atlantic City combined. Place your bet, sir."

Sinani slid ten black $100 chips forward onto two spots.

The dealer glanced at the pit boss before expertly flicking cards onto the table. "Good luck on that ace, sir. I can remember when the Ho-Chunk Nation used to earn money selling caramel apples to tourists every night at the Indian Ceremonial Dance north of town. Not any more. Now they own the town. Tribes all over the country lobbied state governments for the right to gamble on sacred land and provide for their people. What a crock. Hardly any of the profit goes to poor and underprivileged tribal families. It all funnels back to the original investors. And many of them already own shares in the Nevada and New Jersey operations. One of the wealthiest lives in Singapore. Nice hands, sir. Congratulations. You're really on a roll."

Sinani noticed that a crowd had gathered. He tossed the dealer a healthy tip and abruptly collected his chips. He couldn't afford any unwanted attention. Besides, he needed to sleep. The drive to San Diego would take at least twenty-four hours.

Milwaukee Marriott

Tom Ross was curled up on a folding cot in a laundry room next to the NTSB's communication center. Industrial clothes dryers gently hummed through their cycles.

Ron Hollings backed through the swinging doors with two paper cups of coffee. He set one cup one the floor under the cot. "Hal Cowen is filming the cockpit. We're trying to patch in the live tape feed. It should take another twenty minutes or so if you want to watch. It looks like it's in decent shape."

Ross sat up and let out a huge yawn. "Did the Itasca team form up yet?"

"Uh-huh. About an hour ago."

"That was quick." Ross inhaled the coffee vapor deep into his nostrils. He gingerly took a sip. "Ugh, this is horrible. One of these days I'm going to find the person who wrote those asinine guide-lines about saving coffee from prior investigations and strangle him with my bare hands. How many people did we have to give?"

"Just three. There was a contingency list of retirees willing to come back in an emergency."

"Retirees?" Ross said incredulously. "God help us."

"Yeah. Nobody even knew there was such a list, but then mul-tiple airline crashes tend to gobble up resources. I guess they had to do something in case of another nine-eleven."

"My back is killing me," Ross said, stretching for his toes.

Hollings shook his head. "You look like hell, Tom. Why don't you just sleep in your room? We can handle things. Besides, it wouldn't look real good in the media with the NTSB's lead investi-gator napping in a laundry room."

"I'm not the lead investigator anymore," Ross said matter-of-factly. "You are."

"What? But how? Why?"

"Don't ask. You probably wouldn't believe me anyway. Suf-fice it to say that I'm going on a special assignment. Trust me, I'd much rather watch underwater recovery operations, but I've got my first TV interview in fifteen minutes. Buzz me when it's ready. Where's Neela?"

"In her room with her cameraman. She's been working in there all day. Tom, this is crazy. Are we really supposed to start approving news stories? We're investigators, not editors."

"I'll handle that," Ross assured.

"Thank God. Nobody at NTSB has any experience with TV reporting. It's so early in the process that we don't even know the topic."

Ross poured his coffee into a maintenance sink. "The topic is me."

Chapter Forty-eight

Oval Office

Chief of Staff Bard fingered through several folders trying to determine which crisis to bring up first. With an ever-slanted eye on election politics, he decided on economics. "Mr. President, the major airlines are planning to make a joint statement at 1:00 P.M. United, Midwest, Northwest, American, Continental, Delta and Southwest."

"Damn," the president cursed, hearing the last name. "I was hoping they could weather it somehow. They were doing so well."

"I'm afraid they're all going to announce that they can't survive the weekend without some sort of emergency financing. By then their cash reserves will be exhausted. I'm afraid the numbers are horrid. There are rumors that they'll need upwards of fifty to sixty billion in loan guarantees."

"Then it's our job to get it for them," the president said firmly. "Andrew, please stop saying you're afraid. We're all afraid for God's sake. It is what it is. The fabric of our very economy is unraveling before our eyes and we're powerless to stop it. This is a living economic and political hell. No—it's more than that. It's economic terrorism and extortion rolled into one. Whoever did this planned it beautifully. Think of it. They've placed the responsibility for the economic impacts right in our laps. We can't confirm or expose known details, and therefore have no choice but to injure the economy. All the blame shifts to us until we figure out how the terror is being perpetrated. Meanwhile, we have to be the bad guy. And we certainly can't go to the American people with two anonymous phone calls. If we allow air traffic to resume, knowing that more attacks are possible...it would be criminal." The president strode to the window and stared out at the southern skyline. "One nation under God...one nation held hostage."

A phone on the president's desk chirped.

"Mr. President, it looks like the Milwaukee incident was caused by a bomb or some type of explosive," Bridge's voice announced.

"Good grief, man, we already know that," the president rebuked him. "Dammit, I'm sorry, Samuel. Please continue."

"We can confirm that it came from underneath the cockpit."

"The cockpit? From where...inside? Or do you mean a missile?"

"Inside is a possibility, sir. We don't know any more at this time. I wanted to remind you that we're giving the first interview via our embedded media relationship. It's scheduled to air on all major networks later this evening. Hopefully it will—-"

"Excuse me?" The president shifted the phone. "Our embedded what?"

"Cale, er..Mr. President, we talked about this," Bridge said firmly. "Jack Riley was forced to make an arrangement with the news reporter who received the initial terror warning. She's the only non-governmental person who's heard it. We've given her access to certain investigative information and have allowed her to do some on-site broadcasts in return for her silence. Thankfully, she's agreed. I'm uncomfortable with it too, sir, but if Jack says it's for the good of the investigation, then that's good enough for me."

"Her silence," the president muttered. "Why on earth would anyone agree to that? Is Riley involved with her?"

"Absolutely not," Bridge assured. "I think he's smarter than that."

Too bad, the president thought to himself. He was almost disappointed. A tawdry personal scandal might help focus the nation's attention elsewhere. He thanked Bridge and hung up the phone. "Has Congress approached us?"

Bard rolled his eyes and nodded. "Benvenito is resurrecting his draft of the Airline Recovery Act to get a jump on the loan requests. He's also broached the subject of going national again. He said he's got people willing to form up in committee to create the framework. He wants to know your reaction."

The president groaned out loud. "Damned socialists and their knee-jerk ideas. For the life of me I'll never understand how such highly educated politicians can be so dumb. Can you imagine the U.S. government controlling what is arguably the world's most service oriented business? A national airline would be a disaster. Do you know what the real problem is? Some people in Congress need a good old-fashioned history lesson. In a socialistic society, government controls business. In a communistic society, they own it. In other words, there is no difference."

"Is that an official or unofficial reaction?" Bard collected his

206

folders.

The president slumped into his chair and gazed outside. "I should have been a farmer. You know, for all his military heroism and political savvy, George Washington was a farmer. And an extraordinary one at that. Up there at his Mount Vernon plantation tending the land and his horses. Sitting on his porch swing overlooking the Potomac. The man loved horses. He even built a sheltered manure pit right off the main house because he knew the value of fertilizer. I'd like to send a wagon full up to Capitol Hill. How's that for my reaction?"

Milwaukee Marriott

"Tom Ross, I'd like you to meet my cameraman, Terry Lee," Griffin announced and then collected her purse. "I'll be right back. Terry will try and tell you that he's related to Tommy Lee the rock star, but don't believe a word of it." She smiled and closed the door.

The men exchanged handshakes.

Ross took a seat on the sofa and eyed Lee warily. He noticed the diamond in Lee's left ear lobe and his penchant for tattoos. "The guy who married Pamela Anderson?"

"That's my cuz," he replied, tightening the legs of a tripod.

"So, how long have you worked with Neela?" Ross asked.

"Long enough to know that she's the sweetest person in the world. You interested?"

"I might be." Ross narrowed his eyes. "Are you?"

"Nah, I'm just a friend. A friend who wouldn't want her to get hurt again. I guess you could say that I'm sort of a big brother and chaperone rolled into one."

"What do you mean again?"

"I take it you don't know about Dennis."

Ross shook his head.

"Ex-drinker and ex-wife beater. Three separate times."

"Are you serious?"

"Big time. Dennis was, is a Milwaukee cop. The worst kind. A tough guy with an attitude and an alcohol problem. Neela knew it and still married him. She thought he'd change. Right after she signed on with Fox he went on one of his binges and smacked her around pretty good. The first week on the job she wore an eye patch

207

and blamed it on a bicycle accident. The second time she stayed home. Even then she still wouldn't report it. When it happened a third time she had the sense and the guts to file official charges. It was a big day for paperwork and the Milwaukee news media went nuts. All Dennis got was a four-week suspension without pay and Neela got publicly embarrassed. It hurt her reputation real bad. I don't think she'll ever let a man get close to her again. So, Mr. Ross, if you're into physical violence in a relationship, then I suggest you look elsewhere. She doesn't need another Dennis. But be warned, she's taken enough self-defense classes to kick the hell out of most men no matter how big they are. Trust me, you don't ever want to get her mad."

"I've never hit a woman in my life," Ross said adamantly. "I'm not that kind of person."

"Neither was Dennis at first, so consider yourself warned."

"Fair enough, Mr. Lee."

"Call me Terry."

The door opened and Griffin walked in with a bag from the hotel gift shop.

"Are you sure this is such a good idea?" Ross asked. "Why me?"

"Because," Griffin said matter-of-factly. "It'll give the segment instant credibility. Don't be so shy."

"I'm not shy," he huffed. "I've been on camera before."

"Then you know the routine." She turned to Lee. "How does he look?"

"He's cool." Lee adjusted the lighting and casually motioned to the top of Ross's head. He mouthed the word 'lump'.

Griffin reached into the bag and produced a bottle of extra hold mousse. She gave Ross's hair two squirts and brushed through it.

Chapter Forty-nine

Griffin clicked her microphone. "The Marriott Hotel at Mitchell International Airport in Milwaukee, Wisconsin. The National Transportation Safety Board or NTSB has established temporary headquarters. I'm here with Thomas Ross, the man in charge of investigating the airline tragedies that occurred in Milwaukee on Monday morning and in Itasca, Illinois on Tuesday." She turned to him directly. "Mr. Ross, what can you tell us about the so-called black boxes that have been recovered? Will they provide any clues of what caused either incident?"

"Yes and no. We've recovered two CVRs, cockpit voice recorders and two flight data recorders or FDRs. Both sets are in good condition. We've analyzed the Midwest boxes and preliminary results have shown that the flight controls and instruments were functioning normally during the plane's takeoff. But shortly after that, there was an indication of a problem with two of the major systems: maneuverability and thrust. The data indicated that..."

"Excuse me, could you elaborate?"

Ross noticed Griffin's perfume and nearly lost his concentration. "Sure. We found that the number one engine had lost all capability to produce turns due to a failure of the engine's compressor. In layman's terms, a jet engine does four things: suck, squeeze, burn, and blow. Something literally stopped the air from being squeezed or compressed. Something very violent. Secondly, we know that the aircraft lost its ability to yaw, er..laterally turn its nose from side-to-side. That movement is controlled by a vertical fin or rudder. It appears that something dramatic happened to Flight 309's rudder. And that means it was unable to align the nose with the flight path. We also know that the loss of control happened at a specific point in time. The data shows that it was instantaneous. What we don't know is how or where the problem originated. It could have come from a variety of places including something as simple as a stripped screw that allows the rudder to move back and forth. That's only a theory right now. We're still recovering the physical pieces."

"Correct me if I'm wrong, Mr. Ross, but that sounds similar to the accident that happened in the Belle Harbor area of Queens, New

York two months after 9/11. Wasn't that also a rudder problem?"

"Yes, unfortunately, that's true. American Airlines Flight 587 took off from John F. Kennedy Airport and lost an entire section of its tail. We concluded that it was caused by a combination of improper pilot pressure on the rudder pedals and a concentrated vortex of air created by the jet wash of an earlier departure. It was both operator and manufacturer-related. At this time, we're not ruling anything out."

"In his press conference on Tuesday, the president would neither confirm nor deny any terrorist linkage. Is that still true?"

"I certainly can't speak for the president or the FBI, but at this time there are no indications that these crashes were caused by anything other than mechanical failure. The Midwest flight's voice recorder supports further evidence of that. Conversation between the pilot and first officer is relaxed and normal up to the point where they discover something is wrong. Sadly, the time element between that discovery and the actual crash itself was very brief. There simply wasn't a lot of talk. That's fairly strong evidence that there was no pilot duress or unauthorized persons in the cockpit."

"Doesn't it seem incredible that two different aircraft have crashed under nearly identical circumstances?"

"I wouldn't say it's incredible, but it is highly unusual," Ross clarified. "Flight 309 was a Boeing MD-80 and Flight 241 was an Airbus. However, it's important to understand that while the aircraft are different, their flight control systems and mechanics still have many similarities, especially in physical components and parts. And those similarities may then also be vulnerable to similar failures. If it is a mechanical or physical defect in a common component, then I'm confident we'll find it."

"How long would it take for a mass replacement of such a defective part?"

"Good question. It would happen airline by airline. I can't begin to estimate the timeframe. I do know that the maintenance staffs in the entire industry would work day and night to correct that defect. I don't want to speculate, but it would take awhile."

"Thank you, Mr. Ross." Griffin turned to the camera. "Incredible or highly unusual, we'll have to wait and see. Meanwhile, stay tuned for regular updates. Reporting from NTSB investigation headquarters in Milwaukee, this is Neela Griffin, Fox News."

Lee turned off the camera. "Nice take, Neela. This is wild

stuff. The other stations know we're here and they're really pissed. How come Fox gets such preferential treatment?"

"Never mind about that." Griffin turned to Ross. "Do you want to edit this or can I release it as is?"

"It's fine; let it go."

"There's a deadline on this in four hours." She ushered Lee to the door. There'll be more to come. I'll call you."

Ross rose from his chair. "I'm impressed. A lot of people are uncomfortable with our findings on Flight 587. You certainly did your homework. How has reaction been at your news station? Are you still a problem child?"

"Are you kidding? They're treating me like I'm Katie Couric. It's been a complete turnaround. I can do just about anything I want with segment topics and timeslots. They did think it was a little unusual that I was given private access to such a sensitive investigation, but then everyone in this business realizes that that's where the media is heading. It's certainly a good way to present the truth. Remember, we're fair and balanced. My colleagues did wonder why I'm staying here when I live just twenty miles away. Other than that, it's all good."

"I saw a flyer on the fund raiser that you're hosting tonight for some of the families. How are you holding up...I mean, can I help with anything?"

"I'm a little tired, but other than that, I'm okay." She gave a quizzical look and then she smiled. "You're even busier than I am, but that was really sweet. Thanks for asking."

"Alright, lady, I've had enough. Don't move." She froze. Ross gently placed his hand under her chin. His kiss was soft, but firm. She didn't resist.

A warm sensation flowed through her body and her cheeks turned deep pink. Ross let his lips pull away slowly. Trancelike, the couple stood an inch apart with their eyes closed. The moment was interrupted by vibrating.

She swallowed hard and had to catch her breath. "What was that for?"

"Your cologne or body lotion or whatever it is. I can't think straight when you wear that." He silenced his pager. "I just want you to know that this is something that I'm not used to. I've never been through anything like this before and I feel good knowing that you're the person I'm involved with...I mean, that you're the person who's involved with me, I mean…the one who's working with me on this investigation. I'm glad I met you."

She nearly broke into laughter. "I'm glad I met you, too."

Ross was noticeably relieved. "We never really had the chance to, well, if both of us could find the time, would it be alright if we had dinner?"

"Are you asking me out on a date?"

He paused thoughtfully. "I want to be sure that I thoroughly researched the issue using approved NTSB procedures. Let's see…a subject male has just invited a subject female to partake in the consumption of nutrition at a public establishment that serves such nutrition. Personally, I told myself that I would never become involved with anyone at work, but that referred to employees within the same company. And finally, the subject female is kind, intelligent, caring, and very attractive. Yup. I'm asking you out on a date. For the second time. And I really hope you'll accept."

She smiled sympathetically. "I'm sorry, but someone called me earlier. I've been invited to do something special."

His heart sank. "Special?"

"Uh-huh. The Fox News Channel. The cable people in New York," she clarified. "I think they might offer me a position."

"Neela, that's wonderful," he offered a weak congratulation. He was comforted by the suitor's name, but not the location.

"I have to drive out there, but I'll take a rain check, okay? I really want to have dinner with you and I promise I will when I get back, if you let me listen to that CVR."

Ross cocked his head suspiciously. Before he could respond his pager buzzed again.

Chapter Fifty

Ross hurried downstairs to an NTSB staffing room. Hollings was talking with Ian Goodman from the Association of Retired Aviation Professionals (ARAP). On the surface, such a meeting would seem like an unholy alliance based on the grief Goodman had caused the NTSB and the FBI on prior investigations, namely his theory that a SAM-6 missile brought down the infamous TWA Flight 800. But Ross didn't care. Goodman was an expert in jet armaments, including hand-held ground-to-air weaponry.

Hollings turned off the room lights and clicked a TV monitor. The video showed veteran FBI dive team member Hal Cowen descending into Lake Michigan just two hours earlier. Cowen had been the first man into the icy Potomac after Air Florida's Flight 90 had slipped off Reagan National's runway in 1982. When contacted to assist with the Flight 309 recovery operations, Cowen respectfully declined. He could no longer handle the mental stress of removing human remains from wreckage. This recovery would be especially trying as most victims were strapped into their seats. The overall effort was painstakingly slow as each square foot of the underwater crash site was officially considered a crime scene. The pace was unbearable for victims' families. Cowen did agree to do general site filming.

The video scene played out.

Armed with a SeaViewer underwater remote camera, Cowen straightened a tangle in the 150' cable and drifted down forty feet to the right side of the Midwest fuselage. As with all underwater filming, the light conditions tended to filter out yellow and red thus giving images a bluish tint. The lake's maximum visibility at that depth was sixteen feet and the plotting had revealed that the main wreckage was contained within one square mile. Cowen fanned his spotlight and caught the silvery flash of Coho salmon cruising past at thirty-three feet, following the oxygen-rich layer of the lake's thermocline. He concentrated the beam at a large piece of wreckage in the distance. The cockpit was laying on its side. Incredibly, there didn't seem to be much damage until he spotted a black star-like streak. He swam closer and ran his hand along the exposed edge of a large gaping hole where the nose landing gear used to be. He

213

panned up to the roof.

"Pause it right there," Goodman requested. "I think I'm wasting your time, gentlemen. This was definitely caused by an explosion, but based on the apparent direction of the blast, I think it came from inside that plane. There's not a single impact point or trauma anywhere else. It's all on the bottom side of the hull at the gear."

"Is there any possibility that internal sparking ignited the fuel?" Hollings wondered.

Goodman crossed his arms defensively and shook his head. "You and your sparking. Is that all the NTSB ever thinks about? Let me be frank. There's no way. Jet fuel vapors are not explosive until the temperature reaches 185 degrees. Even then, it's not enough for a violent explosion. And really, Ron, this plane was full of fuel. Certainly, anything set off inside the wiring or air conditioning compartments or even the center tank would have taken out that entire section. It's all still there. And you can unequivocally rule out a missile."

"How so?" Ross asked

"A blind man could see it in a minute," Goodman said confidently. "The roof. A missile would've blown right through the cockpit, windshield and all. There's simply too much of it intact. Secondly, Stingers are heat seekers. Not super efficient, but enough to do the job especially at low altitudes, slow target speeds, and defined heat sources. There's the clincher. There's no heat anywhere near the point of impact. And this jet certainly wasn't taking any evasive maneuvers. Besides, witnesses would have seen a vertical smoke trail from ten miles away. Gentlemen, you've got a real problem on your hands. It almost seems as though something was... placed in there."

"Placed there?"

"And I bet the physics would support it, too."

"Inside the cockpit?"

Goodman shrugged. "It's as good a place as any to start investigating. If I were you, I'd tell your friends at the FBI to take a hard look at two groups in particular."

"Who?"

"The flight crew and mechanics."

U.S. No-Fly Zone Day 3

Thursday, May 21st
8:30 P.M.

Sinani lowered his eyes off Interstate 15 and squinted into his dashboard at the Camry's odometer. He recently had it repaired, but it was stuck again. In daylight, the Nevada desert was hauntingly colorful. The sun had nearly disappeared below the horizon and the scenery reminded him of his birthplace. The desert west of Cairo also radiated black from rocks that littered the landscape. Rocks with imprints of strange fossilized animals. His father had told him that the desert was once an ocean and some animals had lost faith so God dried the water and turned them into stone. His father warned that would happen to anyone who lost faith.

He noticed the distant glow of Las Vegas. He would stop there for the night.

O'Hare Aerospace Center

Rosie Burke pressed her toe on the wheel brake lever of her cleaning cart and turned the handle on the office door. It was locked. She read the nametag and wondered what LLC stood for. Probably some legal mumbo-jumbo, she thought. It didn't concern her. She pressed three buttons on the access keypad. The door popped open and she flicked on the lights.

"No, leave that office alone," a supervisor shouted from the other end of the corridor. "PC Doctors never signed up for cleaning."

She waved acknowledgment and reached for the light switch. She glanced around the room briefly, curious at the fact that there was nothing there. Nothing on the desk, no pictures, no papers, no evidence of use or occupancy at all. Just an empty office that someone had prepaid for the next six months. She pulled the door shut and moved on.

Chapter Fifty-one

Milwaukee Marriott
Friday, May 22nd
9:10 A.M.

Jack Riley paced the floor in his Command Center office with his cell phone in his ear waiting for his home answering machine to beep. His daughter had recorded the announcement and was into long-winded greetings. She'd make an excellent lawyer.

Agent Cheng appeared in the doorway.

Riley covered the mouthpiece and waved him in. "I'll just be a min...hi, honey, it's me. I'm going to try and sneak away tomorrow afternoon. I should be home around four. Call me if you can. I love you. Bye."

Cheng smiled. "If I don't call mine every day, then I catch hell, too."

"Hell I can deal with," Riley chuckled. "One time I was gone for five days and didn't call once. When I got home our horse stable had increased by two occupants and our savings had decreased by $18,000."

Cheng noticed the photograph on the wall behind Riley's desk. "So that's the famous fish picture I've been hearing about. What's it supposed to be? I don't see anything but someone's reflection in water. Is it you?"

"Look closer," Riley said, printing an e-mail message. "Below the surface."

Cheng approached the photograph and stared deeper. "Ohmygod, it is a fish. Wow, it's a huge fish. His mouth looks big enough to swallow someone's head."

"Yeah, I know," Riley said matter-of-factly. "Someday it'll be the other way around, pal. Does Mitchell International videotape its departure gates?"

"Every one. So does O'Hare."

"Even from the inside?"

"Inside and out."

"Tell Mr. Cortez that I want the tapes of Flight 309 the whole time it was parked. From the security checkpoints to the ramps. I

216

expect them in this office in one hour."

"What is it, Jack?" Cheng wondered.

"NTSB thinks someone might have placed an explosive device inside the cockpit. In a box or some type of container that wouldn't arouse any suspicion. Something that had the ability to force an explosion downward. We need to check it out."

"That's interesting," Cheng commented.

"No it's not; it's scary."

"Why is that?"

"Read Cortez's status." Riley reached for the printer tray and gave the document to Cheng. "A Midwest ticket agent at the gate saw the captain carry a metal container on board. She said it looked like a kid's lunchbox."

U.S. No-Fly Zone Day 4
Las Palmas, Canary Islands

"Enter," Professor Faiz Al-Aran acknowledged the knock on the door of his Q5 luxury suite on board the Queen Mary II. He closed the cover on his laptop and rose from a desk that was positioned neatly between two balcony doors. He had chosen not to use the room's desktop PC for two reasons: the ship had no Internet access except through their telephone system; and with three data centers monitored by full I/T staffs, emails that encountered system, server, or transmission failures would appear in paper copy outside his cabin door.

A steward appeared with a food service cart. "I'm terribly sorry about the regulations, sir," the man apologized in a stout British accent. "We've slid into port so quickly I'm afraid the luncheon grill had to be turned down. We couldn't manage your pancakes. We did find a bit more fruit. We know how you enjoy the papaya."

"Thank you, Kerry," Al-Aran replied, sitting down on the sofa. "What is the weather forecast?"

"Oh, I suspect another day of sun as usual. The Canary's are known for it. Will there be anything else?"

Al-Aran lifted the cover off one of five silver-capped dishes. "I was thinking of sport fishing. Something large and aggressive."

"Very good, sir. I know an Australian gent who runs a reliable business out on Lanzarote. He charters boats up to sixteen meters long, and four to five wide. He rents a variety of smaller craft, too. He's a gruff little chap, but honest and very knowledgeable. He'll put you on tuna, marlin, wahoo, and several species of shark. Mako, blue, and hammerheads rule these waters. The locals say you can't even dangle your legs overboard if you value your feet. We'll be pulling in there tomorrow so you'll have a good ten to twelve hours free. It's on the north end of the big island near Orzola. I'll send someone 'round with a map." He nodded graciously and closed the door.

Al-Aran filled a plate and returned to his laptop. It was 16:50 GMT.

Las Vegas, NV
Pink Flamingo Hotel and Casino

Sinani checked his watch and booted his laptop. He logged onto CNN.com and jotted down the first two characters of the first three headlines.

Airlines face economic........
Financial losses mount........
President's poll numbers........

His userID for the session would be AiFiPr. Next, he entered the words 'Internet Dating Service' into the search browser and, confirming the date, scrolled to the 22nd result; a website entitled 'Love/Adventures & Romance'. He entered the site's chat room and silently verified the meaning of the one ID present. Friday May Twenty-second, FMT0522. It was Al-Aran.

AiFiPr has logged in.

FMT0522: Greetings from the Atlantic. It looks like I'll be able to fish for a trophy after all. I've always wanted to catch a shark.

AiFiPr: I'm glad to hear that you're enjoying your cruise; my aunt certainly did. Tell me more.

FMT0522: I'm enjoying it immensely. So much so that I haven't paid much attention to world events. In fact, I've never even picked up a newspaper. Too busy relaxing. Of course, we've all heard about the airline difficulties.

AiFiPr: It seems everyone here is suffering.

FMT0522: Any idea on when things might get back to normal?

AiFiPr: I don't think anyone knows.

FMT0522: Too bad. What about you...do you have any upcoming vacation plans?

AiFiPr: I've been thinking about southern California. Perhaps L.A. or San Diego.

FMT0522: Good. The weather should be warm and dry this time of year. It's a nice area if you can afford it. Take care.

AiFiPr: I can and I will.

Sinani closed his laptop and proceeded to pace the floor like a caged animal at feeding time. He paused only to peer through the curtains at the sparse traffic on the Strip below. He had called a delivery service that advertised a 24/7 in-room dinner buffet. It had been well over an hour. Irritated, he removed a navy-blue Entomopter from his suitcase and inserted a wing into a socket. He turned it back and forth while pulling at the same time. It suddenly slipped out. A design flaw that confirmed the fact that he couldn't afford to bump into hard objects in flight.

There was a knock on the door. Dinner had arrived.

It wasn't food.

Chapter Fifty-two

Sinani opened the door just as a short, pug-faced woman in a one-piece white sundress finished speaking his room number into her cell phone. "Who was that?" he asked sternly.

"Just my boss," she replied. "He likes to know that I'm at the right place. Don't worry; it's cool." She tucked the phone into her purse and waddled through the doorway. "My name's Roxy. What's yours?"

"Fred," he quipped, peering into the corridor.

"Sure, Fred," she said indifferently, snapping bubble gum across her lips. "Are you a cop?"

"No, are you?" He closed the door and turned the deadbolt.

"Not me, hun. I just deliver fast food." She drew the curtains shut and unabashedly pulled off her dress revealing no underwear or bra. She reached into her purse and held up a sealed condom. "Are you hungry tonight?"

I was until I saw you, Sinani thought, noticing strong body odor. Advertised as a beautiful college escort, the woman was simply a street whore, probably in her late forties. Even through the dim lighting, he noticed unattractive stretch marks on her thighs and stomach. Her breasts sagged like empty wine sacks. Her face was hardened by makeup and time, and her mouth purported a constant frown. Strawberry blonde and matted, her hair appeared stiff from excessive spray.

Satisfied that she wasn't law enforcement, Sinani removed his shirt and pants. He laid them neatly on a chair and spotted the *Qur'an* peeking out from his jacket. Frustrated, he fell to his knees and buried his face in his hands.

"Hey, no big deal, hun. It's okay; shit happens. Want me to help?"

"I don't need your help," he snapped. He retrieved his clothing and slammed the bathroom door.

Roxy fought back into her dress and inspected the room. "You still owe me one-fifty, hun. I guess you can tip me if you want," she said as an afterthought. "Hey, this is cute. Pretty color. What is it anyway?"

Sinani finished dressing and hurriedly tightened his belt. He walked to the table and nonchalantly placed the Entomopter back in its case. He peeled two one hundred dollar bills from his money clip and tossed them on the bed. "Keep it."

"Thanks, hun," she cooed, stuffing the payment away. "So, I bet you're a salesman here for a convention. Wait...no, you're a teacher and that was a model for a biology class. Really, what is it? Some kind of bug?"

"Right, I give lectures about bugs."

"Fred the bug man," she joked. "You're kinda' weird in a nice way. Can that thing really fly? Wouldn't it make a great pet? I love parrots, but I hate it when they shit all over. One time my girlfriend's cockatoo bit my boob really hard. Wanna see the scar?"

Sinani clenched his jaw muscles and unlocked the deadbolt. "I've had a long day."

"Sure, no problem. If you're ever in the mood, give me a call." She slung her purse over her shoulder. "Bye, Fred the bug man."

Sinani shook his head disgustedly and closed the door. He walked to the windows and drew open the curtains. The temperature outside was 87 degrees and the Strip was still eerily quiet. Perhaps the blackjack dealer in Wisconsin was right. The flight ban had definitely made an impact. He watched Roxy approach a man standing across the street. They talked briefly and then strolled off together.

Sinani set the Entomopter case on the floor and noticed something on the table. Gaudy red with gold metallic lettering, the business card said, 'Triple-D Escorts: Delicious and Discreet'.

He tore the card in pieces and set his cell phone alarm for 5:00 A.M. He reached for his *Qur'an* and propped up a pillow on the bed. They forgot dumb.

U.S. No-Fly Zone Day 5
Saturday, May 23rd
Itasca, IL

It was both a human and an environmental disaster. Unbelievably, rival groups argued about which was worse. A quiet and peaceful respite framed by major expressways and suburban commotion, Songbird Slough was a 360-acre wetland and wildlife preserve fed by the surrounding 1000-acre watershed. A home for contented mammals and lush vegetation, the Slough was best referred to as a wet prairie. Sadly, huge sections of blue joint grass and tussuck sedge were now flattened and burned by Airbus debris that was scattered over an area the size of two football fields. There were no survivors. The plantlife that managed to avoid the initial heat and flame assault succumbed to residual chloride left by 8,000 gallons of diluted aqueous film-forming foam. Thanks to the defined perimeter, local authorities were able to rapidly isolate the preserve and thus maintain the integrity of the site.

A member of the debris recovery team specializing in hydraulic and power systems, NTSB investigator Jeff Munz waded through thick cattails and stopped to examine a piece of round metal tubing half-buried in muck. Using a small shovel, he carved away a top layer and exposed what used to be the plane's nose landing gear. He spotted the charred remains of the piston shaft covered in black melted rubber, presumably from one of the tires. Something caught his eye. He could barely see it, but it was there. Color. Like a skilled archaeologist, he scraped further with his hand and stared at the red feather-like object. He used a pair of padded tongs to grip an exposed corner. Remarkably, whatever it was lifted off and away from the rubber intact. He laid it flat into his gloved palm. There was a notched t-stem at one end that appeared to be made from some sort of hardened plastic. The other end was flexible. A curved thin object six inches long with an intricate design of leaf-like filaments. It reminded him of an elongated ear or some type of wing. A bird wing.

He drew out a plastic evidence bag from his jacket kit and placed the object inside.

Chapter Fifty-three

Milwaukee, WI
Midwest Airlines Maintenance Hangar

TSA Investigator Patricia Creed lifted her briefcase onto the conference room table and ran her finger down to the next name on her list. A man was pacing in an outer hall, occasionally glancing through the doorway. She waved him in.

Matt Driesen closed the door and took a seat. Thin and fit in his mid-thirties with prominent Germanic facial features, he wore a set of deep blue coveralls with a pair of airman's wings sewn above the chest pocket. His hands were crackled with dried grease.

Creed scanned her clipboard notes. "Mr. Driesen, I'm Tricia Creed. I understand that you just had a company service anniversary. Congratulations."

"Yes, ma'am. Fifteen years," he acknowledged warily. "I hope nobody tries to blame me for something that I worked on."

"Matt, just relax. We're not here to blame anyone." She casually touched a button on a small tape recorder. "My name is Patricia Creed-Riley with the Transportation Security Administration and I'm assisting the FBI's investigation of the Midwest Airlines crash. Mr. Driesen, I'm going to ask you some questions related to your work responsibilities. This is nothing more than a general interview. It's very routine and I want you to feel comfortable."

Driesen's face was taught, but he managed a nod.

"How long have you been an airline mechanic?"

"All fifteen."

"Have you ever received a security reprimand?"

Driesen folded his arms and he let his knee bounce repeatedly. "I got my first one last month."

"And why was that?"

"I walked outside through one of our hangar exit doors and forgot to make sure it closed behind me. The wind was blowing hard that day and one of your TSA people was sitting in the parking lot over at UPS eating his lunch. He saw the whole thing and wrote me up on the spot. It cost me $150.00."

"How did that make you feel?"

223

"How do you think it made me feel?" He snapped. "Especially when he gave me this big lecture on how we all need to watch out for terrorists and everything. We started shouting at each other. Pardon my language but the guy was a real asshole."

"Did you feel the fine was justified?"

Driesen shifted uneasily and then looked over his shoulder. "Between me and you, all the security people and their terror alerts are a big waste of time. Most of them walk around thinking that they're better than everyone else. Just because they've got a federal badge they think they can stop you anytime and ask if you've seen anyone or anything suspicious. I guess it's their job or something, but it still seems pretty dumb to me. They check some workers over and over and forget about others. I mean, they'll look to see if the person has an ID, but never real close. One of my buddies cut a picture of Howard Stern's face and taped it over his own photograph. He wore it for a whole month and nobody even noticed. They just get used to seeing the same people. But the worst thing is that no one checks us when we come in and out of the building at shift change."

Creed sat forward. "Can you be more specific?"

"Sure I can, but I don't want to get locked up or anything."

"Nobody's going to lock anyone up, Matt."

"Okay, but you can't say where this came from, agreed?"

"Agreed."

"Over three hundred people work here on two shifts. Mostly mechanics and their supervisors. Nobody ever checks us when we come into the building. I could bring a thermos full of gasoline in my lunch pail and stick it any place on any aircraft and nobody would ever find it. Nobody. I know these planes inside and out and I have access to every inch of every system. Sometimes during routine maintenance, I get into places that hardly anybody has ever been or even knows about. One time I accidentally left an extension drill next to the hydraulic pump shafts. If that drill rolls, we're talking serious damage to rotating parts with the potential for a complete loss of fluid and pressure. The plane left Milwaukee for Pittsburgh and was gone for a whole weekend. Needless to say I didn't get much sleep because guess who the passengers were? The whole Brewers baseball team. Luckily, it came back around and I found my drill again and got it the hell out of there. But you see what I mean? That could've been an explosive, chemical, or even worse. Nobody checks us for anything. It's really scary to think that there might be mechanics on other airlines all over the country or even the world who could hide something in a hundred different places without anybody knowing."

American Legion Post 154

The first thing agent Cheng noticed as he entered the bar area was that at 11:00 A.M. every seat was filled. The second thing was the reason why.

The only bartender on duty, thirty-five year-old Marianne Alby had an average face and muscular arms, but that's not what everyone was staring at. When she scooped ice or opened a beer locker, her blue jean shorts exposed firm cheeks and her loose tank top gave veterans a bare view of her full perky breasts. She enjoyed the tease as much as they did. By shift's end her tip jar was always overflowing.

"I'll need to see a membership card," Marianne said matter-of-factly, setting two mugs on the rail and pulling a beer spigot. Cheng produced his ID. She glanced at it briefly and topped off the second mug. "What can I get for you, Mr. FBI?"

"How about a bowl?" He nodded toward a sign on the wall behind him that read 'Homemade Turkey and Dumpling Soup—$2.00.'

"Anything else?"

"Thank you, but I just have a few questions about a Mr. Jerry Watts." Cheng fingered his notes. "I understand he was also known as Chief."

Conversation throughout the bar stopped. Heads turned.

Marianne pressed a bar towel into her eyes. She quickly composed herself and brought Cheng his soup. "What would you like to know?"

"I'm investigating the crash of—"

"You feds already came through here the day after that plane went down," a long-haired patron wearing a metal neck brace shouted from across the room. "They interviewed everybody. The government's got no respect for people in mourning. We all know it was a damn missile so why are you hassling us?"

"Sir, I'm not hassling anyone," Cheng calmly responded. "I'm

225

simply revisiting the area because I have a few more questions. This is a private post, right? Military veterans only?"

"Not just any veterans," the man hissed. "We're American Legion. That means we served during a declared war. It sets us apart from our VFW brothers."

"I never knew that," Cheng admitted, stirring his soup. "So you probably see all kinds of veterans come and go?"

"If you're asking what I think you're asking, then hang on." The man stood up from his barstool. "Anybody seen any terrorists in the neighborhood?"

"Yeah, there's one down at the 7-11," another voice rang out. "I'd like to add him to my collection."

"Go get 'em, Stan," someone else shouted.

Marianne whispered to Cheng. "That's Stanley Wosniak, Wisconsin's most-decorated Vietnam vet. He had 380 confirmed kills. He's kind of crazy. He used to cut the ears off Vietcong and wear them as a necklace. He even sent trophies home to his mother. He doesn't like too many foreigners."

"I can see that," Cheng whispered back. "So, no new faces or suspicious people hanging around? No new war buddies that just happened to show up? Nobody asking questions about airport security or bad-mouthing the U.S. government?"

"Nope. Nobody new around here except Mikey." She gave a distant look. "Chief used to call him that."

Cheng pushed his soup aside and opened his notebook.

"Don't bother about him," she assured. "He's just a college kid who rented the apartment upstairs for the summer. He's nice, but kind of geeky."

"Is he here?"

"He's never here. He's always traveling somewhere. Mostly back and forth to Minnesota to see his girlfriend. He seems pretty whipped."

"What's her name?"

Marianne pursed her lips. "Good question. I've only met him a couple times myself. He never talked much about anything."

"You said he lives in back?"

"Right above us. I suppose I could let you see the place, but your people already did that. They searched through every building on this block."

She plucked a key from the cash register and escorted Cheng

upstairs.

Dirty clothes; fast food bags; a sink full of dishes; empty soda cans; videotapes and games piled inside cardboard boxes. Computer textbooks and manuals were stacked on the kitchen table along with notebooks and folders. A typical college student.

Cheng opened the refrigerator.

It was empty.

Chapter Fifty-four

U.S. No-Fly Zone Day 6
San Diego, CA
Sunday, May 24th
11:05 A.M.

Sinani turned off the Camry's engine and yawned deeply. He approached the entrance of Nick's Velvet Touch Escort and Massage and glanced at what he thought was refuse heaped on the sidewalk. An arm suddenly rose up holding a filthy foam cup. Sinani stepped around the man and opened the door. A blast of scented perfume stung his nostrils. Inside, there was a carpeted foyer complete with two sofas presumably where customers waited for service. Stacks of pornographic magazines littered the room.

A woman appeared. She was a large heavy-set Mexican-American with long black hair and a deep brown complexion. Bare-foot, she wore a white frilly top and a white miniskirt. She sat down across the room and purposely exposed her red panties. "Do you need a date, senor?"

"No thanks," he answered. "I'm looking for Mr. Karkula?"

"Who wants to know?"

"My name is Dean."

She contemplated that for a moment. "Are you the Dean on the answering machine? The one who calls so early in the morning?" He nodded repeatedly. She glanced at a clock on the wall. "I'm glad to meet you. Nick's in the back. He's usually up by ten, but now that the airport is closed he sleeps longer."

"I take it you're Marissa?" Sinani extended his hand. He noticed her perfectly-manicured nails and gold metallic polish. "We finally meet. I knew it. I could tell by your voice that you were a nice looking lady."

A smile flashed across her dark features. Compliments were rare here, especially from non-paying customers.

Two faces peeked through thin bamboo strips in a rear doorway. Marissa whispered something in Spanish and the strips split open. "My kids," she said sheepishly. "I couldn't get no babysitter. Nick doesn't mind as long as they don't bother the customers."

The children filed into the room and stood politely in line.

"This is Amber; she's eight, and this is little Jo-Jo. His real name is Jeremy, but we call him Jo-Jo. He just turned five." Her long nails combed through the boy's hair. "Say hello to Dean."

Amber peeped a greeting. Jo-Jo hugged Sinani's leg tightly.

"He likes you," Amber announced. "He only does that to people he likes."

Sinani whisked him into the air. "Hello, Jo-Jo. How old are you?"

Five fingers pressed into Sinani's nose. They smelled of sweet syrup. "Our house has a swimming pool. It's called a motel. Are you going to marry my mommy?"

"Jo-Jo," Marissa called out a mild reprimand.

Sinani smiled and lowered the boy.

Marissa clapped her hands twice. The children scurried away. "I know a motel isn't the best for them, but it's only temporary."

"I love kids," Sinani remarked. "I wish I could have some of my own someday. I guess I haven't found the right woman."

Marissa's smile faded and she actually took a step back. Too many men appeared in the neighborhood under court ordered placement. Ex-convicts, recovering drug addicts, sexual predators. Pedophiles were the worst.

Sinani sensed her wariness. "I'm sorry, I'm from Minnesota. I'm finishing up my degree. I'll be living in the apartment upstairs for a semester."

Relieved, her smile returned. So did her interest. "A degree in what, senor?"

"Music, actually. Someday I want to open my own store. You know, sell instruments and equipment, give lessons. And you are Marissa...?"

"Sanchez. It's good to have goals in life. Amber likes music, too. I bought her a toy organ for her birthday. She takes it everywhere. Maybe she could play it for you sometime?"

"I'd like that," he said. "I don't know much about the area and I wish I could find someone who could——"

"I would be happy to show you around," she quickly offered. "I've lived here all my life. Seaport Village is really nice because you can walk along the ocean. There are lots of shops and restaurants. Our zoo is one of the best."

"That sounds great, Marissa. I really appreciat——"

"What you want?" A deep male voice interrupted the conversation. "Massage is $60. Cash or credit card. No checks."

Sinani turned. "Morning, sir. I'm Dean."

"So?"

"I rented the apartment upstairs?"

"Oh, you finally show up," the man growled. "I am Nick Karkula."

They shook hands.

A thick-necked Pole in his mid-fifties, Karkula's hair was unkempt and his face was covered in gray stubble. His stained muscle shirt exposed a carpet of body hair. His eyes were thin slits and his face was puffed and round which made him seem almost teddy bear-like, but that was not his disposition. Grizzly was a better choice. He let out a resounding belch.

"You're such a peeg," a woman's voice sang out from the kitchen.

Karkula raised his middle finger high in the air. He turned to Sinani and lowered his voice. "My wife, Tamara. She's crazy bitch and real pain in my ass. She just get out of hospital. It was actually nuthouse, but I no can say that. If she act crazy, you let me know, okay? I send her back."

"I'll try and remember that," Sinani said. "Did you receive my deposit? It was a cashier's check."

"Sure, I get it. I cash it, I spend it. But first I make copy so I know who to throw out on his ass if you make damage like those last pigs. I sleep late. You break anything, you pay. No drugs and no parties." He noticed Marissa in the next room. "Hey, I don't pay for you to sit all day on your fat ass. If you got no customers, then you clean. And tell your two little pigs to make quiet that TV."

She hurried into the back room.

Karkula found a blackened cigar stub and lit it. He reached in his pocket and tossed Sinani a key. "Door is outside next to ours. This neighborhood is shit and so are the people. Keep it locked or street pigs will find your bed. You don't touch Marissa either; you can do better. Don't ask for me to move your crap; don't sell me anything because I don't buy nothing. Don't ask for money and don't ask for ride. I no do that. If you don't have no car, then call taxi. If you do have car, some pig steals it in one night."

"Thanks, I'll be fine," Sinani assured. "Some friends from school might come by later this week to help me move in. I just wanted to get a few things settled before—"

"Ya ya ya. You do that." Karkula blew a thick smoke line and waddled through it. "No parties."

Sinani turned for the door.

"Pssst." Marissa appeared with a scented candle. "You might need this. Don't worry. Nick calls everyone a pig. If someone rips off your car, then I'll give you a ride. Nobody around here would steal a minivan."

Sinani acknowledged the offer with a wink. He walked outside and turned the key in the latch. Upstairs, the apartment reeked of urine that seemed to emanate from the mattress. He lit the candle and opened three double-hung windows. The view showed a deserted San Diego International Airport and Runway 9/27.

Chapter Fifty-five

Riley was sitting in his office with the lights out and his head tilted back in his chair. He was trying to sleep, but his mind wouldn't stop racing. He chewed on an unlit cigar and repeatedly flicked a disposable lighter.

There was a gentle tap on the door. Tom Ross peeked inside.

Riley spun around. "Hit that wall switch for me will you?"

Ross complied and sat down.

"Where have you been hiding?"

"Neela and I have been analyzing the cockpit voices from Flight 309. Neither of us can figure out the relevance of the captain's last word. Starbucks. As far as I know, it's not an aviation term or codeword. She wants to write a human interest piece on it. Have you ever heard it before?"

"Yeah, every time I need caffeine," Riley quipped. "You like her, huh?"

"I do," Ross admitted, pausing thoughtfully. "I like her a lot. We've become friends."

"Right, and what about your other lady friend—Riley almost said wife—and her mild-mannered daughters?"

Ross leaned back and crossed his arms. "It's funny. Neela and I have had some heart-to-heart conversations and we both enjoy each other's company. It's amazing how much we have in common, especially with bad relationships. You're marriage is obviously successful. What's your secret?"

Riley shrugged off the compliment. "There's no single recipe, pal. And I'm certainly not an expert. But if I had to narrow things, then I'd say hard work and honesty are at the top of the list along with faith, morals, and traditional values. The usual stuff. The question is…can a news reporter have morals?"

Ross rolled his eyes at the subtle dig. "I guess I'll have to find out."

"Does she like kids?"

"She loves kids, but there was an accident and she can't have any. It's such a shame."

Riley gave a distant glance outside his window to the north end of Mitchell International. "How could someone do it?"

"Do what?"

"Kill kids. It just doesn't make sense. Did you know that there were twelve high school sophomores on board that Midwest flight? They were part of a science class headed to the oceanographic institute at Woods Hole in Cape Cod. The more I think about it, the more I realize that terrorists are just plain cowards. What I don't understand is how they can live with themselves afterwards. Indiscriminate subway and bus attacks in London and all those restaurant and hotel suicide bombings in Israel. Then there was that Russian-Chechnyen school hostage situation a few years ago. When some of the terrorists started balking at the operation because kids were involved, their compatriots shot them. Talk about cannibalistic. And speaking of Russia, remember those two Tupelov airliners that crashed south of Moscow? Both were confirmed as coordinated terrorism."

"Impossible to determine," Ross said flatly. "The wreckage from one of those planes was scattered over thirty-five kilometers. That's got to be a guess."

"Who needs wreckage?" Riley asked smugly. "You've got to give the Russians credit. Their Federal Security Service (formerly KGB) made the decision based on a single circumstantial fact but it's one hell of a fact. A RESURS-DK-R imagery satellite owned by Sovinformsputnik Company in Leningrad detected dual heat fluxes from the Tula and Rostov-on-Don crash regions at precisely the same instant. That my friend was coordinated." He flicked his lighter.

"Are you thinking that our terrorist is somehow connected?"

"I'm not sure what to think other than there's a timing element involved."

"You seem pretty confident," Ross observed.

"I'm confident of two things: I'm going to catch our mystery cell phone caller, and I'm also going to catch my fish."

"You and that fish," he chided. "What did he ever do to you?"

Riley held up his hand. "This Bic lighter cost a whopping dollar ninety-nine. I used to have a beautiful stainless steel Zippo engraved with my daughter's portrait. She spent ten months in El Salvador teaching English to village children. An artist there presented it as a thank you gift. He gave it to her and she gave it to me."

"I don't get it. What's a Zippo lighter got to do with a fish?"

Riley removed the cigar from his mouth. "My one and only vice. It's a spiced Nicaraguan blend called Acid Blondie. They're delicious. They make traditional Cubans taste like rotten seaweed. One afternoon in Duck Key, I launched my boat; I anchored in my favorite spot; I baited some lines and then I sat back with a fresh Blondie. I reached for my Zippo and accidentally dropped it into the water. Thank God it landed on a reef ledge only four feet down. No problem; I can reach it. I bent over and this big ugly fish—-my fish—-came out of nowhere and sucked it down. He ate my friggin' lighter. It must have been the reflection or something. It scared the hell out of me. My daughter gave me that lighter as a special gift and he took it away. So, don't tell me about determination or anger or confidence. I will get our terrorist and I will get my lighter back."

"Somehow I tend to believe that," Ross chuckled, producing a plastic bag from his briefcase. "Speaking of confidence, we're close to confirming that there was in fact an explosion in the aircraft's cockpit section either below the throttle or near the landing gear. We found traces of potassium in the burn residue."

"Potassium? Did you do a lab test?" Riley asked.

"There was no need. Our portable scanner took accurate measurements at the scene. It uses an ion spectrometer to spot TNT, Semtex, PETN, and a whole range of nitrates. Potassium is one of the major flags for unstable explosives not common to the elements you'd expect to find on or near jet fuel burns."

Riley examined the bag. "And this?"

"Preliminary tests show that it's some kind of molded composite. Nothing unusual. It could be anything. The configuration doesn't fit with any known explosive model because it's too thin. These are some sketches of what it might look like if it were whole."

Riley frowned at the drawings that ranged from an oversized ear to a six-inch bat wing. He set the object down. "Excluding the passengers, a total of twenty people had contact with Flight 309. One fueler, three baggage handlers, two mechanics, two caterers, two maintenance workers, two rampers, three agents, and of course the crew. None fit an obvious profile. One mechanic replaced a brake temperature fuse and we've got a copy of his log. Do you have anything else?"

Ross produced a set of transparencies and placed one face down on a projector. He pointed the light at a bare wall. The outline showed a remarkably detailed photograph of Flight 309's fuselage cut away to expose the cockpit section. "My people believe that both planes crashed due to a dramatic loss of control caused by a rudder failure. The Midwest flight data recorder showed evidence of a shutdown that originated here." He used a pencil-thin marker to make two circles connecting the nose landing gear to the vertical tail fin. He fingered through the transparencies and placed another on the projector. "Here's a closer look at a potential point of impact caused, in our preliminary opinion, by an explosive. Notice the direction of the outward burns. This was further evidenced by the distortions in the hinges and riveting on the gear bay doors. Everything was forced outward."

"So what's your conclusion?" Riley wondered. "How did it happ—?"

Ross cut him off. "NTSB doesn't conclude anything. We figure out cause. You can conclude whatever you want. In this case, an aviation action. I've just told you what we believe happened. The facts support damage caused by an internal explosion. Unfortunately, that opens an even bigger box of unanswered questions."

"Such as?"

"A Flight 800 theory of sparks or electrical shorts igniting fumes seems unlikely. There's a truckload of speculation and witnesses in that case alone, especially with regard to missiles. Donaldson is in his grave, but he's still a thorn in our side. I simply can't afford to go into why it happened. And I won't cross the line between pure investigation and criminal intent. That's your job. I do have my own theory."

CDR William S. Donaldson, USN (deceased) challenged the U.S. government's conclusions on what caused TWA Flight 800 to crash into the Atlantic Ocean on 17-Jul-1996. The Boeing 747-100 literally exploded in mid-air shortly after takeoff from JFK International Airport killing everyone on board. Hundreds of witnesses reported evidence of offensive targeting that originated from either the ground or the water. There was also indisputable presence of PETN, an explosive compound found around a gaping hole in the plane's fuselage.

Riley was frustrated. "Okay, Tom, it's not a missile. So give me

235

your opinion."

Ross popped a handful of pumpkin seeds into his mouth. "This was criminal. Someone planted a bomb inside or underneath that cockpit. A timed device with enough power to rupture the flight control cables. That's my opinion. It's your job to find out how."

Chapter Fifty-six

San Diego, CA
Seaport Village Shops

Kevin Jones was both anxious and nervous as he opened his guitar case and lifted his instrument to his lap. He plucked each string with his thumb and then strummed a progression of C, D, and G chords, his favorite way to verify in-tune status. He set the guitar back in its case and approached a popcorn vendor wagon next to the seawall overlooking San Diego Harbor. He purchased a large bag. In a scene straight from Hitchcock's film 'The Birds', wings and beaks instantly appeared. The seagulls were remarkably bold and fought angrily over the morsels that he tossed onto the walkway. One hopped onto the guitar case. When Jones tried to pet the seemingly friendly visitor, he was given a nasty warning. It was all about popcorn.

Behind him, a crowd had gathered around a gazebo in a park-like area. There was music pumping through two amplifiers. Curious, Jones moved closer. It was another guitar player. His voice was smooth and his timing was crisp. People were clapping to the rhythmic beat of a low and heavy bass drum.

One-two-three-four-one-two-three-four-bomp-bomp-bomp-bomp....

"Ceeelia, you're breaking my heart...
You're shaking my confidence daily...
Oh, Ceceeelia, I'm down on my knees...
I'm begging you please to come home...
Come on home."

"Sonofabitch, he's singing Simon and Garfunkel," Jones spoke to himself. "Damn, why can't I do that? I can. I know I can." He eased closer keeping a watchful eye on his guitar.

"This guy's good, eh?" A bystanding young man commented. "I love guitar music; I've always wanted to play."

"Playing is the easy part," Jones noted. "Unfortunately, not

237

everyone can sing."

"That's so true. When I sing, foxes usually howl."

The song ended. The crowd responded with loud applause.

Surprised at remembering the breed, Jones faced the man. "Fennec foxes?"

"Yes, especially when there's a bright desert moo..." Sinani turned warily. "I'm sorry, were you talking to me?"

Jones's face lit up like a beacon. "Is your name Omar? Omar Yassin? I'm Kevin. Kevin Jones." He pumped Sinani's hand vigorously. "The Entomopter. Remember? You called me the other day from Saudi Arabia about performance in sand and maximum leg grip pressure. I can't believe it. What the hell are you doing in San Diego? I thought you were beta testing in some oil field. Are you finished?"

"Kevin, what a surprise," Sinani stammered. "Of course. Dr. Al-Aran's project. A funeral...my...um...one of my relatives passed away. My aunt. She lived here...north of here. We...it was a long illness."

"Oh, man, I'm sorry," Jones offered. "But how did you get all the way to California with the flight ban and all?"

"Mexico. I flew into Tijuana and drove up from there. If you've never done that it's an interesting experience."

"I bet," Jones agreed. "This whole country is going through scary times, especially the economy. You have to let me buy you dinner or something. I'd love to hear about the test results. I've been so busy that I've lost touch with the Entomopter team. How long are you in town?"

"I'm sorry, Kevin, but I can't. There's a family thing tonight and I have to leave early tomorrow."

"That's too bad," Jones said and glanced at the time. "So tell me. How did D-Fly perform?"

"Well, to be honest, it was rather disappointing. Average at best. The initial flights looked promising, but I'm afraid we simply expected a little too much. The machine doesn't hold up very well in sand. The wings kept popping out of their sockets, too. Ultimately it proved uncontrollable."

"Really?" Jones's reaction fell somewhere between surprise and embarrassment. Then it turned defensive. "That's bizarre. What exactly were you trying to accomplish? You shouldn't have had any problems."

"Our team documented everything so we do have a record for any required enhancements. I could send you a copy."

"Nah, don't bother," Jones reconsidered. "I've got enough on my plate."

"It was nice meeting you." Sinani cut the conversation short. He extended his hand. "Perhaps we can play music together sometime."

"Sure," Jones said with a puzzled look. "I've got a condo two blocks from the beach. Gotta keep up my image."

Sinani smiled and awkwardly turned away.

In the distance, shopping bags in hand, Marissa appeared on a pathway with her children. Sinani nonchalantly shifted their direction toward the parking lot.

Jones returned to his bench feeling as if he were owed a better explanation. They'd done extensive testing in a wind tunnel to simulate dust storms whipped up on the Martian landscape. Certainly more violent than anything in Saudi Arabia. The Entomopter had performed beautifully.

Marissa buckled her children in the minivan and distributed two chocolate pretzels. "Who was that man you were talking to? The one with the ponytail?"

"Someone I knew from high school…in Minnesota," Sinani answered, starting the engine. "Why do you ask?"

"I'm just jealous," she admitted, climbing into the passenger seat. "You've been to so many places and I've never been out of San Diego."

"I know how to fix that."

"What do you mean?"

"I mean we should just pack up and get away," he suggested. "The kids would love a vacation."

Marissa gave a perplexed look. "So would I, but Dean, I just met you. Besides, I can't leave Nick. He would never go for it."

"Did you hear what I said? You don't think, you don't worry, you just do it. There's nothing for you here, especially working in a disgusting massage parlor for a loser like that. We'll take a nice long trip and then find a new place to live. Somewhere that's not so crowded. Maybe we'll come back here or maybe we won't." He lifted her hand. "Don't say a word to anyone about us, okay? Especially Nick. I'll handle him."

"Dean, please? He's mean. He's the reason Tamara had a nervous breakdown in the first place. He always complains about other people, but he's even worse. When he drinks he gets really nasty. She keeps a gun in the house and said she would use it if he hurts her again. I think she's serious."

"In the house where?" Sinani asked sternly.

She hesitated. "Her laundry basket. Under a towel."

"Is Nick right or left-handed?"

"Left, I think. Why do you want to know that?"

"In case he would ever swing at me. It's always good to be prepared."

Marissa felt her heart race with excitement. Hope was something she rarely experienced. She had always wanted a better life, but never had the financial means or the opportunity. This was a complete whirlwind. She could easily pack up and leave. She had no personal property except her minivan, and no close family ties. Her children could adapt to anything. "What about you?" She wondered. "You just got here. What would you do about the apartment or school? Nick would really be...."

"I have a confession to make," Sinani interrupted. He looked into her eyes. "There's something special about you. I've always said that when I found the right woman, I'd know it. A woman who is kind, beautiful, and who would make a good wife. I know it sounds crazy, but I'm telling you the truth from my heart. Something happened to me the first time I heard your voice on the phone. Let's just get away. Please let me prove it. I can finish college anywhere. It doesn't have to be here. I have money saved. Almost eighty thousand dollars. You won't have to work another day and you can have anything you want. We'll find out about ourselves. I mean, if there's really something there. I promise I'll take care of you and your family, Marissa. Trust me, okay?"

She laid her head on his shoulder. "I will take care of you, too, Dean. I can't believe how lucky I am. This is like a dream."

Chapter Fifty-seven

Oval Office
Wednesday, May 27th
7:42 A.M.

"I want you to listen to something," the president said, opening a window. The south wind carried the chants from the National Mall into the complex. "Now I know how Lyndon Johnson felt during Vietnam."

"There's another protest tomorrow." Transportation Secretary Minka flopped the Washington Post onto the president's desk. "Machinists. United announced a second mass layoff. We may have to reconsider."

The president stared at the Washington Monument, hands clasped behind his back. "You mean end it, don't you?"

"Sir, I took the liberty of projecting some numbers. If the shutdown were to last fifteen days, aviation bankruptcy filings would reach their highest levels ever. Of the two hundred carriers registered in the U.S., all would seek protection. As you know, filing bankruptcy just means that creditors are held at bay until a company is better positioned to repay. Unfortunately, we're at the point where even that might be impossible, even with loans. People are losing confidence. If something isn't done, the sheer weight of the economics might not support a recovery. I know how you feel about polls, but the latest show that ninety percent of Americans believe that we should lift the ban regardless of the potential for additional loss of life via another crash. Of those, only three percent said they'd personally take the risk. That tells me that airfreight should be allowed to resume immediately."

"Tell me how we frame it," the president asked.

"We frame it by telling the truth."

"The truth? That we don't have the first damn clue about what or who is killing our citizens?"

"Well, sir, we don't say it exactly like that. We say that we're doing everything possible to prevent further losses. That's number one. Secondly, we inundate the major airports with visible military as a precaution. Every bag is opened and scanned, every passenger is questioned and searched, every plane is inspected before it leaves the ground, and everyone who comes in contact with an aircraft is monitored visually. That will get us flying again with credibility. Passengers need to feel safe. And when I say inundate, I mean it. We'll get state governors to mobilize National Guard units to stand side-by-side with federal forces. That should mitigate any Posse Commitatus concerns." Minka poured the president a cup of coffee. He helped himself to a glass of wine. "My father taught me a simple lesson about a wolf and a deer. If you face a terrible position, with no way out, it is better to fight like a wolf and lose with honor, than to run. Hokey, yes. But dammit, sir, it's true. If I come back to my den and find a bear eating my pups, then I'll fight to the death. In other words, I would rather go out in ball of fire. It simply comes down to honor. With respect to the economics, last month my mother had ninety thousand dollars in a mutual fund. Yesterday it was worth seventeen with no end in sight. "Sitting here doing nothing is like planning a Haida hunting party day after day and never going out after the Grizzly. We need to get back in the air."

The president took all this in. "You speak as eloquently as always, my friend. Give me a few moments alone."

He folded his hands and recited the Lord's Prayer. Finished, he repeated one phrase out loud. "But deliver us from evil."

U.S. No-Fly Zone Day 10
San Diego KFMB Channel 8 Breaking News
Thursday, May 28th
8:00 A.M.

"...the tremendous amount of military personnel that will be deployed in every airport facility in the country. This will include mobilized and armed National Guard units. Once again, for those of you just tuning in, effective at midnight tonight, the flight ban in all fifty states that has been in place for the past nine days will be lifted, but with certain restrictions: First, there will be a staggered resumption of flights beginning with non-passenger transportation and domestic, followed one day later with internationals. The decision announced just moments ago by the White House was met with resounding support from labor and business groups all across the country. We have some reaction from the airlines as well as local business owners. We go now to our affiliate in ..."

Georgia Tech

Professor Michael Robertson paged through his appointment calendar. It resembled a crossword puzzle of inked out dates and times for meetings that were scheduled, cancelled, and then rescheduled to coincide with the potential for flying again. He pasted a sheet of blank paper over one three-day period and jotted down yet another entry: Collegiate Remote Control Exhibition in Disney's EPCOT Center Pavilion. The event would bring flying competitors from schools all over the country. He was the master of ceremonies and overall program coordinator. Disney's animatronics engineers wanted the Entomopter to fly up to the tip of the Magic Kingdom's castle vis-à-vis Tinkerbell during the evening Parade of Lights show.

The phone chirped.

"Michael, thank God you're there." Dr. Garton's voice was frantic. "I just spoke to Milt Vandenbaum in the Treasurer's office. He has no record of that Saudi check. Apparently no deposit was ever made. We've already contacted the Bank of Riyadh and they're in the dark, too. Dammit, I knew we should have used a wire transfer. Michael, we need those funds. We've already started drawing against the balance. Where is Dr. Al-Aran?"

"Faiz has been on vacation since the eleventh and I have absolutely no idea where. He's supposed to be back on the first. He was handling everything, including the funding. I never even saw the check."

San Diego International Airport
Friday, May 29th
6:05 A.M.

"May I have your attention, please," a voice announced over the public address system. "This is the first call for America West Express flight 6550 to Las Vegas leaving from gate number thirty-nine. Please have your boarding passes ready and we also have a special surprise for each passenger. Thank you for flying America West and welcome back."

"Check it out," Chuck Meyer said, slinging his carry-on bag

strap over his shoulder. "They're handing out scratch-off tickets and two rolls of quarters. I told you this would be great. That's forty bucks in our pocket already. I'm going to hit it big today. I feel it."

Lindsey Meyer rolled her eyes. "Sure, I hear that every year. Just don't go crazy like you did on your last birthday. I think you can take off the cowboy hat."

"It brings me luck. And don't worry; I can handle it."

"I am worried," she shot back. "I'm worried about you; I'm worried about our kids; and I'm worried about this flight. See for yourself. Everyone in this terminal looks scared. What if something happens? I just have a funny feel——"

"Nothing's going to happen," he interrupted. "Think of how lucky we are that our tickets are still good. Besides, there's more security in here than passengers. I think I counted twenty bomb-sniffing dogs. Everywhere you look there's a soldier." He whispered into his wife's ear. "I promise we'll be fine. And I promise that I'm going to win enough to pay for the babysitter."

"Okay, then give it to me."

"My hat?"

"Don't be cute," she said firmly. "There's no way I'm letting you near a TYME machine if you start losing."

He reluctantly slid out his credit card.

One hundred passengers had each paid $99.00 for a 'quickie', a one day gambling excursion to Las Vegas, departing in the morning on an A320 Airbus and returning by 11:00 P.M. the same day.

The couple found their seats and sampled free champagne. They kissed. An annual event on Chuck's birthday, this was their third trip in as many years. One precious day away from work and the kids. A nice break before the weekend.

"Good morning ladies and gentlemen. My name is Captain Vetter and I'll be at the control column today for a short flight into Las Vegas. We've just been cleared for departure and our flying time will be approximately seventy-five minutes at just under twenty thousand feet. We don't expect any turbulence; the ride should be nice and smooth. The temperature is already eighty-nine degrees heading for a high of 115." The passengers groaned. "I guess it'll be another scorcher in Sin City. Enjoy your quickie and thank you for choosing America West. We'll be on our way shortly. Flight attendants, prepare for departure."

The aircraft rose into the air and veered northwest through 2,500 feet. Vetter gently banked the plane over Sea World.

"Yeeee-hah!" Chuck screamed, waving a scratch-off ticket high in the air. "I won. I won two hundred fifty bucks!"

Applause filled the cabin.

A woman leaned across the aisle. "This must be your lucky day."

It was.

Passengers on the right side of the plane let out a collective gasp at a FedEx jet flying parallel and to the north. It was smoking from the underbody and tailing down and away crossing Interstate 8. Some turned away while others watched in horror as it struck the water in Mission Bay, its wings collapsing backward like some cormorant fishing bird diving for breakfast.

Oddly, there was no indication that anything had disturbed the early California morning. The streets were strangely quiet, much like a proverbial beach-calm before the first tsunami wave hit from some distant seabed shift.

Sinani calmly shut the apartment window and dialed his cell phone. "I'm on my way. Do me a favor and get me two Egg McMuffins and two hash browns okay? I'm starved." He clicked off and gave the room a cursory look.

Out on the street, he loaded his gear into Marissa's minivan. He rolled down the windows in his Camry and placed the keys conspicuously on the hood. He glanced at the darkened windows of the Velvet Touch. Nick and Tamara had had a violent night. They'd both be sleeping in today.

Washington Hilton Hotel
National Prayer Breakfast

The president had finished his remarks and was sitting with leaders from the Urban League and the National Council of Churches. The Umbato Choir from Uganda had finished a second set of hymns. Eerily reminiscent of a scene that occurred on the morning of September 11, 2001 in the Emma E. Booker Elementary School in Sarasota, FL, Chief of Staff Bard hurried to the table and bent next to the president's ear.

Guests were riveted by the action.

The president nodded twice and made a point to examine a spoon before calmly stirring his coffee. His facial color had turned ghost-like. He neatly folded his napkin and then rose from the chair. "Folks, I apologize, but something has come up."

Sinani drove the minivan south towards Chula Vista and pulled into the Travel Inn Motel on Third Street and Broadway where Marissa and her children were waiting, McDonald's bags in hand. They reached the I-5 freeway and merged into the northbound traffic. Sinani checked the rearview mirror and then turned on the radio.

Marissa immediately turned it off.

"Why did you do that?" He wondered. "I wanted to hear the news."

"No you don't," she replied. "I want to hear about us."

She placed her arm around his neck so her fingers could toy with his ear. She set a warm breakfast bag between his legs and seductively withdrew the items. "Did you miss me last night?"

"Of course," he smiled, setting the cruise control for five miles over the posted limit. He turned and gave her a kiss. "So, where would you like to go?"

"Any place you want to take me as long as it's out of California. I hate this state," she said, resting her head on Sinani's shoulder and gazing through the windshield. The abusive, whoring way of life gave way to a new beginning. She'd never been treated like this before. He was the first person in a long time who really seemed to care. "Dean, could we go far away?"

"Sure, far away. Any place at all. You decide."

"I've always wanted to see the Statue of Liberty. How about New York City?"

Sinani bit into his sandwich and checked the rearview mirror again. "New York City sounds like a winner to me."

Chapter Fifty-eight

Oval Office

"Did you say Federal Express?" The president shouted into the speakerphone, shaking with anger. "Dammit, Samuel, I don't care if there were only four people on board. This is indiscriminate anarchy. Do something!"

Bard hurried into the room with a handful of faxes. "Mr. President, the airports are in panic. You need to re-establish the country's no-fly zone. Passengers are already refusing to board planes. The American people think that you want the airspace open and are putting the economy ahead of lives. They're blaming you for the deaths."

The president snatched the documents and read one. Uncharacteristically, he tore the rest violently and flung them to the floor. "Get Minka to reinstate the order, please." He swallowed hard, forcing himself to adopt a softer tone. "Do you hear me, Samuel? We're going back to full groundstop—now."

"Yes, sir," Bridge answered. He clicked off.

The president turned to Bard. "Get me General Myers."

"Sir, please, you cannot deploy the military on U.S. soil without declaring a state of emergency," he warned. "And even then you need explicit requests from state governors. It would be viewed as a severe intrusion into—"

"To hell with states' rights," the president shot back. "And to hell with the law. This is a national crisis and I'm going to take action. I want a presence. An overwhelming presence at all airports. We need to screen everything and everyone."

"Sir, there's no need," Bard said calmly. "The airports will shut down voluntarily. All you need do is reinstate the order. That will show you're in charge."

The president glared at him. I am in fucking charge. But of what? An incompetent Homeland Security Department that can't stop aircraft from crashing to the ground like paper toys? "I want five hundred soldiers positioned at every airport. I want them to hand search every single passenger and open every piece of luggage." He nodded confidently. "The military will assist the airlines.

247

They'll board every aircraft just like the Israelis. Soldiers, scanners, even polygraph machines if we have to. Everything. We'll open every single piece of luggage on every single plane, then put it through the detectors, and then let the bomb dogs have their way. Or better yet, we'll simply disallow all luggage. That'll work. It has to."

"Mr. President?" Bard interrupted the tirade. "Two pilots and two mechanics are dead. This was in fact a cargo jet en route from San Diego to San Francisco for routine maintenance."

The president looked at his chief of staff quizzically. "What's your point?"

"There was no luggage, sir. It was empty."

Milwaukee Marriott

"Are you insinuating that my children need counseling?" Marcia seethed. "You smug bastard. Don't you ever suggest that to me again. When are you coming home?"

"I don't know," Ross answered, shifting the phone to his other ear. "I've never seen anything like this before. We've never had two investigations running simultaneously. This is entirely different than 9/11 because at least with those crashes, we knew the cause. We don't have enough people to support the work. I can't just up and leave."

"Damn you and your misguided loyalty. Can't you even answer a simple question?"

"I'm sorry; it's the best I can do."

"The best you can do," she said disgustedly. "I hope you can hear me because I'm going to tell you something about your best. I think you're a failure. And a miserable one at that. A failure to me as a partner; a failure to my daughters; and a failure as the head of this household. You've left me alone for the last time. I won't be here when you get back...click."

Ross paused a moment before touching the redial button. The answering machine made an intermittent beeping sound and then there was silence. He was about to speak when he heard voices in the background. Grunting and sexual. One was Marcia's; the other was male and unfamiliar. He folded his phone and when he did he felt a sudden euphoria. An opportunity for a clean break and a fresh direction. For the first time in months, he had clear insight into who he was and what he wanted from a relationship. Good riddance.

There was a knock on the door.

248

Riley stormed in and clicked the TV remote. "I've been trying to call you. There's been another crash. Who the hell have you been talking to?"

"Nobody. Just a bad connection."

The screen showed a helicopter's view of Mission Bay.

"The damn media know what's happening even before we do," Riley observed.

Ross's face was drawn and he knelt to the floor. "Whoever's doing this has us running all over the country. The NTSB can't handle it anymore, Jack. We need help. It's gone beyond our ability."

"It's about to get worse," he said, seeing a news scroll announcing financial market closings. "Bridge said the president is ordering another shutdown until the military is in place at all major airports. He wants armed soldiers on all commercial flights. One more thing... Congress is calling an emergency session and your organization is on the agenda. They're thinking that the NTSB can do more good in this crisis by assisting law enforcement task forces versus staying so isolated. If the recommendation is accepted, then you and your teams will be reporting to me until further notice. All other investigations and work efforts will stop and resources will be redirected and made available to Homeland Security. We need the expertise, pal."

"Firearms on aircraft is a horrible idea, Jack. Is that even legal?"

"Nobody knows anything. The whole country's in chaos."

"What do you need from me?" Ross asked.

"Physical evidence." He examined the bag on the tabletop containing the mysterious red plastic piece. "Do you still think this has significance?"

"I don't know what to think anymore," Ross said. "One thing's for sure...it came from somewhere or something and we need to find out what."

Riley's cell phone chirped. After a brief conversation, he flipped the phone shut. "Unbelievable. There is a God."

"Now what?"

"Someone had a webcam operating in Mission Bay that captured the flight path. We've got live but delayed video of the explosion. It came from under the cockpit."

249

Chapter Fifty-nine

La Crosse, WI
Sunday, May 31st

A pink neon vacancy sign burned brightly against the night backdrop. Sinani turned the minivan off of County Highway 16 and pulled up the block-long driveway to the office of Nelson's Motor Lodge. He gently shook Marissa's shoulder. "Wake up; we're here."

She yawned. "What time is it?"

"Ten o'clock."

"Where are we?"

"Wisconsin."

"I've never been to Wisconsin." She turned to her children in the back seat. "How long have we been sleeping?"

"Since Nebraska."

"Everything is so quiet and cold," she said, opening the door and peering outside. "It's almost June and I can still see my breath."

"The Midwest isn't California. And La Crosse is a college town. Most students leave for the summer. I used to stay here when I visited friends. The University of Wisconsin campus is only three miles south. You can't see much at night, but there are bluffs right behind us. The Mississippi River is just across the road." He popped the rear hatch. "Do me a favor and check in. We should be in room number twelve."

"Okay, Dean, but I don't have a credit card."

"You won't need one."

Marissa ran a brush through her hair and then shuffled into the motel's office. There was a handwritten note and a key taped to the counter:

SANCHEZ FAMILY————-
PLEASE FILL OUT THE GUEST REGISTRATION CARD AND LEAVE IT ON THE COUNTER. WE'LL HAVE COFFEE AND HOMEMADE CINNAMON ROLLS HERE IN THE MORNING. YOU CAN PAY THEN. ENJOY!

Marissa collected her children and walked to the room. There were two double beds and the interior walls sparkled with white gloss paint. "Are these people for real leaving everything unlocked?"

"Refreshing isn't it?"

"Crazy." She gave off a noticeable shiver. "Someone will rip them off."

"People aren't like that here," Sinani yawned deeply. "They trust everybody."

Marissa tucked her children in bed. "Dean, do you really think we're a family?"

He turned the dial on the wall heater and then draped a blanket over her shoulders. He rubbed her arms vigorously. "From now on we'll always be a family."

"I love the way you say that to me."

"I love to say it." He kissed her cheekbone and then her lips. "Hungry?"

"I'm too cold to be hungry. How long are we going to stay here?"

"Just tonight. There's another resort two hours from here with an indoor pool. I already made reservations. The kids will love it." He handed her the TV remote. "I'll be right back. I know a good Chinese place."

Sinani sped down the highway until he spotted a darkened shopping center. He parked at the far end of the lot. He retrieved his laptop from his travel bag and logged onto the Internet. At CNN's website, he jotted down three headlines:

> Chaos in the air……..
> America under siege……..
> President invokes war powers……

Sinani entered the words 'Internet Dating Service' into the search browser and clicked on the 31st result. The chat room was filled. He mouthed the words Sunday, May 31st and scrolled down. Four screens later, he found who he was looking for.

ChAmPr has logged in.

251

SMT0531: Hello. I almost gave up on you.

ChAmPr: How is the cruise?

SMT0531: Excellent. Your recommendation was perfect.

ChAmPr: And the itinerary?

SMT0531: Better than I could have imagined. I've decided to take three more long vacations. You've done such a good job so far that I want you to pick the itineraries for them, too. Feel free to send recommendations. I'd like to start the next trip in late June. I'll leave the date up to you. For now, I believe we have one more stop.

ChAmPr: Cunard Cruise Lines always saves the best for last. It should be very memorable. A fitting end to a successful trip.

SMT0531: I wish there was a way to repay you. Perhaps we could meet sometime?

ChAmPr: That would be nice. If you're ever in New York City, then stop in. I live at 0112 18th Street in West Pinehurst. I look forward to seeing you.

Sinani logged off.

The red neon lights of the China House Restaurant flashed in the distance.

Chapter Sixty

Milwaukee Marriott
2:30 A.M.

Riley sucked the last liquid from a plastic diet Coke bottle and neatly replaced the cap. Numb from eighteen hours of non-stop video meetings with field teams, he sat on the floor in his hotel room staring dejectedly at a stack of unread investigation reports. He yawned at the television. The sound was barely audible, but he managed to hear a cable news roundtable guest claim that the airline crashes were caused by shoddy maintenance and that the president and his administration were culpable for not adequately funding the FAA and its safety inspectors.

Riley tossed the bottle across the room at Tom Ross asleep in a chair. It landed directly on top of his head giving off a loud, but harmless bonk. "Turn that idiot off before I throw something at him. News commentators who allow people to spread their bullshit without any supporting facts should be shot."

Ross snorted awake and reached for the remote. "When can I go back to my old job?"

"When the skies are safe and not a minute before," Riley said, rubbing his eyes. "Did you ever have that pain in your side looked at?"

"It hasn't bothered me lately, but I gave up the pumpkin seeds. And speaking of pain, I'm going to ask Marcia and her kids to leave. I just haven't figured out how."

"Is that a good thing?"

"It's a very good thing." Ross stretched. "I'm beat. I'll be in my room. My bed is calling."

Riley turned his head suspiciously. "Your bed or Neela's?"

"Mine," Ross answered firmly. "Besides, she's still in New York. She's driving back Tuesday."

"That job offer?"

"Uh-huh. And get this...she's supposed to be interviewed on Fox's national morning news show. They want to hear about her embedded assignment. She's really getting popular. Unfortunately, I'm not real keen on long distance relationships. We'll have to see." Ross pressed what he thought was the remote's On/Off button. Instead, it was the Favorites button and the screen flipped to the Discovery Channel. He found the right button and the screen went black.

"You know what they say…love will find a——wait, turn that TV back on." Riley stood up. "Did you see that?"

Ross complied and raised the volume.

A narrator was standing inside a sports stadium underneath a football goalpost. Something was in his hand.

".....the Mars project due to NASA budget cuts. The Entomopter is the brainchild of Professor Michael Robertson who designed the flying insect under a research grant from Georgia Tech here in Atlanta. As you can see from the size of this wing, the unit is quite small, but still capable of carrying a built-in camera and an array of sensors. In fact, the D-Fly, as it's known on the project team, can carry up to double its weight in rock samples from the Martian landscape. Unfortunately, even the best flying inventions never get off the ground. Next, we'll look at some of the military's high-tech remote control land robots."

Decatur, GA
4:30 A.M.

Linda Robertson sat up in bed, awakened by what sounded like voices and radio static. She fell back to the pillow wondering why the boys were up so early. The bedroom door cracked open and she heard the sounds again. She nudged her husband. "There's someone in the house. It's your turn."

The door opened further. Michael groaned and rose up on his elbows. "That's far enough, buddy. I don't care how big of a gun you have. If you come in this room then I'm going to tie you to a tree outside and squirt you with the garden hose." There was silence. "I'm serious. My gun is bigger than yours."

The door burst open and five federal officers armed with assault rifles surrounded the bed. A second team swept onto the premises.

Linda pulled the covers up to her face and gasped in disbelief as they whisked her pajama-clad husband outside and into a waiting vehicle.

FBI Special Agent Harlan Ellis strode into the room and laid an envelope on the bed. He spoke in a soft southern drawl. "Ma'am, you need to be advised that this is a federal warrant served by authority of the U.S. attorney's office to detain a Mr. Michael C. Robertson. Your husband will be at the FBI offices on Century Parkway in Atlanta. If y'all have a lawyer, then you can call the number on the back for further information. Y'all need to get up and get dressed, ma'am. We need to search this room."

Atlanta, GA
10:30 A.M.

Riley stood outside a secure detention cell and peered through a thick glass window at his prisoner's physical appearance. He opened the door and nodded to the two agents inside. They removed the hand and leg restraints.

"I sure as hell hope you're in charge, mister," Michael said, rubbing his wrists.

"My name is Jack Riley and as a matter of fact, I am."

"Well, you're going to pay, Mr. Riley, because I demand to call my lawyer. You had no right to do what you did to me. Why won't anyone tell me anything? I'm going to sue you and your whole damn government agency whatever it is."

"Homeland Security," Riley clarified, pulling up a chair.

"I don't care; I want my lawyer. His name is Ray Mills."

Riley produced an evidence bag and slid out a piece of red plastic. "Do you know what this is?"

Michael gave the item a brief glance and then turned away.

"Sir, I don't have time for games," Riley said sternly, repeating the question.

"Of course I know what it is. It's part of a wing. An Entomopter wing."

"Could you explain exactly what . . ."

"Entomopter. Get your own damn dictionary and then my lawyer. I won't say another thing to you or anyone else."

Riley moved closer. "Sir, this Entomopter wing was recovered from the wreckage of United Flight 241 in Itasca, Illinois. It was stuck to one of the landing gear tires. We believe it had something to do with the crash. We also presume that someone smuggled it aboard

255

or otherwise placed it on that plane. What we don't know is how or why. We hoped that you might be able to provide the answers."

Michael pointed his finger. "Mister, you've got some nerve. You storm into my home, place me in handcuffs in front of my wife and children and then cart me off to jail like I'm Timothy McVeigh. I've been sitting in this stinkhole for over five hours and no one has said anything to me about why. I want a public apology and I want my lawyer."

Agent Cheng cracked the door. "Jack, could I see you a minute?"

"Excuse me," Riley said, stepping into the corridor.

Cheng opened a notebook. "This guy is a research professor at Georgia Tech. He has an exemplary academic record and recently received worldwide attention in the scientific community for inventing some kind of flying insect. There's a bunch of them in the campus laboratory. I've got one right here. It's called an Ento..."

"Mopter." Riley examined the unit.

"Uh-huh. Entomopter. How'd you know?"

"Anything else?"

"According to his wife, he hasn't been out of Atlanta since they got back from Italy. He won some award there. She's a teacher and seems credible. She's also really pissed. Maybe they're both in on it?"

Riley gave Cheng a doubting look. "Dammit, we need to be smarter. Why did Ellis have to drag him out of his house like that? That's all we need is a front-page photograph of federal agents manhandling another innocent citizen. If he's not involved then we're going to be up to our eyeballs in lawsuits. Do me a favor and track down a local attorney named Ray Mills. He'll want a piece of us, too."

Cheng jotted the name. "There's one more thing. His wife is on her way down here with a busload of students. The media is already setting up outside."

Riley returned to the holding cell with the Entomopter and a cup of coffee. "Professor, I just wanted to tell you that we probably could have brought you here in a more respectable manner. And if you're not involved, then I'll give you your public apology. It may take awhile. Please try and be patient."

Michael slammed his hand onto the table. "Involved in what?"

"The loss of three aircraft and the death of 264 citizens."

Michael tried to digest that and then turned his head incredulously. "You think...the airline accidents...that I...for God's sake do I look like some Arab terrorist?"

"Looks can be deceiving, sir. They're not all Arabs."

"Alright, that was inappropriate," Michael admitted. "I'm sorry, but truly, the Entomopter is nothing more than a robotic exploratory tool. I built it exclusively for NASA. It was supposed to be part of the manned mission to Mars until it got cancelled. That's all there is. I have absolutely no idea how that wing ended up in your debris. The units aren't secret and neither are the parts. Anyone could have picked one up and walked off with it."

Riley stirred his coffee and eyed the device. "This can really fly?"

"It can fly," Michael affirmed.

Riley lifted the insect and felt the leg torque.

"For carrying tools or rocks. They can also hold the unit in position. On the roll bars of the Mars rover for example."

That raised Riley's curiosity even more. "Anyone else make these?"

"I can name at least a dozen other universities, but on a much smaller scale. For its size ours was the first of its kind. We had high hopes until—"

"Mars got cancelled. You mentioned that before." Riley set the Entomopter down. "So, if this can carry a rock then why not something else?"

Michael knew what Riley was thinking. "I'm sick and tired of people assuming that my invention can instantly adapt to all these weird applications. It's not a military device."

"What do you mean weird applications?"

"A pie in the sky security and monitoring venture that has some people on campus blinded by dollar signs."

Riley leaned forward. "What kind of monitoring?"

"Oil rigs and other fixed assets. One of my colleagues is in charge. I don't care to even bring it up."

"Oil rigs where?"

"In the desert outside Dhahran, Saudi Arab—"

Riley stood up from the table, tipping his chair. "What did you say?"

Michael's mind raced. His mouth twitched and he shook his

257

head repeatedly, mumbling to himself.

"Sir, I asked you a question," Riley pressed. "What did you just say?"

"Saudi Arabia," he answered softly. "We gave five Entomopters to someone from Saudi Arabia."

"Who did?"

"The university...my project ...my colleague ...no, not possible."

Riley turned and sprinted for the door. "His name. What is it?"

Michael couldn't speak. He just stared at his invention.

"Professor Robertson! What is his name?"

"Al-Aran. Faiz Al-Aran."

Chapter Sixty-one

Queen Mary II

"Would you repeat that, please?" Captain John Francis asked the caller on the other end of the telephone. He calmly walked across his cabin and touched his finger to a computer screen's navigational icon. He perused the ship's course and speed.

"The Court orders you to return to port, senor. Immediately." Alberto Tadich spoke in broken English. The National Court was Spain's anti-terrorism agency.

Francis had served in Britain's Royal Navy and was a NATO strike force commander before an arrogant German general relieved him. He carried a grudge against foreign authority ever since. He bristled at the Spaniard's tone. "Orders me? On what grounds? Do you really expect the world's largest passenger ship to simply up and turn 'round without any explanation? We're on an extremely tight schedule."

"It is my duty to inform you of this instruction, Capitan. You must return to Las Palmas."

"Then you've done your duty, sir. I'll take the request under advisement. Good day." Francis clicked off. His face had a smug expression. The ship had already reached international waters.

Chief Officer, Clifton Remmers knocked on the cabin door. "Captain, sir, we've just gotten word from London. It seems they'd like us to detain one of our passengers. A fellow by the name of Al-Aran. They say it's urgent and to use extreme caution."

"This is absolute madness," Francis grumbled, snatching the dispatch from Remmer's hand. "Send a detail at once."

"Right away, sir." Remmers reached for his communicator. "I think it's something about the U.S. flight ban, but I'm afraid they wouldn't let me in on the details."

Francis touched his computer screen's security icon and scrolled through the passenger list. Al-Aran's name came up highlighted and flagged by the ship's Smartcard System as a non-returning passenger on embarkation. "Belay that, Clifton," Francis reversed himself.

"Sir?"

"The chap never reboarded which means he's still in the Canarys. It's their problem now."

Lanzarote Island
Greef's Charter Fishing

"Al-Aran, Al-Aran...he's that tall wog of a dark-skinned fellow," Rollin Greef recalled. A Popeye-like man dressed in dock shorts and knee-high rubber boots, Greef had a filet knife slung over his back and his hands were stained with fish blood. "Now I've got him. He's out on one of me small runabouts. He took a tub full of squid and half a dozen rods. I thought he was a bit of a dill to go shark fishing alone, but he kinda' persuaded me if you get my meaning, eh?"

"In other words he gave you money," Cheng clarified.

Greef smiled briefly and spit a huge stream of tobacco juice over the dock rail. He reached in his pocket for a tin container. "You look a little knackered, mate. Where did you say you lit off from?"

"Atlanta."

"Care for a pinch of durry? Might perk things up a bit." Cheng declined. Greef stuffed a wad in his cheek. "This Al-Aran must be in some big trouble if the American FBI sets off on a 4,000 mile walkabout."

"How long has he been fishing?"

Greef craned his neck at the boathouse clock. "All of five hours now. I'd say he should be heading back this way any time."

Atlantic Ocean
28° 47′04.80′′N   13° 12′52.58′′W
33 Miles Southeast of Orzola

Faiz Al-Aran removed a hand-held GPS receiver from his briefcase and verified his positional coordinates. He checked the time and peered through binoculars. To the south, a freighter appeared on the horizon. Its silhouette grew steadily larger until gray-white lettering was visible. He flung the receiver and binoculars in a wide arc and watched them plop into the water narrowly missing a curious pilot whale that had come to investigate. Next, he heaved the squid overboard and churned the runabout's propeller through the blood-soaked entrails. The first shark appeared in less than a minute. Finished, he stripped off his clothes and laid them in a pile on the floor. He pressed the engine's throttle and headed for his rendezvous.

The freighter had slowed to four knots.

Pacing the big ship's speed, Al-Aran shut off the runabout's engine and leaped to the portside boarding ladder. Three crewmembers watched with mild amusement as the naked seafarer scrambled up to the main deck.

The runabout drifted away aimlessly.

A tall dark-skinned seaman in a white turtleneck appeared on the freighter's bridge and eyed Al-Aran suspiciously. He lit a pipe and took several deep puffs as he walked down the metal steps. A package of clothes was tucked under one arm. "Why do you board the Abuzenima, the finest ship in the National Navigation Company? And why are you so far from shore in the trade lanes? Surely you have had bad luck, but I'm afraid you will be with us for a while. Rabat is another five hundred miles. Do we know each other, senor?"

"My name is Faiz Al-Aran." He shivered. "I am a friend."

"My name is Captain Ramon Naimi and I choose my friends carefully."

Al-Aran slipped into the clothing and then pressed his face into a towel, gathering himself. *To his crew he is Captain Ramon Naimi, but you must change the letter in his name from O to A. A simple but effective code we have used for years. He will have your new identity and you will become family.* "May God be with you Raman."

"Come we'll dine together." The captain smiled, embracing Al-Aran. "You must tell me of the interesting work God's people have done in Ameri. . ." He lifted his binoculars. "Your runabout, senor. You left something on the console. A briefcase. Do you wish to retrieve it?"

Al-Aran tightened the belt around his waist. "Your brother Ali is well and sends God's love."

Chapter Sixty-two

Wisconsin Dells, WI
8:20AM

Situated on the western bank of the Wisconsin River four miles from the downtown dam, River's Bend Resort featured authentic log cabin accommodations, a bar and restaurant, and a complete line of watercraft rentals. Ho-Chunk Casino had drained the area's minimum wage labor pool and that forced the resort's owner to live on-site in back of the combination office/bait shop. He was a small wiry man with a drawn and weathered monkey face horribly distorted by TB (tourist burnout). A makeshift FOR SALE sign hung in the window.

Marissa and Amber waited in the minivan while Sinani and little Jo-Jo walked inside and approached the counter.

"Well, my ass is grass," the owner spoke dejectedly into a corner-mounted TV. "I might as well close the doors right now and get it over with."

"Excuse me?" Sinani said. "Are you open?"

The owner pressed the TV remote and lowered the volume. "Yeah, but I don't know for how long. The president's called out the National Guard and closed the airports again indefinitely. I've never seen anything like it. News reports yesterday said the odds of three planes crashing in five days are a billion to one. It's towel heads, no doubt about it. They're shooting lasers or something. Goddamn country's gone crazy with fear and I can't blame it. I won't fly again. No way. And that don't look good for the travel business. This place'll go cowshit for sure. Every single one of my reservations cancelled this morning. Every one."

"I'm here," Sinani smiled.

"Yeah, well you're the exception and I sure appreciate it. The fishing's never been better. They're really killing 'em down by the dam. You'll have the place to yourself. What's the name?"

Jo-Jo bent over an aerated bait tank and managed to snatch a slippery minnow. It easily wiggled onto the floor.

"Hey, don't you do that," the owner barked. "Those cost money."

"I'm sorry about that; he's with me," Sinani apologized. "How much are you asking?"

"Three dollars a dozen. The river shiners are four dollars."

"For the resort?"

"Two million." The man perked up. He instinctively peered outside expecting a Lexus or Mercedes. His smile quickly faded and he reached underneath the counter for a real estate broker's card. "If you want to know any more then you should call this number. Anything else?"

"Sanchez," Sinani said. "I called last night."

The man tapped an entry into his computer and reached for a room key. "Yessir, Mr. Sanchez. Family of four, two days at one forty each plus tax comes to $294 even. Cash or charge?"

Sinani peeled out four hundred dollars. "If it's alright, I'd like to reserve a pontoon boat. Is one available?"

"One pontoon for $75.00. They're a lot of fun." The man eagerly calculated a new total and made change. He produced another key attached to a yellow foam float. "She's tied to the pier and all ready to go. Our name is on the side. The life preservers are under the seats and there's a cooler on board. Let us know if you need ice."

"One more thing...how long is that casino open?"

"No idea," the owner lied. "But our buffet starts in half an hour. Here's a couple of videotapes for the kids, no charge. You're in number three. Right on the water."

They found their cabin and unloaded.

Amber and Jo-Jo headed for the playground swings.

Alone, Sinani and Marissa drew together in a warm embrace. She pressed Sinani's head into her cleavage and slowly rocked back and forth in a stationary dance. Content in the arms of her newfound lover, she stared dreamlike through balcony doors at the Wisconsin River's fast-moving current. "This place is beautiful. I feel so good when I'm with you."

"Marissa?"

"Yes?"

"I'm going to a casino tonight."

"Win something for me."

North Lanzarote Island
Greef's Charters

Las Palmas town authorities and curious locals crowded the dock as Rollin Greef secured his recovered runabout. In the Canarys, the drowning of one cruise ship passenger carried more significance than the capsizing of overloaded migrant rafts from sub-Sahara Africa. Tourists meant money.

Greef scampered up the dock steps carrying what were presumably Faiz Al-Aran's personal belongings consisting of clothes and a brown leather briefcase. "Not one sign of him. The poor dumb bastard's a shark biscuit by now. I've never in me life seen a bloke try and swim with man eaters as if they was dolphin. That's like ringing a dinner bell."

Cheng took the briefcase and immediately flipped the latches.

"Whoa now, mate." Greef backed away. "There's one helluva camera mob watching and we need to think about this. Something weighty is in that case and if this Al-Aran rigged up a nasty surprise, then I don't fancy having my donger blown off. Not to mention scrubbing all these sticky beaks off my dock."

"Good points," Cheng acknowledged in a low voice. "I need to get off this island quietly and back to the States. I don't have time for the media here or the hassles of evidence protocol. Is there a back road to the airport?"

"Hmmm, it's possible, mate," Greef paused. "Lanzarote or Arricife?"

"Lanzarote."

"Any brass headed to my pocket?"

"Five hundred, U.S. And you don't remember a thing."

"A tidy sum, but these locals might want a say. Never know… some might even go berko for their own investigation." Greef's eyes narrowed. "I was a fair truckie in my younger days, but if we could just take my water tinnie everything would be ace. That way nobody'd know where we was off to. All we need is a little misdirection. You run these blokes off my dock, mate and we've got a deal."

Cheng noticed a young policeman standing in front of the crowd. "Where's the nearest law enforcement headquarters with x-ray capability?"

"Las Palmas, senor. I will inform them that you are en route with evidence."

Cheng motioned for the policeman to come closer and then whispered into his ear.

The policeman whispered a response in Spanish and after he did, he gulped and stumbled backwards. "Please, senor, if there is such a thing then we must ask everyone to...you must be careful not to—-"

Cheng lifted the briefcase high in the air and shouted, "Bomba."

The crowd scattered and as it did, Cheng and Greef sprinted waterside for the charter boat Ana Segundo. In a flash, Greef had the lines untied and the engines started. He flattened the throttle on the Cobia 211 Bay Skiff and the hull planed out into the open ocean. Top speed was 25 knots. Lanzarote Airport was 27 miles.

Alone in the front of the boat, Cheng set the briefcase on his lap and gently opened the cover.

Oval Office

"Hot damn, now we're getting somewhere," Secretary Bridge announced to the president. "We have a laptop computer, names, and a possible method. We've been concentrating on the inside of these aircraft when all along the threat has been outside. It's a goddamn bug."

The president nearly laughed. "Have you lost your mind?"

"A remote control flying bug capable of carrying who-knows-what kind of explosive and attaching it to an engine or wing near a fuel tank or some other vulnerable position." Bridge rifled through a set of faxes until he found a photograph. "Here, this is your aircraft killer."

The president winced. "Entomopter? What in God's name is an Entomopter and what maniac designed it?"

"He's no maniac. He's a well-respected professor at Georgia Tech. Believe it or not this Entomopter was built for your Mars mission. It was supposed to help survey planetary landscapes and carry soil samples."

"Are you sure that your people have proof?"

"Riley has a name, address, and description of a potential conspirator. He's a Saudi-American named Faiz Al-Aran. We think he's on the Queen Mary II. At least he was registered as a passenger, but he may have temporarily disappeared somewhere in the Canary Is-

265

lands. Riley's working with the Spanish authorities. They'll find him. The State Department has a request in to the Saudi embassy for sight detainment of another individual named Ibrahim Al-Assaf who supposedly works for their oil ministry. He arranged the transfer deal with Georgia Tech. That's the good news. Unfortunately, there are some unconnected dots. Witnesses have confirmed that a man fitting Al-Aran's description was on that ship. But if that's true, then it's unlikely that he personally committed any acts. And that means he's working with unknown accomplices inside the U.S. Secondly, we still have no idea on the exact method used. We're confident that the Entomopter device is involved, but we don't know how. Riley's teams are focusing on airport exteriors. Ramps, baggage areas, runways, taxiways, tarmacs, secured and unsecured perimeters. Especially structures with visual access."

"What's the bad news," the president wondered.

"We've had three crashes," Bridge said. "Before he left the country, Al-Aran walked off Georgia Tech's campus with five Entomopters."

"Did you say five?"

"Yes, five."

Chapter Sixty-three

Milwaukee Marriott
FBI Command Center

"One pissed-off inventor, one flying bug, and one Saudi-American professor who for some strange reason turned himself into shark food." Riley rapped a large felt eraser on the edge of the conference table. "Dammit, there is no way this Al-Aran could have acted alone. I want his conspirators. Names and descriptions. We haven't come up with a single solid lead in this investigation and I'm sick of it. I want a suspect list and I don't care how or who is on it. How many interviews have we done?"

"We have Al-Aran's laptop," Cheng reminded. "Our best people are looking at it."

"Yeah? And who's the FBI's best?"

"A fellow by the name of Bruce Baltis. And he's not with the Bureau. He works for New York's Criminal Justice Division's cyber security group. He's the guy who single-handedly wrote an integration program that connects state fingerprint identification systems to the FBI's national system. You really should go out there if nothing more than to show a presence. It's become the focal point of the investigation. Baltis is analyzing the laptop's hard drive as we speak. He told me that he found some interesting e-mail. Something about unusual names and user IDs. And if I might make a suggestion, I don't think it's appropriate to share that with your female Fox News friend."

Tom Ross entered the room and caught the end of the conversation. He nodded at Cheng. "Are you talking about Neela?"

"I was just saying that I'm uncomfortable sharing too much information with her, especially from Al-Aran's computer. I think whatever we get from it should be kept confidential." He turned to Riley. "As far as names, first you need a list of suspects and right now that's impossible. All we've got is raw data. There are no suspects."

"Then I want numbers," Riley demanded. "How many?"

Cheng exhaled a deep breath and reached for a stack of papers. "Mitchell International has a ten-mile perimeter with one hundred eighteen military, civilian, and commercial structures. So far our agents have interviewed people who live, eat, work, and touch those structures. Truck drivers, delivery personnel, transients, renters, and old and new homeowners. We even tracked down customers who were filmed by restaurant security cameras. Just like you requested. Any one of them could have had access to a rooftop or vantage point from which to maneuver and guide an Entomopter onto a runway. Take your pick. There's over two thousand names."

Riley turned to Ross. "Okay, Mr. NTSB, I want you to start thinking of a way that we can use Neela to our advantage. Perhaps even a little disinformation." He approached a magnetic dry erase whiteboard and uncapped a thick black marker. He jotted a series of columns from one to five. "Mr. Cheng, do we know how many businesses around Mitchell's perimeter are foreign-owned?"

Cheng shrugged.

"Alright, that's list number one." Riley turned back to the board and labeled column two as HIGH VANTAGE POINTS. I want names of anyone who had access to an area that overlooked a runway. Does anyone fit that?"

"We never looked at it from that perspective, because we didn't know about the Entomopter."

"Number three, a link to the military," Riley continued. "I want a sorted list of people we interviewed who are currently or have been in the service. Number four is..." He turned and wrote UNUSUAL CIRCUMSTANCES. "Strange behavior, a practical joke, accident, injury. Anything that could be attributed to a terrorist training mishap. Even a suspicious or untimely death."

Cheng dug through a set of notes. "A Milwaukee detective did report some commando activity in the woods south of here."

"Say again?" Riley perked up.

"A paintball tournament."

Riley was not amused.

"I'm sorry, Jack but this is impossible. We need at least two to three input days so we can do some system searches. Sifting through all this paper will just bog things down. Where do we even start?"

"We start with damn Mitchell International," Riley cursed. "Our perpetrator was in the vicinity somewhere and then he vanished. Something tells me that that observation lot on the north side of the airport is involved. It's vulnerable as hell. That Georgia Tech professor said the Entomopter runs off of a laptop program. Maybe our guy just sat there and controlled the whole thing from a vehicle right out in the open."

"No way," Ross observed. "He would've been spotted by security cameras."

"Who covered the north side perimeter and associated buildings?"

Cheng straightened in his chair. "We ran into some disgruntled military personnel at an American Legion Post so I went back there myself."

"And?"

"Nothing. They're disgruntled alright, but other than a bad case of racism, the place was clean. One of their employees passed away recently on the premises. I guess you could consider that an unusual circumstance. His name was Chief, er..Watts. He managed the place along with an upstairs apart..." Cheng's voice trailed off.

"What is it?"

"Nothing. I guess he was pretty well-liked."

"How'd he die?"

"A massive heart attack. His friends said he drank too much even when he wasn't celebrating his birthday. They found him on the floor dead on the morning of the eighteenth."

"His birthday?"

"Uh-huh, the big six-oh. Talk about bad timing. It happened right after the party. Witnesses said he played poker until five in the morning. What a way to go."

"Hmpf," Riley said, drumming his fingers. "Anything else?"

"Not really. We interviewed all the regulars except for some college kid who lives above the bar. He was out of town."

"Above the bar as in high vantage point? What's his name?"

Cheng searched for his notes. "Waleu. Mike Waleu."

Riley wrote the name on the board. "That's one. Who else?"

Cheng shook his head. "Jack, don't do this. We're talking two thousand names attached to the Milwaukee investigation alone. The follow-ups could take months."

"I need a damn conspirator and I need a damn cigar." Riley walked to his suit coat hanging on a rack by the door. The pockets were empty. Frustrated, he flung the eraser across the room. It missed Cheng's head and struck the whiteboard erasing the 'l' in Waleu's first name. "I'm sorry, David. When's the last time you had any rest?"

"Not since I got back from Lanzarote," Cheng replied. "I can't sleep on a plane, especially over water."

"Go get some. We'll finish up here. Mr. NTSB and I will run out to New York and meet with this Baltis character. Where is he?"

"The Manhattan field office," Cheng responded, letting out a deep yawn. He collected his documents.

Ross retrieved the eraser from the floor and set it in the whiteboard's metal tray. He uncapped a marker and rewrote the missing letter 'I'. He started for his chair and then froze in mid-step. He turned back to the whiteboard and erased the letter again.

HIGH VANTAGE POINTS
M KE WALEU

Ross easily recognized MKE as Mitchell International's three-letter FAA airport designation code. He wrote another word below, alternatively matching letters to Waleu's name like some federal Wheel of Fortune. He stood back. "Uh, Jack, you might want to look at this. Can I go back to my old job now?"

Riley approached the board. His mouth hung open at the revelation.

HIGH VANTAGE POINTS
M KE WALEU
M I L W A U K E E

"Mr. NTSB, I want you to call your reporter friend and tell her to meet us at the Javits Building, 26 Federal Plaza in New York City. Mr. Cheng, I'm afraid you're not going to get any sleep in the foreseeable future. I want the following alert issued to the Milwaukee, O'Hare and San Diego teams: Any airport perimeter building that has recently rented space or reported a fatality of any kind is to be locked down by local law enforcement until cleared by Homeland Security. Seal off entire blocks if necessary. Go." Riley took the eraser and swiped the whiteboard clean.

Chapter Sixty-four

Ho-Chunk Casino North Parking Lot
10:30 P.M.

Surah 86. The Morning Star, The Nightcomer

1. By the Sky and the Night-Visitant;
2. And what will explain to thee what the Night-Visitant is?
3. It is the Star of piercing brightness;
4. There is no soul but has a protector over it.
5. Now let man but think from what he is created!
6. He is created from a drop emitted,
7. Proceeding from between the backbone and the ribs:
8. Surely God is able to bring him back to life!
9. The Day that all things secret will be tested,
10. Man will have no power, and no helper.
11. By the Firmament that returns in its round,
12. And by the Earth which opens out for the gushing of springs or the sprouting of vegetation,
13. Behold this is the Word that distinguishes Good from Evil:
14. It is not a thing for amusement.
15. As for them, they are but plotting a scheme,
16. And I am planning a scheme.

Sinani was reading his *Qur'an* by penlight and was startled by the face peering through the minivan's window.

Abderrouf Jdey slid inside. "May God preserve and strengthen his soldiers. I live and die for God."

Sinani studied the man's appearance. Their physical characteristics were remarkably similar, but Jdey's facial hair and clothing were dangerously stereotypical. Too many young Middle-Eastern males were tagged by wary law enforcement due to an inability to fit in, especially with 9/11 hijacker video images burned into America's psyche.

"Shave your beard," Sinani ordered. "You must learn to dress in a more...Western manner." He meant slovenly. "No more suitcoats or expensive shoes. Old jeans and a cap with a college or sports logo. Nothing that draws attention. Find a female companion and try to appear as a student."

Jdey unbuttoned his shirt collar.

"You are aware of the turmoil in the skies?"

"Praise God." Jdey lifted his head and hands. "When you called, I knew it was of our doing."

"It is not yet finished," Sinani cautioned. "We must bring one more aircraft to its death. In this I will need your help. It has become too dangerous for me. My face may have already been discovered."

"I understand," Jdey replied. "The aircraft...how is it done?"

"First, what is the name of your meat processing company in New York City? And do you have contacts knowledgeable in stock-yard operations?"

"Hunt's Point Cooperative. Three soldiers and I have worked there for two years. It is in the Bronx. We have earned their trust. What kind of operations?"

"Midwestern feedlots."

Jdey's eyes narrowed. "I will work on the information my-self."

"Good. The next phase of our struggle must continue. That is why we have selected you. First, you must dedicate your mind to a device and learn its nuances and technicalities. You must know enough about its specifications to replicate it. I will teach you."

"An explosive device?"

"It is like nothing you have seen. The council has expressed great confidence in you alone. But you must listen to my instructions carefully and do exactly as I say. Write nothing, but commit these words into the soul of your memory. A mechanical insect caused those aircraft to fall from the skies. A remote-controlled device that operates from a base station via a laptop computer. There is a small camera inside the insect's nose that allows it to see. The insect is powered by liquid fuel and controlled in the air by simple frequency. It has movable legs and an ability to cling onto a target and deposit an explosive. Its name is Entomopter."

"Entomopter," Jdey mused. "Fascinating. Think of the power of one thousand such insects. We could attack one thousand targ—"

"In time we will consider it, but for now we are not interested in attacking one thousand anything." He rebuked Jdey. "We must proceed on a calculated basis. I will teach you how to operate the

272

device and together we must destroy one remaining aircraft."

"Forgive me. One target only."

Sinani continued. "I have killed three and this has caused the infidels overwhelming pain and suffering. Just one more and our enemies will feel the full force of God's might. The council has already approved further actions."

"Where will Entomopter strike?"

"LaGuardia International. There is an apartment. You will take the insect there and study it. I will meet you in sixteen hours and you can teach me of America's beef industry while we wait for the president to open the skies."

Sinani explained the Entomopter's controls and functionality.

Jdey briefly examined each component and practiced assembling the wings and fuel packets. "Friend, I am overwhelmed," he admitted. "This is truly a gift from God."

"It is more than a gift. Our work can no longer be carried out indiscriminately. There is a saying among the Western infidels that suggests change is inevitable. It is true. We too must change in order to survive. Our holy war must be guided by new technologies. Technologies that our children will carry into the next generation and beyond. Remote control devices such as these will lead the way. Do you know American history?"

Jdey pondered the question, proud that someone of Sinani's status would ask for his opinion, but embarrassed that he couldn't respond.

"America's native people could not compete with their invaders because they lacked technological skills and abilities. Thus their culture perished. They had no will to learn or adapt and therefore were conquered. The day will come when great numbers of God's people will migrate here. We are the new invaders and we will learn and master technology. We will live among the infidels; we will conduct business with them; we will gain their trust and, upon the great Day of Judgment, we will kill them wherever they are. It is so written in the Holy *Qur'an*. God is great."

"God is great," Jdey repeated.

"Here is the apartment key. An old woman lives below. Do not let her see your face. She is harmless, but perceptive. If she interferes, do what you must without killing her. She must remain alive." Sinani reached in his pocket and fished out a small plastic case. It was tightly wrapped and addressed to Mrs. Timmons. "Place this

273

inside the woman's mailbox. It is a payment. I will join you in sixteen hours. God willing, another infidel aircraft will soon fall from the sky."

"Sixteen hours," Jdey confirmed. "God has given us a manifest victory."

Chapter Sixty-five

New York City
Javits Federal Building

Computer Technologist Bruce Baltis was ensconced in a glass office in the FBI's Information Technology Center. A hulking brilliant man with a baby's face and oversized forehead, his dainty fingers expertly typed commands on three separate keyboards. He finished his input and then tilted one monitor. The screen showed a mass of numbers and cryptic program language. "I'm running dual, but parallel environments. Al-Aran's laptop has an older version of Windows 98 and I found retained dialogues in both the cache indexes and files. There's also a ton of cookie history. See for yourself."

"Can I have it in English?" Riley asked.

"Sorry. Every message Al-Aran sent or received on the Internet is still identifiable. In this case via the e-mail registers. He left a cyber trail that a blind man could follow. There are multiple IDs. The first one is someone called Praying Man, probably Al-Aran and his first conversation was in a public vacation chat room with someone called Air Babe. There are other IDs present and also conversing. Several days later, the communication pares down to just two users. But those IDs are different and vary in character type and length. Some appear to contain a simple numeric calendar date. I haven't figured out the rest."

"Okay, `so Praying Man is Al-Aran and he liked to talk with women on-line," Riley agreed. "Are you telling me that this is all about Internet dating?"

"Possibly. Al-Aran or somebody used this laptop to access those kinds of sites. But millions of people do that. It could be just harmless interactive browsing."

"Harmless my ass," Riley shot back. "I'm not assuming anything."

"Well, that's good because a minute ago you assumed Air Babe was female. In reality it's simply someone communicating with Al-Aran at one point in time. There are other IDs sending messages, too. And those are all six characters long with no apparent pattern or meaning. The last one was named ChAmPr. Whoever that is, he or she mentioned an address right here in New York City, but that's another thing that doesn't make sense. I've lived here all my life and I can't picture West Pinehurst."

"Are you sure?"

"Positive. There is no such place."

"Then it's got to be some sophisticated signal or code," Riley observed. "How long will it take you to crack it?"

"Code, yes, but hardly sophisticated. These people are definitely playing word games, but something feels odd. They just don't seem that smart."

"How can you tell?"

"Take the conversation between ChAmPr and someone called SMT0531, for instance. The house number ChAmPr mentioned in West Pinehurst was 0112 18th Street. For one thing, no physical mailing address starts with a zero. And anybody can create an anagram like Mike Waleu if you start with a city's name. The difficulty comes into play when you first try and identify all potential names. There could be thousands and the only limitation is the number of letters."

"You're losing me," Riley cautioned.

"Think about it. There are no rules for a person's name. It can literally be anything, especially a phony one. This guy may be slick, but so am I." Baltis rolled his chair across the room and touched a mouse on another computer. The screen saver opened to a running program. The status bar said 9% completed. "This program takes a city crash site word-name like San Diego or Chicago and crunches out all possible anagrams. Then it compares the results to identical first and last names found in U.S. databases. If we don't get any American hits, then we'll go international."

"Criminal databases? What if he has no record?"

Baltis smiled slyly. "Criminal files are only the tip of an information iceberg. In addition to all the data available to law enforcement, there's a whole other public universe of sacred information. I'm talking the really personal stuff. The kind that's harvested and managed by the three amigos."

"Who?"

"The three credit bureaus. Experian, Equifax, and TransUnion. The biggest data gods I know. Scary big. Beyond the usual financial information like loans, debt balances, payment history, employment, credit ratings, and salary, they also gather and store data on personal human habits. The search programs are the most sophisticated and intuitive anywhere. That means they'll help you even if you screw up the input. Instead of returning 'not found' errors, they'll flip data around and make suggestions. Believe it or not, you can enter a person's first and last name and find information from ten years ago right down to last known addresses and job history. Their financial list alone is around ten thousand files."

"Do we have access?"

"Sure, the FBI has access, but not the navigation skills." Baltis moved to yet another PC and brought up a logon screen. He entered a usercode, company ID, user ID, and a 16-character password. The system immediately asked a question about his mother's maiden name, and a final one about his deceased family pet. He swung his chair back to the second PC and filled in the address blocks. He left the zip code field blank. "Let's see if we get lucky."

0112 18th Street, West Pinehurst, NY appears to be incorrect.

We assumed you meant 2110 81st Street, East Elmhurst, NY 11370?

"Si, senor," Baltis responded and clicked yes. The program continued searching for approximately twenty seconds and then produced several lines of data along with a map point location. "Gotcha. Equifax keeps automobile registrations in its motor vehicle repairs database. They provide that data to companies who sell repair warranties and roadside protection to customers. Follow? If you take your car in for service, somebody somewhere knows about it. It's all about keeping track of customers and their personal preferences. Let's see what we have…on April 9th, Queensboro Toyota in Jackson Heights repaired the odometer on a 2000 Camry. The owner listed 2110 81st Street as his home address. Someone by the name of…Kenneth Wory."

"I'll be damned," Riley whispered to himself. "Ken Wory… New York."

Baltis drilled further into the selection and brought up a Google-Earth satellite view of the surrounding neighborhood. The residence was located directly across the street from LaGuardia International.

Chapter Sixty-six

San Diego, CA
Nick's Velvet Touch and Massage

FBI Special Agent Ben Jeffers flicked his cigarette in a long arc into the center of Pacific Highway just as Cheng's vehicle pulled up. They shook hands. "Am I glad to see you," Jeffers said."This building matches your alert criteria, but San Diego PD isn't very happy about us barging into the middle of a double domestic homicide. Their assistant chief, Cheryl Bryden is really upset and she wants answers. It's one thing to take over an investigation, but to simply lock down a fatality scene and not let anyone in or out?"

"Did you tell her it was a Department of Homeland Security priority?" Cheng asked.

"Yes."

"Did you tell her that if she'd talk to her own DHS Liaison she'd understand that this might be connected to the airline crashes?"

"Things are moving so fast that I'm not sure I know what's going on." They walked inside. "You'll need this."

The foul odor of human decomposition was strong. Cheng placed the charcoal-lined dust mask over his nose and mouth. "Who found them?"

"A utility meter technician had a key to the basement," Jeffers said. "The medical examiner figures they've been here for at least four days."

Cheng stepped into a bedroom and briefly examined the bloodstained carpet.

"Karkula. Nicholas, F. and Tamara, L. Ages fifty-four and fifty-five," Jeffers said. "Apparently, the husband killed his wife and then himself. She was shot once through the chest; he was in the kitchen shot once in the head at close range. Obviously a murder-suicide. The gun was still in his hand. According to police records, this place had its share of violence. Neighbors said they were always screaming at each other."

"What's upstairs?" Cheng asked.

"An apartment. But no one lives there; it's vacant."

"Employees?"

"Mostly female drifters that come and go. Hookers and addicts that work a few days for cash and then leave. Usually with customers. Hard to keep track of the movement."

Cheng drifted into the kitchen and spotted a file cabinet next to a desk. He slid out the top drawer and casually fingered the folders, stopping at one curiously labeled: Pigs. One document was a copy of a cashier's check. The signature was sloppy, but readable. It was issued by a bank in Milwaukee.

Javits Federal Building
Information Technology Center

"S-o-g-i. Dean Sogi. San freaking Diego," Riley translated into his phone. "Anything else?"

"Someone rented an office at the O'Hare Aerospace Center on the airport's east side," Cheng explained. "The building's access logs showed that the tenant was there early on the morning of May 19th and then never showed up again. The timeslot fits with the Airbus departure. The name on the lease is Ghoacci, another anagram for Chicago. First name John."

"Damn, that's beautiful work, David," Riley said. "You get two out of two. Now all we need is a descript——"

"We've got it," Cheng said. "He was caught on a lobby camera. Medium complexion, male. Thin with short black hair. He's young. The image is a little blurry, but enough for a bulletin. Jack, I think we're dealing with the same person in all locations."

"Sonofabitch." Riley pumped his fist once and made a long kissing sound into the phone. His eyes narrowed and his face grew stern. "That's for you, mister. Nationwide alert to all law enforcement. Let's flush this little bastard into the open."

"The media, too?"

"Uh-huh. Our Fox News reporter is in the next room." Riley closed his phone and headed for the door. He turned. "No offense, Mr. Baltis, but you can unplug your programs. We've got the names."

"Mr. Riley?" Baltis said. "My cousin lived in Queens real close to that address. She died on 9/11. She never made it out of the first tower. I hope the guy you're looking for is at home and I hope you

279

nail him."

FBI Operations Center

The 23rd floor was buzzing with staff agents and members of New York's Joint Terror Task Force assigned to the operation. Riley took a seat in a large conference room next to the man in charge of the New York field office. Special Agent Robert Farino bore a striking albeit hairier resemblance to his second cousin ex-Mayor Rudy Giuliani and also shared a family trait for tenacious prosecution of evil. Farino began the briefing with introductions. "You all know Jack Riley from DHS. The gentleman in the back is Tom Ross from NTSB; and next to him is Ms. Griffin from Fox News."

Heads turned.

"Both of them are with me and will be observing this operation," Riley added matter-of-factly. "It's about time we got some positive press for a change."

Farino continued. "The subject's address is in Queens in an upper flat in the middle of a residential neighborhood. Older homes, relatively quiet, people keep to themselves. NYPD has had the site under close surveillance since we got the notification. No one can go in or out without us seeing. There are seventy-five officers and an unmarked armored personnel control carrier ready to move on the premises. We're receiving radio updates from two tactical officers who managed to position themselves on the porches of the two adjacent houses."

Riley winced. "Dammit, I thought we agreed not to do that? I don't want to spook him. Why'd you have to get that close?"

"I gambled, Jack," Farino admitted. "Both of those officers are carrying handheld T-rays. I figured we'd want to know how many perpetrators we're dealing with."

"Excuse me," Griffin interrupted from the back of the room. "What's a T-ray?"

Farino looked at Riley. He nodded.

"Tetrahertz radiation or T-ray is an experimental gun that shoots a pulse of radiation at a target location and receives a digital image in return. It's like an x-ray that can see through fog, smoke, and even walls."

"How thick of walls?"

"Up to twenty five centimeters."

"Ten inches," Ross whispered to Griffin.

"That's incredible," she commented. "How long have you had that abil—"

Farino's radio crackled. He held a brief conversation and then stood. "Okay, people, listen up. We've got two suspects inside that flat. One appears to be inactive and one is active. He's been in a sitting position for the past twenty minutes."

"Doing what?" Riley asked.

"Unknown. The frames only show that the subject's hands and arms are repeatedly moving to and from different positions. He could be sitting at the kitchen table reading a newspaper, petting a cat, or simply eating."

"Or arming an Entomopter."

Farino nodded. "Or arming an Entomopter."

Chapter Sixty-seven

East Elmhurst
8:15 P.M.

The order was for quiet transport—flashing lights, no sirens—during the NYPD escort from downtown Manhattan to LaGuardia. Twenty-two minutes later, Farino's Ford Expedition and fifteen other assorted Terror Task Force vehicles pulled off of Grand Central Parkway and into a staging area one block south of the suspect's location.

Farino left the keys in the SUV's ignition and opened the rear door. He rifled through an equipment bag and handed Riley a bullhorn. Riley knew what he was thinking and pushed it back. "Nice try, pal but I want you in charge of this assault with one condition: human intelligence is more valuable than any physical evidence so tell your people that they are to do everything possible to capture these guys alive. The use of lethal force is discretionary."

"What should we do?" Ross spoke up from the back seat.

"Absolutely nothing. I want you and Neela to stay inside this vehicle and observe," Riley ordered, handing Ross a pair of binoculars. "It's the brick two-story in the middle of the block." He gave Neela a direct look. "No wild ideas; no close-ups and no heroes, okay? You can shoot all the photos you want from here, but please stay safe. The suspects are in the upper unit with the walk-out porch. We don't know who they are; we don't know their firepower; and we don't know what's going to happen. I'm already second-guessing my decision to bring you two out here. These bastards murder innocent people and I guarantee they'll have no qualms about killing more. This could get public and loud very quickly."

"We'll stay put," Ross promised, extending his hand to Riley. "Be careful."

"My teams are in position," Farino announced. "An elderly woman owns the property and lives downstairs. She's not home."

"Do we have an interpreter?" Riley asked, sliding into a Kevlar vest.

"He's standing by," Farino confirmed. "His name is Rooze."

"Rooze?"

"Agent Firooz Ghanbarz. He's fluent in thirteen Arabic dialects." Farino glanced at his watch. "Two minutes, Jack. Is there anything else?"

Riley took Farino's arm and gently escorted him behind the SUV. Riley sat on the vehicle's bumper and lit a cigar. "I'm not a very sensitive man and I'm certainly not into drama. But I remember the president's speech to Congress and the nation on September 20th, 2001. This city was in shock and the rest of the country was gripped with fear. He stood at that podium and talked about American resolve. The kind that Todd Beamer and those other brave heroes mustered on Flight 93 over Pennsylvania. With no weapons and virtually no hope of surviving, they faced and overpowered an unknown number of hijacking sons-a-bitches. Sometimes I think we've lost our resolve and then it comes back stronger than ever. Todd's wife, Lisa was sitting in the audience pregnant with their daughter, Morgan. I wanted to hug her so bad my heart just ached. When I heard the president speak those words for the first time my whole body shivered. They were Todd's words and I'll never forget them." He stepped on his cigar and glanced heavenward. "It is about freedom and this is for you, pal." He turned to Farino. "Let's roll."

Law enforcement personnel and vehicles converged on the suspect's house from three directions. Two helicopters with thermal capabilities appeared overhead, focusing spotlights onto the roofline and upper windows. Agents in full tactical gear formed a defensive line across the street.

The interpreter, Ghanbarz lifted a bullhorn. "Attention, you are surrounded. Show yourselves with your hands in the air. We are authorized by the United States government to use deadly force if you do not comply."

No response.

He spoke Arabic. "God is a peace lover and will look upon you with forgiveness. Show yourselves and he will be merciful."

Nothing.

Farino put his radio to his ear and then turned to Riley. "Something strange is happening in there. The north T-ray officer is still scanning two suspects. One is active and the other is in a prone position with no movement at all. We may have some sort of victim."

A face appeared in the flat's upper window.

Riley reached for the bullhorn. "This is Jack Riley, United States Homeland Security. Step outside with your hands in the air and you will not be harmed."

Incredibly, the window slid open. The curtains drew back.

After an agonizing fifteen seconds, something small and black moved through the opening and slowly fluttered off the porch down the middle of the street. Riley raised his binoculars. Barely visible against the night backdrop, the bird-like object paused, circled and then paused again as if it were hunting something. Riley's stomach sank as the object descended toward the task force staging area and disappeared under Farino's SUV.

Ross was fiddling with his binoculars adjusting a stubborn focus dial. "I feel so useless just sitting here."

"There are two more of those vests in the back," Griffin noted, lowering a window and peering outside. "Do you think it would be alright if we—"

"No way," he said firmly. "They told us to stay here and that's exactly what we're going to...wait, hang on. Something's happening."

"Can you see Jack?"

"Uh-huh...I think so. He's on the phone."

"Maybe it's over?"

"Possible," Ross agreed, glancing over his shoulder at her. "Neela, this probably isn't the best timing, but I need to tell you something. Before this does come to an end I just wanted to say that I hoped we might...if there was a way that we could work things out and still see each other even with me in DC and you in Milwaukee, I mean...I don't have all the answers, but could we both at least promise to try? I really enjoy being with you."

A ringtone chirped once, then twice, then a third time.

"I've got something to tell you, too." She touched his hand and smiled. "Are you going to get that?"

Ross finally realized it was his cell phone and thought not to answer, but then he did.

"The Entomopter!" Riley's voice screamed. "It's underneath you!"

Ross's heart nearly burst from his chest. He didn't think, he didn't hesitate. He reached Griffin's body and in one sweeping motion lifted her into his arms and lunged through the door for the curbside grass. They hit the ground hard, his weight slamming binoculars into her abdomen forcing the air from her lungs in a short violent grunt.

The potassium chlorate explosion easily ruptured the SUV's plastic fuel tank. A millisecond later, twenty gallons of gasoline unleashed a horrific secondary explosion that sent hardened chunks of debris and shrapnel spraying laterally. The last thing Ross remembered was shielding Griffin's head at the risk of his own.

Hurtling end-over-end like some tumbling metallic toy, the Ford Expedition finally came to rest on its roof. Engulfed in flames, black smoke mushroomed skyward. Fiery droplets rained down like some spring storm in hell.

There was momentary quiet before a barrage of tear gas and stun grenades shattered the flat's windows. Seconds later, smoke illuminated by muffled explosions billowed through the interior.

The assault abruptly stopped.

The front door opened. A youthful-looking adult male appeared waving a New York Yankees baseball cap. Thin and barefoot, he sported an odd combination of a baggy Boston College sweatshirt and black dress pants. Eyes and nose dripping with burning moisture, he placed the cap on his head and slowly stepped off the concrete stoop.

A chorus of metallic breeches clicked in unison.

"Do not shoot; it is over," he coughed in broken English. "God is our judge."

"Get down on the ground."

Six agents pounced on the man, immobilizing his arms and legs.

One officer appeared and immediately focused a hand-held T-ray scanner at the man's body. The unit's black and white video screen showed a spaghetti-like mass and eight dark rectangular lumps taped to the suspect's torso. The face of a digital clock showed movement.

00:07...00:06...00:05...00:04

"Wired!"

The suspect lifted his head and as he did, his eyes made contact with Riley standing thirty feet away in the street. It was a moment frozen in time. The man's stare was lifeless and cold. Then he smiled. A split-second later, he detonated.

285

The concussion blast of the first homicide bombing on U.S. soil lifted Riley's body horizontally and slammed him to the pavement on both knees.

Riley opened his eyes and his first thought was that his head was split open. His second thought was that the roadway had somehow turned soft and he had sunk into wet concrete. His vision was blurred and his brain was overwhelmed with a pattern of pinpoint lights. Then he realized he was lying on a stretcher and staring into the sky. There was movement around him, but sounds were muffled. He flexed his jaw and pain waves pummeled his eardrums. He turned and saw three emergency medical technicians lifting a male body into an ambulance. His vision cleared and he recognized the face of his friend, lifeless and at peace. Griffin was sitting inside the vehicle sobbing.

"Oh my God, why?" Riley cried, limping off the stretcher.

"Sir, he still has a pulse, but we need to go now," a technician said, holding Riley back. "They're waiting in the ER."

The technician spoke into his radio; the ambulance pulled away.

Riley sat down on the curb and put his head in his hands.

"Are you alright, Jack?"

"Did we lose both suspects?" Riley asked, composing himself.

"There was only one," Farino gently advised. "The second body was the landlord. She was blindfolded and tied up in the bathtub. She's on her way to the hospital. I think she'll be okay."

Chapter Sixty-eight

Elmhurst Hospital
ER Waiting Area
11:40 P.M.

Patients and staff stood quietly staring into television screens at breaking news. Something about an FBI drug siege in Queens.

Griffin was sitting on a couch next to a beleaguered young woman whose seven-year-old daughter had accidentally fallen with a pencil.

ER physician Derek Feldman walked through a pair of double doors and made his way toward the two women. "Your daughter is very lucky. The pencil missed her eyeball and punctured the area next to the bridge of her nose. She'll wear a patch for a while, but she'll be fine." He turned to Griffin and sat down, flipping a page on his clipboard. "Ma'am, are you Mrs. Thomas Ross?"

Her eyes welled up and she felt a wave of nausea. "Is he...?"

"Why don't you ask him yourself?" Feldman smiled. "He's got a nasty gash just above the left temple, but he's stable. He's going to be okay. It's a good night for near misses. He's been asking for you. Follow me."

Riley reached the second floor nurse's station. An attending doctor escorted him to a patient room and waved him inside.

Sedated but awake, Mary Timmons was trying to grasp a plastic water container on a tray next to her bed.

"How do you feel, ma'am?" Riley whispered, bending a flexible straw to her mouth. She drew four long sucks.

"Sleepy," she peeped, out of breath. "Are you the police?"

"My name is Jack, ma'am." He gently touched her forearm, careful to avoid the deep purple bruises. "Mary, I need to ask you some questions about Kenneth Wory. It's important." She nodded once. He leaned closer. "Can you tell me what happened tonight?"

"For the life of me, I don't know," her voice cracked. "I went upstairs to see if Kenneth was hungry and when I walked in he pushed me to the floor. He put a sack on my head and dumped me in that tub. He never said a ting. I couldn't believe it was happening.

287

Then he taped me. It was all I could do to breathe. Is he…gone?"

"He's dead, ma'am. Could you describe him?"

"Why would Kenny do such a ting?" Tears streamed down her cheeks. "Such a handsome lad. Always so neat and polite. He finally remembered my coins."

"Coins?"

"In the mailbox yesterday and now they're in me sweater on that very chair." She pointed her finger. "Kenny always said he'd bring them home. I knew he would."

Riley rifled the pockets and found a small plastic case.

Amaze your friends with Scotch and Soda.

"Ma'am, did Kenneth ever have any visit—?"

There was no response. She had drifted asleep.

He left quietly, conferring with staff briefly before making his way to Ross's room. Griffin was sitting at his bedside and Riley gave her a gentle hug. "I guess you got one helluva story."

"I'm glad it's over," she said, pressing moisture from her eyes.

"How is he?" Riley whispered.

Ross's head was wrapped and his eyes were closed but he responded by raising his thumb.

"You scared the hell out of us, Tom. How do you feel?"

"Like I've been kicked in the head by one of your horses," he said weakly, barely moving his lips. "You?"

"My knees are banged up and I can't hear worth a damn, but that might be a blessing."

"Can I go back to my old job now?" Ross spoke louder.

"Anytime, pal. I'm finished with you."

"What about yours?" Ross asked. "That night at the Outback Restaurant. You said you'd tell me about your retirement job sometime. In the Keys."

"He's all drugged up, right?" Riley asked Griffin.

"A little bit. But now I want to know, too."

"I'm going to push a little cart and sell popcorn," Riley announced matter-of-factly.

Ross gave off a loud snort and then he winced.

"Go ahead and laugh. Mallory Square vendors in Key West make a grand a day, cash. It's a couple of years away, but I figure I'll need to do something to feed all my horses."

Ross struggled to his elbows. "The perpetrators. Did you get them?"

"Him," Riley corrected. "It looks like Waleu, Sogi, Ghoacci, and Wory were all the same person. I doubt if we'll ever know his real identity. We'll draw up a composite sketch and share it with known witnesses. He was pretty much blown to pieces. Can't say that I'll lose any sleep over it."

"What's that?" Griffin asked, noticing something in Riley's hand.

"Some kind of magic coin trick that we need to analyze. I guess our terrorist was pretty good at slight-of-hand."

Griffin placed her hand in front of Ross's face. "How many fingers?"

Ross smiled broadly. "Are we ever going out on a date?"

"No sense rushing things." She kissed his cheek and gently adjusted his pillow. "I've accepted a job in Washington working for Fox's DC bureau. Who knows? We might even be neighbors."

"I guess I'll leave you two alone." Riley winked at Ross. "I've got to tell the president that his country can start flying again."

Chapter Sixty-nine

Port of Rabat
Cargo Vessel Abuzenima
Captain's Quarters

"We must part ways, Faiz, but only for a short time. I assume your struggle will continue?" Captain Naimi reached into his desk for an envelope. "Your new life. You are now Habib Saloume named from the rural village of your birth in Senegal. The real Habib served on my crew and was lost in a storm three years ago. He had no friends or family. You could be his twin; your image is perfect. Do the authorities have your fingerprints?"

"You might say that I was one of many who managed to avoid the bureaucracy." Al-Aran set his pipe down and examined the documents. "I have never seen Aljezur. Are you sure it is safe?"

"My friend, I am a man of faith and I support your work, but I do not wish to know the details. I will provide everything that you require in life as a service to my brother, Ali. In Portugal you will lack nothing. You may raise vegetables and peanuts and assist with my animals. I have a small but reliable servant-staff. On my land, your time is your own. The town of Aljezur is filled with tourists who mind their business. No one will ask anything of you. You may walk in and among the stores freely. You may sip wine and browse the world's information in our new Internet café. The region is completely uneventful. It will be as if the old professor no longer exists." He glanced at his watch. "The Abuzenima sails for Lisbon today. After some business in Antwerp I will return and we will both rest. Perhaps the time may come, senor when you admit you have done enough for God."

"Perhaps," Al-Aran agreed. "But only God can determine that. In twenty-one days I must travel to London."

"As you wish. There is a map of Aljezur with your papers. I am happy to assist."

Al-Aran rose for the door. He paused. "Your farm…what animals do you raise?"

"Goats and a small herd of livestock. Primarily for meat."

"You are a fortunate and prosperous man, Captain. And you

may take comfort in the fact that your meat does not come from America."

Duck Key, Florida
Tom's Harbor Inlet
10:00 A.M.

Riley reached for his cell phone and touched a speed dial number.

"Tom Ross."

"I can't believe you're back to work," Riley chided. "Tell your boss your head still hurts and you need more medical time."

"Effective this morning, the entire U.S. Congress is my boss," he announced. "I was just named the NTSB's permanent Investigator-in-Charge."

"Aren't we moving up in the world?"

Ross laughed. "What about you? How's the vacation?"

"Life is good. I'm sitting under a Tiki hut and Charlene's flying in tonight on a private jet compliments of the Secretary of Homeland Security."

"That's not enough. For what you did it should be Air Force One."

"I suppose," Riley said half-heartedly.

"Jack, what's wrong?"

"Mixed emotions, pal. I can't put my finger on it, but I just feel kind of empty about the way things turned out. You know, falling into place the way they did. It just seemed too perfect."

"What the hell are you talking about? What's wrong with perfect? You led an investigation...a successful investigation that stopped a terrorist. A terrorist who killed Americans. He was a real threat. A threat that almost brought this country to its knees."

"He did bring the country to its knees."

"You know what I mean. It could have been worse, Jack. A lot worse."

"Frankly, I wanted more," Riley admitted. "Like a name, for instance. We never even knew his real name, not to mention where he came from or how he was able to operate so freely right under our noses. Think about that. How many more are out there? It reminds me of when I was a kid in Georgia. We used to play in the woods

291

near a creek. Then one day a cottonmouth snake bit my friend and the next thing you know the whole place was roped off. He lost his right leg. They found and killed a snake, but never knew if it was the snake or if there were others. They simply assumed. They hung signs and told us not to go there anymore, just to be safe. Something bothers me about that Saudi professor, Mr. Shark Food. I keep thinking that he played us. What if he set the whole thing up?"

"You have absolutely no evidence to support that," Ross said. "And for the sake of argument, if Faiz Al-Aran is still alive, he's a marked man all over the planet with no place to run or hide. Someone will pick him up."

"But it proves my point that there might be a helluva lot of snakes out there, pal," Riley quipped. "Poisonous snakes."

"Alright, I order you to snap out of this negative funk. Get your butt into your boat and go catch Osama. You hear me?"

"Yessir, loud and clear. I'll call you when I get back in town. We'll have you and Neela over for barbecue and a horseback ride. Deal?"

"Deal."

Riley gulped the last of his orange juice and gazed north to the King's Bridge that separated the Gulf of Mexico from the Atlantic Ocean. A light breeze gently tickled the U.S. flag above his pier. He turned the handle on a hydraulic lift and the L-shaped aluminum beams lowered Just-Duck-Key to the water. The boat's engine started faithfully and he eased the craft forward. It took only minutes to reach his fishing hole off the main canal halfway between his dock and the open ocean. He pointed the bow into the tide flow and dropped anchor. The iron flanges gripped the coral bottom and held firm. He methodically rigged four lines with chunks of fresh ballyhoo and set each rod in a holder. He sat back in a padded captain's chair and peeled the blue foil wrapper off an Acid Blondie cigar. He tasted one puff and his cell phone chirped. It was his home number.

"Good morning," Charlene Riley's voice sung. "How's the weather?"

"Seventy-eight and sunny. There's a nice breeze blowing in from the Gulf. I miss you. Are you packed?"

"Just about. Are you sure this is alright?"

"Trust me. All you have to do is show up at Dulles. The Secretary's jet will be there fueled and ready to go. It's his way of saying thanks."

"How long is it?"

"A little over two hours. It's exactly one thousand miles, so you should get into Marathon Airport around six. Don't eat. We're having something special."

"Aren't you the romantic one?"

"Hey, you deserve it. We both deserve it. I'm looking forward to a relaxing vaca—" One of the fishing lines twitched. "Damn, don't be mad sweetie; gotta go."

He clicked off and set the phone on the console. When he gripped the rod the line instantly went limp. He waited a few seconds and then reached for his phone. It chirped before he could dial.

He brought the phone to his lips and spoke seductively. "Sorry, sweetie. One more thing...be sure and bring that black negligee I bought for your birthday. The see-through one from Victoria's Secret. Dammit, you've got a great body and I want it all."

There was a moment of silence.

"I don't know about great, but I have been working out," the president's voice finally spoke.

A series of waves bounced off the canal seawall and rolled the boat sideways. Riley dropped the phone, but quickly retrieved it. "Mr. President, I'm sorry. I didn't know it was you."

"No harm done, son. I just wanted to offer my personal thanks for what you did for the country. You made us proud."

"Thank you, sir. I appreciate that, but I had a lot of help. It's bittersweet though, I mean, I wish we could have discovered and prevented those attacks beforehand. It would have, well, the economic problems and all. I hope you know what I mean."

"I do, Jack, and I tend to agree. War is bittersweet. I pray that the American people can think in those terms. It'll help us all recover."

"Yes, sir."

"Jack, how old are you?" The president wondered.

"Forty-four. Why do you ask?"

"That's a good young age. It's rather comforting to know that you'll be around a bit longer. I suspect that we'll need all the sharp minds we can muster if we expect to truly win the war on terror. Anyway, thank you again from my heart. Have a good vacation and enjoy that...birthday present."

Chapter Seventy

Riley set his phone down and as he did, he noticed movement again on the same fishing rod. This time it was different. The line was straightening. He gently lifted the rod from its holder; he lowered the tip and then heaved backwards.

The fish nearly pulled him into the water and Riley could hear the rod's graphite filaments crack. In an instant the air was filled with high-pitched buzzing. The line peeled out as the fish classically headed for a deep hole next to the seawall.

It was him.

The line went limp and Riley quickly reeled up the excess. The monster on the other end wouldn't budge. After ten minutes, his arms ached from the stalemate and he felt rather stupid just standing there. Something had to give. The pressure would either force the fish out of its rock sanctuary or snap the line.

He gathered his strength and pulled.

Something actually moved.

A wave of excitement ran through Riley's body and he felt like shouting. When a 100-pound fish acted like deadweight, it was as good as caught.

Twenty-five feet away, Osama's massive body broke the surface like some steel barrel. Seemingly beaten, the giant grouper fanned its tail slowly and the movement actually brought it closer.

Riley spied the net on the boat's canopy, but decided to use a four-foot gaff hook instead. He wrapped his hand through a thick leather loop on the handle and leaned over the water. "Come to papa," he squealed, barely able to contain himself. "I'm gonna grill your fat ass."

The fish would have none of it.

With one strong flap, Osama's tail turned him back for the seawall. Riley managed to alter the path slightly and as he did, the monster headed straight for a docked 48-foot Sea Ray Sedan Bridge. The name on the stern was appropriate.

D E V I L F I S H

Riley couldn't see below the surface, but he knew that the fish had circled the yacht's propeller. Strained beyond limits, the line gave off a firecracker-like snap and the momentum sent him backwards onto his butt. His head smacked into the console sending his cigars tumbling to the saltwater on the floor.

A little girl wearing oversized glamour sunglasses and her mother's floppy straw hat appeared on the Sea Ray's bridge. She leaned over the railing and shook her head. "You're not a very good fish catcher, mister. He got away."

A U.S. Interstate Highway

"I never knew this state had so many cows," Marissa said, observing a large herd grazing in the flat grassland.

"It ranks eleventh," Sinani noted. "Kansas, Nebraska and Texas are the top three. Most of the beef cattle in this region are from a Brahman strain. They can handle the excessive heat and humidity. Soon we're going to visit some animals."

"Really? I'd like that."

"Yup. Quite a few as a matter of fact. Farms, zoos, parks, and then some forests."

She looked at him oddly. "I thought you were studying computers and music in college. How come you know so much about cows?"

"I dunno, I guess I read it somewhere."

She leaned over the seat. "See the cows, honey?"

"Are we almost there yet?" Jo-Jo whined impatiently.

"Just a little while longer."

"Mommy, do you want to hear my new song?" Amber asked.

"Sure I do."

She braced the toy organ on her lap and used two fingers to press out the tune.

"Amber, that's beautiful. Who taught you that?"

"Dean did," she beamed. "Mommy, is the world big?"

"Of course it is. It's very big."

"Then Dean lied because he said it was small and that a lot of people from far away were all coming to live in Amer..."

"Amber," Sinani scolded. "What I said was that people from all over the world like to visit America because there's so much free-

295

dom and so many things to do and see. We're going to a special place where there'll be lots of people from other countries."

"Can we stay there for this many days?" Jo-Jo begged, holding up four fingers.

"That's up to Dean, but I think it will be okay."

Sinani checked the rearview mirror and eased the minivan into the right-hand lane. He turned his head and winked. "If you're a good boy we'll stay there for twenty-one days—-uh-oh, look who I see."

Jo-Jo's eyes grew wide and he covered his smile with both hands at the sight of a large billboard. On it, two symbols represented a simple but universal code that every child could decipher. One symbol was a large black arrow that pointed south. To the right of that arrow, three offset circles formed the beloved ears and face of Florida's most famous mouse.

Amber set the organ aside and laid her head on her pillow. She sang the words softly from memory. Sinani joined in.

> "It's a world of laughter, a world of tears;
> It's a world of hope; it's a world of fear;
> There's so much that we share,
> That it's time we're aware,
> It's a small world after all."

Order Form
Soft Target: The Air

For additional copies, please complete the order form below and mail to:

**Dan River Press
Order Department
P.O. Box 298
Thomaston, ME 04861**

Paperbacks are $18.95 ___how many?　　　　$_____

Hardcover are $39.95 ___ how many?　　　　$_____

Autographing $5.00 per copy___how many　　$_____
Inscription desired:_____

_____

SHIPPING: $3.95 FIRST COPY, PLUS .65 EACH ADDITION-
AL TO SAME ADDRESS. TOTAL　　　　　　$_____

Total Enclosed　　　　　　　　　　　　$_____
Ship to:

　　Name:

　　Address:

　　City/State/ZIP
**If you have one of those little address labels to yourself, please
toss it in, it cuts way down on errors. Visit us at www.joelnar-
lock.com
or www.americanletters.org**